FOR BETTER OR FOR CURSE

THE MAD KING'S DAUGHTERS #1

TANYA BIRD

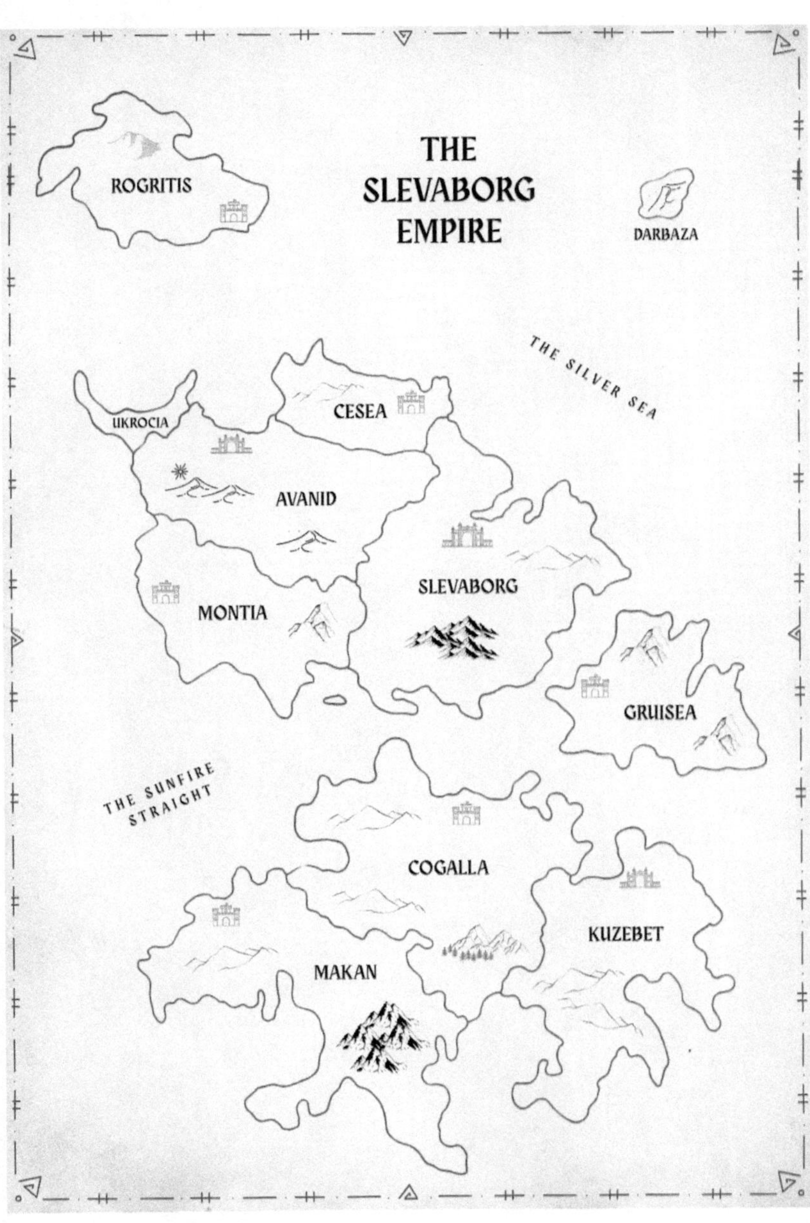
THE
SLEVABORG
EMPIRE
ROGRITIS
DARBAZA
THE SILVER SEA
UKROCIA
CESEA
AVANID
SLEVABORG
MONTIA
GRUISEA
THE SUNFIRE
STRAIGHT
COGALLA
KUZEBET
MAKAN

PROLOGUE

$\mathcal{A}$isha would never forget the smell of her mother burning. The eerie hiss of fabric dissolving in the flames. The sweat trickling down her face and hairline as the fire intensified. Two blazing gold saucers that barely resembled her mother's eyes.

She flinched when the queen flung her head back, eyes squeezing shut against the blinding heat. Then came the smell of singed hair. Aisha covered her nose and mouth in a vain attempt to block it. She didn't have enough hands to cover her ears as well. Her mother's screams were drowned out only by the strangled cries of her father, pinned to the ground by guards.

It took four men to keep him down.

They say the initial pain is the worst, before the flames burn the nerves. The victim dies from suffocation as the respiratory tract fails. But that's not how her mother died. Someone merciful relieved her of her suffering, despite the overwhelming presence of holy warriors.

Aisha flinched a second time when an arrow struck

the Queen of Avanid through the heart. Through blurry eyes, she saw her mother go limp, head tipping forwards. The collective gasp of the crowd had Aisha drawing a shaky breath and looking around. Her father had stopped fighting. Stopped shouting. Stopped moving altogether. His eyes were open but hollow. Dirt caked his lips, and blood coloured his teeth.

Her gaze travelled to her elder sister, Zara, white-faced and holding their one-year-old brother so tightly he was crying. Zara's hand wrapped his small head, shielding his view, her own wide eyes reflecting the flames. The only reason Omar had travelled with them to Slevaborg was because he was still being nursed.

Who would nurse him now?

The holy warriors still had their swords drawn, blades bloody after slaughtering the guards who had fought until their dying breath to save their queen from this fate.

'Mama,' Lilah called, palms still pressed to her eyes.

Aisha looked down at her younger sister, whose shoulders rose and fell with each heaving sob. Thank the gods her two youngest sisters had remained in Avanid, spared the trauma of watching their mother die and their father's heart shatter into a million pieces.

'Mama.'

Lilah's distress roused Aisha's physical body. She drew her sister close, holding her tightly. 'Shh' was all she could manage to say. One small sound against a world on fire.

It's what their mother might have said.

Zahvik stepped up onto the platform beside the fire, seemingly unaffected by the heat from the flames. He wore a white thobe with a deep hood that partially covered his face. Slevaborg's sectarian. 'Let this serve as warning to every covenweaver across the empire, whether she be a peasant or a *queen*: If you invite the devil to our lands, we will stamp him out.'

This was the first time Aisha had heard her mother referred to as a 'covenweaver'. She had always referred to herself as a healer. Her knowledge of medicinal plants was unmatched. She saved lives. She had saved a life that very morning.

And it had cost her own.

'*Good intuition is the mark of a good healer,*' she had told Aisha earlier that day. '*Ignore the labels used by others.*'

They had labelled her a covenweaver.

'Mama,' Lilah cried into Aisha's chest.

All Aisha could do was hold her tighter. What other comfort could a ten-year-old possibly offer an eight-year-old when her own limbs and mind were like jelly? They *both* needed their mother. The next best thing was their father, but he remained on the ground despite the warriors no longer holding him.

'Baba, get up,' Zara said, standing over him with a crying baby. 'Get up!'

He didn't get up. Or he couldn't.

Thankfully, their carriage driver had been spared. He came forwards and helped the king to his feet. His hands shook violently, and his eyes darted nervously about, as if he were expecting someone to stop him.

When Zahvik stepped down from the platform and came towards them, the driver paled but kept hold of the king. Zahvik looked between the girls.

'I am deeply sorry for your loss,' he said with what

sounded like genuine sympathy. 'I pray you and your family heal and find comfort in the fact that the devil no longer resides in your home.'

King Bilal blinked, fat tears rolling down his cheeks and disappearing into his dusty beard.

Zara's face twisted with anger. 'You killed her!' She might have lunged at the man if she had not been holding Omar.

The baby cried harder, startled by her raised voice.

Zahvik gestured to a nearby warrior, and a moment later, they were surrounded by armed men. The warriors pushed the carriage driver aside, took hold of the king, and began dragging him to the waiting carriage. The girls hurried after their father, Zara shrugging free of warrior hands each time they reached for her.

'Don't touch me!' she shouted at them.

Aisha was too broken to shout at anyone. Too numb. She barely noticed the hand on her shoulder. She was faintly aware of Lilah still clinging to her waist and her brother's wailing, though it sounded distant due to the ringing in her ears.

The driver climbed up atop the carriage and gathered the reins as the family was ushered inside. The door closed half a second before it lurched forwards. Zara sat opposite her sisters, and her eyes locked with Aisha's. Neither of them knew what to do next, what to say to their siblings, or how to help their father, who was curled up on the carriage floor, gripping his hair as though he meant to tear it from his scalp.

The girls jumped when a figure appeared at the window of the moving carriage. A boy, maybe fifteen years old. Holding tightly to the door with one hand, he extended the other. In it was their mother's crown. Zara reached out and took it, her eyes meeting the boy's. Then, without saying anything, he let go of the door and disappeared from sight. They never heard his feet hit the ground, because the pounding of hooves drowned everything else out.

Everything except the crying.

'Mama.' Lilah spoke the word into Aisha's tear-soaked robe.

Aisha gathered her sister close as feeling returned to her fingers. But with the return of feeling came the return of emotion. It seemed to hit her all at once, knocking the air from her lungs as it arrived. She pressed her eyes closed when it turned to nausea.

Another sob from Lilah. 'Mama.'

Mama.

CHAPTER 1

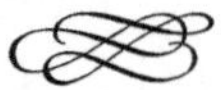

The sound of hooves approaching on the stone roadway drew the sisters to the balcony. They rarely received visitors, and they were all keen for a glimpse of the Crown Prince of Gruisea.

'Which one is he?' Lilah asked, looking between the faces of the men, now visible.

Aisha was also having difficulty distinguishing the young royal from his guards. They were all dressed in the same cream thobes with matching headscarves. It seemed they weren't taking any chances with the holy warriors along the borders, who were now roaming the city as though it belonged to them.

'I think that's him on the left,' Yasmin said over the top of her cat's head. Her other cat sat beside her foot like a guard dog.

Aisha narrowed her gaze. 'How do you know?'

'Because he looks the most miserable.'

Aisha pinched her.

'Ow.'

'It's true,' Safiya said behind them, arms crossed and feigning disinterest. 'Everyone knows Gruisea's royal family is the dullest in the empire.' She was against the plan to place Lilah in his path. If she had her way, none of them would ever leave Khorasan Palace. But that wasn't the world they lived in. An unwed princess in the Slevaborg empire was a wasted opportunity. Smart alliances were the only path to survival. Even King Hamza of Gruisea knew that. It was why he wed his only daughter to the Crown Prince of Kuzebet the day she had come of age.

Prince Tariq had not risked crossing the sea and entering Avanid for a few pleasantries and a cup of tea. Trade was the word being passed around court. The Emperor had Gruisea's limestone mines in a chokehold. But there was a second reason he had come in person.

The prince was on the hunt for a future queen.

Aisha snuck a glance at Lilah, who was peering over the guardrail. She was everything one could want in a queen: smart, graceful, loyal, charismatic, intuitive. And her beauty would bring any man to his knees. She was the ultimate bait for any prince.

'Is he here?' Omar shouted as he leapt out onto the balcony.

Safiya caught him mid-leap. 'If Zara sees you running on the balcony'—she wrestled him into a secure hold—'she'll blame us.'

Being the eldest, Zara was burdened with the responsibility of worrying about everyone in the family. She had only been eleven when she took on the role of mother to five children. Plus, she had to look out for the current king while protecting the *future* king.

Zara was the closest thing Avanid had to a queen.

'I can climb down from here,' Omar said, looking up at Safiya. 'I've done it before.'

Safiya clamped a hand over his mouth in response.

He was twelve years old with five older sisters. Some boys might call that hell, but Omar enjoyed being the youngest and the only boy. He wasn't fussed about the king part—yet.

The prince had been the queen's parting gift to Avanid before her execution. Five daughters, three miscarriages, and a stillborn son whom she had held for two days. Then Omar arrived—early, true to his character. Healthy despite his small size. He only got a year with her and no memories to show for it.

'Back from the guardrail, all of you,' Zara said as she stepped out onto the balcony. Her gaze went from Omar to Safiya. 'Will you let him breathe, please?'

Safiya's hand remained in place. 'He can breathe just fine through his nose.'

Shaking her head, Zara continued forwards to get a look at the prince—since no one was moving back as instructed. Yasmin made room for her, and Omar pulled free of Safiya's grip, pushing between them.

'Which one is he?' Zara asked.

Lilah wrapped her arms around Omar. 'They're all dressed the same, so we don't know.'

One of the men chose that moment to look up in their direction, spotting them all on the balcony. Everyone took a fast step back—except Aisha, who held his gaze despite the nervous pounding of her heart. That was him, the prince. Somehow, she just knew it.

'In the middle,' she said.

They all took a step forwards, Lilah at the front.

'How do you know?' she asked.

Aisha didn't have an answer. Her mother's strong intuition, perhaps.

Safiya made a face. 'Hope your children get your nose.'

'Ignore her,' Aisha said. 'You can't even see his nose because it's covered.'

Zara leaned forwards and whispered, 'Keep your voices down. If he hears you, it will be a long wait for the next prince to arrive.'

Aisha took Lilah's hand.

'Down to the courtyard,' Zara instructed, adjusting the silk folds of her skirt. 'All of you. Make sure you're there to greet our guests.' She ran a hand over her hair to smooth it despite not one strand being out of place. 'I'll get Baba.' With that, she left the balcony.

Safiya ushered Omar, and Yasmin set the cat down and followed.

When Lilah went to move, Aisha held her in place.

'I'm fine,' Lilah said, sounding defensive.

Aisha searched her sister's eyes. She was afraid. Of course she was. 'Trust yourself when you meet him.'

Lilah offered a reassuring smile. 'It doesn't matter what I think. It matters what he thinks.'

The words struck Aisha like a knife. 'Don't say that.'

'It's true.' She squeezed Aisha's hand. 'We need this.'

Her beautiful sister, with all her beautiful human parts, reduced to an asset for trade.

'I'll remain at your side the whole time. Fill every awkward silence. Ensure the light is hitting you at just the right angle. Whatever you want.'

Lilah laughed. 'I appreciate that.'

Looping her arm through her sister's, they went inside.

* * *

He was taller than Aisha had expected. A full head above Safiya. His watchful guards stood back, but within hearing range. As the women approached, his gaze met Aisha's for the second time before shifting to Lilah.

'May I present my sisters, Lilah and Aisha,' Safiya said, gesturing to each in turn.

He bowed, which was unnecessary, but it gave Aisha a moment to get a proper look at him. Even fully covered, she could see the outlines of a strong body. This wasn't a man who sat idle. The only visible parts were his hands. Veins traced the backs of them like desert rivers. When he straightened, she noticed his eyes were moss green up close, ringed with bright gold. The shadow of stubble gave him a rugged edge.

'This is Prince Tariq,' Safiya said, in case it wasn't clear to anyone.

'Welcome to Khorasan Palace, Your Highness.' Lilah wasted no time. 'How was the journey here?'

His eyebrows knitted together. 'Challenging.' He looked at Aisha, whose turn it was to say something. Instead, Omar beat her to it.

'Is it true that if I were born in Gruisea, I would already be considered a man?'

Tariq assessed him. 'That depends on how old you are.'

'Twelve.'

The corners of Tariq's eyes creased. 'Not quite.'

'At what age can a man marry?'

'Certainly not at twelve.'

Aisha placed a hand on Omar's shoulder, silencing him. 'I understand this is your first time in Avanid. What are your thoughts so far?'

When he looked at her, it was like staring into a rich forest.

'It appears to be a very well-organised kingdom,' he replied.

Clearly, he was trying to be polite.

'I hear the scenery in Gruisea is breathtaking,' Lilah said.

'It's a little more rugged than Avanid.'

'I can't even remember the scenery outside,' Yasmin said, looking off in the direction of the wall.

An awkward silence followed.

Aisha cleared her throat. 'Shall we head to the garden and see if the king has arrived yet?'

Tariq gestured for them to lead the way, but Lilah walked at his side while the others walked behind them, watching. His party of guards followed at a distance.

'How long have holy warriors been posted inside your borders?' Tariq asked Lilah.

She kept her eyes on the ground in front of her. 'Almost a year now. What remained of our army moved inside the walls.'

He looked around. 'I see.'

Lilah went for a subject change. 'Do you sail often?'

Aisha pretended she wasn't listening to every word exchanged.

'It's enjoyable when the seas are calm,' he said.

'And when they're not?'

A frown settled on his face. 'Less enjoyable.'

Zara and their father appeared ahead, Zara's emerald dress trailing behind her as she walked. The king walked with a slight limp, a symptom of his sedentary life. He left his quarters only when forced.

Tariq stopped before King Bilal, bowing. 'Your Majesty.'

'Your Highness,' Bilal said, finding a shaky smile for their visitor. 'Welcome.'

'Thank you.'

Bilal looked around at his family. 'I see you have already met everyone.' He gestured to Zara. 'This is my eldest, Zara.'

'Welcome to Khorasan Palace, Your Highness,' Zara said, bowing her head. 'How wonderful that we were finally able to make this meeting happen.'

He responded with a polite nod.

'Come,' Bilal said. 'Sit. Rest.'

They all made their way over to the table where a servant was laying the last of the refreshments. The autumn breeze was a refreshing change from the scorching summer heat that had lingered for far too long.

'Yasmin, why don't you take Omar for a walk?' Zara suggested.

The youngest siblings excused themselves and wandered away.

Everyone else took a seat, Lilah next to the prince. Zara poured some tea.

'Thank you,' Tariq said.

The king discreetly wiped his already sweaty hands on his robe. 'And how is your father?'

Tariq drank before answering. 'He's well, thank you, and sends his respects.'

'Good, good.'

Tariq cleared his throat. 'I hope you don't think me rude for getting to the point of my business,' he said, shifting in his chair, 'but our ship isn't safe in your port, as you know.'

Bilal's face reddened at that. 'I understand. Please, go ahead.'

'As you're likely aware,' Tariq began, 'we have the largest supply of limestone in the empire. I'm currently trying to gauge demand.'

Zara frowned. 'Gruisea has been exporting all over the empire for decades. How's it possible that you don't have that information?'

There was a beat of silence before he responded. 'All trade goes through Slevaborg now. The Emperor chooses which information is passed on.'

Did he say all *trade?* It was worse than any of them had realised.

'I see,' Zara said, taking the opportunity to steer the conversation. 'It sounds like you need more than figures. While information is a great foundation, foundations don't build fortresses.' She paused. 'If Gruisea and Avanid are to survive the threats encroaching on us, then perhaps we need to align more closely.'

And there it was—Avanid's hand laid out for him to see.

The subtle tightening of Lilah's shoulders was the only sign of her discomfort. Small, but enough to draw Tariq's attention. His green eyes seemed to darken as he set his cup down on the table with a soft clink.

'Go on,' Tariq said, looking around at the captive audience.

'One of mutual benefit and longevity,' Zara continued in a steady voice.

The prince nodded. 'I see.' His gaze returned to Lilah, staring at her as if he were deciphering a puzzle. 'Such an alliance would require deep trust.'

Zara nodded in agreement. 'In times like these, trade is no longer enough.'

Aisha swallowed down the odd sense of guilt and complicity at the trap being set. All while her father sipped his tea and said nothing. He'd been letting Zara make big decisions for years, and this was no different.

Tariq sat back, fingers drumming on his thigh. 'Since we've established we don't have time to waste, what is it that you're proposing?'

Bilal cleared his throat, and when everyone looked at him, he reached for his cup and drank.

Frowning, Zara turned her attention back to Tariq. 'Gruisea has a proud history of great queens. Women who have stood alongside their kings, not merely as ornaments but strategic partners in governance.' She paused. 'Lilah here embodies all the traits a crown prince like yourself would seek in a wife.'

The conversation was going exactly as planned, and yet Aisha had never felt more uncomfortable. She could only imagine how hard it was for Lilah.

When Tariq didn't speak, Zara continued. 'Lilah is a paragon of grace and dignity. She has been trained in diplomacy from a young age, mastering the art of negotiation along with other relevant skills. Her intellect is matched only by her compassion.'

Tariq's gaze went briefly to Lilah, his expression unchanging.

'She understands the weight of duty,' Zara added. 'She knows what it means to serve her family, her people, and the greater good.'

'From behind walls,' Tariq replied casually.

His words had Aisha speaking up in defence of her sister. 'I'm sure you're aware of the reasons for that, Your Highness.'

Green eyes locked on hers once more. 'A queen must understand the realities of the world outside the walls of her keep. Gruisea is not Avanid.'

'Lilah is a quick study,' Zara said. 'Adaptable.'

His gaze shifted back to Lilah. 'And yet your sisters speak for you.'

Flustered, Lilah opened her mouth to reply, but no words came out.

Aisha was tempted to step in and fill the silence, but this was Lilah's moment.

'I—' Lilah cleared her throat when her voice cracked. 'I

would do everything within my power to rise to the occasion, for the sake of our families and kingdoms.'

Tariq shook his head. 'You wouldn't survive.'

Safiya, who had done remarkably well to remain silent up until that point, could stay quiet no longer. 'Do they not teach decorum in Gruisea?'

Tariq shrugged. 'I thought we all agreed not to waste each other's time.'

Lilah reached for her cup, but her hand was trembling and it slipped from her fingers, smashing on the ground. She stared down at it in horror.

A servant rushed forwards to clean the mess, and Aisha instinctively bent to help. Apparently Tariq had similar instincts, because they both reached for the same shard of porcelain, fingers meeting. On contact, a sudden wave of heat surged up Aisha's arm, and the ground blurred and faded. The sound of her sisters' voices dissolved, replaced by the sound of waves lapping against a wooden hull. The tang of salt filled her senses. Looking around, she realised she was aboard a ship, the deck swaying gently beneath her feet. Aisha gripped the railing for balance, eyes drawn to the horizon, where a rugged coastline beckoned her. Then she saw him, standing a few feet away as the wind whipped his hair.

Tariq.

When he looked in her direction, the scene disappeared. The ground and broken cup were before her once more. And Tariq's face, mere inches from hers, staring.

Aisha bolted upright, her pulse pounding in her ears. She took hold of her chair to stop herself from swaying. Thankfully, another servant arrived, filling the space between her and the prince, silently sweeping up the mess with a small broom.

Aisha looked around to see if anyone else had noticed. Safiya and Lilah were out of their chairs, politely excusing themselves. Understandable given the humiliation. But Zara was looking straight at Aisha, head tilted and an all-knowing look on her face. It had been a long time since Aisha had experienced a vision. She thought she had shut that part of herself down—just as Zara wanted.

When Aisha could take the stares no longer, she rose. 'Please excuse me.' She managed a smile, though she still felt dizzy. 'I'm just going to check on Yasmin and Omar.'

Tariq stood courteously, despite his far from courteous words earlier, and bowed his head.

Aisha left, trying not to hurry but desperately needing a moment. She was almost at the main doors when she heard Zara call her name. 'Aisha, *stop.*'

Her feet obeyed her sister against her own wishes. *Damn feet.* Aisha turned, slowly, and watched Zara approach. Her face appeared calm, but her eyes gave away her true state. She stopped in front of Aisha and looked around before speaking.

'What happened back there?' Her eyes moved over Aisha's face as if looking for lies before she had even opened her mouth.

'She was clearly nervous, and the cup slipped—'

'You know very well I'm not asking about that.'

Aisha had no choice but to disappoint her with the truth. 'I should have worn gloves. I didn't think. It had been so long.'

Concern was etched on Zara's face. 'You saw something.'

'I don't know.' A lie. 'It's been over a year since—'

'What? Suddenly you can't recognise it when it happens?' Zara gave her a doubtful look. 'Enough of that. I need to know what you saw.'

Everything Aisha was about to say would ruin all their plans. 'I was on a ship. Sailing towards an unfamiliar place.' She swallowed. 'Tariq was there.'

Zara's eyes widened a little. 'You were on a ship? With the prince?'

Aisha nodded.

There was a long, thoughtful silence before Zara said, 'We can fix this.'

'What do you mean?'

Zara held on to her hips, turning in a circle as she worked through the implications. 'You can go to Gruisea in her place.'

Aisha blinked, shocked. '*What?*'

Stopping, Zara asked, 'You're sure it was you on that ship?'

'Yes.' The word was a whisper.

Zara nodded, as though deciding on something. 'Then you will take her place.'

Aisha stepped back from her sister's words. 'No. You're putting too much faith in what I saw.'

'Have they ever been wrong? These visions of yours?'

Aisha tried to think of one time they had been inaccurate in order to back herself but came up blank.

'What about when Omar cut his foot,' Zara continued, 'and you saw the whole thing the day before it happened.

Was any detail incorrect? The colour of his trousers, perhaps?'

Aisha exhaled. 'No.'

'Then this path has already been decided, hasn't it?'

A thousand thoughts and feelings hit Aisha at the same time. 'You heard what he said. He doesn't want a wife raised inside walls.'

'We already know he will want you.'

'But why?' Aisha shook her head. 'He doesn't know anything about me.'

Zara looked around as though the answer lay somewhere in the courtyard. 'Well, Baba always said he knew from the moment he laid eyes on Mama.'

The comment threw Aisha. Zara never spoke of matters of the heart because it wasn't practical. They had all assumed that part of her had been suffocated years ago.

'I just know we need to take full advantage of this attraction before it wanes,' Zara added. Then, softer, 'We're running out of time.'

That sounded much more like the sister Aisha knew.

'So I'll go back in there and get this deal done,' Zara said, the strength returning to her voice.

Aisha glanced in the direction of the garden. 'And if we're wrong?'

'I can be wrong.' Zara took a slow step forwards, closing the distance between them. 'But your vision *can't*.'

ntent
CHAPTER 2

The Mad King of Avanid seemed surprisingly... sane. Yes, he sweated too much for the climate, and he gripped his robe as though it was the one thing keeping him upright, but the rumours of his mental deterioration had been somewhat exaggerated. He was more than capable of coherent conversation—even if he clearly wished he were elsewhere.

Tariq's gaze drifted to Kaidon, his anxious bodyguard who was pacing nearby, then to Aisha and Zara, visible through the archway at the edge of the garden. It was abundantly clear that the eldest princess was the one making all the decisions.

'They are all good girls,' Bilal said, rocking slightly in his seat. 'I just want them safe.'

The king looked in need of a lie-down.

'I understand,' Tariq said. 'You've been successful so far.'

When Bilal met his gaze, Tariq saw the pain in his eyes.

The story went that a decade after his wife's death, the king was still grieving. That grief had consumed him entirely. It was visible in every crevice of his face. Even his clothes resembled those worn by a widower. Despite his advisers urging him to remarry, his heart and soul remained bound to his dead wife.

A covenweaver.

Many women had since met the same fate. The Emperor had no tolerance for people with abilities he couldn't control or possess—especially women.

The two sisters glanced in his direction, confirming that they were talking about him. It had been clever to suggest Lilah as a match, knowing his parents were seeking a pliable wife. But Tariq hadn't travelled to Avanid for a *good* wife. He had come in search of a covenweaver.

Aisha turned to go indoors, and Tariq watched her retreating back, wondering if he had imagined the change in her when their hands had touched, the way her eyes glazed over and her pupils expanded.

'Apologies, Your Highness,' Zara said as she took her seat. 'Everyone seems to be dispersing.' She glanced at the king. 'What did I miss?'

Bilal didn't appear to hear.

Tariq gestured towards the garden. 'I was just admiring your carved wall.'

Zara looked over at it. 'My mother's design. She was quite the artist.'

Bilal seemed to come back to life at the mention of her, staring at the wall as though seeing it for the first time. 'She really was.'

Zara reached for his hand, giving it a gentle squeeze, the way one might a child's.

'The craftsmanship's a testament to Avanid's dedication to artistry,' Tariq said, keeping the conversation moving.

Zara lowered her head in gratitude. 'Thank you, Your Highness.'

Conscious of time, he brought the conversation back around. 'I was wondering if you could tell me about Princess Aisha.'

That had Bilal looking up.

Zara sat back, assessing the prince. 'She's as educated and capable as her sister.' She paused before adding, 'And just as beautiful, as I'm sure you've noticed.'

He had noticed. But he wasn't about to let a pair of pretty brown eyes impair his judgement. There was no way of confirming that Aisha had abilities without putting her in danger. Covenweavers hid behind safer words like *healer*, *confidant*, or *mentor*.

'Aisha's attributes are endless,' Zara continued. 'And she's not spoken for—*yet*.'

It seemed Zara didn't mind which sister he wanted, so long as it was one of them.

'She doesn't have any current marriage prospects?' Tariq asked.

Bilal closed his eyes. 'It is the rumours. He wants them all to burn.'

Zara's hand shot out, silencing him with a simple touch. 'People love to talk.'

'They lie,' Bilal said to no one in particular.

Another squeeze from Zara.

'I try not to pay too much attention to rumours,' Tariq said, eyes on the king. 'With your blessing, Your Majesty, I'd like Aisha to accompany me to Gruisea.'

Bilal slowly lifted his gaze, staring at the prince with the most tortured of expressions. But before he had a chance to respond, Aisha rushed into the garden, looking slightly panicked.

'Nasir's here,' she said to Zara. 'Requesting an audience.'

Kaidon must have recognised the name, because he gestured to the other guards to move in. Tariq had to assume they were referring to Nasir Handal, the head of the Slevaborg Mission to Avanid. A so-called peace-keeping ambassador, who was more of a highly trained spy.

Our time is up.

Rising, Tariq said, 'I'll leave you to—'

Too late. Nasir walked in before he was fully upright, apparently unable to wait. He was dressed in a decorated red tunic and flanked by a guard. His sharp gaze locked on Tariq, though his expression didn't change.

'Apologies,' he said, stopping a polite distance from everyone. He looked at Zara then. 'I was unaware you were entertaining.'

It was the first time Tariq had seen Zara look uncomfortable, though she hid it well. She held the High Verran's gaze for a moment longer before saying, 'I believe you've met Prince Tariq of Gruisea.'

'A very long time ago.' Nasir nodded politely, his jaw tight. 'You're a long way from home, Your Highness.'

'I am,' the prince replied.

Nasir's gaze flicked to Kaidon. 'What brings you to Avanid?'

If he thought Tariq was going to share that information, he was deluded. 'Private business.'

Nasir's eyebrows rose slightly. 'I wasn't aware Avanid had any private business.' He looked back at Zara.

'He means *family* business,' she said, keeping her tone light.

'The royal family's business is everyone's business, is it not?' Nasir replied.

The king chimed in with 'Not when it comes to matters of the heart.'

Nasir was silent a moment. 'And whose heart would that be?' The question was asked to Zara.

She drew a breath. 'What's the reason for your visit, High Verran?'

Nasir turned his attention to Tariq. 'I received word that an unidentified ship had docked in the port. The ship's currently being searched.'

Kaidon moved to take a step, but Tariq stopped him in his tracks with a small movement of the hand. 'Searched for what reason?'

'Safety.'

Zara briefly pressed her eyes closed.

'It's standard procedure when unmarked foreign ships arrive in Avanid's ports—unannounced,' Nasir added.

Tariq's temperature gently rose. 'I assume you mean unannounced to Slevaborg?'

'The prince just arrived,' Aisha said. 'We've barely had time to serve him tea, let alone notify authorities.'

Nasir cast her a doubtful look. 'Believe it or not, this is

actually a courtesy visit.' He looked back at Tariq. 'There are men waiting for you at the port.'

There was no stopping Kaidon this time. He marched forwards, hand going to his weapon. 'What men?'

Nasir's guard drew his sword, which had Aisha stepping in front of Zara.

So, she's the protective type.

'Enough,' Tariq said, careful not to raise his voice in someone else's house.

Nasir gestured to his guard. 'Let's keep our weapons in their sheaths. There's no need for any of that.'

Beads of sweat had formed on the king's brow. Zara noticed.

'I appreciate you coming by,' she told Nasir. 'Was there anything else?'

The High Verran observed the king for a moment, then lowered his head. 'I apologise for the interruption, Your Majesty.' Then to Tariq, he said, 'Have a safe journey back to Gruisea.'

Tariq nodded in place of a response.

Bowing, Nasir said, 'Your Majesty. Your Highnesses.' His gaze returned to Tariq as he rose. Then he turned and left, with his guard trailing behind him.

Once the men were gone, Zara turned back to Tariq. 'You should return to your ship as soon as possible. We have no way of protecting you outside these walls.' She glanced in the direction where Nasir had exited. 'He was doing us a favour by coming here. If the Emperor's men find you, there's a risk they'll take you across the border for questioning.'

Despite everything Tariq knew about the Emperor, he

was still shocked by the control he had over Avanid. 'We didn't get very far with our trade talk.'

Bilal wiped his forehead.

'We'll provide you with all the information we have,' Zara said. 'If it's direct trade you want, we'll consider any fair proposal you bring to us.'

Tariq could feel she wasn't done.

'After the wedding,' Zara added.

And there it was.

'It is too dangerous,' the king said quietly.

Zara's expression softened. 'It has to be now.' Then to Tariq, she said, 'You must take Aisha with you. This might be our only chance.'

When Tariq looked at Aisha, he expected to see complete shock on her face but was surprised to find only concern.

'We haven't finished that conversation either,' Tariq pointed out. 'Princess Aisha hasn't even consented.'

'Aisha will do whatever she can to benefit the kingdom,' Zara assured him. 'Isn't that right, sister?'

Aisha stared back at Zara, while the king stared at the ground. 'Yes.'

Tariq struggled to hide his surprise at how quickly and easily she agreed. 'It's a bold move to hand her over to strangers.'

'Now's the time for bold moves,' Zara replied. 'And we know you're a man of honour.'

Tariq set his gaze on Aisha. He could see her heart beating through her abaya.

'Once you have the king and queen's blessing, write to us,' Zara said. 'We'll announce the betrothal together. I'm envisioning a large wedding in Gruisea, with royalty from all over the empire in attendance.'

So she wanted a spectacle—a middle-finger salute to the Emperor.

'Your parents will approve the match?' Zara asked cautiously.

Tariq could feel Kaidon's eyes burning holes in the back of his head. 'Gruisea's strength depends on such alliances. They know it as well as I do.' At least he didn't lie.

'Should anything change,' Bilal said, 'you must return her safely to us. I want your word on that.'

Not a madman, but a father. 'You have my word, Your Majesty.' He looked at Aisha, who was doing her best to remain composed. 'We'll be departing shortly if you choose to come with us.'

It would surely go down as the worst marriage proposal in history. There was no softness to his words, just the grinding weight of duty.

'I…' Aisha swallowed when her voice came out hoarse. 'I'll go pack my things.'

Her response didn't even include the word *yes*.

'Pack light,' he said. 'Whatever you can fit into one bag on the back of your horse.'

Nodding, she turned away. Tariq made a point of not looking at Kaidon, though he was confident he could guess his bodyguard's expression.

'I'll come and help you prepare,' Zara said. 'And tell the others the good news.' She followed her sister, leaving Tariq standing with the king.

Tariq was at a complete loss as to what to say next.

'In a different world, at a different time, they would marry for love,' Bilal said, filling the silence for him.

How the hell was he supposed to respond to that? King Bilal's love story was one of the greatest and most tragic of its time. And Tariq had followed it with *We'll be departing shortly if you choose to come with us.*

He didn't know where to look. 'I'll keep her safe.' There weren't many other assurances he could offer to make the man feel better about handing over his daughter. 'You have my word.'

Bilal nodded, the motion sluggish. 'I would ask the palace guards to escort you to the port, but I do not want to draw the attention of holy warriors in the region.'

'My men will provide all the protection we need.'

Another nod. 'Cover your faces. Keep them covered until you are safely on the ship.'

'Of course.'

Bilal turned away. 'Excuse me.' He gestured to one of the servants to follow him as he exited the garden.

Only Tariq, his men, and a handful of servants remained now. Kaidon walked up beside him and said in a low voice, 'You sure about this?'

'Mostly.'

'*Mostly?*' Kaidon did a quick check to ensure the servants had not heard him. 'It's a long way to drag her only to find out she has no abilities.'

Tariq was well aware of the fact. 'There's a reason they've agreed to this. We're all playing the same game. We're just playing for different reasons.'

'Isn't the point to play for the same side?'

'Tell that to my sister who spills all her husband's secrets in her letters to the queen.'

A sigh slipped from Kaidon. 'Because the queen *demands* it of her. Who's brave enough to tell your mother no?'

Tariq didn't reply.

Kaidon glanced in the direction of the other guards. 'Are we going to assume the princess can stay on a horse?'

'We'll find out soon enough.'

CHAPTER 3

The next thirty minutes of Aisha's life passed in a blur of voices and people running back and forth in front of her. Safiya and Zara couldn't seem to agree on what to pack.

'She'll need something nice for when she meets the king and queen,' Zara was saying.

'There's no carriage,' Safiya replied. 'If it doesn't fit into this bag, it can't go.'

Barely anything could fit in that bag. It would all need to be left behind—like her family.

'This is all my fault.' That was Lilah, crying on the bed. 'If I hadn't dropped the cup—'

'This has nothing to do with a broken cup,' Zara said, straightening and looking at her. 'The gods have another plan. Now stop your incessant sniffling and go fetch a hairbrush.'

Lilah wiped her face and got to her feet, doing as she was told.

'Will we come to the wedding?' Omar asked. He was

seated on the floor, red-faced from trying to hold back tears.

'You won't,' Yasmin said. She was by the window with her parrot perched on her shoulder.

'Why not?'

'Because the holy warriors will shoot you in the back as you're boarding the ship,' she replied matter-of-factly.

Safiya threw a shoe at her, careful not to hit the bird.

'Go pick that up,' Zara said tiredly. 'It's going in the bag.' Then to Omar, 'We'll all attend the wedding so long as it's safe to do so.'

Aisha stood, unmoving, by the door. These were her final moments with them all together in one familiar room. She didn't want to do or say anything that would end it early.

Seconds ticked by.

'It's time to go.' That was Safiya, suddenly in front of her, the bag in hand.

Aisha wasn't ready, but that didn't matter.

Next thing, she was standing in the courtyard, her siblings to her left and a horse to her right. How long had it been since she had ridden a horse?

She looked around for her father, but there was no sign of him yet. Tears threatened to spill over, but she wasn't foolish enough to let them. No point turning a difficult moment into a traumatising one.

Despite Safiya's calm façade, her fingers were turning white on Omar's shoulders. Yasmin had brought her lizard outside with her and was focused on that. Lilah was barely composed. She stood with her hands open at her sides, face red from crying, not saying a word.

'You have everything you need for the journey,' Zara told her. 'Prince Tariq has assured me you will be well taken care of at Azura Castle.'

Aisha nodded.

'We have to go,' Tariq said, leading his horse over to them.

The devastation that hit Aisha had her holding on to her horse for balance. She didn't know where to begin with the goodbyes.

Lilah rushed forwards, wrapping her arms tightly around Aisha. 'I'm sorry,' she whispered.

Aisha pulled away and held her at arm's length. 'Everything is the will of the gods, remember?'

Lilah pressed her lips together to stop from crying, then nodded.

Omar was next, his strong arms going around her waist. Aisha kissed the top of his head, then signalled for Yasmin to join them. Aisha was careful not to squash the lizard as she hugged her youngest sister.

'Listen to Zara,' Aisha told them.

They nodded as they stepped back.

'They say the Gruisean leopard will be extinct soon,' Yasmin told her. 'Maybe you can save them.'

Aisha forced a smile. 'Maybe.'

Safiya was looking everywhere but at Aisha.

'Safiya,' Aisha said gently.

Pressing her lips together, Safiya stepped up and threw her arms around her sister, then whispered, 'There's a dagger in your bag if they try anything.'

Aisha closed her eyes, holding on for a second longer before stepping back and looking at Zara.

'How will you manage everything without me?' Aisha asked, her throat closing.

Zara gave her a strained smile. 'You were always going to leave these walls eventually.'

'You'll come back to visit us?' Omar asked.

Aisha mustered a convincing smile for him. 'That's definitely the plan.' She glanced at Tariq, half expecting him to contradict her, but he didn't.

When Zara didn't make a move towards her, Aisha went to her instead, aware of the tension in their bodies as they hugged. 'Take care of them,' she whispered before kissing her sister's cheek and turning away.

'Write to us,' Lilah said.

Aisha nodded, too close to tears to speak.

One of the palace guards approached Zara. 'There are holy warriors combing the city.'

Tariq exchanged a glance with his head guard, then approached Aisha, pulling her headscarf up. 'Cover your face.'

She did as she was told. She was still tucking her hair in when Tariq took hold of her waist and lifted her onto the gelding. 'Can you ride?' he asked as he stuffed her foot into the stirrup.

'Yes.' She tried to sound confident, but the sudden contact had caught her off-guard.

His eyes searched hers. 'Can you ride *well*?'

'Well enough.'

He finally took a step back. 'Good.' He then returned to his horse, mounting in one fluid motion and gathering the reins as he gave instructions to his men.

Baba.

Aisha looked around for her father, still nowhere to be seen, then at Zara. She must have read Aisha's thoughts, because she shook her head.

He wasn't coming.

He was likely in his quarters with the curtains drawn, unable to face the moment.

'Let's move out,' Tariq said.

Her horse began moving without her doing anything, following the others. Aisha looked back at her siblings just as Lilah burst into tears. Her gaze snapped forwards, unwilling to watch the aftermath.

Tariq's horse moved into line with hers. 'Don't leave my side,' he said, looking at her. 'Understand?'

Everything about the moment terrified her. It was her first time outside the walls in years, and she was doing so with a group of strange men. 'Yes.'

A few heart-racing minutes later, the gates appeared before her, and she couldn't look away from them. Tariq nudged the sides of his mare, and she lengthened her stride. Aisha's horse matched the new pace.

The gates opened, and Tariq signalled to his guards. The men formed a protective circle around the two of them. Aisha looked back as the gates began to close, losing her balance in the process. Tariq's hand shot out, catching her elbow and righting her.

'Keep your eyes *ahead*,' he told her.

Colour filled her cheeks.

The palace was located in Orinthia, Avanid's capital. The streets outside were alive with sounds and colour. The clamour of hooves on cobblestone mixed with the shouts of merchants selling everything from eggs to fine jewellery. People glanced in their direction but quickly lost interest when they realised they weren't holy warriors.

Fear bounced in Aisha's belly as she held on to the front of the saddle. It grew the further away from the palace they got. The smells changed, and her surroundings became unrecognisable. She may have been surrounded by guards, but she was entirely alone.

Reality tightened around her neck.

She stole a glance at him, her future husband. His features were hard-edged as he scanned their surroundings. She looked away when his gaze slid to hers.

The party continued through the maze of streets, the aroma of spices and fresh bread creating a heady smell that Aisha found nauseating. The buildings around her felt like they were leaning in.

They passed a market where a group of musicians were playing instruments. But then the music waned, and a strange hush fell over the area. Aisha felt the ripple of tension spread along the street, prompting the head guard to raise a hand, signalling some sort of warning. Tariq gestured to a nearby alleyway, and the guards pressed in around them. He grabbed her reins as horses appeared. The riders wore white surcoats banded with scarlet, chainmail visible beneath. Verses were carved into their bracers so that every movement flashed with prayer.

Slevaborg's holy warriors.

They were nothing more than the Emperor's soldiers wrapped in scripture. Gods, how long had it been since she had seen them up close? Her breath caught in her throat, her pulse beating in her ears.

'Princess.'

She flinched at the word from Tariq's mouth. When she looked at him, she was met with the same intense stare as earlier, after her vision.

'You're shaking,' he said, gesturing to her hands.

She looked down and saw that he was right. She quickly took hold of the saddle again to still her hands. 'It's cold in the shadows.'

He let her have that lie, his eyes returning to the road.

The head guard walked his horse to the edge of the alleyway and looked both ways before signalling to the others. The horses began to move again, and Tariq let go of her reins.

When they returned to the street, people looked at them with suspicion now, likely realising that the warriors were looking for them. Tariq must have noticed this too, because he told his head guard to 'Pick up the pace.'

No one spoke again until they reached the outskirts of the city, a stark transformation from the bustling streets behind. The noise faded, replaced by the gentle rustle of desert winds and the occasional call of a raven overhead. Aisha had not seen the desert in over a decade, since her mother was alive, when it had all felt safe. Nothing had felt safe since that day. Her father had kept the fear alive for good reason.

Tariq remained at her side as they made their way through vast stretches of golden sand. Aisha marvelled at the raw beauty of the setting, with its towering date palms along the horizon. Aside from the occasional cluster of nomadic tents, there was nothing but space and gentle sunshine.

'How far to the port?' she asked.

Tariq met her gaze. 'You don't know how far your own port is?'

Aisha's cheeks heated. He thought her sheltered. What kind of princess didn't know the distance from her own capital to the sea? She shifted in the saddle. 'What I meant to ask is how long will it take to get there?'

He was about to answer, but then his head turned sharply. He appeared to be listening for something. Aisha followed his gaze across the shimmering dunes, wondering what he had heard that she didn't.

'Shit,' said the head guard.

Aisha heard it then—the pounding of hooves in the distance.

Tariq wheeled his mare around with a clipped signal to his men. 'Let's get off the road.'

'How do you know who it is?' Aisha asked.

'We don't,' his guard replied. 'Which is why we're getting off the road.'

Tariq sent her gelding forwards with a sharp slap to its flank. The horse lurched after the others. 'Ready for a gallop?'

'What? No—'

'Lean forwards and hold on.'

Then they were off, the guards thundering into formation around them.

Aisha lowered herself against the horse's neck, grabbing handfuls of mane as sand and sunlight blurred together. Risking a glance over her shoulder, her stomach dropped as horses crested the horizon. She reminded herself that she had seen herself and Tariq on the ship. That meant they would make it.

She just needed to stay on the horse.

* * *

Tariq remained close to Aisha, bracing for her to tumble off her horse. But to his surprise, she stayed on.

'We'll head west for a bit,' Kaidon called over his shoulder, signalling to the other men.

Tariq snuck another glance at Aisha, who was holding on for dear life while the horse's mane whipped her face. Then he looked over his shoulder to see if they were being followed.

Damn it.

The group had trailed them off the road and into the desert. They had to be warriors.

'Are we being followed?' Aisha yelled into the wind.

'Don't worry about what's behind you. Focus on what's ahead.'

She looked at him then. 'But this isn't the way to the port.'

It certainly wasn't the most direct way. 'We'll get there. Eyes ahead.'

Kaidon dropped back to ride behind Tariq and Aisha. As the prince's bodyguard, he would ensure any arrows aimed at the prince went through him first.

Sand lashed Tariq's face as he pushed his horse faster. 'Nasir must have alerted them,' he shouted over his shoulder at Kaidon.

That had Aisha looking at him again. 'He wouldn't do that.'

He would have rolled his eyes if it weren't for the sand pelting him. He gestured for her to face forwards.

They continued at that speed for a number of minutes, slowing only when they reached the stony ground that separated desert and coast. Their horses heaved with exhaustion, their necks covered in foamy sweat.

'I think we've lost them,' Kaidon announced.

Tariq looked back. 'Thank the gods. The sooner we board, the better.'

They continued at a slow trot, pushing the horses through their fatigue. The smell of seaweed and brine signalled they were close.

'I can smell the sea,' Aisha said, sitting taller in the saddle.

Tariq noted her eager expression. 'When was the last time you visited the coast?'

Her eyes met his. 'Never.'

His eavesdropping guards exchanged glances.

'Not even when you were younger?' Tariq asked, unable to comprehend the idea of never laying eyes on the sea.

Aisha thought for a moment. 'I travelled inland a handful of times. To Montia and Cesea.' She swallowed. 'And Slevaborg.'

And since then, she had spent her entire life inside the palace walls, a small utopia designed to block out the harsh reality of the world on the other side. Tariq might have felt guilty about removing her from that world if it weren't for the growing occupation of their land. Zara seemed happy to hand any one of her sisters over in order to secure the alliance. He suspected that the king would have preferred to keep his daughters safely inside the walls. There was no fight left in that man.

'I heard you can see the ocean from Azura's walls,' Aisha said. 'Is that true?'

'Yes' was all he said.

When they reached the top of the next hill, they slowed to a walk. He heard Aisha suck in a soft breath. Stretching out before them was the Silver Sea.

'Wow,' she said. 'The world feels much bigger suddenly.'

It was the kind of view Tariq took for granted, having grown up in Gruisea with its endless coastline. But he tried to see it through her eyes. The silhouettes of ships in the harbour. The endless, glittering surface.

'There will be plenty of water to stare at from the ship,' Kaidon said, nudging his horse into a trot.

They began their descent towards the dock below, leaving a cloud of dust behind them.

A scatter of whitewashed buildings huddled along the curve of the bay, their flat roofs faded by the salt and sun. Narrow lanes wound between them, nets hanging from doorways like tattered curtains.

When they reached flat ground, Tariq spotted holy warriors patrolling the area on foot, their faces stony as they watched their surroundings. Their ship was on the other side of them.

Kaidon rode up beside Tariq. 'Got a plan for getting past our new friends over there?'

'I'm thinking.' Tariq looked around. 'First, we need to

get the princess safely aboard that ship. I'll draw them away.'

Aisha whipped her head in his direction. 'What about you?'

'I'll follow once you're aboard.'

She looked far from convinced. 'If they catch you—'

'Your sister will have no difficulty finding you another prospect,' he finished.

Her face fell at his words, and Kaidon looked away.

'Get her on the ship and set sail immediately,' Tariq told him. 'Don't delay.'

Aisha shook her head. 'Your Highness—'

He dismounted and handed Kaidon the reins of his horse. 'Go.'

Kaidon hesitated before joining the other guards in ushering Aisha into the shadows to wait. Meanwhile, Tariq lowered his headscarf and walked straight towards the ship, confident he would be spotted before reaching it.

And he was right.

The two warriors stilled to watch him for a moment, then conversed.

'Halt!' shouted one of the men.

It was time for a little game of cat and mouse. He glanced their way, then pivoted in the opposite direction.

'I said halt!'

I heard you, arsehole.

Tariq broke into a run, and the chase began.

He darted into the busiest alleyway he could find, hoping to blend in with the crowd. But that plan fell flat when all the shop owners stopped their conversations to watch him. He definitely stood out in his foreign clothes.

Behind him, he heard the shouts of the warriors in pursuit, prompting him to turn down the next alleyway and dash into one of the shops. A woman seated at a small table looked up at him in surprise.

'Which way did he go?' he heard one of the warriors shout—too close for comfort.

The woman looked past him, in the direction of the voice. 'I don't want any trouble.'

'Me neither.' He stepped up to the table. 'I just need a place to hide until they pass.'

Her eyes narrowed on him. 'Where's your accent from?'

He didn't have time for questions. 'Please.'

The woman looked him up and down, then let out a resigned breath. 'Get under the table over there. Quickly now.'

He dove beneath a cloth-covered table half a second before the warriors stepped into the shop, looking around.

'Good afternoon,' the woman said. 'Looking for something for your wives?' She picked up a brass trinket tree and held it up for them to see. 'To hold her rings.'

Tariq watched through a gap in the fabric as the warriors stared at the item in her hand before looking around the shop. He held his breath as their gazes brushed over the table where he was hiding. After a few painfully long seconds, they left the shop without saying a word.

Releasing the breath he'd been holding, Tariq waited a few seconds before poking his head out.

'It's all right,' the woman said. 'They've gone.'

Now he had to get back to the port and on that ship before it sailed away.

He crawled out from under the table and stood, brushing dust off his thobe. 'Thank you for that.'

'Now are you going to tell me where you're from?'

He looked around before replying. 'Gruisea.'

She gave a knowing nod. 'That explains why they were searching the ship.' Waddling over to the table he had emerged from, she picked up a garment made of rough wool and handed it to him. 'Put this on.'

He opened it up and looked at it.

'Fisherman's robe,' she explained, looking him up and down. 'Help you blend in.'

He gave her a tight smile. 'Thank you.' Then he slipped it on.

She stepped back to see him properly. 'Much better.'

Tariq reached into a pocket to retrieve some coins to pay her, but she waved him off. 'Any enemy of the holy warriors is a friend of mine.' She winked. 'Don't you have a boat to catch?'

With a quick nod of gratitude, Tariq left the shop, stepping into the bustling laneway and heading back the way he'd come. He needed to get aboard that ship.

CHAPTER 4

*A*isha's fingers were turning white on the ship's railing as she searched the crowded dock, her gaze darting from face to face. Every second that passed without seeing him made her grip a little tighter. She couldn't go to Gruisea without the prince. And if she got off the ship, she didn't know how she would get back to the palace.

'Where is he?' she said quietly to the guard beside her. 'I can't see him.'

The crew was already raising the sails, the canvas snapping as it caught the breeze. Ropes creaked and pulleys groaned as sailors shouted instructions to one another.

'He'll make it,' the guard said confidently, though it was clear from his rigid jaw that he was concerned.

Aisha looked at him properly. 'What's your name?'

He pulled his gaze from the dock to look at her. 'Kaidon.'

'I really hope you're right, Kaidon.'

Seconds dragged by.

'There,' Kaidon said suddenly, pointing to a man moving through the crowd.

Aisha strained her eyes, not seeing him.

'In the fisherman's cloak,' Kaidon said.

She narrowed her gaze on the hooded figure with his head bowed, moving purposefully towards the ship. 'It seems he stopped to do some shopping.'

'Pull anchor!' Kaidon called to the crew.

As quickly as relief arrived, it vanished when Aisha spotted three holy warriors shadowing the prince. They assessed him carefully. If they stopped him, for even a moment, it would all unravel.

'He's being followed,' she told Kaidon.

He looked out, then slammed his hand against the rail. 'Gods damn it.'

Before she could second-guess herself, Aisha tugged a filthy woollen blanket from a pile of cargo stacked near the railing and threw it over her head and shoulders. The stench of old fish and mildew made her throat close in protest.

'What are you doing?' Kaidon asked with an edge in his voice that suggested he already knew.

She gathered the blanket tighter so that only her face was visible. 'Making sure he gets on the boat.'

Kaidon grabbed her arm. 'I can't let you do that.'

She looked him in the eye. 'Need I remind you that we're still in *my* kingdom? This ship is docked in Avanid waters. I have authority here, and you don't. Now, unhand me.' The words came out more confident than she actually felt.

Kaidon reluctantly let go of her.

Aisha walked straight down the gangway and into the crowd, her heart hammering and throat dry. Then, clearing her throat and pointing, she shouted as loudly as she could, 'It's the princess! Princess Aisha! I just saw her! Over there!'

Heads turned instantly, murmurs rippling.

The people of Avanid were starving for royal appearances, and Aisha felt bad for taking advantage of the fact. But everything she was doing was ultimately for them. Everything she was doing, and everything she was leaving behind.

'Is that her?' a woman cried, pointing in the direction Aisha indicated.

The crowd surged like a tide, people tripping over one another in their eagerness to catch a glimpse of one of Avanid's hidden jewels. The holy warriors had stopped walking, their gazes following the wave of movement. They followed the flow of people.

Aisha slipped through the shifting bodies, the woollen blanket scratching against her cheeks. She moved quickly, searching for Tariq. She found him fighting against the current. When his eyes met hers, the hard lines on his face deepened. He was not happy. He pressed towards her, and she towards him, until they met in the crush of bodies.

'Why didn't you stay on the boat?' he whispered.

'They were tailing you.'

Someone bumped into her, and Tariq drew her closer to him.

'I know,' he said. 'I had a plan.'

She exhaled sharply. 'Well, I didn't know that.'

Gripping her hand tightly, he began pushing his way through the tide of people towards the ship. The gangway was already being hauled in, wooden beams groaning as the crew dragged it aboard.

'We need to move,' Tariq said as they broke free of the crowd.

'Leave it!' Kaidon was shouting, his voice sharp as steel.

The crew looked around, confused.

'Run,' Tariq told her, his tone urgent.

The pair sprinted as the plank slid to the edge of the dock. Aisha let the blanket fall off her as Tariq pushed her forwards, propelling her. They leapt just as the gangway left the dock.

Oh gods.

They were going to end up in the water.

Her feet slammed onto the boards, skidding danger-ously. For a terrifying second, she pitched backwards, but Tariq caught her. The crew held the gangway steady as Aisha and Tariq hovered above the water.

Taking hold of the rail, Kaidon stretched an arm towards Aisha. 'Grab on.'

Tariq pushed her towards the extended hand, clearly more confident that Kaidon would catch her than she was. Kaidon caught her wrist, swinging her up onto the ship. Aisha grabbed a handful of Tariq's thobe in the process, bringing him with her. They collapsed on the deck, breathless and trembling. Aisha met Tariq's gaze, but neither spoke. The ship creaked as the sails filled with wind and the deck lurched beneath them.

'Well,' Kaidon said, panting, 'I guess that's one way to depart.'

He extended his hand to Aisha once more, and she took it, rising unsteadily. Her chest rose and fell as she looked back at the dock. The holy warriors now stood at the water's edge, their faces dark with recognition. But they were too late.

A raw ache welled in Aisha's chest. She was really leaving. No more siblings sneaking into her bed after a bad dream. No more quarrels with Safiya or lectures from Zara. No more games with Omar or jump-scares from Yasmin's pets appearing underfoot.

The final thread was unravelling.

Tariq rested his elbows on the rail, the breeze tugging at his hair as he stared back at the warriors. 'Kaidon will show you to a cabin below decks,' he said. 'You'll be safe there.'

Aisha looked at him. 'Safe from what?'

'The crew's stares,' he replied without looking at her.

She looked around the deck, noticing for the first time the men staring at her. 'How long's the journey?'

Tariq straightened. 'If the weather's kind, four days.'

She glanced at the shrinking dock, where the holy warriors were now walking away. 'I'm sure I'll find a way to keep myself entertained.'

'Show the princess to her cabin,' Tariq said to Kaidon.

Kaidon inclined his head. 'This way, Your Highness.'

When Aisha went to follow the bodyguard, Tariq said, 'Thank you, by the way.'

She looked back at him.

'For trying to help,' he said. 'Even if it was ultimately to help yourself.'

She searched his eyes, unsure how to respond to the backhanded gratitude. Aware that the crew was still scrutinising her, she walked away without saying anything further.

CHAPTER 5

The first day at sea, Aisha remained in the small cabin with the door locked, listening to feet pounding above. In the evening, Kaidon brought her food, but she had no appetite. She drank the water, then attempted to sleep, waking every hour in a strange sort of panic, forced to remember where she was over and over again.

Aisha emerged the next day to the quiet rhythm of activity on deck. She ignored the stares of the crew. They would have to get over the novelty of a princess on board, because there was no way she could remain below decks for another three days.

If Tariq was unhappy about her emergence, he hid it well. He spotted her from the other side of the deck, then walked over to her.

'Morning,' he said.

'Good morning.'

He looked around before saying, 'If you're looking for food, Kaidon was about to bring you some.'

'Actually, I was looking for fresh air.'

He nodded. 'Did you sleep well?'

'Yes,' she lied. 'You?'

'Well enough.' Another awkward look around. 'I'll leave you to your… air.' With that, he left, busying himself with other people and things. It seemed he had no interest in spending time with the woman he had chosen to be his wife.

The sea stretched out endlessly, a blanket of dark blue with choppy waves that made the ocean look alive. Aisha leaned against the ship's railing, eyes on the horizon where the sky and water met. But her gaze kept returning to Tariq, whether he be absorbed in a conversation with his guards, reading something, or liaising with the crew. His expression was always serious, as if every minute of the journey demanded it.

Occasionally, their eyes would meet, and he would give a polite nod before turning to the next task. She left him to it, wandering the parts of the ship where she wasn't in anyone's way.

At the end of the second day, Kaidon brought a tray of food to her cabin again, and this time she was hungry enough to finish it.

On day three, she woke with a gasp when she landed on the floor of her cabin. It was pitch-black, and it took her a moment to realise that she had fallen out of bed because the ship was rocking from side to side. Climbing to her feet, she held on to the wall for balance as she felt around for the latch on the door and slid it open. She made her way up the narrow steps to the deck to see what was going on. Cold wind whipped her hair across her face as she looked around. A wave crashed against the ship's side, sending a sharp spray of water over her.

'Get below decks!' a crew member shouted at her.

Realising how dangerous it was, she did exactly that, retreating back down the stairs to her cabin. She slid the latch back into place and sat on the bed in the dark, hugging her knees and waiting for the weather to pass.

But it didn't.

The sunrise brought with it rougher waves that slammed into the ship with a force that made the walls shudder around her. The fear and loneliness Aisha had felt was replaced with seasickness. She tried lying down and closing her eyes in hope of relief, but that only made it worse. Nausea climbed her throat, sharp and unrelenting. She fought it, but the ship lurched again, and she knew she was going to be sick.

Stumbling out of bed, she fell against the door, her vision blurring. When she opened it, she came face to face with a soaking-wet Tariq holding a pail. Water dripped from his hair down his face. They looked at each other in the grey light.

'In case you don't have your sea legs yet,' he said, extending the pail to her.

She slapped a hand over her mouth in a desperate attempt to not be sick in front of him, but it was no good. Grabbing the pail, she vomited while he watched on.

'I'm so sorry,' she said, beyond mortified.

'Even the strongest of stomachs are being tested right now.' He looked up. 'Half the crew are currently emptying theirs.'

The cold air coming down the stairs was bliss on her face.

Tariq gestured for her to go back inside. 'I'll stay with you.'

'You don't have to do that.'

Taking the pail, he turned her around and guided her back into the cabin. 'I need to take care of this. I'll be back in a minute.'

Embarrassed, and thoroughly ill, Aisha did as she was told.

Tariq returned with a clean pail, leaving the door open behind him for fresh air. They sat side by side on her bed with their backs pressed against the wall, listening to the storm.

'Are you cold?' he asked.

'No, I'm fine.' She drew her knees up and leaned her head back, closing her eyes and breathing deeply, trying not to notice the rise and fall of the ship.

It was no good. She returned to the pail at Tariq's feet and was sick again. He reached out to hold her steady.

'Don't look,' she said, waving him away.

'I assure you, I'm not.'

She wiped her mouth with the back of her hand, fighting back tears. Thankfully, she had nothing left to bring up after that. She sat with her nausea, wishing she was anywhere else but on the ship. While Tariq certainly wasn't her first choice for company, his presence eased the sharp edges of everything she was feeling.

As the hours dragged on, the storm's fury lessened. The waves became smaller and less frequent.

'Do you want some air?' Tariq asked when all was still.

She nodded weakly. 'I'm guessing *you* do.'

A ghost of a smile appeared on his face. 'Let's go.'

The deck was a wreck of seawater and tangled ropes. Barrels had broken loose and were being dragged back into place. The sails hung heavy and soaked, straining against the rigging. The crew moved like ghosts through the aftermath, their clothes plastered to their skin and steps sluggish from hours of fighting the storm.

Tariq guided Aisha to the base of the mainmast, where they sank down onto the damp boards and leaned back against the solid post. The clouds began to thin and break apart, and light spilled over the deck. It was too bright for her, so she closed her eyes.

'You should start to feel better soon,' Tariq said beside her.

Aisha barely registered his words as she fell into an exhausted sleep.

When she woke, the sky was a brilliant blue. She blinked, adjusting to the stark light. That was the moment she realised her head was resting on Tariq's shoulder. The fabric of his cloak was rough and wet, yet warm. Not only had he remained there as her pillow, but he'd changed his position to provide better comfort.

A flush of awkwardness washed over her as she carefully sat up, running a hand over her wild hair. 'Sorry.'

There was the faintest hint of amusement in Tariq's eyes.

'And thank you for... all of that,' she said, her voice hoarse. 'That must have been very unpleasant for you.' When she looked over at the pail, she was both relieved and embarrassed to discover that someone had rinsed it clean.

Tariq rested his wrists on his knees. 'I've endured worse.' He exhaled. 'Feeling better?'

She nodded. 'I'm trying *really* hard not to breathe in your direction right now.'

The corners of his mouth twitched before he looked ahead again.

The deck was now tidy. At the stern of the ship, Aisha spotted Kaidon sitting with the other guards.

'Is everyone else aboard all right?' she asked.

'Yes.' Tariq stood and extended a hand to her, pulling her to her feet. 'You should try to eat something. It'll help settle your stomach.'

'I will.' Her legs were like jelly beneath her, and she prayed they would hold, as she had embarrassed herself quite enough.

The prince watched her for a moment longer, then bowed his head before walking off to join his men.

Aisha's eyes followed him as she considered whether she was any closer to knowing him. She knew he was dutiful. Tending to her while she was ill was proof of that. However, his actions lacked warmth. Though what did she expect three days into a new relationship? At least he was respectful. Many women in her position didn't even get that.

With a heady exhale, Aisha returned to her cabin and prepared for another day of solitude.

CHAPTER 6

$\mathcal{A}$s dawn approached on their last day at sea, Aisha stood at the ship's bow, watching the distant peaks of Gruisea take shape on the horizon. They rose sharp and blue, and she felt a mix of relief and apprehension. It was to be her new home, yet she didn't know anyone there, except for Tariq. She had never met the king or queen but suspected they were like every king and queen before them. They were there to do a job and happy to sacrifice members of their family in order to uphold the institution. Why else would they marry their only daughter off at the tender age of sixteen?

At least Zara had let them all grow up first. Yasmin was sixteen, and Aisha couldn't imagine her as a bride, as someone's *wife*. She was still very much a child, and they were all happy for her to remain one for as long as possible.

Aisha glanced right to where Tariq stood further down, looking out at the same view. They had barely exchanged more than a few polite words since the storm.

When he looked in her direction, she quickly looked away. To her surprise, he wandered over to join her.

'Almost there,' he said, stopping a few feet from her. His gaze fell to her gloved hands resting on the rail. 'Are you that cold?'

She looked down. 'It's a lot colder than in Avanid.' In truth, she was terrified of skin-to-skin contact on the day she would be meeting the King and Queen of Gruisea. The last thing she needed was another vision.

Tariq let the subject go.

They stood together in silence for the final hour of the journey. Aisha told herself it was a good thing that they didn't need to fill it with polite conversation. 'Companionable silence,' her mother had called it. That sounded much more palatable than 'having nothing to say'.

Gruisea's coastline was a stark contrast to Avanid's, with its imposing cliffs towering over churning waves. Mist curled around the base of the cliffs, where the water struck in angry bursts. It had its own natural fortress.

A hawk circled in the sky above, its dark silhouette gliding effortlessly. It was different to the elegant falcons back home. Larger, more primal.

'Thoughts so far?' Tariq asked.

Her gaze went to the patches of green clinging to the cliff sides. 'It's beautiful.'

'Nature can be a little stark and unyielding here,' he said, 'but you get used to it.'

That was reassuring.

The sea in the harbour was much calmer than any other parts. Fishermen were out in their boats, casting nets. Dockhands waited to secure the ship, calling out to the crew as they prepared to guide it to a safe berth. Ropes were tossed, and the ship appeared to creak in protest as it was reined in.

Aisha held tightly to her one bag as she waited to disembark.

'Don't worry, Your Highness,' Kaidon told her as he walked by, 'your exit should be far less eventful than your entry.'

She crinkled her nose. 'That's a relief.'

She followed Tariq down the gangway, exhaling when her feet met the dock. However, the relief she felt was short-lived. Soon after her feet touched solid ground, she felt said ground sway beneath her. It was as though the tide had followed her ashore. She gripped her bag, her stomach rolling.

A glance over his shoulder had Tariq stopping to observe her for a moment. 'I see you haven't got your land legs yet.'

She blinked, trying to comprehend what she was hearing. 'That's because I've been busy getting my sea legs.'

He took the bag from her. 'As far as your body's concerned, you're still at sea. It might feel as though the land's moving for a while.'

'Oh, perfect.' She looked around at everyone else, seeing no problems. 'Just me, then?'

Amusement flashed in Tariq's eyes. 'We're used to sea travel. Do you think you can make it to the horses?'

Horses? She cried inwardly. Hadn't she been punished enough?

As if reading her mind, Tariq said, 'It's just a short ride to the castle.'

She thanked the gods for that.

They made their way over to the waiting horses, and Aisha went straight to the smallest one. The saddle had a crest imprinted on it: a hawk gripping a miner's pick and hammer. She traced a finger over the hawk's wings. 'I thought Gruisea's crest bore swords.'

Tariq and Kaidon exchanged a glance before Tariq said, 'It was recently changed.' He mounted his horse. 'You'll ride with me.'

She was about to insist that she was fine to ride solo, but then the ground swayed, so she kept quiet.

Tariq rode up beside her, extending a hand. She took it, and he pulled her up onto his horse as if she were a bag of wheat.

'Hold on,' he said.

They rode at a gentle trot along a winding road that skirted the coastline before turning inland. The path wove through pine trees, where shafts of sunlight broke through, creating wild patterns. They emerged at the base of a slope, and when they reached the top, Aisha could see the entire city below.

'Chaldea,' Tariq said, stopping their horse so she could take in the view. He pointed. 'And Azura Castle.'

The castle was built back from the clifftop, its dark stone turrets and high walls blending with the rocky terrain. Blue banners with the hawk insignia lifted in the breeze. The rest of the city was variations of brown and grey. No colour.

The horse moved forwards again.

As they descended into the city, the streets narrowed into winding lanes. Market stalls sagged under meagre displays. Wilted vegetables and neutral-coloured cloth. Children ran about in threadbare tunics. Their mothers called to them, wrangling them in while dropping into hurried bows. People stopped what they were doing to acknowledge the prince, but it seemed more polite than excited.

Aisha recalled her time in Orinthia as a child, the way people's faces lit up at the sight of the royal family. It had been a long time since she had ridden through open streets. The whole empire had changed since then.

She made a point of smiling at anyone who met her gaze, but they responded only with suspicion. It was fair enough. She was a stranger sitting on the back of the prince's horse, and she looked like death warmed up. She probably looked like his prisoner.

As they approached the gates, Aisha saw the tension settle in Tariq's shoulders. That took her from nervous to terrified. Were his parents expecting him to return with a bride? And even if they knew, they would most definitely be scrutinising his choice.

The guards at the gate swiftly opened them when they saw Tariq. The inner courtyard came into view, busy with attendants and a few elaborately dressed men who watched their arrival with curiosity. He stopped the horse, and a groom appeared to help Aisha down.

Tariq dismounted soon after. 'I think it best I meet with the king and queen privately before introducing you.'

That answered her earlier question. At least it would give her a chance to freshen up. 'Where should I wait?'

Before Tariq had a chance to answer, a well-dressed

man with neat greying hair strode into the courtyard, his gaze immediately locking on Aisha.

'That was quick,' Kaidon said under his breath.

Aisha tried not to look as scared as she felt.

The man stopped in front of the prince, bowing. 'Welcome home, Your Highness.'

'Thank you.' Tariq gestured to Aisha. 'May I present Princess Aisha of Avanid.'

The man appeared to freeze for a moment before bowing again. 'Welcome to Azura Castle, Your Highness.'

'Thank you,' she said.

'Numair is the castle's steward,' Tariq explained.

'I see.' She could already tell the man had more opinions about Tariq's guest than was appropriate for his rank. 'It's lovely to meet you.'

He bowed his head slightly, then looked at Tariq. 'The king and queen are waiting for you in the garden.'

Tariq looked in the direction of the main castle. 'Of course they are.'

'And your guest,' he added.

Kaidon coughed, then pressed a hand to his chest. 'Excuse me.'

Tariq let out a long exhale. 'I guess we'll go straight into introductions, then.'

It was clear by his expression that he didn't have a choice in the matter.

They made their way through a series of arched corridors that opened to a garden. Colour at last. The space was meticulously maintained, filled with flowers and shaded by olive trees. A marble fountain trickled softly in the centre. The king and queen were seated at a table to the right of it. They looked up when they heard people approaching.

Queen Farrah's gaze swept slowly over Aisha, pausing on her gown, unpinned hair, the shadows beneath her eyes. Her expression tightened at the edges, lips pressing into a line that said more than words ever could.

King Hamza rose, extending his hand to his son. Tariq walked over to him, kissing the back of it, then touching his forehead to it. Hamza didn't extend his hand to Aisha.

'And who is this with you?' Farrah asked, still staring at her.

Tariq stepped back. 'This is Princess Aisha of Avanid.'

Still, the king didn't extend his hand. Silence settled like a noose.

'She will be staying with us here at the castle,' Tariq added.

Farrah didn't so much as blink. 'Why?'

Hamza waited for Tariq's reply with a confused look on his face.

'Perhaps we could let the princess settle in and discuss this later,' Tariq said.

'I would rather discuss it now,' Farrah replied coolly.

Aisha felt very hot in the gloves suddenly.

Tariq took a moment to gather his words. 'We're exploring the possibility of a future together.'

Aisha's eyebrows pinched together at his choice of phrasing.

'Out of the question.' Farrah spoke each word with precision.

Tariq pinched the bridge of his nose. 'Mother—'

'We told you before you departed that we have a suitable prospect in mind,' Hamza said.

Aisha felt her seasickness returning. Or was it land sickness? She looked at Tariq. 'Is that true?'

His hand fell to his side. 'I never agreed to it.'

'You do not have the privilege of *disagreeing*,' Farrah fired back.

The king gestured for calm.

Aisha drew a breath, but there didn't seem to be enough air in the garden.

'Fine,' Tariq said. 'If you insist on doing this now—with an audience. Princess Aisha comes to Gruisea with the strength and wisdom necessary for the changes I envision.'

'*You* envision?' Hamza said, his voice dropping dangerously. 'You do not rule this kingdom yet, son.'

'But I will one day,' Tariq replied.

For a long moment, the only sound was the trickle of the fountain.

The queen turned her attention back to Aisha. 'What is your age?'

'Twenty-one.'

Farrah gave her a disapproving look before focusing on Tariq again. 'When you suggested we strengthen our relations with Avanid, this was not what we envisioned.'

Aisha sucked in a breath, prompting everyone to look at her. 'Should I go, perhaps?'

Farrah raised her chin slightly. 'If you cannot handle uncomfortable conversations, then you *really* should not be here.'

'Enough,' Tariq said quietly.

Hamza took over the lecture. 'Do you honestly think we did not explore every option for you?' He paused for effect. 'That we did not thoroughly research every eligible woman within the empire for the future King of Gruisea?'

'I don't doubt it,' Tariq said, 'but I must have a say in the future of this kingdom if I'm to rule it eventually.'

Farrah's gaze slid to Aisha, colder this time. 'How did you do it?'

Confused, Aisha asked, 'Do what?'

'Seduce a sensible man. I would not have thought you pretty enough, but perhaps I am wrong.'

Tariq tensed up at that. 'If you speak to her like that again, we'll leave.'

Tutting, Farrah looked at her husband. 'She has changed him already.'

Aisha had no idea what to do or where to look.

'The girl is a Nazari, for goodness' sake,' Farrah continued. 'Her mother was a covenweaver. Do you honestly expect our people to trust her?'

Aisha's temper flared. 'My mother was one of the most beloved queens of her time.'

Farrah stared back at her. 'I know all about your *beloved queen*. I know everything about your family. Like the fact that your eldest sister did not shed a tear as she burned.' She paused. 'Because she knew what she was.'

Aisha felt like the floor had been pulled out from under her. 'How dare you,' she breathed.

'You don't have to listen to this,' Tariq said, taking Aisha by the arm and turning her around. 'Let's go.'

'You have not been excused,' Hamza said.

Tariq ignored him.

The sound of the fountain faded behind them, replaced by the scrape of Kaidon's boots and the pounding of her own pulse. Aisha bit the inside of her cheek to keep her composure, swallowing hard against the burning heat in her eyes. She refused to cry in front of Tariq.

The prince looked back at Kaidon. 'Run ahead and find out which room Numair has prepared.'

The guard jogged ahead.

Aisha pulled her arm free of Tariq's grip and turned to face him. 'You should have told me.'

'About the match?' He shook his head. 'I never agreed to it.'

'You should have told me anyway.' She glanced over her shoulder. 'You should have told me about all of it. About them.' Her eyes filled with accusation. 'You knew how they would react, and you let me go in there unprepared.'

He searched her eyes. 'I didn't expect my mother to bring up your family's history. For that, I'm sorry.'

'For *that* you're sorry?' She laughed despite nothing being funny. 'Why did you bring me here, knowing they would reject me?'

She was met with silence.

Gods, she had been such an idiot not to ask more questions before coming. Her vision hadn't shown anything beyond the journey.

'They're not used to people going against their wishes,' Tariq said. 'They just need some time to get used to the idea.'

She nodded slowly. 'Why *did* you go against their

wishes? Please tell me I'm not part of some rebellious phase or game you're playing.'

'They wanted me to marry Imperial Lady Katryne,' Tariq said.

Her face went slack as the name registered. 'The Emperor's niece?'

A small nod.

It took her a moment to speak. 'Why would they willingly tie themselves to that family?'

'You're a smart woman. I'm sure you can figure that out.' He leaned in and lowered his voice. 'This isn't a game to me.'

A throat cleared, and Aisha looked down the corridor to find that Kaidon had returned.

The guard glanced between them. 'The princess's chamber is ready.'

Aisha didn't trust her own voice, so she simply nodded, then walked over to him—without looking back at Tariq. Kaidon proceeded to lead her through the winding halls of Azura Castle.

She wanted to believe she was strong enough to face whatever was ahead of her, but the humiliation was making her doubt herself.

'Here we are,' Kaidon said, stopping in front of a door.

Before he could say another word, Aisha walked straight in and closed the door behind her. Leaning against it, she sank to the floor and cried.

CHAPTER 7

Two days passed, and Aisha didn't leave her rooms. Meals arrived on trays carried by silent attendants who left as quickly as they came. She spent many hours with her forehead pressed against the cool glass of the narrow window, watching the world outside. She missed the chatter of her siblings and the endless company. All she heard now were her own thoughts—and they weren't kind.

A knock at the door startled her. Rising quickly, she smoothed her gown and went to open the door. Tariq stood there, tall and composed, with dark circles enclosing his eyes.

'You haven't left your rooms,' he stated plainly.

She folded her arms. 'Where should I go?'

'Anywhere you like. It's not a prison.' He exhaled. 'Unless, of course, you've changed your mind and wish to return to Avanid.'

He was testing her. Gods, she wanted to take him up on that offer. But then what? Nothing would change if

68

none of them were prepared to sacrifice their happiness. Avanid needed this wedding to happen. 'I've not changed my mind. Have you?'

He shook his head.

'I'm surprised your parents haven't changed it for you,' she said.

He looked past her into the room. 'I've arranged a feast tonight. We call it a majlis, a gathering to welcome new guests and show honour.' He paused. 'It's important the king and queen see you accepted by the nobility. If the court welcomes you, it will show people that this union has merit.'

Aisha didn't know whether to be reassured or alarmed by this. 'What would I need to do at this… majlis?'

'Meet people. Talk. Maybe dance.'

She frowned. 'I don't know any of your dances. Lilah knows all of them, along with your traditions and customs.'

He leaned against the doorframe, appearing to relax a little. 'Princess Zara was rather confident in her plan, wasn't she?'

Aisha dropped her gaze. 'Lilah was the obvious choice.'

'Not for me.'

She couldn't find it in her to look up.

'I'm confident they'll like you,' Tariq said.

She forced herself to meet his gaze. 'Your reassurance would mean more if the king and queen weren't so blatantly opposed.' She watched the discomfort play out on his face. 'You knew they wouldn't approve. You just didn't communicate it.'

'Would you have come here if I did?'

'No.' She bit her lip.

He lifted his shoulders in a shrug. 'Then I did the right thing.'

Aisha unfolded her arms. 'I need to know you won't just throw me to the sharks tonight.'

'I'll remain at your side throughout the whole evening, if that's what you want.' He sounded sincere.

She stared at him. Of course she had to say yes. She couldn't hide away in her room forever. 'I'll need something to wear.'

He straightened, nodding. 'I've organised a permanent attendant for you. I'll send her to help you. Whatever you need, she'll organise it.'

Aisha felt her hostility towards him lessen. 'Thank you.'

'I'll see you later.' With that, Tariq left.

Later that afternoon, Aisha had just finished having a wash when there was another knock at the door. Wrapping herself in a robe, she walked over to the door.

'Who is it?'

'Your attendant,' a woman answered.

Aisha opened the door to find a tall attendant standing there, silks draping her arm and tray in hand. The scent of herbal tea drifted into the room. The woman's hair was cropped close to her head, her posture precise, her eyes light brown. Aisha guessed her to be in her late twenties.

'Your Highness,' she said, inclining her head to show respect without the tray moving at all. 'My name is Maryam. Prince Tariq sent me to help prepare you for the evening.'

Aisha stepped aside. 'Come in.'

Maryam entered, setting the tray on the small table by the window. Steam rose from the hammered-brass pot. She poured the tea, her movements as controlled as her expression.

'To calm the nerves,' she said, handing a cup to Aisha.

The porcelain was warm to the touch and instantly comforting. 'Thank you.' Aisha carried it over to the dressing table.

Maryam busied herself with the folds of fabric she had brought. 'These silks were selected for their quality and colour. Gruisean nobility normally wear subtler shades, but this soft blue will honour your Avanid heritage.' She held it up to show it.

'It's beautiful,' Aisha said, finding a smile.

'I am pleased you like it. Now we can begin.' Maryam gestured towards the dressing table. 'Take a seat. I will start with your hair.'

Aisha felt herself relax into the female company she had missed so much.

Maryam's fingers moved through Aisha's hair with practised ease. At one point, she started to hum, and it reminded Aisha of Lilah. Always humming. She watched the attendant pin her hair back in the mirror.

'Now for your face,' Maryam said when she was done.

She went to mix powders in a small dish, then traced colour over Aisha's eyelids with a soft brush. Then she used kohl to darken the lashes and added a rose colour high on her cheeks.

Satisfied with her work, Maryam wiped her hands on a cloth before fetching the silks draped across the bed. The gown shimmered when she lifted it. The fabric felt luxurious against Aisha's skin as she slipped it over her head. Maryam adjusted the folds and smoothed each crease until it lay perfectly. She then added heavy jewellery at Aisha's throat and wrists.

Aisha found the weight suffocating.

When she was finished, Maryam stepped back to look at her properly. 'I believe you are ready, Your Highness.'

Aisha stared at her reflection in the mirror, and a stranger stared back. It was all so unfamiliar. 'They'll approve of this?' she asked Maryam, turning to her. 'The nobility?'

Maryam's eyebrows rose ever so slightly. 'Yes, Your Highness.' She returned the empty cup to the tray. 'When you are ready, I will escort you to the banquet courtyard. The prince is waiting for you there.'

Aisha didn't think she would ever feel ready.

She looked around for her silk gloves, hoping Maryam wouldn't ask about them. The attendant watched her put them on but didn't say a word.

'Are you ready, Your Highness?' Maryam asked.

'Ready.'

* * *

Tariq paced in front of the doors that opened to the banquet courtyard, exchanging pleasantries with passing guests as they entered. He could feel the quiet whispers already brewing on the other side. Kaidon was standing off to one side, watching him.

'She should be here by now,' Tariq said.

'It's early,' Kaidon replied. 'The guests aren't going anywhere.'

Approaching footsteps had Tariq looking up again. His feet stilled when he spotted Aisha walking towards him. Her dark hair had been pinned back, and colour edged her eyes, making them look sharp and luminous. His gaze fell to her painted lips, then to her gown, light enough to catch the glow of the hall's lamps. The neckline was modest, edged in silver thread, with long fitted sleeves that tapered to her wrists. A wide belt cinched her waist, with delicate chains trailing down the front. It was beautiful, but it was also deliberate. Bold enough to remind the room she was Avanid royalty and restrained enough to silence accusations of ostentation.

He also noticed the gloves.

'You're staring,' Kaidon whispered to him. 'In a creepy way.'

Tariq quickly averted his gaze, not looking at her again until she was standing in front of him. The stirring in his chest was most unwelcome.

'What do you think?' Aisha asked, turning in a circle.

He ran his eyes briefly over her. 'You look nice.'

Out of the corner of his eye, he saw Kaidon look up at the ceiling. The words had come out flatter than he'd intended. Perhaps he was trying to make up for the fact that he'd been caught staring. It wasn't the gown—it was her. It had been the same when he first arrived at Khorasan Palace, when he had spotted her on the balcony. She had a way of holding a person's attention.

Perhaps it was one of her covenweaver abilities.

'Thank you.' There was definitely disappointment in her voice. 'You look nice also.'

He regretted his choice of compliment. Nice was not beautiful, and she *was* beautiful. But it was too late to do anything about it now.

His own attire was simple in comparison: a tailored indigo tunic trimmed in gold thread, a leather belt with a silver clasp, and black trousers.

'Anything I need to know before we go in?' she asked.

He glanced at the doors. 'I'm sure I'll think of something once we're in there.' He offered his arm. 'Just follow my lead. Tell me you're thirsty if you need to exit a conversation at any point, and we'll go and get you a drink.'

She took his arm as if she had done it a hundred times before. The warmth of her touch reached him through the fabric.

Kaidon stepped up to the doors and pulled them open. Tariq felt the weight of the nobility's eyes on them as they entered, speculating. Aisha carried herself well, back straight and head high. He prayed that strength would last the evening.

'Let's start with an easy one,' he whispered, steering her towards some members of his family. They paused their conversation when they saw him approaching. 'May I present His Excellency Eyad and Her Grace Kalila. My aunt and uncle.' He gestured to Aisha. 'This is my esteemed guest all the way from Avanid, Princess Aisha.'

Aisha bowed her head. 'It's a pleasure to meet you both.'

Kalila's smile was immediate. 'What a pretty thing you

are.' Then to Tariq, 'Much prettier than I was expecting from your mother's description.'

Aisha was quick to reply. 'In the queen's defence, she met me straight off the ship after a bout of seasickness. Her assessment at the time was probably fair.'

Eyad barked out a laugh, nearly spilling his drink. 'A royal with a sense of humour is a rare find these days.' He leaned towards Tariq. 'I must say, I am a bit surprised *you* picked a funny one.'

Tariq clapped him on the back. 'Thank you for that.'

'Not much of a sense of humour, this one,' Kalila told Aisha. 'Takes after his mother.'

'Hamza is not much better,' Eyad said. 'Though there is not a lot for him to laugh at right now.'

Concerned that his aunt and uncle were about to reveal too much, too soon, Tariq interjected. 'You'll have to excuse us. We must keep doing our rounds.'

Aisha took hold of his arm again. 'It was lovely meeting you both.'

As they walked away, Tariq brought his head closer to Aisha's. 'Safe to say they liked you.'

'If they're all that easy, it'll be a great night.'

Tariq glanced in the direction of his parents, who were seated at the far end of the courtyard, keeping an eye on the pair as they carried on their conversations.

One by one, the prince introduced Aisha to everyone in attendance. He remained careful with his words, acknowledging her rank, offering praise, but never naming her as his chosen bride. Not yet. The whispers were sharp enough already. No need to hand his parents the blade.

Aisha was far too good at her part. Charming when appropriate, poised under scrutiny. His mother must have seen it too, because her sharp eyes rarely left them.

'We're almost done,' Tariq whispered as they crossed to the final group.

Aisha looked around, smiling. 'Your mother hasn't stopped staring.'

'Great. Then she's witnessed how well you've been received.'

They crossed to the couple by the fountain, the last introductions of the evening. He inclined his head as they came to a stop. 'Lord Daman, Lady Selene. May I present Princess Aisha of Avanid.'

Selene's painted smile didn't falter, but her first words landed like a knife. 'Ah, the Mad King's daughter. What a lucky escape.'

Tariq had left them to last for that very reason. He felt Aisha's fingers press into his arm at the words. He gave her a moment to recover in case she wanted to respond herself, and when she didn't speak, he did. 'I had the pleasure of meeting King Bilal recently.' He kept his tone light. 'He was very welcoming. A true family man.' He stared at Selene, calm but pointed.

Selene's smile tightened. 'I think it is lovely that the Emperor let you enter Avanid.'

Lord Daman muttered something about the fine weather, attempting to move the conversation along, but it was too late for that. Aisha couldn't seem to recover.

Swallowing, she finally found her voice. 'Would you excuse us? I'm rather thirsty.'

Tariq inclined his head again. 'Forgive the fleeting

introduction, but we were just on our way to get some refreshments.' He guided Aisha away before the pair even had a chance to reply, waiting until they were well out of earshot before speaking. 'Don't take anything that woman says to heart.' He snatched a drink off a passing tray and handed it to Aisha as they came to a stop. 'She's well-known for stirring up trouble.'

Aisha stared into the cup of mead. 'Is that what people call him? The Mad King?'

He didn't know how to answer her. Of course she didn't know. How could she? 'Some people.'

'People here?' She looked up. 'Or people everywhere?'

His eyes moved between hers. She wanted to know if it was only Gruisea laughing behind her father's back or the entire empire. 'They're just rumours.'

Her eyes filled with tears. 'He's not crazy. He's just sad.'

The way her voice broke at the end had him looking away. He unfortunately locked eyes with his mother in the process, and she began making her way over to them—at the worst possible time.

'There she is,' Farrah said. 'The desert flower.'

Aisha blinked to clear her eyes. 'Your Majesty.'

'I know you have already met a lot of people this evening,' Farrah said, 'but I wanted to introduce you to Gruisea's Divine Sectarian.'

Aisha's eyes widened.

The queen gestured to Jamil, who was speaking with someone nearby. The sectarian excused himself, then turned towards them, the familiar sweep of his white robes brushing the floor. Jamil assessed Aisha on the walk over, taking in far more than he ever revealed.

'This is Princess Aisha,' Farrah said when he joined them.

Jamil extended a hand to Aisha, his thin fingers steady, expectant.

Aisha stared at the hand as though it were a blade aimed at her throat. It was clear she didn't want to take it. And Tariq knew why.

Farrah's brows lifted slightly when she didn't move. 'Something the matter?'

'No,' Aisha said on an inhale. Slowly, she took hold of Jamil's hand and brought it to her lips, then touched her forehead to his skin.

Tariq didn't miss the tremble of her hands. Nor did his mother, who watched each movement like a hawk.

'Your Holiness,' Aisha said, straightening. 'It's an honour.'

Jamil inclined his head. 'May the gods bless and keep you safe during your time here in Gruisea.'

Aisha clasped, then unclasped her hands. Tariq wasn't willing to stand by and watch her struggle any longer.

'We were actually just leaving,' he said. 'I'm going to escort the princess back to her chamber.'

Farrah looked Aisha over. 'Tired so soon?'

'Yes,' Tariq said, answering for her.

Aisha bowed her head. 'Your Majesty. Your Holiness.'

Tariq placed a hand at her back and guided her towards the exit, moving through a murmur of whispers. He ignored them, knowing Aisha had done everything right in winning their approval. Kaidon fell in behind them, silent and watchful.

They didn't slow down until the doors swung shut

behind them and the noise of the courtyard faded. Tariq's hand fell away when he saw her shoulders relax. They walked in silence.

When they reached her chamber door, Aisha turned and looked up at him. 'I'm sorry about that.'

'There's nothing to apologise for.'

She looked like she had more to say. 'I haven't had the best experiences with sectarians.'

'I know.' Sectarians were responsible for the burning of covenweavers. For the burning of her mother. 'I suspect the queen knows too. I'm sorry about that.'

Aisha shook her head. 'She just wants the best for you.'

'You don't have to defend her to me.'

She fell silent.

'You haven't eaten anything all evening,' he said. 'I'll have a tray sent to you.'

She nodded and brought her gaze back to his. 'What will happen now?'

Now, the nobility would gossip relentlessly, discussing every reason why she was right for the role and every reason she was wrong for it. They would scrutinise every detail of her appearance and every word spoken.

'Now we let them get used to the idea of you.' He took a step back. 'Goodnight.'

Aisha inclined her head. 'Goodnight.' She disappeared inside her rooms.

Tariq headed off down the corridor, and Kaidon fell into step with him.

'Where are you going?' he asked.

'The servants' quarters.'

Kaidon didn't need to ask why.

When they arrived at Maryam's room, Tariq rapped once on the door. Maryam opened it, her short hair catching the lamplight as she looked between them. She stepped back to let them in, closing the door behind them.

'Forgive the intrusion,' Tariq began.

'It is quite all right, Your Highness. Go ahead.'

Tariq hesitated. 'Now that you've spent time with the princess, I need to know it's her.'

Maryam's gaze flicked to the closed door behind him before answering. 'Yes,' she said, nodding. 'It is her. Aisha is the woman from my vision.'

CHAPTER 8

The following morning, Tariq went to visit his parents, who were eating their breakfast outdoors.

'Have some fruit,' his mother insisted, tapping the edge of the platter with her fingernail.

He ate to keep her happy. She watched him while his father sipped his drink in measured silence.

'Our guests were surprisingly accepting of the princess last night,' Farrah said. 'I would even go as far as to say some *liked* her.'

Here we go.

'Then perhaps we can make the betrothal official,' Tariq suggested.

His father looked over his cup at him. 'Let us not be hasty.'

'Hasty?' Tariq leaned back in his chair. 'The two of you were betrothed without ever meeting. And Amani shared a pot of tea with Prince Farid before news of their match was shouted from every rooftop.'

'Well, more caution is needed at present.' Farrah eyed Tariq for a long moment. 'Aisha was rather nervous around His Holiness last night.'

'And why do you think that is?' he questioned.

'I am interested in why *you* think that is.'

'Because her mother was murdered by a sectarian.'

'Her mother was *sentenced* to death because she was a covenweaver,' Farrah corrected, 'and was foolish enough to use her so-called gifts during a visit to Assur Qasr.'

Tariq drew a breath for patience. 'Did you bring Jamil to Aisha last night as some sort of test?'

Farrah tutted. 'How little you think of me. Your sister would never suggest such a thing.'

'King Lugman has nothing but praise for her,' Hamza chimed in.

No one mentioned the fact that Amani spent her first year in Kuzebet begging to return home.

'A few polished conversations are not proof of a suitable queen,' Farrah said. 'Perhaps I will spend some time with the princess today and get to know her better.'

That had Tariq on alert. 'Alone?'

Farrah looked him straight in the eyes. 'Yes, alone.'

His gut was telling him it was a bad idea, but he also knew he couldn't keep them apart forever. Their futures were entwined. 'Fine, but please be kind.'

She feigned offence. 'The fact that you feel the need to say that is insulting.'

He rose from the table. 'If you'll excuse me, I have some business in the city.'

Hamza merely nodded.

'We shall see you later,' Farrah said, turning her attention back to her breakfast.

Tariq offered a small bow before making his way across the garden, rejoining Kaidon at the gate. The guard cast a quick glance at the king and queen before asking, 'So? Is there to be a wedding?'

'Yes.' Tariq gave him a sideways look. 'They just haven't agreed to it yet.'

'Ah. Well, at least you know now that you brought the right bride back with you.'

Even before Aisha's apparent vision, Tariq had known it was her. He began walking. 'My mother's planning on spending some time with the princess today.'

'I suppose that's inevitable if she's to join the family.' Kaidon paused. 'Do you ever worry that you're putting too much faith in one attendant's vision?'

'Every day,' Tariq said plainly.

Maryam had been tending the queen a few months earlier when she'd had the vision. She had risked her life in telling him. He could have—*should* have—turned her over to Jamil, who would have sentenced her accordingly. Instead, he kept her secret, because she was part of a movement that wanted a different future for Gruisea.

A movement he was also a part of.

They went to the stables to collect their horses, then headed into the city.

Chaldea unfolded before them in layers that no longer fit together. The marble façades and tiled roofs of the merchants' quarter gleamed, while just beyond, cracked plaster and sagging timber told another story. Everywhere else, fountains were dry and the cobblestones beneath his horse's hooves were uneven from neglect. The gulf between the wealthy and the miners was widening.

Nobles drifted about in embroidered robes, their perfumes taking over the air, while ragged children lingered in alleyways, watching them. Tariq felt the quiet resentment beneath the hollow greetings he received.

They slowed their horses to a walk when the road turned to dirt, marking the outskirts of the city. When they reached a building with multiple horses tethered out front, they dismounted. Inside, a group of men were waiting for them, their faces showing signs of frustration.

Malik marched straight up to Tariq when he spotted him. 'Did you hear?'

Kaidon intercepted him gently. 'Easy now.'

'They took Kanin on his birthday,' Malik shouted around the guard. '*On his birthday.*'

Tariq knew whatever he said wouldn't be enough. 'I'm sorry.'

'You're sorry? He's *ten years old* and destined to spend the rest of his life in a black hole.'

Kaidon forced the man to take a step back. 'No, he won't. Remember, the prince is here because he wants to change that.'

Malik waved Kaidon's words away before walking off to calm down.

Rauf, one of the older men who attended, folded his arms across his chest and looked at Tariq with scepticism. 'Some of the children are struggling to lift the tools, yet they're forced to labour for up to nine hours.'

They had every right to be angry, but he was careful to keep his expression neutral. He wanted to rage with them, cry with them, but he was the Crown Prince of Gruisea. He was supposed to be enforcing his father's laws, not secretly scheming to change them. 'You've likely heard that Princess Aisha is here in Gruisea. Avanid will be our first direct trade route. I only ask for your patience.'

'We've been very patient,' Malik said bitterly. 'I was patient when I took off my uniform and laid down my weapons because King Hamza asked it of me. I was patient when he sent me to work in a mine. I was patient when the hours increased and the days grew longer.' He sniffed, hard. 'Now you come for my children, and I find myself running out of patience.'

'We have men ready to rise,' Rauf said.

The other men in attendance, the ones listening carefully, all shouted their support.

'When will trade with Avanid commence?' asked one of the men. 'The others will quickly follow suit once they see it can be done.'

'We need a wedding followed swiftly by a new trade deal,' Malik said.

Tariq was about to say he needed more time, then thought better of it.

'Our children's hands bleed. Their lungs fill with dust,' Malik said, his voice quieter this time.

Tariq felt powerless. 'I'll speak to the king about the hours.'

Malik's eyes blazed in his direction before he looked away. 'If the king won't listen, then maybe he shouldn't be king.'

'Careful,' Kaidon said. 'Be very careful.'

Rauf slowly shook his head. 'The king would rather

watch us suffocate underground than stand up to the Emperor.'

Tariq looked around the room before his gaze settled on Malik. 'I'm on your side. But remember, that's my family. Don't threaten them again.'

Silence.

'I'll update you as soon as I can,' Tariq said. 'If any issues arise in the meantime, reach out to Kaidon.'

The men mumbled a few barely coherent words in response. Then Tariq and Kaidon left and returned to the horses.

The pair rode in silence back through the city. Tariq barely noticed the people he passed this time. His mind kept replaying the conversation he'd just had. The situation felt heavier with each passing mile.

'You can only do so much,' Kaidon said, seemingly reading his mind. Or perhaps his mood.

Tariq adjusted his grip on the reins. 'It won't be enough.'

The castle rose before them, and they both stared at it.

'Will the king reduce the hours in the mine if you ask him? Given we're barely meeting Slevaborg's demands as it is?'

'Unless he's prepared for strikes or civil war, he'll have to.'

They entered the gates of Azura Castle and made their way to the courtyard. Tariq dismounted and handed the reins to the stable hand.

'Don't worry, Your Highness,' the boy said. 'I put the princess on Basma. Quietest horse we have. Scared of nothing.'

Tariq stared at the boy. 'Princess Aisha took a horse?'

'Not by herself, Your Highness. She went with the queen and her guards.'

Tariq exchanged a concerned glance with Kaidon before asking, 'Where did they go?'

'I... I don't know.'

Seeing the panic on the boy's face, the prince gave him a reassuring clap on the shoulder before walking away.

Kaidon caught up to him. 'When you said the queen was going to spend time with her, I thought they'd take a walk or have a game of cards.'

'I should have known.'

'She won't send the princess off a cliff, will she?'

'You joke,' Tariq replied, 'but I wouldn't put it past her.'

'Who's joking?' Kaidon looked over his shoulder. 'Want me to search for them?'

That had been Tariq's first instinct also, but whatever point his mother was trying to make, she would find a way to make it. 'No.'

He stopped walking when a realisation hit him.

'What is it?' Kaidon asked, turning to him.

Tariq shook his head. 'I know where they are.' He looked Kaidon in the eye. 'She's taken Aisha to the mine.'

*A*isha adjusted her grip on the reins and snuck a glance at Queen Farrah riding alongside her. They had been riding for nearly an hour, the castle shrinking behind them until it disappeared from sight. Four guards trailed closely.

When the queen had sent an invitation for her to join her on a morning ride, Aisha had expected a leisurely walk through the city. But then they'd left the city entirely, the landscape becoming more and more isolated. Cobblestones turned to rocky paths, and the scenery turned to harsh, barren terrain. And still barely more than a few words spoken between them.

'Your Majesty,' Aisha said, 'may I ask where we're going?' She kept her tone light despite the growing unease in her chest.

Farrah kept her eyes ahead. 'You shall see soon enough. Patience is not your strong suit, I see.'

Not when she felt like her life was in danger. The lack of detail had Aisha worried that she was about to have an 'accident' resulting in the queen returning to the castle *alone*. She held her breath every time one of the guards' horses moved closer to hers.

The path narrowed, winding between sheer rock faces that funnelled the horses into single file. Dust stung Aisha's eyes as they descended, the air growing chalky and bitter-tasting.

Then she saw it.

An entire hillside had been gutted, torn open. Timber scaffolding clung to the rock, propping up entrances to tunnels. People moved in endless lines, stooped, exhausted, their faces white from the dust. The clang of pickaxes rang out, broken by the occasional shout of an overseer.

Aisha pulled her horse up to take it all in.

'Welcome to Dareth Mine,' Farrah said, stopping beside her. She sat tall in the saddle as she surveyed the scene. 'It is the largest in Gruisea. The backbone of Gruisea's wealth. Without it, our kingdom would crumble.'

It was the first time Aisha had seen a mine, and it made her stomach turn. An endless grind of human suffering.

'Let us take a look around,' Farrah said, nudging her horse into a walk.

Aisha had no choice but to follow.

As they made their way between the wagons, the horses attached to them snorted and shuffled their hooves. The men paused their work briefly to look at them, then continued loading without so much as a polite nod.

Aisha looked from face to face. Some workers were quite slim and short, and she wondered how they managed the weight. Then a slow realisation came over her. Those were not men—they were children. *Young* children. Some around the same age as Omar, carrying loads far too heavy for their tiny frames.

A small breath escaped Aisha, drawing Farrah's attention.

'Peace and prosperity come at a cost,' the queen said. 'And it requires a strong stomach.'

Aisha looked around at the weary faces. 'Some of these boys look too young to be working here.'

'The youngest are ten,' Farrah replied.

Aisha blinked in disbelief. '*Ten years old?*'

'The minimum age for mine work used to be sixteen. However, we were forced to lower it in order to meet demand.'

Questions flooded Aisha's mind. 'What would drive a parent to send their child to work in a mine at such a young age? There must be safer ways to earn money.'

There was a beat of silence before Farrah answered her. 'It is not a decision for parents. It is a decision made by the crown.'

Aisha stared at the queen, her breathing shallow.

'Every boy over the age of ten, excluding those born into noble households, is now required to work for the benefit of Gruisea's future,' Farrah explained.

'In Avanid, we call that child labour.'

Farrah laughed. 'You do not get to claim moral superiority with me. When the Emperor came for Avanid's resources, your father opened the borders and handed them anything they wanted.'

'That's not true—'

'Your father is a weak leader,' Farrah said matter-of-factly. 'I am sure it hurts your feelings to hear that, but it is the truth.'

Aisha shook her head. 'Enslaving young boys does not equate to strength.'

Farrah's nostrils flared, but she didn't respond.

Aisha watched a nearby boy drag a block of limestone across the wagon floor. 'Why did you bring me here? Was it to shock me into leaving?'

'To show you the truth about who we are.' Farrah's voice was quieter now. 'Tariq would not bring you here because he is ashamed. He clings to a version of Gruisea that no longer exists.' Her gaze drifted back to Aisha's. 'If you wish to be the Queen of Gruisea one day, then you must pursue it with your eyes wide open.' She paused. 'Marriage is a business transaction. Your kingdom aligning with this kingdom in an attempt to hold on to the things we have left.' She looked away on an exhale. 'So look around you. Ask yourself if you can bear to inherit this, to uphold it. If the answer is no, then you must decline Tariq's offer of marriage and return home.'

An older man shuffled by, his shoulders rounded under a heavy basket. He looked so exhausted. Aisha watched him dump his load before heading back in the direction from which he had come.

She wanted to ask Farrah why they didn't push back on Slevaborg's demands for more supply, but she already knew the answer. Holy warriors would be swarming

Gruisea within the month. That would turn Gruisea from an overworked kingdom into an unsafe one.

'I would like to return to Azura Castle now,' Aisha said.

The queen studied her for a long moment before swinging her horse around. 'Of course.'

They didn't speak on the return journey. Aisha saw her surroundings through entirely new eyes. The city now felt like an extension of the mines, the misery spilling over.

As they neared the castle, they passed the army barracks. Aisha noticed this time that the gates hung open. There were no soldiers drilling in the yard, no thud of boots or sound of steel. The place was empty. Not a single soldier in sight. She looked down at the crest on the saddle, with its pick and hammer.

The castle gates opened to receive them, guards bowing as they passed through. When she finally slid from her horse in the courtyard, her legs were like jelly from being in the saddle for so long—and perhaps other reasons.

'Thank you for your company,' Farrah said to Aisha as she removed her soft leather riding gloves.

Aisha searched her eyes, then bowed her head. 'Your Majesty.'

The queen walked away, leaving Aisha trembling in the courtyard.

* * *

Aisha rounded the corner of the corridor and slowed when she spotted Tariq waiting at her chamber door. He was leaning against the stone wall, arms folded and expression unreadable. He straightened when he saw her.

For a long, weighted moment, neither of them moved, the dirty truth between them. He knew what she had seen, and she knew he had wanted to keep her from it.

'How long have you been waiting?' she asked when she finally resumed walking.

'Not long. Kaidon informed me you were back.' He looked her over. 'We should talk.'

She nodded. 'Fine, but not here.'

They didn't say a word until they were out of the main castle and safely among the olive trees. Only then did she turn to face him, her heart beating faster than usual. 'When were you planning on telling me that your dynasty is built on the backs of children?'

His jaw tightened. 'I gather from your question that you visited Dareth Mine today.'

She crossed her arms. 'You should have told me what sort of place you were bringing me to.'

'I know what you're thinking—'

'I doubt that.'

He exhaled. 'I wanted to give you time to settle in first before burdening you with all of this.'

'That translates to you thought you could trap me here and that I would accept any circumstances for Avanid's sake. You definitely overestimated our desperation.'

Anger flickered in his eyes. 'I chose you because I believed you were strong enough to face it.'

'Face what, exactly?' she asked. 'A kingdom so broken it enslaves its own children?'

He stepped closer. 'Gruisea's position is fragile. Every-thing I do—*everything*—is to protect my people.'

She forced herself to remain in place. 'Where are all the soldiers?'

Confusion flashed in his eyes. 'What?'

'We passed the barracks. They're empty. Where are all the men?'

His eyes closed for a moment. 'In the mines.'

Another piece of the puzzle fell into place. 'No ruler would order their army to lay down their weapons and take up tools unless they were bending to the will of another.'

'You would know,' he fired back. 'It was Avanid that paved the path for the rest of the empire.'

His words stung, but not because they were false. '*We* didn't have a choice.'

'Neither did we.'

'My father couldn't fight.'

'And mine refuses to.'

Aisha's chest rose and fell—hard.

Tariq stepped back and looked around, collecting himself. 'The queen took you there in an attempt to scare you.'

Her eyes burned. 'Well, it worked.'

His features softened into something resembling empathy. 'I have a plan for change.'

She searched his eyes. 'Why do I get the feeling the king and queen aren't on board with your plan?'

His silence was his answer.

Aisha let out a huge breath. 'Go on, then. Tell me of this plan.'

He immediately appeared uncomfortable. The discomfort was followed by more silence.

'I see.' She dragged her teeth over her lip. 'So, I'm just supposed to trust you?'

He relaxed slightly. 'Yes.'

A small laugh escaped her, even though nothing was funny. 'Imagine you were me. Imagine leaving your family and travelling to a foreign kingdom because you thought it would help the people you left behind. Then imagine finding out they can't even protect themselves, let alone help anyone else.' Another awkward laugh. 'We're slaves to the same master.'

They both looked off in different directions.

'Nothing's official,' he said. 'No announcement of any kind has been made.' His expression turned serious. 'You can leave and return home if that's what you want.'

Quiet stretched between them, taut as a bowstring.

Aisha drew herself up, meeting his eyes with as much steadiness as she could muster. 'I think it best that I return to Avanid.'

Her words hung in the air like a blade.

Tariq studied her face for the longest time before nodding. 'So be it.'

Then he left her standing amid the olive trees with tears spilling down her cheeks.

CHAPTER 10

Tariq stormed into his mother's private chambers, his boots striking the polished stone floor with force. The room smelled faintly of jasmine and parchment, sunlight spilling through the arched windows onto silk-draped walls. Everything was orderly, precise—like the woman who ruled it. His mother was seated by the window, sipping tea as though she hadn't just attempted to dismantle his future.

'You took her to the *mine?*' His voice was low, dangerous.

The queen's guard had followed him in, an apologetic expression on his face. Farrah set her cup down with delicate precision and waved him out.

'Yes, I took her to the mine. I see you are upset about that.' She gestured to the chair opposite her. 'Would you care to sit? This angle has me straining my neck.'

He ignored her invitation. 'Not approving of my choice is one thing, but deliberately sabotaging it is something else.'

Farrah sighed and turned in her seat to face him. 'The girl must comprehend the realities of her future—the burden as well as the opportunity. I did her a favour.'

'She just got here,' Tariq said. 'She's missing her family. I was giving her a moment to breathe.'

'If you feel the need to shelter her from reality, then I am afraid she is not the right person for the job.'

Tariq raked a hand through his hair, eyes closing. 'It's not sheltering. It's courtesy. She's my responsibility.'

Farrah rose. 'It is your responsibility to ensure Gruisea's safety and stability in the future, and it is my responsibility to see to those things *now*.' She paused, letting her words settle. 'If the princess cannot stomach the sight of children working in a mine, she will not survive the weight of this crown.'

Fury simmered in his chest. 'Even the strongest among us are struggling to watch children in those mines.'

Farrah's eyes moved between his before looking away. 'The alternative would have been war, and you and I both know we would not have won.'

Tariq exhaled, his shoulders falling an inch. He didn't have it in him to have that fight over and over again.

'I will give you this,' Farrah said. 'There is kindness in her. I believe she will make a good mother.' Her gaze returned to him. 'I just do not think she will make a good queen.'

He slowly nodded. 'I actually came to congratulate you.'

'On what?'

'On getting exactly what you wanted.' He wet his lips. 'Aisha's returning to Avanid.'

Farrah's expression didn't shift. Not a flicker of regret. 'If that was all it took to deter her, then the alliance was never meant to be.'

His jaw tightened as he turned on his heel. He didn't give her the satisfaction of looking back.

Tariq threw open the doors to his mother's chambers and stalked out, his heart pounding.

Kaidon was leaning casually against the wall opposite and didn't appear at all surprised by Tariq's dramatic exit. 'You look ready to break something.' He straightened. 'I gather it didn't go well?'

Tariq charged past him, forcing Kaidon to jog after him. The air in the corridor felt too heavy. He needed space to breathe, so he headed for the garden.

Once they were outside, Kaidon asked, 'What happened?'

Tariq stopped in the shade, turning in a circle. 'Aisha's leaving, and my mother's thrilled.'

'You can't just let her leave,' Kaidon said.

'What choice do I have? I can't force her to stay.'

Kaidon let out a noisy exhale. 'Maryam saw the wedding. Can visions be wrong?'

'I don't know.' Tariq shook his head. 'We don't even know the specifics of what she claimed to see. I've put far too much trust in this woman, and look where it's gotten me.'

'I can't think of a reason she would lie.'

Tariq touched his temple, where a headache was forming. 'She's a covenweaver, for the gods' sake. We're supposed to hand her over to the sectarian, not follow her down to the underworld.'

Kaidon's gaze shifted past Tariq, narrowing slightly. 'I think someone's ears were burning.'

Tariq followed his line of sight and found Maryam standing at the far end of the path, hands folded neatly in front of her, watching them.

'Should I bring her over?' Kaidon asked.

The last thing Tariq was in the mood for was another cryptic pronouncement, yet he found himself nodding.

Kaidon went to her. They exchanged a few words, then Maryam followed him over to where Tariq was waiting.

'Your Highness,' she said quietly. 'I thought you would seek me out. Since you have not, I have come to you.'

Tariq drew a breath. 'I gather the princess has informed you that she's leaving?'

Maryam's expression tightened. 'She did not have to tell me.'

'Ah.' Tariq shifted his weight. 'Then you *saw* her leave.'

She considered her words carefully. 'I saw her board a ship, yes. But when, I cannot say.'

Her words struck surprisingly hard. 'That's not terribly useful, is it?'

Maryam didn't appear to take offence. 'I have seen her wearing a wedding gown, here at Azura Castle. That I do know.'

He had no idea what to do with that information. 'So, I'm supposed to force her to stay?'

Maryam's gaze didn't waver. 'I do not think that is necessary.'

He waited for her to say more, and when she didn't, he asked, 'I don't suppose you've seen another way?'

She appeared sympathetic. 'The gods brought her here. She is yours to keep, or yours to lose.'

The ambiguity was too much for him.

'The queen has shown her all the reasons she shouldn't stay,' Kaidon said, joining the conversation. 'Maybe you should show her the reasons she should.'

Tariq waited for him to continue.

Kaidon frowned back at him. '*You* have to come up with the reasons.'

He'd been afraid of that.

'What does she enjoy?' Kaidon asked.

'I don't know.'

'You must know something about her by now,' he pushed.

Tariq thought. 'She needs dresses. Perhaps I could take her into the city to shop for fabric.'

Kaidon appeared to like that idea. 'So, she enjoys shopping?'

'No idea,' Tariq replied.

Maryam pressed her lips together.

Noticing, Kaidon said, 'Maybe you could help him out by telling him what he'll choose.'

She frowned up at him. 'The Sight does not quite work like that. And the prince does not need my help.' She looked at Tariq. 'His heart will guide him.'

Kaidon snorted, then cleared his throat. 'Sorry.'

Tariq looked off in the direction of the castle. 'I'll go to her in the morning. Hopefully I come up with something in the meantime.'

CHAPTER 11

Sleep had eluded her. Now Aisha sat at the table near her window, arranging the bits and pieces she had gathered on her walk earlier: leaves, flowers, bark. It was something she always did with her younger siblings back in Avanid. They would find things in the gardens and create pictures with them. And when they were done, they would return everything to the garden.

She had just finished arranging a colourful butterfly when there was a soft knock at the door.

'Come in,' Aisha called out.

Maryam stepped inside, balancing a brass tray. Steam drifted from the spout of the teapot. She crossed the room and set the tray on the table. 'Some tea and fruit, Your Highness.' She then proceeded to pour the tea. When she was done, she looked over at the bag Aisha had gotten out. 'You are still planning to leave, then?'

Aisha drank before answering her, savouring the warmth of the tea. 'It feels like the only sensible choice.'

Maryam observed her a moment. 'Does it?'

Why did that simple question make Aisha choke up?

Maryam tilted her head. 'Perhaps you are not ready to decide. It is all right if you need more time. Time to see more, to know more.'

Aisha sat back, her fingers tight around the cup. 'At what point is it too late to turn back?'

'*After* the wedding.' Maryam's mouth curved up.

It was the first time Aisha had seen her attendant attempt humour. She liked Maryam. There was something about her that felt safe, familiar even.

A knock sounded at the door. Maryam went to answer it for her. Tariq stood in the corridor, freshly washed and looking every bit the prince in his dark blue tunic and riding trousers. He looked past Maryam, green eyes meeting Aisha's.

Maryam excused herself, then slipped past Tariq.

'Can I come in?' he asked.

Aisha got to her feet. 'Of course.'

He stepped inside, leaving the door open behind him. She felt oddly nervous.

'I wondered if you might like to see some more of Gruisea before you leave,' he said. 'Something other than corridors, courtyards, and mines.'

That wasn't what she had been expecting him to say. Her first instinct was to refuse, but there was something in his tone that stopped her. Something quiet. He sounded like a man trying rather than a prince commanding.

'See what, exactly?' she asked.

His gaze drifted to her butterfly construction on the table. He stepped forwards to see it better. 'What is that?'

'Nothing.' Aisha moved to stand in front of it. 'Just something I do to entertain myself.'

Undeterred by her repositioning, Tariq stepped around her so he could see it. 'You made this?'

She turned on an exhale. 'I did.'

He reached out and touched a piece of bark, withdrawing his hand when it moved. 'Sorry.'

'Don't be. It's supposed to be disassembled at the end.'

He continued to touch various parts of it. 'Seems a shame to mess it up.'

She straightened the piece of bark. 'The joy's in the doing.'

Tariq lifted his gaze. 'You know, there's an oasis about an hour's ride from here. It has some of the most exotic foliage in the kingdom. Would you like to see it?'

The offer took Aisha by surprise. It was spontaneous and thoughtful, something just for her enjoyment rather than serving some purpose. 'Oh.' She glanced at the bag sitting on the bed. Packing would take her all of five minutes, so there was no real rush. 'All right.'

He looked as surprised as she was by her answer. 'Great. Well, I'll have Maryam bring you something suitable for the ride.' He began backing up to the door. 'Meet me in the courtyard when you're ready.'

Then he was gone.

Maryam brought her a linen kaftan with fitted trousers, then braided her hair, humming as she worked. 'Enjoy yourself,' she said before leaving the room.

Aisha found Tariq waiting in the courtyard with Kaidon and another guard. The guards bowed their heads in greeting before mounting their horses. Tariq was holding the reins of two horses, one of which was presumably hers.

'Ready?' he asked.

'Ready.'

He helped her mount, then wrapped his fingers around her ankle to adjust her foot in the stirrup. In that fleeting touch, Aisha realised he no longer felt like a stranger. His voice, his manner, the weight of his hand against her skin—it had grown familiar.

The ride to the oasis was far more enjoyable than her trip to the mine with the queen. The company felt safe, so she was able to relax.

City turned to countryside, to scattered palms and clusters of mudbrick houses. Children emerged from them, following the horses and asking them questions.

'Where are you going?' asked one young girl.

'Prince Tariq is taking me to see an oasis,' Aisha told her.

The children exchanged excited glances.

'You shouldn't have told them where you were going,' Tariq said when the children stopped following. 'They'll all be waiting at the oasis for you.'

And he was right. The children were already there when they arrived.

'They know all the shortcuts,' Tariq said as he dismounted.

Aisha slid down from her horse, taking in the sight before her. The water was so clear it reflected the palms and sky like a mirror. Wildflowers dotted the sand in splashes of red and yellow, and reeds swayed at the edge of the water.

The children rushed forwards in a noisy cluster, calling to Aisha to come see this and that. She took the hands of the smaller girls and let them lead the way. The men had no choice but to follow.

One of the boys ran up to Tariq, and Aisha was surprised when the prince called him by his name, Sadiq, resting a hand on his shoulder. So he did know people outside the nobility.

'Can I go on your back?' Sadiq asked.

Aisha nearly fell over when Tariq swung the boy up onto his back without breaking stride, carrying him without saying a word. Judging by how comfortable the boy was, she suspected it wasn't the first time. She found herself watching them.

'What are we going to do now?' one of the girls asked, as if she had been part of the plan all along.

'What's your name?' Aisha asked.

'Yara.'

'Well, Yara, we're going on a treasure hunt for beautiful things.'

The girl's eyes widened with excitement. 'We are?'

That got the attention of the other children, who all gathered closer to listen.

'But there's no treasure here,' a boy said, his voice laced with scepticism.

'What do you mean?' Aisha gestured to their surroundings. 'Nature has treasure everywhere. Any beautiful thing you come across.' She stopped walking. 'But there are rules. You're only allowed to collect things you find on the ground.'

'That's not treasure,' Yara complained.

Aisha scooped her up and placed her on her hip. 'Maybe not yet, but it will be when we're finished.'

'How?' Sadiq called to her.

Aisha glanced in his direction. 'We're going to create masterpieces for the exclusive viewing of those of us present today.'

'Out of things on the ground?' one girl asked.

Aisha nodded. 'You need to trust your inner artist.'

Yara was all in at that point, wriggling down from Aisha's grip and running off to begin her search.

'Are you going to do it?' Sadiq asked Tariq as he was placed on the ground.

'I'm going to try.'

Aisha's insides warmed when he said that. She had assumed he would only watch.

They spent some time collecting items, then Aisha showed them all how to start arranging them into familiar things. The children pressed in around her, tossing bright petals and smooth stones, eager to see what she would create with them. Tariq had to keep gently pulling the children off Aisha so she wouldn't get crushed by their enthusiasm.

Eventually, everyone settled down to create their own.

'Yours isn't very good,' Sadiq told Tariq when he was done.

Tariq feigned offence. 'Are you saying I'm not skilled in the art of bark-and-petal pictures?'

'Yes,' Sadiq replied simply.

The older children laughed, and Aisha joined them. For the first time since arriving in Gruisea, the heaviness in her chest eased just a bit.

When the sand was covered in makeshift butterflies, trees, animals, and various kinds of suns, the children raced off to splash around in the shallow water. Aisha brushed sand from her hands and looked over at Tariq.

'They adore you,' she told him.

Tariq watched the children play for a moment. 'Not as much as they adore you, apparently.' His gaze travelled back to hers. 'Thank you for this, by the way. I'm sure they'll talk about it for years to come.'

She shrugged. 'This is what childhood is supposed to be.'

He dropped his gaze when she said that. It was guilt. Guilt for all the boys whose childhood ended at ten years old.

'Do you want to have a look around?' Tariq asked, looking up again.

She nodded.

Tariq went to fetch his saddlebag and told Kaidon to keep an eye on the children in the water. Then the two of them set off along the faint trail along the water's edge.

The air was cooler in the shade, and the tranquillity was unmatched.

'I've seen oases in Avanid,' Aisha said, 'when I was younger. But nothing like this.'

Tariq looked up at the canopy of trees above them. 'My father first brought me here when I was six or seven. He told me this place is a reminder of how even in the harshest conditions, life finds a way to flourish.'

'I didn't know the king was one for poetic sentiment.'

'He has his moments.' Tariq stopped and pointed up at the trees above. 'Look. A sooty falcon.'

Aisha followed his line of sight and spotted a bird perched on a high branch, its sleek grey and white feathers shimmering in the sunlight. 'It's gorgeous.'

They watched it spread its majestic wings and take flight.

'Are you hungry?' he asked.

She looked at the saddlebag he was carrying. 'You brought food?'

'Credit goes to Maryam. I usually forget to eat during the day.'

'Ah.'

Opening the saddlebag, he pulled out a tightly rolled blanket and laid it out on the ground, gesturing for her to sit. He then retrieved a small bundle of food wrapped in cloth and a flask. He opened the flask, smelled it, then offered it to her. 'I think it's honey wine.'

Aisha took it from him. 'I'm guessing there aren't any cups in the bag.'

'Afraid not.'

She removed her gloves before drinking.

Tariq opened the food parcel, revealing some flat-bread, dried fruits, and cheese. Once he was seated comfortably, she handed the flask back to him, watching his lips press against the same place hers had been moments earlier, without any hesitation. They ate with the gentle sounds of the spring as a backdrop.

When Aisha was finished, she leaned back on her hands and looked at Tariq. 'Tell me about your sister.'

He held the flask out, and when she shook her head, he placed it on the blanket between them. 'Amani is the perfect daughter. Not only is she married to the future

King of Kuzebet, but we've also just learned she's pregnant. Now she's the extra-perfect daughter.' He followed the comment up with a smile that didn't quite reach his eyes.

'Do you think she's scared?' Aisha asked.

'Of the birth?'

'All of it. She's barely eighteen with no family nearby.'

Tariq picked up the flask. 'If you say that to my mother, she'll tell you how blessed she is to have her husband's family to care for her.' He drank before saying, 'Your father seems in much less of a hurry to marry his daughters off.'

'I think if he had his way, we'd never marry,' Aisha said in a joking tone, even though it was the truth. 'Zara, on the other hand...'

He watched her a moment. 'Which sister are you closest to?'

'I'm close to all of them for different reasons. Zara keeps me anchored. Lilah keeps me sane. Safiya keeps me stressed.'

Tariq's mouth turned up.

'And Yasmin...' She remembered the exact feel of her youngest sister curled against her. 'Yasmin keeps me guessing. She has a way of seeing the world that makes one think they're seeing it wrong.'

He was silent a moment. 'And what about Prince Omar?'

'Oh, he's the worst parts of all of us,' Aisha laughed. 'Impulsive, mischievous, reckless.'

'But he's also twelve, so there's still hope.'

Her smile faded. 'Those boys are too young to be working in mines. But you already know that.'

Tariq's eyes moved between hers. 'Yes.' He held out the flask to her, and she took it. 'My family built this dynasty to endure, no matter the cost. Whereas I refuse to let Gruisea endure like this.'

He sounded sincere.

'So, you plan on changing these laws when you're king?' she asked.

'I would like to change them before then.'

She drank, then passed the flask back to him. When her fingers met his this time, a chill ran through her, and the world dimmed. A rush of images, sharper than memories, played in her mind. She saw herself standing with Tariq in the centre of a grand hall, dressed in ceremonial robes. Their hands were clasped, their gazes locked. Around them, a sea of faces blurred into obscurity. It was the connection she felt with Tariq that she was most aware of. The absence of fear. Only certainty.

The vision left as abruptly as it had come. Aisha blinked hard, grounding herself back in the present. Her forehead was slick with sweat. *Oh gods.*

'Are you all right?' Tariq asked, his brow creased with concern.

She nodded, swallowing down her nausea. 'This is why I don't drink wine during the day.'

He rose and tipped out the wine, then walked down to the water's edge to fill the flask. Returning, he handed it to her. 'Here.'

She took it and drank. The water tasted of wine, but

she swallowed it anyway, desperate to cool the heat in her chest. 'Thank you.'

'Are you sure you're all right?'

Aisha nodded again, though her head felt light. She tried to pull herself together, but her trembling hands weren't helping.

Tariq leaned forwards until his face was mere inches from hers, searching her eyes. *Seeing too much.*

'Stay,' he said. 'Stay and marry me.' The gold in his irises flickered like sunlight on metal. 'Together, we'll fix it.'

The air between them stilled. She couldn't breathe. Couldn't think.

Say no, reason whispered. *Wait.*

But the vision urged her towards him.

She released a shaky breath. 'All right,' she whispered. 'I'll stay and marry you.'

Tariq found his mother seated in the garden playing cards with one of her attendants. Farrah placed her hand of cards on the table when she saw him coming, then excused her companion.

'There you are,' Farrah said when he reached her. 'You were gone all day yesterday, and then you were training with Kaidon all morning.'

He took the seat her attendant had vacated. 'I train with Kaidon every morning.'

'For what reason I have no idea. Enjoy the peace your father has provided for you.'

It infuriated him that she acted as though obedience to the Emperor meant they were safe. He knew better than to lay his weapon down.

'Where were you yesterday?' Farrah asked, looking him over.

'With Aisha.'

Her eyebrows rose slightly. 'Oh, it is *Aisha* now, is it?

How very familiar. I thought the princess would be busy packing.'

Tariq didn't take the bait. 'I've come to tell you that she's staying here in Gruisea, and I would like to publicly announce our betrothal.'

Farrah's mask of composure slipped for a second. 'Given she is prone to changing her mind, perhaps we should wait.'

'No need. We'll also need to set a date for the wedding so guests can plan their travel.'

For a moment, Farrah didn't speak. The sound of the fountain filled the silence. 'It must have been some day out yesterday,' she said eventually.

He didn't reply.

She turned her teacup so that the handle was at the right angle. 'If you are certain the princess will support you in carrying out the work we are doing here, *and* you know she is capable of forging a different path to that of her mother, *then* perhaps I could discuss it with your father.'

He gave her a knowing look. 'I wouldn't be having this conversation with you if there were any doubts.'

As though summoned by the mention of him, the king entered the garden at a fast walk, eyes locking on Tariq. The prince recognised that look. Something was wrong.

'What is it?' he asked, rising.

'It is the Ashwaq Mine.' Hamza came to an abrupt stop in front of him. 'The workers are striking. I need you to travel there and fix the situation quickly. We need that mine open and running in order to fulfil our obligations.'

The stress on his father's face made Tariq genuinely

sad. He had looked up to the man his whole life—until the day he hadn't. Now he was just another frightened man, like so many others across the empire. 'Have they given a reason for the strike?'

Hamza wiped sweat from his brow. *Sweat.* 'There are some safety concerns. The foreman has tried to reason with them, but the situation has escalated.'

'Then perhaps the safety concerns are valid,' Tariq said.

'They may be, but we still need a functioning mine while we address them.' Another wipe at his brow. 'Better you go. They are more likely to listen to you.'

What he was really saying was that they were no longer listening to him. He had thrown away the respect of his people when he had signed the new trade deal with Slevaborg, and the only reason they listened to Tariq was because he represented future change.

'If production halts, the ripple effects could be catastrophic,' Hamza said, sounding defeated.

'No pressure,' Tariq muttered.

The queen spoke up at that. 'You are the crown prince. The position comes with responsibilities, as you well know.'

Tariq gave a defeated nod. 'Very well. I'll handle it.'

'Today,' the king said. 'I want that mine up and running by the morning.'

What a mess.

'I understand.' Bowing, he left the garden.

'Where are we going?' Kaidon asked when they reunited.

'Ashwaq.'

Kaidon winced. 'I heard about the strike.'

Tariq didn't slow down. 'I'm not thrilled about leaving Aisha alone here after breaking the news of her staying.'

'Understandable.'

'I need to tell her I'll be away for the night.' He glanced over his shoulder. 'And warn her that the queen may take full advantage.'

A smirk came and went on Kaidon's face.

'What are you smiling at?'

Kaidon raised his hands defensively. 'It's just amusing watching this marriage of convenience turn into something else.'

Tariq looked at him. 'What are you talking about?'

'I'm talking about the fact that you like her.'

Tariq rolled his eyes forwards again. 'Of course I like her. She's intelligent, capable—'

'Funny.'

'Yes.'

'Beautiful.'

Tariq sighed. 'I was pointing out the important things.'

'Always so practical.'

Tariq ignored him.

When they reached Aisha's chamber, Kaidon hung back to give him the illusion of privacy. She answered the door wearing a loose embroidered robe. Her hair was braided to one side, falling down her shoulder, and her face was scrubbed clean. Was he imagining it, or was she growing more beautiful every time he saw her?

'Your Highness,' Aisha said, looking confused. 'Is everything all right?'

He was so busy staring that he had forgotten to speak.

'Yes.' His gaze fell to the part of her collarbone that was visible, then shot back up again. 'Well, no. I came to tell you I'm going to Ashwaq for the night. There's a matter the king has asked me to deal with.'

She leaned her weight on one foot. 'You're going today?'

'Yes.'

'Oh.'

Her lower lip disappeared between her teeth, and he watched it until it was freed.

'Then I'll come with you,' she said.

That had him looking up. 'What?'

'I'll come with you to Ashwaq.'

So he hadn't misheard. 'It's a mining village. There's nothing there.'

She shrugged. 'You'll be there. Maryam will help me pack.'

Tariq didn't know how to respond. 'It's a four-hour ride.'

'I'll bring water.' Her face fell a little. 'Please.'

He realised then that she would rather sit on a horse for four hours and visit another limestone mine than be alone at Azura Castle.

'We can bring extra guards,' Kaidon said—which did not help.

Tariq ignored him. 'The workers are striking. It's really not safe.'

Aisha's expression turned almost pleading. 'If my options are alone here with your mother or an unsafe mine with you, I'll take my chances in the mine.'

Kaidon chuckled quietly.

Tariq stared at her for a long moment before exhaling. 'Fine.' He caught the flicker of relief in her eyes when he gave in. 'We leave within the hour.'

Aisha stepped back into her chamber. 'I'll be ready.'

The door closed softly between them, and Tariq stared at it before turning to Kaidon. 'Thanks for backing me up.'

'I figured it would be more bonding time for the two of you.'

Tariq shook his head. 'Go round up the guards for the journey.' He headed for his quarters. 'Let's not take any chances.'

CHAPTER 13

It was clear Tariq had wanted Aisha to remain at the castle, but she would be easy prey for his mother with him away. He claimed he wanted a partner for this life, so a partner was what he got.

As the sun disappeared behind them, the temperature fell. Aisha retrieved her cloak from her bag and wrapped it around herself.

'Regretting coming yet?' Tariq asked, watching her.

'No.' She looked over at Kaidon, who was wise enough not to look back. Two additional guards also accompanied them.

A few more hours passed in silence before the trees thinned and gave way to barren slopes. Aisha sat a little taller in the saddle as the village came into view. It was even smaller than she was expecting.

Ashwaq was more like a settlement forgotten by time. Buildings leaned into one another, smoke curling from their chimneys. The streets were empty, and all was silent.

Aisha snuck a glance at Tariq, who wore a hardened expression. 'Is it usually this quiet?'

'Never *this* quiet,' he replied.

As they entered the heart of the village, Aisha felt eyes upon her. She spotted people looking out at them from behind wooden shutters. They came to a stop in what appeared to be the main square, though it was nothing more than a widening of the dirt road.

Kaidon dismounted first, his hand resting on the hilt of his sword as he surveyed their surroundings. Tariq walked straight over to Aisha to help her down.

'Stay close,' he said.

A door creaked, prompting the guards to reposition themselves. A man stepped out from the shadow of a low-built structure, his expression cautious rather than welcoming. He looked middle-aged, though it was difficult to judge with miners, as hard labour ages a person. A thick beard covered his jaw. His eyes narrowed on Tariq.

'Your Highness?'

Tariq's hand fell away from Aisha's back, and he went to greet the man. 'Jibran.'

The man laid his hand across his heart and gave a small bow. He looked past Tariq to Aisha as he straightened. 'Who is this?'

A door crashed open before Tariq could answer. Aisha sucked in a breath as a man stumbled out into the square, his face gaunt and eyes wild. A knife gleamed in his hand, the blade catching the last scraps of light as he came towards them.

'Murderers!' the man shouted, his voice hoarse but carrying. His eyes were fixed on Tariq. 'You send our boys to the mines. My son's dead in the ground because of you!'

Kaidon drew an inch of steel and moved forwards.

'Stand down,' Tariq instructed, stopping all three guards in their tracks. He stood calmly as the knife glinted closer.

'You sit in your fucking castle with your feasts and your finery while my boy rots beneath the stone!' The man's grief poured out in broken words. 'He was twelve. Twelve!'

'All right,' Jibran said, his face tight. 'You've said your piece. Now put the blade away.'

'Shut your mouth!' the grieving father replied, rounding on him for an instant before focusing again on Tariq. 'Prince, king, emperor—it doesn't matter. You're all part of the same disease.'

Aisha stood frozen. She was both afraid and captive to the man's anguish.

Tariq approached him, slowly. He didn't reach for his weapon or call for his guards, instead meeting the man's gaze with a steadiness that seemed to quiet him. 'Give me the knife.'

'You don't deserve to live,' the man rasped, his hand trembling as his grief overtook his rage. 'Should be you in the ground.'

Tariq continued closing the remaining space between them, dropping his voice lower. 'Don't make your wife mourn her son *and* her husband.'

The man's shoulders collapsed. His grip faltered. In a single, controlled motion, Tariq seized the man's wrist, turned it, and eased the knife free. It landed with a soft thud in the dirt. The man began to sink to the ground, and Tariq grabbed hold of him. The father sagged against him, sobs tearing from his chest as Tariq kicked the knife towards Kaidon, who snatched it up.

The sound rang through her. Raw, unbearable, and so painfully human.

'Get her out of here,' Tariq said to Kaidon.

The guard was at her side a moment later, an arm locking around her as he led her away from the scene at an almost run.

'Put her in there,' Jibran said, pointing to a small hut with a warped door.

Aisha looked over her shoulder at Tariq, who was still holding the grieving father, before she was ushered inside.

'Lock the door and stay away from the window,' Kaidon instructed before the door slammed shut between them.

With her heart racing and palms sweating, Aisha stared at the closed door for a few more breaths before looking around. It was a single room with a small iron stove in the corner and a rickety table with two mismatched chairs near the window. A bed sat in the centre.

She didn't know what to do next—besides stay away from the window.

Walking over to the bed, she sat on the edge of the hard mattress and watched the door.

Minutes passed by.

Aside from the occasional sound of muffled voices in the distance, all was silent. Then came a soft knock.

Aisha walked over to the door, hand on the lock. 'Who is it?'

'Jibran' came the familiar voice.

Aisha unlocked the door and cracked it open. Jibran stood holding a wooden tray. She immediately opened it the rest of the way. One of the guards who had travelled with them was standing guard at the door, eyes scanning the area.

'For you, Your Highness.' Jibran spoke barely above a whisper. 'Best I could do.'

She took it from him. 'Thank you.' When he went to leave, she asked, 'Is the prince all right?'

He faced her again. 'There are some heavy conversations taking place. I'm sure he'll join you as soon as he can.' He turned and left.

'Lock the door,' the guard said, glancing in her direction.

She did.

Aisha set the tray on the bed, then dragged the table away from the window so she could eat at it. She stared down at the tray, which held some flatbread, dried fruit, and a small dish of warm fish. A bowl of steaming water and a washcloth were also included, which she was most grateful for after the long ride.

She washed her hands and face, then sat picking at the food. The room was lit by a single lantern, which cast flickering shadows on the walls. She watched them as she ate. When half the food remained, she set it aside in case Tariq returned hungry.

The night stretched on, but despite her exhaustion, she couldn't sleep. She lay on her back, staring at the uneven ceiling and listening for any sound of his return. It must have been past midnight when the door finally rattled. She got to her feet, blinking against the haze of fatigue, and opened the door without checking it was him.

Tariq's shoulders were rounded with fatigue, and his cloak was covered in dust. His eyes moved over her before he asked, 'Did I wake you?'

'No.' She stepped aside to let him in, then locked the door.

He took his cloak off and hung it on a loose nail on the door.

'I saved you some food,' she said, gesturing to the table.

'You didn't have to do that.'

'I wasn't sure if you would get the chance.'

He held her gaze for a long moment, then walked over to the table, sinking down in a chair. Aisha sat in the other one and watched him clean his hands and face. There wasn't much that could be done about the dust clinging to his hair. She pushed the tray of food towards him.

'Thank you,' he said without looking at her. He tore off a piece of bread and used it to pick up the fish, eating quietly.

'Is the man all right?'

He swallowed before answering. 'No. Nor are the others who lost family earlier in the week.'

She swallowed. 'What happened to them?'

'One of the tunnels collapsed. Despite new reinforcements, they're understandably hesitant to return there.'

Aisha stared at the tray. 'It's still so raw for them.'

'And yet the mine will open in the morning.'

His tone made it clear he wasn't happy about that. 'Why the urgency?'

'Because we have an agreement with Slevaborg that we must honour'—he reached for more food—'at any cost.'

It wasn't just Avanid bending over backwards to keep the Emperor happy.

Done with the food, Tariq leaned back in his chair and looked at her. 'You should get some sleep.'

'So should you.'

He looked over at the bed. 'I'm sorry about all this. If I'd known the state of things here, I never would have agreed to you coming.'

'I insisted, remember?'

He rose from his chair. 'You take the bed.'

'There's enough room for both of us.'

He stilled and looked at her. 'That's a rather scandalous suggestion.'

She noted the hint of teasing in his tone, softened by exhaustion.

'I won't tell anyone if you don't.'

Tariq walked over to the bed and sat on the edge to remove his boots. Aisha averted her eyes as he stripped down to his sirwal, but not before seeing the outline of him. He wasn't broad in the way of men who spent their lives labouring, but every curve spoke of discipline.

She waited for him to get into bed before extinguishing the lantern and following him. He moved as far over as was possible without falling off and opened the blanket for her.

'Thank you,' she said as she climbed in, remaining as close to the edge on her side as possible.

They lay on their backs, staring up at the roof in the dark.

After a long silence, Tariq said in a low voice, 'I'm sorry that you'd rather be in this godsforsaken place than back at the castle. I hope that changes once we're married.'

Aisha's eyes traced the uneven ridges of the wooden beams above them. 'I'm sorry for what happened earlier. I'm beginning to understand the difficult position you're in.'

Silence.

'I know this probably doesn't mean much,' she said, 'but I think you handled the situation with that man perfectly. With dignity and empathy.'

More silence followed before he finally said, 'Thank you. That means more than you realise.'

She listened to the steady rhythm of his breaths, the quiet rise and fall of his chest against the blanket, as she drifted off to sleep.

CHAPTER 14

Grey light filtered through the slats of the window, cutting across the rough walls. Aisha blinked a few times as she got her bearings. She was in Ashwaq. She was in Ashwaq and in bed with…

Aisha became aware of the warmth. Warmth and weight. Looking down, she saw an arm draped over her. Her lungs stilled when she felt Tariq's body, solid and grounding, pressed to her back. His sleepy breaths were slow and even against her hair. Sometime during the night, that careful distance between them had well and truly disappeared.

She recalled being cold at one point, drawing the blanket up to her ears. Perhaps he had noticed. Or perhaps she had drawn him in too.

She lay still, studying his fingers lightly curled around the fabric of her abaya. If she moved, he would move, and for whatever reason, she wanted him to stay where he was for a little longer.

Perhaps he had been cold also.

Whenever she pictured their marriage, she had never pictured this part. She'd spent plenty of time imagining how they would look together in public and what they would achieve politically but not given much thought to the private moments.

She held her breath when Tariq stirred, his arms curling around her, drawing her closer until every inch of her back was pressed against every inch of his chest.

Breathe.

She probably should have exited the bed, saving them both from embarrassment. But that's not what she did. She knew the exact moment he woke, because his body tensed. He was supposed to withdraw his arm, but he didn't.

Neither of them moved.

He likely thought she was still asleep. Perhaps he wanted to try the moment on, like she had.

Summoning her bravery, she turned to face him, moving slowly so she wouldn't scare him away. His grip loosened, but his arm remained around her. He watched her with a relaxed expression.

'Are you warm enough?' he asked, his voice rough with sleep.

Aisha was hot and cold all at once. 'Yes.'

His gaze never left hers. 'Good.' He shifted slightly, but not enough to break the strange, fragile moment. His hold on her wasn't possessive, just present.

Aisha studied his face in the soft light. He looked different without his usual frown. Younger, maybe. Less like someone carrying the weight of a dynasty.

'Have you ever imagined what it would be like?' she asked.

He frowned. 'It?'

'Waking up together.'

He considered the question for a moment. 'I figured we would sleep separately.'

'Oh.'

'My parents have always slept in separate quarters.' He searched her eyes. 'But something tells me yours didn't.'

'Never.' She found a smile. 'Of course, this is Gruisea, so we'll do things the Gruisean way.'

He was silent a moment. 'I wouldn't mind doing some things the Avanid way.'

She felt herself melting. Tentatively, she reached up and brushed her fingers along his stubbly cheek, studying the tiny details of his face. Tariq didn't pull away. Instead, he leaned into her touch. She traced the line of his jaw, his skin warm against her fingertips. Never had she touched a man in such an intimate way. When his gaze moved to her lips, she felt her stomach dip.

'Are you going to kiss me?' she asked, needing to know if she was reading the situation correctly.

His throat bobbed. 'I'm definitely thinking about it.'

Her curiosity outweighed her fear of an unwanted vision. So far, so good. She tilted her head up slightly, an invitation. One he accepted. He closed the distance between them, his lips brushing hers. Gentle, hesitant. Her eyes sank shut of their own accord as a new kind of warmth washed over her, and she moved closer to him. He responded by deepening the kiss.

Aisha inhaled sharply as all the heat gathered. Her fingers curled into the fabric of his sirwal, and—

A knock at the door sent her scrambling away from him. Tariq caught her by the elbow just before she fell off the bed. They stared at each other, breathing fast.

'One moment,' Tariq called out to the person at the door. He dragged a hand through his hair as he exited the bed, then threw his clothes on.

Aisha got out of bed also, walking over to the table and standing awkwardly next to it, as if she had spent the night in that very spot. She touched her lips, which still tingled.

When Tariq opened the door, Kaidon was standing there. The guard looked from him to Aisha, and his mouth tugged up at the corners.

'Well, good morning,' he said, a coy edge to his voice.

Tariq's eyes narrowed in annoyance. 'What is it?'

'I came to tell you that the miners are returning to work as we speak.' He looked pleased. 'You did it.'

Tariq was still for a long moment. 'Good.' He nodded slowly. 'That's good.'

A frown settled on Kaidon's face. 'Really? Because you don't look very happy.'

'The king will be happy.' Tariq reached for his boots. 'That's what matters.' He looked back at Aisha. 'I need to go to the mine and speak with Jibran before we leave. You can wait here.'

She didn't want to be left alone again. Joining him at the door, she said, 'I'll come with you. Shame to come all this way and never see the mine.'

He looked torn but then nodded. 'Get your boots.'

* * *

The mine looked like a jagged wound carved into the rocky hillside. The air near the entrance was thick with dust stirred up by the line of workers filing into the main tunnel. Their faces were already streaked with grime despite it being the start of the workday.

Tariq and Jibran were talking a few feet away from Aisha and Kaidon. She noted the tension in the prince's posture.

'I want men working on the additional reinforcements today,' Tariq said, trying to compete with the noise of shuffling feet.

Jibran folded his arms across his broad chest. 'The king won't like it. He wants the miners *mining*.'

'He wanted the mine open.' Tariq gestured to the entrance. 'It's open.' When Jibran let out a noisy breath, Tariq clapped him on the shoulder. 'It's *open*.'

Aisha's gaze drifted over the workers in their tattered clothing, exhaustion carved into their faces. Every time she saw a young boy, her stomach would twist. The youngest ones still had those small hands that should be used for playing, exploring, and learning how to write. The saddest feature was their eyes, hollowed with routine.

She made eye contact with a boy walking by. His tunic was too large for his thin frame, the sleeves rolled up past his elbows. He stared at her with a dead expression, and she felt a pull to follow him.

'Where are you going?' Kaidon asked when she began walking off.

Tariq's gaze shot to her. 'Aisha.'

She barely heard him as she reached for the boy's hand, stopping him before he joined the line of workers. The moment her fingers wrapped around his, everything shifted. The people around her vanished, and darkness swallowed her. The cool morning air was gone, replaced by thick, suffocating heat. Dust and sweat filled her nose and coated her throat. The flickering light of oil lamps cast trembling shadows on the walls. Her hands were small and calloused.

She was *inside* the mine, but not as herself.

A deep, low groan reached her from somewhere within the mine, then the ground beneath her began to shake. The other workers paused as dust rained from the ceiling.

Another groan, followed by a sharp, deafening *crack*. Shouts rang out. Someone grabbed her arm, jerking her forwards.

'*Run*,' someone shouted, right before dust exploded into the air, burning her throat and choking her lungs.

The sun blinded Aisha as she returned to herself, wrenching her hand from the boy with a violent gasp before stumbling backwards. Strong arms caught her.

'You're all right,' Tariq said quietly into her ear. 'Easy.'

She couldn't breathe. Why couldn't she breathe?

He turned her around to face him, eyes searching her face for clues as to what was happening. 'Breathe,' he told her.

She finally sucked in a ragged breath, her lungs awakening. Then she began to cough.

Kaidon appeared next to them, looking concerned. 'What the hell just happened?'

The boy. Aisha whipped her head around, searching for him, but he was nowhere to be seen. 'Where is he?'

'Who?' Tariq asked.

'The boy.' Her eyes locked on the mine. 'We need to get him out.'

Kaidon followed her line of sight. 'You mean the boy who ran off?'

Aisha looked back at Tariq, eyes pleading. 'You need to get them *all* out.'

His eyes moved between hers, confused. Then a look of understanding settled on his face. He drew her closer to him. 'What did you see?'

Her entire body went cold when he asked that.

'What did you see?' His grip on her tightened, as though he meant to squeeze the answer from her.

Why was he asking her that?

'Aisha.' Her name came out of him like a plea.

Oh gods. He knows.

Tariq lowered his voice. 'If you want to save them, then tell me what you saw.'

Her gaze swayed to Kaidon. He, too, was waiting for her reply. They both knew.

Gritting her teeth, she looked back at Tariq. 'The mine's going to collapse.' She grounded her feet. 'You need to get everyone out.'

Tariq's eyes widened slightly. Then he nodded, as though deciding something. Releasing his grip on her, he looked over at Jibran. 'Clear the mine! I need every single person out of there—now!'

Jibran raised his hands in an exasperated gesture. 'I just sent them in there.'

Tariq waved Kaidon into action. 'Get as many people out as you can.'

Kaidon took off at a run.

'Have you lost your mind?' Jibran asked, marching over to Tariq. '*You* were the one who wanted—'

'And now I'm telling you to get them out of there.' Tariq looked over at the supervisors loitering nearby, eavesdropping. 'Move! Clear that damn mine!'

The man looked at Jibran, who threw his hands up in defeat. 'Go. Do it.'

Panic bloomed inside Aisha. It felt like nails were being dragged across her brain. The shouts of the foremen echoed against the rock, urgent and sharp, until finally, workers began to exit the mine. They looked around at one another, confusion on their faces.

'I hope you realise how difficult it's going to be to get them all back in there,' Jibran said.

Tariq looked back at Aisha. 'I'm going to help. Stay here.'

A low rumble reverberated through the ground, making the hairs on the back of Aisha's neck stand up. The pair looked down at their feet, then up at each other.

'Kaidon,' Tariq breathed before taking off at a run towards the mine's entrance.

Aisha followed him, weaving between the people now pouring out.

'Kaidon!' Tariq shouted, pushing through the gathering crowd.

There was a deafening roar before dust and debris exploded from the entrance. Tariq skidded to a stop, hands going into his hair as he watched the cloud of dust rise into the air. Aisha stopped beside him, blinking against the powder.

'I can't see him,' Tariq said, searching.

Movement caught Aisha's eye. A shadow emerged from the dust, solidifying into a figure. It was Kaidon. 'There.' She pointed.

Tariq folded in relief, leaning on his knees for a moment.

'There are still a few inside,' Kaidon said when he reached them, coughing into his hand.

Tariq straightened and took hold of the guard's shoulder as he caught his breath.

Aisha looked around at the clusters of people, confused and scared, and spotted the small boy from earlier, tucked safely beneath someone's arm. Their eyes met briefly before he was ushered away.

Thank the gods.

Dust swirled in the air, clinging to their skin and settling into the folds of their clothes.

'We need the names of everyone who's missing,' Tariq said. 'And clear a space for the injured—away from the dust.'

Kaidon nodded, then dashed off again.

Aisha couldn't hold the question in any longer. 'How long have you known?'

Tariq shifted his weight to one foot as he dragged his gaze to hers. 'I didn't know for sure—'

'How long?'

He looked almost ashamed. 'A while.'

'Is that...?' She struggled to ask the question because she was afraid of the answer. 'Is that why you chose me?'

Tariq's throat bobbed in place of an answer.

She felt sick suddenly. Sick and foolish. 'I see.'

He had deceived her. Lied. He didn't just want a better trading partnership or a strong queen at his side. He wanted a covenweaver.

CHAPTER 15

The silence on the journey home was intense. Dust still clung to their clothes, a visual reminder of what had happened. They had spent hours helping with the aftermath of the collapse, taking stock of the wounded and searching for the dead.

Seven men and a fourteen-year-old boy had died.

Tariq had to keep reminding himself that it would have been hundreds if it weren't for Aisha. She had saved those lives, after he had sent them back in there to die.

He snuck a glance at Aisha, who was riding beside him. She hadn't looked at him once. Her back was straight as a flagpole, her gaze fixed on the road ahead. The breeze sent loose strands of hair across her face, which she didn't appear to notice.

While they had been fortunate to have the warning, that warning had come at a price. Tariq had been forced to expose his motives for choosing her much sooner than anticipated. He had always planned to tell her eventually, but not at the beginning when they were still learning to trust each other.

He had truly botched that.

Tariq was aware of Kaidon's stare pressing into his back, no doubt wondering how he planned to claw his way out of the mess he had made. He rolled his shoulders, trying to rid himself of the sensation, but it did nothing to relieve him of the weight of Aisha's silence.

They followed the sun on its journey west until Tariq noticed Aisha sinking in the saddle, fatigued. 'Let's stop for a bit,' he told the guards ahead of him.

She sat up. 'Why?'

'Because you need to rest.'

They pulled off to the side of the road. Tariq dismounted and went to help Aisha down, but she quickly slid off by herself. He stopped and looked at Kaidon, who shrugged.

Aisha took her waterskin and wandered away from the group without saying a word, plonking herself atop a rock at the edge of the tree line. He thought about telling her to come back but suspected she wouldn't listen in her current mood.

'Give her time,' Kaidon said, patting Tariq on the back as he walked by him.

Tariq ran a hand down his face, then returned to his horse for his flask. As he was drinking, he saw Aisha brushing dust from her clothes. He wanted to speak to her and fix things between them, but she clearly wasn't ready to hear from him.

As he watched her, the small hairs on the back of his neck rose. He lowered the flask, listening and watching.

His stomach dropped when he saw the brush behind Aisha shift.

Shit.

'Aisha, run!' he shouted, reaching for the dagger at his belt.

But there wasn't enough time to run. She looked behind her as the undergrowth exploded and a leopard sprang from the thicket, a flash of muscle and claws cutting through the air towards her. Aisha fell forwards off the rock in her attempt to get out of its path. Tariq threw his dagger, striking the leopard in the ribs. It tumbled into Aisha, sending her sliding across the dirt. He heard the air leave her lungs.

All four men reached her at the same time, dragging the dying animal off her.

'Are you hurt?' Tariq asked, dropping to his knees beside her.

She shook her head. 'No.'

The colour was gone from her face, so he lifted her limbs, one at a time, just to be sure. Satisfied she wasn't bleeding, he helped her sit up. 'You could have been mauled.'

'I'm fine.' She averted her gaze as Kaidon cut the leopard's throat, putting it out of its misery. 'Did you have to kill her?'

'It's kinder than letting her suffer.' Tariq helped her to her feet but thought she appeared dizzy, so he kept hold of her hand.

Aisha leaned in and whispered, 'There's a cub.'

Confused, he looked around. 'Where?'

'In a den.'

It took him a moment to realise she hadn't physically *seen* the cub but rather had a vision. 'Your Sight works through animals?'

She looked as baffled as he was. 'Apparently, yes. It's never happened before. And we had *a lot* of animals at the palace—thanks to Yasmin.'

Tariq looked over at the dead leopard, noting the mammary swelling and loose belly. 'I should have told you to stay close.'

'I shouldn't have wandered away.'

Their gazes met briefly.

'We need to find the cub,' Aisha said. 'It can't be far, and it'll starve if we don't help it.'

The vision had clearly drained her of sense. 'You want to go looking for a leopard cub? After being attacked by a leopard?'

'Yes.' She pressed a hand to her chest. 'The thing is, I told Yasmin I would try to help.'

He stared at her. 'Help... leopards?'

'She told me they're endangered.'

'Aisha...' He took a small step back from her. 'This isn't some puppy on the street. It's a wild beast.'

'Please.' She took hold of his arm, locking eyes with him. 'The mother's dead because of me. Help me find the cub.'

For a long moment, he didn't speak, just stared back at her, seeing only conviction. Emitting a defeated exhale, he looked over at Kaidon, who was now listening in on their conversation while the other two guards disposed of the corpse.

'Gods, what have you agreed to now?' he said.

Tariq muttered a curse. 'We're going to take a quick look around for the cub before we leave.'

Aisha let go of his arm. 'The den can't be far from here.'

'Mothers will travel up to six miles from their young in search of food.' He watched the disappointment play out on her face. 'That said, I believe the den's nearby.'

That had her perking up. 'Why do you say that?'

'Because leopards normally avoid humans. Females will only attack to protect their young, which we can assume is close by.'

She pressed her eyes closed. 'Thank you.'

When the other guards learned of the plan, they were confused but didn't ask questions. The five of them left the main road and set off in search of the den. Aisha studied the rocks on either side of them as they walked their horses along a faint trail only used by animals, eventually pulling her gelding to a halt.

'What is it?' Tariq asked.

She looked around. 'I think we're here.'

'How do you know?'

She looked at him, and he realised she recognised the setting from her vision.

A soft mewing sound had them all looking south. Dismounting, Tariq handed the reins of his horse to Kaidon. 'Wait here.'

'I'm coming with you,' Aisha said, sliding down from her horse.

He didn't have the energy to object. 'Stay behind me.'

They were halfway up the slope when they heard another mew. Pausing, they looked around.

'There,' Aisha said, pointing to a gap in the rocks.

Tariq walked over to it and crouched down at the narrow entrance, half hidden beneath the tangled roots of a large tree. He peered inside, and Aisha craned her neck behind him.

'Well?' she asked.

At first, he didn't see anything, but then a single curious cub moved into the light. Tariq shook his head in disbelief. 'You were right.'

Aisha got down on her hands and knees in order to reach the cub.

'You can't just crawl into a leopard's den,' Tariq said.

'It seems I can,' she replied, crawling in. She stopped before the tiny spotted cub. When it didn't hiss or shy away, she picked it up. 'A girl,' she announced. 'Probably around two months old.'

The cub stared up at her, its little body trembling.

'It's scared,' Aisha said.

'That makes two of us.' Tariq reached a hand out. 'Pass her to me.'

Aisha passed the cub to him before crawling out. Once she was upright again, she took the cub back and tucked her against her chest.

'Now what?' he asked.

'We have to take her with us.'

'I was afraid you were going to say that.'

'We can feed her goat's milk and release her back into the wild when she's old enough.'

He stared down at the cub. 'She would never survive, as she won't have any idea how to hunt.'

Aisha stroked the cub's little head. 'We'll figure all that out later.'

He knew he would likely regret agreeing to this plan but didn't have it in him to tell Aisha no. 'Fine. Let's go.'

Kaidon eyeballed him as they returned to the rest of the group. 'You're getting soft,' he said quietly as the prince walked by.

Tariq didn't disagree. 'Do you want me to hold that thing so you can ride properly?' he asked Aisha.

'I'll manage.'

Once everyone was back on their horses, they set off at a slow pace.

Very few words were exchanged during the second half of the journey. Only when the castle came into view did Tariq move his horse closer to Aisha's.

'For the record,' he said quietly, 'I've no intention of telling anyone.'

Aisha looked down at the cub, not saying anything.

'I told you I'd protect you,' he added.

That got her talking. 'You brought me here knowing I'd be vulnerable. You don't get to claim protector now.'

He looked forwards again. 'And I suppose you were completely transparent, with your family being so morally superior and all?'

Silence.

Tariq drew a breath. 'We both benefit from this marriage. Let's not allow feelings to get in the way.'

Her expression turned from annoyed to disappointed. 'No feelings. Got it. Just let me know when you need something.'

It had come out wrong. 'You know what I meant.'

'I do, because you were very clear.'

His eyes remained on her. 'The political landscape is precarious, and I'm looking out for *both* kingdoms.'

'Of course,' she said without looking at him.

'Because it's not about us. It's about the people we represent counting on us to find a solution.'

'And personal feelings get in the way of that. Believe me, I understand.' She finally met his gaze. 'How did you find out?'

He could have told her about Maryam, but he'd promised not to expose the attendant for the same reasons. 'The day we met.' It wasn't a lie. 'Our hands touched, and you…' He didn't finish his sentence. He didn't need to.

Aisha was silent for the longest time. 'The queen won't hesitate to hand me over to the sectarian if she learns the truth. In fact, she'd probably be thrilled to do it.'

Her words landed hard because they were true. He couldn't imagine living in constant fear of being exposed for some ability you were born with and couldn't control. 'Well, I won't let that happen.'

'Because you need me.'

'Yes.'

'Without the emotion,' she added.

His eyes searched hers until she looked away. The cub gave a small cry, and Aisha held her closer, her chin brushing the soft fur.

They rode the rest of the way in silence.

CHAPTER 16

Two weeks had passed since their journey to Ashwaq. Two weeks of wedding preparations and avoiding each other.

The city erupted in celebration the day of the announcement. Tariq and Aisha had walked together through the streets, and for a fleeting moment, he had allowed himself to imagine that her smile was for him. But it wasn't. It was for the children tugging at her sleeves and offering flowers to put in her hair. She had never shone as brightly as she did that day. It had left him with the sharp ache of *knowing*.

Amicable would have to be enough.

The late-autumn air nipped at Tariq's face as he and his mother crossed the courtyard towards the gardens.

'I still find it extraordinary that you made the decision to empty the mine minutes before it collapsed,' his mother was saying. 'After sending everyone back to work, no less.' She eyed him sideways. 'Whatever could have prompted such a decision?'

If she was fishing for some sort of admission, she wouldn't get one. 'Sometimes you just have to trust your instincts.'

His mother stopped walking when something ahead caught her attention. 'Should that animal not be in a cage?'

Tariq followed her line of sight to where Aisha and Maryam sat on a pile of cushions amid bright silks draped over a low stone wall. A blur of spotted fur tumbled past Aisha, and her head fell back with laughter. She was really something when she was happy like that.

She had fully committed to the task of raising the cub, whom she had named Mira, finding solace in the tiny creature's unwavering need—or so Maryam said. If only *he* could find some solace. Instead, he preferred to torture himself with thoughts of the kiss they shared right before their relationship spiralled.

'She doesn't pose a threat,' Tariq assured his mother.

Aisha hadn't noticed them yet. Her attention remained on the cub, her expression soft—contrasting the guarded look she wore around him. She tossed Mira a small piece of meat, and the cub caught it with surprising grace.

'What in the world...' Farrah tutted while Tariq watched on, impressed.

Aisha finally spotted them, and the joy on her face vanished. Tariq and Farrah made their way over, prompting Maryam to rise and move a polite distance away. Aisha got to her feet as well, a hand going to her heart as she bowed her head. 'Your Majesty. Your Highness.'

Tariq bowed his head in return.

Farrah glanced over at Maryam. 'I think your attendant is getting far too comfortable for her position, if you ask me.'

'I don't mind,' Aisha replied. 'Much better than being alone.'

'We can organise some more suitable company for you,' Farrah said. 'Lady Selene enjoys cards. I have played with her many times.'

Selene was probably the last person on the planet Aisha wanted to play cards with. The suggestion had Aisha and Tariq exchanging an amused glance. Despite everything that had transpired between the couple, their sense of humour remained intact.

'I'll keep that in mind, Your Majesty,' Aisha said.

Mira padded over to Tariq, nudging his leg with her head. He crouched to pet her, and the cub began to purr. The chill of his mother's disapproval had him straightening.

'I was just saying to Tariq how fortunate his instincts were in Ashwaq,' Farrah said. 'Many lives were saved.'

Aisha kept her expression neutral. 'Yes. He has good instincts.'

Farrah studied Aisha for a few moments before speaking again. 'We have people working very hard to get the mine functional again before the wedding guests start to arrive.'

'I didn't realise that was important for a royal wedding,' Aisha replied.

'Our international friends must see Gruisea at its best. Every mine *must* be functional.'

Aisha glanced at Tariq but said nothing.

Farrah adjusted the sleeve of her gown. 'I shall head to the kitchen and see how the food planning is coming along.' Her gaze fell to Mira. 'Be careful she does not scar your face ahead of the wedding.'

Aisha bowed her head. 'Your Majesty.'

Farrah left behind a heavy silence. Aisha stared down at the leopard to avoid looking at Tariq. He probably should have left as well, but he didn't.

'She knows,' Aisha said quietly.

Tariq didn't have to ask what she meant. She was referring to the comment the queen made about his fortunate instincts while in Ashwaq. 'She doesn't know anything.'

'She suspects.' Aisha finally looked at him. 'And that's dangerous enough.'

Something pulled in his chest. 'I told you I'd keep you safe, and I meant it.'

She simply nodded.

He had an overwhelming urge to take her hand or bring her closer, comfort her in some way. But that wasn't the relationship they had. So instead, he crouched down and petted Mira's spotted head. The purr vibrated against his palm.

After a few seconds, Aisha crouched down opposite him. 'She's really excellent company.'

'My mother?'

She fought against a smile.

'I'm pleased I let you talk me into keeping her, then,' he said.

'You make it sound like you had a choice.'

His mouth curved up. 'I'm pleased Maryam's also proving to be good company.'

Aisha nodded. 'I have Mira to bite my toes and Maryam to bring me tea.' The humour fell flat because it was laced with sadness.

Guilt gnawed at Tariq's insides. She had one attendant, a wild pet, and his mother's scrutiny for company.

'You'll be seeing your family soon,' he said, trying to make them *both* feel better.

Her expression softened. 'I'm counting the days.'

Mira chose that moment to tumble onto her back, batting playfully at Aisha's sleeve. 'You're going to shred my gown.'

Tariq gently pried the cub off her.

'Thank you,' Aisha laughed.

The sound had him looking up. Her laughter died when their eyes met. They both rose and took a small step back.

'I should...' She glanced behind her.

'Yes, you should.'

Her lips parted like she was about to add something, but instead she reached down to scoop Mira into her arms. 'Your Highness.'

Tariq inclined his head. 'Princess.'

He watched Aisha walk away before going in the opposite direction. Kaidon was waiting for him at the far end of the courtyard, arms folded and watchful as ever.

'I see things are still awkward between the two of you,' Kaidon said when Tariq reached him.

Tariq looked back at Aisha, who was playing with

Mira once again. 'I'd like to organise for some of Aisha's sisters to arrive early. She needs them.'

'For wedding preparations?'

Tariq shook his head. 'For her sanity.'

The pair of them began walking.

'You could offer her *your* company, you know,' Kaidon said.

'I'm the last person she wants to spend time with.'

Kaidon waited until they passed a servant coming in the other direction before speaking again. 'If you want my advice—'

'Your longest relationship is two nights. I'm not taking relationship advice from you.'

'Oof. That was rather mean, but I'll ignore your cruelty in order to finish my point.' He sped up to get ahead of Tariq. 'She's hurt because she cares for you. And I know you care for her. You think I don't notice the way you look for her?' He stepped in front of Tariq, forcing him to pull up. 'Why not fix things?'

'The wedding is still going ahead. What more do you want?'

'What more do *you* want?'

Tariq wasn't in the mood for a lecture, even one with valid points. 'Can you reach out to her family or not?'

Kaidon raised his hands and stepped out of his way. 'I'll take care of it.'

Aisha sat cross-legged on her bed, absently stroking Mira as she dozed in her lap. The heartbeat beneath her hand was steady, comforting. Maryam sat nearby on the dressing-table stool, humming while she sewed.

Ten days had passed with barely a glimpse of Tariq. Maryam informed her the prince had returned to Ashwaq for a few days. But what about the other days? Was he avoiding her?

The queen certainly wasn't. She was at every dress fitting, every meeting with Jamil, always there to offer her opinion.

Ten more lonely days.

The decision to keep feelings out of their marriage was a wall between them.

It didn't help that Aisha's thoughts kept circling back to the kiss, to the press of his hand at the back of her neck. To the *warmth*. She had felt something she had wanted to believe in, only to witness its poisoning. A connection born of half-truths and too many omissions. She hated herself for wanting more from a man who had blatantly told her there was no need for it. Yet when she caught glimpses of him across a room, she couldn't ignore the lifting sensation in her belly.

'Please don't feel obligated to stay here,' she told Maryam as she traced a finger over Mira's spotted back. 'I'm sure you have other duties to attend to.'

Maryam's eyes softened with sympathy. 'It is really no trouble.'

A knock at the door made Aisha jump and Mira leap to her feet. Rising, Aisha went to answer it.

It was Tariq.

His posture was composed like always. The morning light sharpened the lines of his shoulders, and a lock of dark hair fell across his temple. He was so effortlessly handsome, and she was trying really hard not to notice. Surely the underlying attraction would be helpful when it came time to produce an heir.

'Hello.' She was annoyed at the level of breathiness in her voice.

'Change into your riding clothes,' he said. 'We're going out.'

The instant excitement she felt when he said that.

'Out where?'

'To the port.' He began backing away. 'Meet me in the mounting yard as soon as you're ready.'

Aisha turned to Maryam, bewildered.

'I will watch Mira for you,' the attendant said, her eyes smiling.

Aisha hurriedly changed into her riding clothes. Her leg bounced impatiently as Maryam braided her hair.

'Go,' the attendant said when she was finished, clearly amused.

Aisha shot up off the stool. 'Thank you.' She gave Mira a quick pat before hurrying out the door.

Down in the mounting yard, she found Tariq and Kaidon waiting with their horses. The groom brought out a chestnut mare for Aisha. Tariq approached, hands going to her waist before lifting her into the saddle. The pressure of his fingers sent heat to her face. He was walking before she had even gathered the reins.

As they were riding to the port, a thought hit her: What if he was planning to put her on a ship and send her back to Avanid? But surely he would have her pack her belongings if that were the case. She pushed the destructive thought from her mind.

Salty air filled Aisha's lungs as they neared the sea. Not long after, she spotted several ships along the harbour, their masts reaching into the clouds. Dock workers and merchants scurried about, shouting and laughing. She looked past them to the horizon. There was no better sight than scenery without walls.

Tariq slowed his horse to a walk as they approached one of the piers. Aisha looked up at the sleek vessel moored there, its crew busy on deck. When he stopped his horse, she rode up beside him.

'Now are you going to tell me why we're here?'

'You'll find out soon enough,' he said before dismounting.

The sun burst through an opening in the clouds as

Aisha was helped from her horse. Her hand went up to shield her eyes. There was movement on the deck, and her gaze narrowed on two familiar figures. Her heart leapt into her throat as recognition dawned.

She gasped.

Standing at the ship's railing were Lilah and Safiya. Aisha blinked multiple times to ensure she wasn't hallucinating, but the image didn't change. Her hands flew over her mouth as she turned to Tariq, trying not to cry. 'What are they doing here?' Her voice shook. 'They're not supposed to be here for another two weeks.'

His expression was unusually soft. 'I thought you might want them sooner.' He swallowed. 'I didn't want you to be alone with everything ahead of you.'

Aisha felt her heart expand in her chest, followed by a rush of affection. She looked back at her sisters, who were preparing to disembark, and took a few hurried steps in their direction before coming to an abrupt stop. She returned to Tariq, throwing her arms around him.

The prince stiffened.

'Thank you,' she whispered, dizzy with gratitude.

Slowly, hesitantly, his arms encircled her. The closeness felt familiar, and for a moment, she forgot that the man holding her with such addictive strength was the same man who chose her for her Sight.

'You're welcome,' he said, his chin brushing the top of her head as he released her. His expression turned serious once more. 'You better go welcome your sisters.' He nodded in their direction.

Aisha turned and ran towards the ship, all propriety forgotten. She reached the gangway just as Lilah and

Safiya stepped off it. Lilah squealed as Aisha crashed into her, hugging the air from her lungs. Tears spilled down Aisha's cheeks as she soaked up the feel of her sister. She reached for Safiya, pulling her into the chaos.

'That might not be wise,' Lilah said. 'Safiya was sick the entire journey.'

Safiya held Aisha tightly. 'I can't believe I have to get back on that thing to get home.'

Aisha laughed, stepping back. 'Gods, I've missed you both.'

Lilah sniffed. 'We've missed you too.'

The three of them made their way over to Tariq, who was patiently waiting.

Lilah's hand went over her heart as she bowed. 'Your Highness. Thank you for your generous invitation and organising transport. We're honoured to be here.'

Safiya bowed her head. 'Yes, thank you.'

Tariq eyed Safiya. 'Rough trip?'

She smoothed her hair back from her face. 'You could say that.'

'Will you be all right to ride to the castle?' Aisha asked.

'If the alternative is getting back on the ship, then yes, I'll be fine.'

Tariq gestured to the waiting horses. 'After you.'

As they prepared to leave, Aisha found she could not stop crying. Not only because her sisters were right here with her, but because the gesture had been so incredibly thoughtful. How on earth was she supposed to keep emotions out of the relationship with all the emotions currently flooding her body?

She rode between her sisters on their way to Azura,

asking questions about home while pointing out landmarks they might find interesting. She noticed that Safiya carried a sword.

'You'll have to remove that weapon when we reach Azura,' Aisha whispered to her sister. 'Kaidon will take care of it for you.'

Safiya's hand went protectively over it. 'I'm not going to stab anyone.'

'While that's pleasing to hear, you're a princess entering someone's *home*. I'm going to need you to act like one.'

'Wow,' Lilah said. 'It's beautiful.'

They all looked ahead at the castle's imposing silhouette contrasting a bright blue sky.

'So, that's the infamous Azura Castle,' Safiya said, taking it in.

The horses moved into a canter, their hooves growing louder as the road turned to stone.

When they arrived in the courtyard, grooms rushed forwards to assist.

Numair appeared, hands folded behind his back. 'The king and queen are waiting for you in the throne room.'

Aisha and Tariq exchanged a knowing look before they all followed after the steward.

* * *

'I thought you were exaggerating,' Safiya said to Aisha after the meeting, 'but you're right. The queen hates you.'

'What gave it away?' Aisha asked. 'Was it the permanent look of disdain or the constant commentary high-lighting all the ways I fall short?'

'It was the breath she drew every time you opened your mouth,' Safiya replied.

'And her expression whenever she said "Avanid",' Lilah added. 'As if the word tasted bad.'

Aisha's chamber was warm with late-afternoon sunlight. It filtered through the lattice windows, creating shifting patterns across the ceiling. The three of them lay sprawled across Aisha's bed, staring up at the pale stone, while Mira slept curled at the foot of the bed.

'She should be thanking you for marrying her son after everything you've told us,' Safiya said. 'If we had known about the true state of things here, we would have steered clear of Gruisea altogether and had you marry a prince with some personality.'

'Tariq has personality,' Aisha said quickly.

'I don't think I've ever seen him smile,' Safiya replied.

Aisha had seen him smile. Sure, it was mostly subtle and fleeting, but always contagious.

She sat up and slid to the edge of the bed. 'He's actually funny—in a quiet sort of way.'

Lilah sat up as well and looked at her. 'What was that?'

'What was what?' Aisha asked, confused.

'That whimsical tone you just used.' Light filled her face. 'Have you fallen for your husband?'

'He's not her husband yet,' Safiya pointed out. 'And of course she hasn't. Did you miss the part of the story where Tariq blatantly said their marriage was a business transaction?'

Lilah waved her words away. 'What he said and what he feels are not the same.'

'You almost sound against us liking each other,' Aisha told Safiya.

Safiya rolled onto her stomach. 'It's much harder to manipulate someone you admire.'

Aisha gave her a disapproving look. 'I didn't come here to manipulate him.'

'I know it's not the nicest word, but that's exactly why you came,' Safiya replied. 'And he knows that. He's just prepared to acknowledge it aloud while you remain in denial.'

Her sister's words landed hard. Aisha sat with them, remembering her conversation with Tariq on their return trip from Ashwaq. She had felt so used at the time, but perhaps he had felt that way all along. Tariq had been speaking the truth, and she didn't want to hear it. The question was why?

Because somewhere along the way, she had developed feelings.

Maybe as early as the journey to Gruisea, when he took care of her during the storm, or the night of the banquet, when she felt his stare like physical touch. Or the kiss in Ashwaq—the one she replayed in her mind over and over...

'Are we realising some things?' Lilah asked in a teasing tone.

Safiya sat up at that. 'Hopefully smart things.'

Aisha was realising that it didn't matter how much she pushed her feelings down to protect herself and their arrangement, they just kept rising to the surface every time she caught sight of him or he said something or did something.

'We kissed,' Aisha blurted. 'We slept together, and we kissed.'

Lilah's expression fell. 'Aren't you supposed to wait until after the wedding?'

'Isn't kissing just part of sleeping with a man?' Safiya asked. 'Wouldn't it be strange if you did it *without* kissing?'

Aisha pressed her eyes shut. 'We didn't sleep together, we *slept* together.'

Lilah blinked. 'I'm quite lost.'

'We shared a bed,' Aisha said on an exhale. 'We slept *next* to each other.'

A look of disgust settled on Safiya's face. 'Why?'

'It's a long story.'

'Did you kiss in your sleep?' Lilah asked.

'Obviously not,' Safiya said. 'Did he snore like an old dog?'

Aisha frowned. 'No.'

'Remember that hound Yasmin had a few years back with the cataracts?' Safiya continued.

Aisha rolled her eyes.

'If he took advantage of you,' Safiya said, 'it would be grounds enough to call off the wedding and return home with us.'

'He didn't take advantage,' Aisha said calmly.

Lilah clicked her fingers. 'Rufun.'

Aisha and Safiya looked at her with confused expressions.

'The dog with cataracts,' Lilah explained.

'Oh, that's right,' Safiya said. 'She kept that thing alive *way* past its expiry.'

Groaning, Aisha covered her face with her hands. 'I regret saying anything.'

Lilah pulled her hands away, forcing Aisha to look at her. 'I'm relieved there's something between you. You deserve some happiness for the sacrifice you made.'

Aisha felt herself relax.

'It's your turn next,' Safiya said, shuffling over to play with Mira. 'There will be royalty coming from all over the empire for this wedding. Zara will be hunting husbands left and right.'

Lilah crinkled her nose. 'You make it sound so predatory.'

'It's about time men had a turn at being the prey.' Safiya winced when Mira bit her mid-play. 'Even Mira agrees. Her mother also died at the hands of a man.'

Aisha sighed. 'A man who was saving *me*.'

Lilah climbed off the bed and walked over to the table, plucking a fig off the tray of food Maryam had brought them. 'Have you prepared for the Promise Exchange? Chosen a dress for the Binding Feast?'

She was referring to the Gruisean traditions that took place ahead of the official ceremony. Lilah had learned all about them before Tariq's visit, because she was supposed to be leaving with him. Thankfully, Maryam had explained them all in detail to Aisha.

'These happen before the wedding?' Safiya asked.

Aisha nodded. 'First, we have the Promise Exchange, where we each ask a promise of the other. It's engraved onto a silver token and exchanged before witnesses. We wear them only if we're prepared to keep that promise.'

That tradition seemed simple enough.

'Then comes the Binding Feast,' Lilah said. 'The couple interact only with each other under the watchful eyes of the nobility. Any disconnect, arguments, awkward moments, or unhappy expressions reflect poorly on the union.'

Safiya laughed. 'How ridiculous.'

Lilah continued. 'At the end of the evening, the guests confirm whether the pair are a good match.'

'So, an evening of fake smiles,' Safiya said. 'Welcome to the life of a queen.'

'And there's a dance,' Lilah said. 'A symbol of how in sync they are.'

Safiya looked over at Aisha. 'Dare I say no one will be watching your feet closer than the queen.'

'Thanks for that,' Aisha said drily.

'Have you learned the dance?' Lilah asked.

'Maryam showed me all the steps.'

'That's not enough,' Lilah said. 'You need to *practise*.' She rose and straightened out her dress. 'Come on. I'll do it with you.'

'And I'll play the role of the queen,' Safiya said, moving to the edge of the bed.

Aisha shot her a tired look.

'Lilah, I'm surprised you still remember the steps,' Safiya said.

'When Zara is your teacher, you don't dare forget.' Lilah dragged Aisha to the centre of the room. 'You begin like this.' She positioned Aisha. 'Imagine I'm Tariq.'

'But try to refrain from kissing her,' Safiya said.

'Chin up,' Lilah said. 'There you go.'

They bowed to each other, then began to step, with Lilah counting, 'One, two, three, four. Back, side, forward, side.' She smiled. 'Good.'

Aisha tried to make her movements graceful and effortless, like Maryam had told her to.

'Look at those narrow hips,' Safiya said with an exaggerated accent. 'How on earth will she birth my son's large-headed sons?'

Aisha stopped dead and turned to her.

'What?' Safiya said. 'I told you I was playing the role of queen.'

Lilah tutted. 'Ignore her. Your children's heads will be perfectly average. Keep your eyes on me.'

As they continued, Mira grabbed hold of Aisha's ankle mid-step, causing her to lose her balance and fall into Lilah. They both went down.

'Is this part of the dance?' Safiya asked.

Aisha and Lilah both burst out laughing. Gods, it felt good to laugh again. And laughing with her sisters was a special kind of good.

Rolling onto her back, Aisha caught her breath, one side of her ribs aching. 'I've missed you both so much.'

Lilah reached out and took her hand, and Safiya came to join them on the floor.

'I hate that our reunion's here in this strange place,' Safiya said. 'And I hate that our next reunion will probably be in another strange place.'

It was true. The next time they were all together again would likely be Lilah's wedding.

'I just wish we were all at home,' Safiya continued.

For all of Safiya's bravado, she was actually a big sentimental softie at her core.

'This was always the plan,' Aisha said. 'We do it for Avanid.'

'And for Mother,' Lilah added, 'who couldn't.'

They fell silent.

Outside, the sun was setting and darkness crept in. With her sisters there, she was in no rush to light the lamp.

'This will all be worth it, won't it?' Lilah asked. 'Dispersed across the empire. Separated from one another.'

Aisha swallowed. 'Yes, it will be worth it.'

More silence.

'Aisha,' Lilah said.

'Mm?'

'Don't forget there's a kiss at the end of the Promise Exchange. The two of you should practise since the king and queen will be present. You want it to look as effortless as the dance.'

Aisha turned her head to her sister. 'Maryam didn't mention anything about a kiss.'

'I'm certain Zara told me it takes place at the end.'

Aisha looked back at the ceiling.

Safiya held her stomach. 'I don't think I can watch.'

Aisha laughed softly.

That evening, despite the rooms across the corridor all made up for Lilah and Safiya, the three sisters slept in Aisha's bed, like they had done so many times throughout their lives.

It was the best sleep Aisha had experienced since arriving in Gruisea.

CHAPTER 18

*T*ariq was walking along the carefully manicured paths in the garden when he spotted Aisha ahead. He half expected her to turn around and walk the other way, but she continued towards him. They stopped a few feet from each other.

'Morning,' he said.

'Good morning.'

She seemed brighter than he had seen her in weeks. 'Did your sisters settle in all right? Maryam said they stayed with you overnight.'

'Did she?' Aisha squinted up at him.

Maryam was only obligated to share visions that were relevant to Gruisea's future, but lately he found himself asking questions about Aisha's general wellbeing. 'I happened to see her before I saw you.' It wasn't a lie.

Aisha searched his face. 'My sisters and I had a lot to catch up on and fell asleep.'

'I see.' He looked past her to the fountain in the

distance, where Lilah and Safiya were seated, watching Mira hunt an insect of some kind.

'Do you have a moment?' she asked.

For her, he seemed to always have time. 'I do.'

She began walking, and he fell into step with her, aware of her sisters' eyes now boring into his back.

'I wanted to speak to you about the Promise Exchange,' she began. 'Have you decided what you'll engrave on your token?'

'Yes. You?'

A nod. 'Yes.' She fell silent for a few strides. 'Do you get to choose what goes on yours? Or did the queen already have it pre-engraved on your behalf?'

'Funny,' he said, suppressing a smile. 'Though we are supposed to choose with the king and queen's wishes in mind.'

She looked up at him. 'Will they want to approve mine?'

'I'm sure my mother would love to, but the tradition has always been that each party asks for what serves their individual interests.'

'It's essentially another trade agreement,' she said.

'A trade agreement of the heart.'

They walked in silence for a moment, the gravel crunching beneath their feet.

'Listen,' Aisha said, clearing her throat, 'about the kiss.'

He slowed mid-step. 'The kiss?'

'The one at the end of the exchange.' Her voice was tinged with nervousness. 'I know this might seem a bit forward, but with the king and queen present, Lilah thought it might be a good idea if we were to… practice.'

He stopped and turned to face her. 'Lilah suggested this?'

'She's very thorough with these things.'

Tariq glanced in the direction of the sisters. They were too far away now to read their facial expressions. 'Is she now?'

'I know it won't be our first time.' Aisha's cheeks flushed with colour. 'But it will be our first time with an audience.'

He tried to hide his amusement. 'That's true.'

Aisha was looking everywhere but at him. 'Do you think a standing kiss will be quite different from when we kissed… lying down?'

He crossed his arms, pretending to think about it. 'I imagine so.'

She nodded thoughtfully. 'I suspected as much.'

Tariq watched her chew that bottom lip as she weighed her next words. He couldn't have looked away if he wanted to.

He should have told her that she'd been set up, that there was no kiss at the end of the exchange, but the memory of her impossibly soft lips against his kept him silent. And since there *was* a kiss on their wedding day, the practice would not go to waste.

'We wouldn't want to appear awkward,' Aisha said.

'No,' he agreed. 'No, we wouldn't want that.'

She looked around. 'Should we do it here? Get it over with?'

'Sure,' he replied.

He waited for her to look at him again and felt his pulse quicken when their eyes met. Her chest stilled as he stepped closer, his shadow falling over her as he reached a hand up to lightly hold her face. Her head tipped back slightly, the muscles in her neck softening. His gaze fell to her lips as he brushed his thumb over her jaw. He leaned in, then waited, giving her every opportunity to pull away.

But she didn't move.

Slowly, he pressed his lips to hers, savouring the heat from them as the world fell silent around them. He should have stopped there. That was plenty for a kiss that wasn't even part of the ceremony. But then she inhaled in a way that made his temperature rise.

He deepened the kiss, his free hand moving to the small of her back, drawing her closer. Aisha's hands landed on his chest. He was expecting her to push him away, but instead, her fingers curled around the fabric of his tunic.

A throat clearing had them stepping apart. Lilah and Safiya now stood nearby.

'Forgive the interruption,' Safiya said, arms crossed. 'We were taking a turn around the garden and didn't see you here… talking.'

'I think they're still talking,' Lilah said, tugging on Safiya's arm.

'No, they have definitely finished,' Safiya replied, her feet rooted to the ground.

Aisha took another unnecessary step back from Tariq. 'I think that's everything sorted for the ceremony.'

'Are you sure?' Lilah asked. 'Because we can go.'

Tariq could still feel the heat of Aisha's mouth, and it was painfully distracting. He realised he needed to tell her the truth about the exchange. When she moved to leave, he caught her wrist. 'Wait.'

Aisha's gaze shot to his hand, then travelled up to meet his eyes.

He led her a few paces away from her sisters and lowered his voice so as not to embarrass her. 'Listen, about the Promise Exchange.'

She waited.

He just had to come out and say it. 'There's no kiss.'

At first she looked confused, but then her eyes widened slightly. '*What?*'

'There's no kiss at the end of the exchange.' He swallowed. 'It's possible Lilah got confused.' Though he didn't believe that for one second.

'Oh.' She looked accusingly at her sister. 'You knew, didn't you?'

Now Lilah appeared confused. 'What?'

'That there's no kiss at the end of the exchange.'

A guilty expression swallowed her sister.

Aisha's gaze returned to Tariq. 'Why didn't you correct me *before*? You let me make a complete fool of myself.'

He tilted his head. 'Why do you think?'

She opened her mouth to reply, but words failed her.

'I know I should apologise,' he said. 'The kiss was—'

'It doesn't matter how good it was,' she said, cutting him off. 'You should have told me before.'

His eyebrows rose. 'I was going to say deceptive.'

Colour flooded her cheeks. She dipped her head, turned, and walked away.

She was halfway to her sisters when Tariq called to

her. 'It was good practice for the wedding ceremony. There's a kiss at the end of that one.'

Aisha didn't look back. She walked straight past her sisters. Lilah and Safiya exchanged a look before following her.

Only when the three of them were out of sight did Tariq release the grin he'd been holding back.

CHAPTER 19

On the morning of the Promise Exchange, Maryam helped Aisha prepare for the ceremony while her sisters went to get themselves ready.

'Here,' Maryam said, placing a cup of tea in front of her.

Aisha picked it up and took a grateful sip. 'Thank you.'

Maryam went to fetch the necklace the queen had sent for Aisha to wear and brought it over to her. It was a family heirloom Farrah had worn at her own Promise Exchange.

'It's beautiful,' Aisha said, staring at it. 'I'm surprised she trusts me with it.'

The faintest smile came and went on Maryam's face.

'Can you help me with the clasp?' Aisha asked.

'Yes.'

Aisha watched in the mirror as the attendant drew it around her neck, concentrating hard on the overly complicated clasp. It was more difficult than either of them was expecting. Maryam's hand came to rest on her neck as she fiddled.

A familiar sensation came over Aisha, her tongue beginning to tingle. The room faded. She saw Maryam standing somewhere dimly lit, her posture rigid, eyes glazed and unfocused, mouth slack. The air around her was alive with some invisible energy, like she was… *seeing*.

The image broke as quickly as it came, and Aisha jolted, then grabbed the edge of the dressing table for balance as the room rushed back into view. When she looked into the mirror, her eyes met Maryam's. The attendant slowly lowered her hands and asked, 'What did you see?'

Aisha didn't reply. She was too confused and afraid.

'You had a vision, did you not?'

A tear slipped down Aisha's cheek. 'I don't know what you mean.'

Maryam stepped closer, and Aisha tensed up. The attendant lifted the necklace to show that she only intended to put it on. Aisha forcibly relaxed her shoulders.

'I know a vision when I see one,' Maryam said quietly. 'How is the nausea?'

Aisha remained wary. *It's a trap.* The queen probably set it for her. And now she was torn between feigning ignorance and blurting out her every truth to someone who might actually understand.

With the clasp finally secure, Maryam moved away. 'You can trust me,' she said. 'And I believe I can trust you.'

Aisha felt her walls weaken. She turned on the stool to face her. 'I saw *you*.' She watched her reaction carefully, but Maryam didn't seem alarmed by that. 'Eyes glazed over. Gone from your own body. You see things too.'

Maryam nodded. 'Yes.' She folded her hands together. 'I saw you before I ever met you. I knew what you would become before you ever set foot in Gruisea.' A faint smile came and went. 'I saw your feelings for the prince before the two of you had even met.'

It took Aisha a moment to respond. 'Why didn't you say something sooner?'

'You know why.' Her tone was kind. 'This conversation alone carries great risk. We must be careful who we trust.'

'I can't believe we have the same gift.'

'The Sight,' Maryam said.

Aisha nodded slowly. 'I won't tell anyone. Not even my sisters. I swear it before the gods.'

Maryam smiled briefly. 'Well, you already know I will not tell anyone.' She drew a breath. 'Your sisters will be by to collect you shortly. Do you want something for the nausea?'

'You saw them coming?'

Maryam shook her head. 'No, Your Highness. You told me the plan last night.'

Aisha's cheeks heated. 'Of course.'

There was a knock at the door.

'We can speak later,' Maryam said.

'All right.' When Maryam went to open the door, Aisha said, 'The nausea always passes.'

Maryam looked back at her. 'Yes, it does.'

In walked Lilah and Safiya, clearly done waiting.

'Didn't you hear us knocking?' Safiya asked, looking between the two of them.

Maryam bowed her head. 'Apologies, Your Highness. We had some trouble with a clasp.'

Safiya turned her attention to the piece of jewellery around Aisha's neck. 'Oh, it's gorgeous.'

Aisha reached up to touch it. 'It belongs to the queen.'

Safiya screwed up her face. 'At second glance, I can definitely see some flaws in the gem's setting.'

'No, you can't,' Lilah laughed, walking over to Aisha. 'You look so beautiful. I've no idea how you'll top this on your wedding day.'

The gown was made of light blue silk embroidered with silver thread that looked like water when it moved. It had short fitted sleeves and a high neckline.

'Yes, very nice,' Safiya said, waving Aisha towards the door.

'You have the token?' Aisha asked.

Safiya nodded. 'Yes. We're good to go.'

'I hope the exchange goes well, Your Highness,' Maryam said, holding out a pair of light blue gloves. 'I shall take good care of Mira until you return.'

Aisha took them from her and slipped them on. 'Thank you.' She glanced in the direction of the sleeping cub before following her sisters.

The trio made their way through the corridors of Azura, Aisha still feeling slightly sick from the vision. She made a mental note to ask Maryam what symptoms she got.

The exchange was to take place in the Temple of Salithar at the southern end of the castle grounds. Salithar was the god of marriage, union, and reconciliation. A figure with two faces was carved into the door. When they entered, Aisha found a small gathering of nobles who had come to bear witness. The king and queen were seated at one end, and Tariq waited beside them. His expression softened when he caught sight of her, and he watched her make her way over.

'Your Majesties. Your Highness,' Aisha said when she reached them.

The king extended his hand to her. She minimised contact as she kissed it, not wanting to risk a vision.

'You are late,' Farrah said, even though she wasn't. She nodded towards Aisha's hands. 'You will need to remove the gloves for the ceremony.'

She had been afraid of that.

Farrah gestured to Jamil, and the sectarian made his way over. Before he reached them, Tariq leaned in and whispered, 'After obeisance. There should be no more contact after that.'

She nodded.

There was more kissing of hands and polite reverences, then Lilah swooped in to take the gloves before the ceremony began.

Tariq must have noticed the slight tremble in Aisha's hands, because he leaned in again. 'It will be over soon enough.'

Jamil cleared his throat, and the room fell silent. 'We are gathered here today to witness the promises exchanged between Prince Tariq of Gruisea and Princess Aisha of Avanid.' He bowed his head and said a prayer: 'Salithar, guide their steps where shadows gather. Let truth be their compass and mercy their strength. May your light guard their hearts and minds.'

He then placed a small bowl of water, with a sprig of fresh rosemary in it, at the altar. A humble offering to Salithar.

Turning back to Tariq, he said, 'Prince Tariq, what is the promise you ask of your future wife?'

Kaidon stepped forwards, handing Tariq a small silver token, engraved with delicate script. The prince focused on the words. 'I want you to promise to always put the collective needs of our people before our individual needs.' He looked in her eyes, adding, 'The people's well-being and safety must always come before our own comfort.'

It was selfless and entirely appropriate. Every queen should prioritise the wellbeing of her people. So when he held the token out to her, like a question, she lowered her head so that he could put it on. Her fingers curled around the token as she looked up at him, feeling the roughness of the engraved words. 'I swear to uphold this promise.'

Applause broke out around them. Aisha snuck a glance at the queen, who was clapping so lightly that she doubted the action was producing any noise.

Jamil nodded approvingly, then turned to face Aisha. 'Now it is your turn, Princess. What is the promise you ask of your future husband today?'

Safiya stepped forwards to hand her the token. Aisha proceeded to read from it. 'I want you to promise to protect my kingdom as you would your own. Promise to do everything in your power to keep it safe from external threats for as long I'm at your side, serving the people of Gruisea.'

There was a collective murmur across the room. Aisha

didn't dare look at the king or queen now. She knew it was a big ask, but it was also the reason she had agreed to stay.

Tariq stared at her for a long moment—so long that Aisha thought he might not accept it. But then he bent so that she could slip it over his head, adjusting it as he straightened. 'I swear to uphold this promise.'

And it was clear on his face that he meant it.

Applause broke out again, and Aisha looked over at her sisters. Lilah was wiping the corner of her eye while Safiya stared off in another direction—her usual tactic for hiding emotion.

When the clapping died, Jamil clasped his hands together, looking between them. 'The tokens will rest against your hearts for as long as the promise remains true. May your words, spoken before Salithar and the witnesses here today, hold fast.'

More applause.

'We're done,' Tariq whispered. 'And no kiss, remember?'

She held back a smile.

The pair made their way to the temple doors. They were about to step outside when a hand caught Aisha's elbow. She whipped her head around and found Jamil.

'My apologies, Princess,' he said. 'I wondered if you might—'

The vision hit her before he'd finished his sentence. She saw Jamil through a haze of smoke. His eyes burned with purpose—

She jolted back to the room to find Tariq now

standing between her and the sectarian, her weight against him. *Oh no.*

'I'm afraid your question will need to wait, Your Holiness,' Tariq said while simultaneously ushering Aisha out of the temple. 'The princess woke with a bad headache, and it appears to have worsened.'

Lilah and Safiya caught up to them once they were outside.

'What happened?' Lilah asked, peering into Aisha's face. 'Goodness.'

'Tariq.'

Aisha recognised the queen's voice and began to panic.

'Take her and keep walking,' Tariq said, transferring her weight to Safiya.

Lilah moved to the other side of her without breaking stride. 'You're trembling.'

'It's normal,' Aisha reassured her. 'It will stop shortly.'

'Why are they happening so frequently now?' Safiya asked. 'And while that sectarian is sniffing around you.'

Aisha had been wondering the same thing. Since arriving in Gruisea, all skin-to-skin contact carried risk. Yet she could kiss Tariq with no problem at all.

'I don't know.' Another question for Maryam.

'What did you see?' Safiya whispered to her.

Aisha shook her head as she tried to remember. 'It was very fast. Jamil. And… smoke.'

Lilah almost tripped over her own feet. 'Smoke?'

'Shh,' Safiya said. 'What do you expect? The man's a sectarian. Burning women is 50 percent of his job.'

By the time Aisha reached her chamber, her heartbeat had steadied, but her thoughts continued to race. The feel of Jamil's hand clung to her skin, cold and heavy. Her sisters settled her on the bed while Maryam went to fetch some tea, sensing something had happened. Or maybe she had seen it for herself.

Aisha made the decision to learn everything she could from Maryam when she returned. If anyone could help her understand the Sight, it was her.

Aisha was done being a passive vessel for her gift. It was time to take control of it.

CHAPTER 20

Maryam was perched comfortably on the edge of Aisha's bed, with Mira curled at her feet. Aisha sat opposite her, hands resting in her lap. The closeness felt natural now, a kind of sisterhood forged in secrecy.

'I don't even know what gifts my mother had,' Aisha said. 'I think she was too frightened to share things with us. She worked with herbs mostly. She always smelled of them. Dried petals, roots, tinctures.'

Maryam was listening intently. 'That sounds like the gift of the Bloom.'

'The Bloom?'

'Herbal weaving.'

Aisha sat with that information for a moment. 'She always told us she was a healer.'

'She was. A very *powerful* healer.' Maryam offered her a warm smile. 'I am certain she would have taught you everything once you started showing signs. That is often when education begins.'

That was both comforting and painful—a reminder of the things they had missed out on. 'Will you teach me about the Sight?'

'It will take more than a single conversation. What are your pressing questions?'

Aisha leaned forwards. 'Why does it happen sometimes and not others? Nothing when I hold my sister's hand, but immediately when the sectarian touches me?'

Maryam nodded thoughtfully. 'It is complicated because there is not only one reason.'

'Then tell me all the reasons.'

Maryam smoothed a crease in her plain gown. 'The first is conflict. The Sight responds most fiercely when there is tension, danger, or contradiction. For example, if you share a kiss with the prince, you feel safe, yes?'

Aisha blinked. 'How do you know we...?' Then it dawned on her. 'Never mind.'

Suppressing a smile, Maryam continued. 'The Sight has no reason to stir during such times. But with Jamil...' She selected her words carefully. 'His choices and his path clash with yours. That friction tears the veil open.'

Aisha *thought* she understood. 'So, danger is the trigger?'

'One of them.' Maryam drew a breath. 'There is also resonance. The Sight is drawn to those whose fates will tangle with yours. The greater the overlap, the stronger the pull.'

'But Tariq's fate and mine is entirely entangled, and I've only had two visions of him since our meeting.'

'That's because the prince is already bound to you. You

do not need visions to know your paths entwine. Though that may change in the future.'

'You mean, if the relationship fails?'

She hesitated. 'Again, it is more complicated than that.'

Aisha fell silent, twisting her fingers together.

'The balance between mind and body is also a factor,' Maryam continued. 'When you are deeply anchored in your body, through closeness, touch, or desire, the Sight quiets. It is grounded. But when your mind floats free, a vision can seize you.'

Aisha's brows pinched. 'So I have no real control.'

A shadow of a smile curved Maryam's lips. 'That is an entirely different conversation.'

Aisha exhaled, leaning back against the pillows. 'Do you feel sick after a vision? Weak?'

'Yes.'

'Why does it happen?'

'That is the cost.' Maryam's tone was gentle. 'You feel it in your body afterwards. Weakness. Sickness. Headaches.' She paused. 'Longer visions may even cause stomach cramps and nose bleeds.'

Aisha had definitely noticed that the length of the vision impacted how poorly she felt afterwards.

'That is another reason why it does not come every time,' Maryam said. 'Your mind saves its strength for what matters most.' Her expression turned serious. 'Whatever fate demands that you see.'

A soft knock at the door had Maryam getting to her feet and Mira twitching awake. Aisha was expecting it to be her sisters, so she didn't even bother moving from the bed.

It was not her sisters.

'Your Majesty,' Maryam said when she opened the door, bringing a hand to her heart and bowing.

Farrah entered before Aisha had a chance to stand, looking around the room as though everything in it displeased her. 'Oh my,' she said when her gaze landed on Aisha. 'You look awfully tired.'

Aisha went to get up, but the queen held up her hand. 'No need.' Then to Maryam, 'Leave us.'

Maryam bowed again and quietly left the room.

Once they were alone, Farrah stepped into the light coming through the window. 'I trust you will be well enough to attend the Binding Feast tomorrow?'

'Of course, Your Majesty.'

The queen took a few steps closer to the bed, eyes travelling slowly over Aisha before pausing on her hands. 'No gloves today?'

The question took her by surprise. 'No.'

'They must be quite the fashion statement in Avanid.'

Aisha hoped Farrah couldn't see her heart pounding through her clothes. 'I wouldn't know. We weren't out in society very often.'

Farrah's eyebrows rose. 'It is certainly an interesting style choice.' She tilted her head. 'We only use them for riding here.'

Aisha forced her face to relax. 'That's helpful to know.'

The queen's gaze swept the room once more. 'You will learn our ways soon enough.' Her gaze drifted to Mira, who had gone back to sleep. 'On the bed?' She tutted. 'Really. You are fortunate she has not injured you yet. Leopards are very unpredictable.' With that, she turned and glided from the room, saying over her shoulder, 'Do rest up. No one wants to see a tired bride.'

When the door closed behind her, Aisha listened for the sound of footsteps fading. Then, covering her face with both hands, she collapsed back onto the pillows.

CHAPTER 21

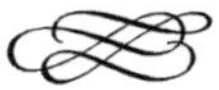

ariq's boots echoed off the stone floor as he made his way down the wide corridor to collect Aisha for the Binding Feast. Kaidon walked beside him. The cool breeze had the tapestries on the walls stirring.

'So, the princess was feeling better when you went to see her last night?' Kaidon asked.

Tariq nodded. 'Though she told me my mother came poking around.'

'Of course she did.'

'Aisha's convinced both she and Jamil *know*.'

Kaidon looked at him. 'The queen doesn't miss much, and Jamil will follow her lead. Hopefully she eases up after the wedding.'

Tariq prayed he was right.

Kaidon fell back as they reached Aisha's door, waiting for them across the corridor. Tariq knocked, and Maryam answered the door, bowing before moving aside. Aisha replaced her in the doorway, and Tariq forgot to breathe.

She wore a deep blue gown, with gold embroidery that climbed like vines along the bodice and sleeves. The neckline was stitched with tiny beads that looked like stars. A belt cinched her waist, highlighting her curves. Her hair was intricately braided and interwoven with gold thread, and a small sapphire pendant rested at the hollow of her throat.

He needed to say *something*, but the words refused to come.

'I can't tell if that's a good reaction or a bad one,' Aisha said, scrutinising his face. 'Maryam assured me this was the right choice.'

'It's… the right choice.' Tariq cleared his throat and tried again. 'You look…' *Come on, words.* 'Breathtaking.'

Light filled her face. 'Thank you. Hopefully the queen doesn't reprimand me for the gloves.' She looked him over. 'Avanid's colours look good on you, by the way,' she said, gesturing to his sky-blue tunic.

'Had it made in your honour.' He stepped forwards and offered his arm. 'Shall we?'

Aisha took his arm, and they set off towards the feast hall.

'Should we have a code phrase like last time?' she asked.

He thought for a moment. 'How about I check in with you by asking if you would like some more wine. If you're fine, say no. If you need time to regroup, say yes, and we can regroup.'

'Better make it a slow pour.'

'That was the plan.'

She looked up at him. 'But not so slow that it reflects badly on our relationship.'

The corners of his mouth lifted.

She faced forwards again. 'It's not work, you know.'

He gave her a questioning look.

'Conversation with you.' She moved closer. 'It's rather easy.'

He could almost hear Kaidon's ears flapping behind them.

'I agree,' Tariq said. 'So we just go in and talk like us.'

'Like us,' she echoed, like she was testing the phrase out.

Aisha brought her free hand up to rest atop the other one, moving closer still in the process. Gods, he loved the feel of her beside him. The world felt so much quieter.

They arrived at the grand double doors, and Aisha increased the distance between them slightly, one hand returning to her side. She pressed her painted lips together, then found a smile, aware that all eyes would be on her once those doors opened.

'Ready?' he asked.

She nodded.

Tariq gestured to the guard waiting to open the doors, and a moment later, they swung open. Sounds of conversation, laughter, and clinking goblets spilled out into the corridor. Dozens of nobles and foreign emissaries filled the space, gathered beneath the soaring arched ceilings draped with blue and yellow silk. Long tables lined the sides of the hall, covered with platters of roasted meats, fruits, and stuffed pastries.

Tariq felt the collective gaze of the court shift the

moment they stepped into view. Aisha's head was high, her expression serene, but Tariq could feel the slight tension in her fingers where they rested against his arm. He made sure to keep pace with her and not scowl back at the staring nobility.

Conversation died, replaced by a heavy silence. Some of the guests smiled at them as they passed by, while others just watched. At the far end of the hall, his parents were seated on a dais. His father wore green robes, his crown weighing down his frown. Beside him, his mother was a picture of icy composure in a maroon gown. Her unblinking gaze followed Aisha's every move.

The pair approached the dais to kiss the hand of the king.

'Please,' King Hamza said, his voice carrying across the hall, 'the evening is yours and yours alone. Demonstrate to all here why they should bless this union.'

Tariq inclined his head.

The queen rose then, apparently with something to say. 'Let us see if you are a *true* match. The people of Gruisea know best.'

Jamil was seated at the table closest the dais, with Lilah and Safiya down from him. They all watched intently. Murmurs stirred, then settled when the music struck up.

Tariq extended a hand to Aisha, and she took it. When they came together, he whispered, 'Should we get the dance out of the way?'

'I practised, you know.'

He placed his palm to hers. 'Not with me this time.'

'No.'

Seeing that they were about to dance, the guests

cleared space for them. Everyone stilled to watch. Tariq waited until Aisha met his gaze before taking the first step. He led, and she followed, skirts swirling around them as they moved.

It was going beautifully until her toe caught his boot. She overcorrected and almost tripped in the process. Tariq righted her before coming to an abrupt, graceless stop. They looked around, then at each other.

'I added a variation,' she said, trying to cover her embarrassment.

'Shall I fall next? For symmetry?'

A smile spread across her face. 'I can't see any other way through it.'

He flicked his gaze towards their audience. 'It might be too late for us. I saw Shariff Mazin utter a prayer.'

A laugh burst from Aisha, and she immediately slapped a hand over her mouth. Tariq couldn't help but laugh also. Her hand fell away when she saw him, and she allowed herself to join him properly. The sound curled around him, warm and disarming. This was his new favourite sight—Aisha forgetting herself and *happy*.

For a few seconds, the hall, the guests, his parents, all faded. There was only the two of them. *Us.* Aisha's hand rested on his chest as she caught her breath. Once they had collected themselves, they resumed the dance.

When the music drew to a close, the guests applauded. It was likely pity applause, but Tariq didn't mind. Everyone then moved to their seats to eat.

Aisha and Tariq sat at the raised table near the king and queen. A servant had already filled their goblets.

'There goes our plan,' Aisha whispered.

'If you drink quickly, we'll be fine.'

Aisha smiled as she removed her gloves.

Tariq reached for some flatbread, tearing it in half and placing a piece on her plate.

'Too soon for the toast?' Aisha joked quietly.

'Just a little.'

The toast came at the end of the evening. Guests would be asked if they blessed the union, and hopefully the majority raised their cups. He glanced in the direction of his parents, who were watching them. 'We're at the whims of the king, I'm afraid.'

They both reached for the large spoon sitting on the tray of lamb at the same time. Neither of them was paying attention to what they were doing, and Aisha's hand landed on top of his. Tariq heard her suck in a breath, and he looked up just as her eyes glazed over and her lips parted. She was no longer looking at him or the hall but somewhere beyond all of it.

Not here. Not now.

He withdrew his hand carefully, making sure the movement wasn't sudden or suspicious. He didn't know whether to look at her or his food or away. Her mouth twitched. Then, like a wave receding, she blinked rapidly and came back to him.

Reaching under the table, he took a firm grip of her thigh and said, 'Focus on me.'

She did, holding his gaze for dear life as she returned from wherever she had been. He wanted to reassure her, to provide reprieve from all the staring, but all he could do was hold her gaze and wait for her to steady.

'How long?' she asked, breaths coming fast.

He shook his head. 'A few seconds. Everything's fine. You're doing great.'

She looked down at his tunic, and her eyebrows came together in confusion. 'Did you say the tunic was made for this feast?'

He looked down at his clothes. 'Yes.'

'Oh.'

When he lifted his gaze, her expression frightened him. He leaned in. 'Tell me what's going on.'

She took a nervous look around and tried to relax her shoulders. 'I don't know.'

'You don't know?'

'I saw you,' she said, looking back at him. 'With Zahvik Barakat.'

It took him a moment to place the name. 'Slevaborg's sectarian?'

She nodded. 'Wearing that tunic.' She reached up to touch his hair. 'Your hair at this *exact* length.'

He stared at her. 'What are you saying?'

The doors to the hall swung open, and every head turned. Framed in golden torchlight stood a tall figure in a white thobe. As he stepped inside, he lowered his hood, steely eyes sweeping the hall.

'That's him,' Aisha whispered. 'The man who killed my mother.'

CHAPTER 22

Aisha couldn't breathe.

The light behind Zahvik made him burn gold at the edges. It was really him. There were more lines on his face and grey in his hair, but everything else... Same height and build, same slow, measured way of walking.

A loud clatter broke the silence. Someone had dropped something, a goblet maybe. A servant hurried over to clean up the mess.

Aisha's pulse roared in her ears as memories of him flooded back in. That day was branded on her soul. Her mother's screams. The primal noises coming from her father. The exact shade of Zahvik's eyes when he addressed them.

She flinched when Tariq took her hand under the table. Only then did she realise she was shaking. Her eyes met Lilah's across the room. A servant was mopping up wine on the table in front of her. She looked as though she had been slapped.

Safiya had never laid eyes on Zahvik before, but judging by her glare, she knew exactly who it was.

'Look at me,' Tariq said.

Aisha dragged her gaze to his.

'Whatever this is, you and your sisters are safe. Understand me?'

She nodded.

King Hamza rose from his seat, a welcoming smile on his face, suggesting this was not a surprise visit. Queen Farrah, on the other hand, looked from the sectarian to her husband, then back again. Her fingers had tightened visibly around the stem of her cup, the only indicator of her internal state.

Everyone watched as Zahvik made his way to the royal dais, flanked by two holy warriors. Their synchronised, armed presence was designed to intimidate.

Zahvik stopped before the king and queen and bowed his head. 'Your Majesties.'

That voice. How many times had she heard it in her mind? In her *dreams*? Smooth as silk.

'Your Holiness,' Hamza replied. 'I must apologise. I had no idea you were arriving today.'

The queen managed to smile. 'We would have sent a carriage.'

Zahvik met her gaze. 'I told the men at the dock not to interrupt this sacred event.'

What did he think he was doing at that very moment? It had been intentional. The entire kingdom could be on fire, and Zahvik would know exactly which direction the smoke was blowing. These people had eyes and ears in every corner of the empire.

Zahvik looked around until his gaze snagged on Aisha. She didn't move. She couldn't. Recognition dawned, and his mouth curved up. His expression was neither cruel nor kind. He was simply making sure she felt *seen*.

Tariq got to his feet, drawing the sectarian's gaze to him.

Zahvik looked him over. 'And you must be Gruisea's Crown Prince I have heard so much about. When King Hamza sent the invitation to foreign emissaries, the Emperor insisted I attend in person to bless the happy couple.' He extended a hand in Tariq's direction, expecting him to come forwards and kiss it.

Aisha gripped the edge of her chair with both hands.

Noticing, Tariq placed a hand on her shoulder. 'Forgive me, Your Holiness, but the Binding Feast tradition requires us to refrain from interacting with guests.'

The sectarian bowed his head. 'We must respect traditions of this land.'

'Numair, would you show His Holiness to his seat?' Farrah said.

The steward came forwards, gesturing to the space between Jamil and Lilah. Aisha watched the colour drain from her sister's face.

'No!' Aisha shouted, shooting up out of her seat.

You killed her! Zara's young voice screamed in her mind.

Aisha fought the urge to cover her ears. Everyone was looking at her now, all with shocked expressions—except for Zahvik. He watched with interest.

All of Aisha's instincts yelled not to let him near her

sisters. And she would honour those instincts like her mother always had. 'I...'

Tariq looked from Aisha to Zahvik. 'We would be honoured if you joined us at our table.'

He had salvaged the mess the only way he could, and she didn't contradict him. She lowered herself into her chair as the sectarian was shown to a seat on the other side of Tariq. The silence that followed was thick and suffocating. It was clear from the expressions of the nobility that they did not know what to make of the situation.

Aisha looked again at her sisters and saw that Lilah's eyes had filled with tears. The damage this man continued to cause their family was unbearable.

Farrah leaned in to say something to the king, the corners of her mouth tight. Her eyes met Aisha's briefly in the process, and Aisha could have sworn she saw traces of sympathy. The king nodded, then got to his feet, drawing the attention of the room. He raised his cup in the air.

Aisha and Tariq exchanged an equally confused look.

'We have all observed Princess Aisha and Prince Tariq here tonight,' Hamza said, his voice booming. 'Now, I ask you, who among us blesses this union?'

He had jumped ahead to the toast.

Aisha's gaze found Farrah's, and she wondered if the queen had told her husband to do it. She didn't know if it was an act of mercy or an attempt to save face, but she appreciated it more than Farrah would ever know.

The guests looked between themselves. Then, one by one, goblets rose. Some with enthusiasm, and some with reluctance, but up they went. More than enough.

'So be it,' Hamza said. 'The union will be made sacred before the gods one week from now.'

Aisha's eyes closed as relief washed over her.

* * *

'Why would the king invite him to the wedding?' Lilah asked, her eyes full of tears once more.

Aisha looked at her. 'The invitation was for foreign emissaries. Due to their relationship with Slevaborg, they could hardly exclude them.'

'The Emperor knew exactly what he was doing when he sent Zahvik,' Safiya said, fuming. 'It's intimidation in its purest form.'

They were seated on Aisha's bed with their knees pulled up, facing one another.

'It's a long way to travel to flex some muscle,' Lilah said.

Aisha didn't mention all the other possible reasons he was there, like psychologically tormenting their entire family or hunting for covenweavers among them.

Lilah was rocking slightly as she thought. 'How are you going to get through this wedding with him watching your every move and breathing down your neck?'

Aisha reached out and squeezed her hand. 'We're not frightened children anymore.'

'You're right,' Lilah replied. 'We're frightened adults.'

Safiya shook her head. 'He doesn't scare me.' She looked at Aisha. 'You did an amazing job tonight given the circumstances. And I was pleased to see Tariq looking out for you. It makes me feel better about the whole marrying him thing.'

Aisha felt for the token beneath the fabric of her gown.

'What are we going to do about father?' Lilah asked. 'He hasn't seen Zahvik since…'

The image of his dusty face and bloodstained teeth flashed in Aisha's mind. She blinked it away. 'He has to come.' Her voice was heavy. 'He has to. The marriage isn't lawful without him.'

Safiya leaned back with a sigh. 'They're so *rigid* with their traditions. What if he were dead?'

'That would be a different matter,' Aisha said, 'but he's alive, so he must consent in person.'

'Getting him here will be one thing. Getting him into the same room as that man will be something else.' Lilah wiped her eyes. 'We didn't want to say anything—'

'Lilah,' Safiya cut in.

'She needs to know.'

'Know what?' Aisha asked.

Lilah waited for Safiya to relax before continuing. 'We weren't going to say anything because you have enough to worry about, but Baba has gotten worse since you left.'

'Worse how?'

Safiya answered that. 'Disorientation, tremors, withdrawal, difficulty making even the smallest decision.'

Silence followed.

There was a knock at the door, and Safiya climbed off the bed, reaching beneath her skirts and pulling out a small knife.

'Safiya,' Lilah whispered. 'Put that away.'

'With Zahvik loose in the castle—no way.' She pulled

the door open and immediately hid the knife behind her back. 'Your Highness.'

Aisha hopped off the bed and went to the door. Tariq was still in his formal robes, fatigue softening the lines of his face.

'Should I be worried that your sister's answering the door with a knife?' the prince said.

Aisha shooed Safiya back from the door. 'Sorry about that.'

'I just wanted to check on you before retiring,' he said. 'I didn't realise you still had company.'

Safiya cleared her throat and went over to Lilah, dragging her off the bed. 'We were just leaving, weren't we?'

Lilah stumbled off the bed. 'Yes. Yes, we were.'

'There's no need to leave on my account,' Tariq said.

'We're truly exhausted,' Lilah said as she passed them in the doorway. 'Goodnight.'

Aisha watched them disappear through the door on the other side of the corridor, then exchanged an amused look with Tariq as she stepped aside to let him in. 'Come in.'

'If you're tired—'

'I'm fine. Just don't wake the baby.' She nodded towards Mira, who was curled up on the divan. She didn't so much as open one eye. 'Have a seat.'

He walked over to the table and slid into one of the chairs, looking her over. 'So, you're all right?'

She poured him some water from the jug and slid the cup towards him before taking the seat opposite him. 'I think so.' She watched him drink. 'Thanks to you.'

He watched her as he placed the cup down. 'The evening was… intense.'

'Nothing ruins the appetite faster than your mother's murderer taking a seat at your table.'

'I'm sorry about that.'

She waved his apology away. 'You did the right thing. Better my table than theirs.'

'That's what I figured.'

'I have you for protection, and they only have me.'

His eyes moved between hers. 'I hope you know my protection extends to everyone you love.'

She felt her eyes sting as tears rose to the surface. 'I know.' The words came out a little choked.

He looked away. 'Just as well with Safiya walking around the castle *armed*.'

'I promise to have a word with her about that.'

Tariq exhaled through his nose. 'I don't mind. I like that she's protective of you.' After another silence, he said, 'There was no colour left on your face at the feast. You were white as a sheet.' His concerned eyes returned to hers. 'I'm glad to see it has finally returned.'

Aisha's throat tightened. 'I never thought I'd have to see him again, and if I did, I thought I'd have time to prepare.'

He slid his hand across the table, the tips of his fingers meeting hers. 'He's going to be here for the wedding.'

'I know.' She watched their fingers touching. 'I'll get through it. I'm just not sure my father will.'

He nodded. 'You should write to Zara and warn her.'

That was all she could do.

At some point, her fingers had entwined with his. She

felt the temperature in the room rise slightly. And when Tariq's fingers flexed against hers, she felt that too.

Standing slowly from her seat, she walked over to him, her bare feet silent on the floor. Tariq tipped his head back to look up at her, that familiar crease forming between his brows. She smoothed it with her thumb.

His hands settled at her waist, palms blissfully warm through the fabric. She found herself imagining their warmth against her bare skin.

Aisha brought her hands to his shoulders, feeling them rise and fall with his breath. For the first time that evening, the tension in her stomach loosened. Her fingers travelled from his shoulders to his collar, brushing against the soft edges of the embroidery. Tariq's grip on her waist tightened, just slightly.

'Do you still think we shouldn't let our feelings get in the way?' she asked softly.

His eyes turned liquid as he stared up at her. 'It was a solid plan at the time.' He reached up to touch her now-messy braid. 'But plans change.'

She lowered her forehead to his. 'Best we keep plans flexible.'

Tariq turned in his chair to kiss her. There was nothing rushed about it, only a slow unravelling of restraint. His hand moved to the back of her neck, drawing her down, and her fingers slid into his hair.

When he stood, she moved with him instinctively, breathing against him. His desire bled into every kiss. He lifted her gently, and her legs curled around him.

Mira didn't stir, and the world outside the room didn't matter.

Tariq held her with care, like he was afraid the moment might shatter if he moved too quickly.

'Do you want to wait?' he asked. 'Until after the ceremony?'

Aisha's lips turned up. 'The ceremony is for *them*. We were bound the day we met, when the gods showed me a future with you.' She slid her hands inside his tunic, feeling for his heartbeat. 'Our hearts have already chosen.'

Tariq's expression intensified as he stared at her. Heat radiated from him, his muscles tensing under her touch. His mouth went to her neck. 'You're so beautiful,' he whispered.

Aisha closed her eyes as teeth grazed her skin. The world fell away, but this time it had nothing to do with a vision.

Aisha sat opposite Maryam on the rug, Mira curled at her feet with her paws tucked under her chin. The cub's slow breath warmed the hem of her gown. Aisha had been meeting with Maryam at the same time every day for the past week, while Tariq trained and before her sisters were up for the day.

'Again,' Maryam said gently.

Aisha drew a breath, slow and even, the way she had been taught. 'Breathe until the tightness in my chest loosens. Let my thoughts stop and sit. If I can get quiet enough here'—she touched two fingers to the notch above her sternum—'the Sight will listen back.'

'Good.' Maryam tilted her head. 'Or?'

'Or I can use conflict. Summon tension to make two futures hold together in my mind until they scrape.' She wrinkled her nose. 'My least favourite.'

Maryam appeared amused. 'It is just another tool you can utilise, like moving in or out of your body, which you *must* practise.'

Aisha nodded. 'Feel the ground when I want silence, and let my thoughts unhook.'

'The Sight sits at the edge between stillness and drift. You will learn where that edge is.'

Mira's ear flicked at a fly that had found its way inside the room.

'And now for the last piece,' Maryam said.

Aisha groaned. 'My mind is bursting already.'

'It will hold,' Maryam assured her. 'This knowledge is very important.'

Aisha tried to focus. 'Go on.'

'You already know the Sight exacts a cost. Do not think of it as a punishment but as the price of crossing thresholds your body does not normally cross. We always try to be respectful of that, but today I want to show you how to spend it on purpose if required.'

Aisha thought she had misheard. 'Do you mean force a vision?'

'Sort of.' Maryam paused. 'You cannot make fate speak, but you can let it know you are ready to hear it.'

A frown settled on Aisha's face.

'You will feel the drain more quickly and for longer,' Maryam said. 'Everyone's body reacts differently.' She sat up. 'You will begin as you do with openness, breath, unclench the jaw, soften the tongue. Then you choose a thread and hold its edges.'

Aisha had no idea what that meant in a practical sense.

'And as you do that, let your body loosen.' She tapped Aisha's wrist lightly. 'Listen to your pulse, then imagine it drifting. You are not leaving your body but merely loosening your grip on it.' She continued to tap on Aisha's wrist. 'It will feel like you are falling.'

Aisha closed her eyes, breathing deep into her belly the way Maryam had shown her. When she exhaled, the air slid past the back of her throat like water. Eventually, the tightness in her chest eased.

'Visualise the conflict,' Maryam murmured.

The door burst open, and Safiya rushed in. 'They're—' She stopped dead when she saw the two of them sitting on the floor, Maryam with her hand on Aisha's wrist. 'What are you doing?'

Maryam withdrew her hand and got to her feet.

Lilah came through the door, eyes landing on Aisha. 'Why are you just sitting there? Let's go!'

'Go where?' Aisha asked.

Lilah's smile was luminous. *They're here.*

It took Aisha a moment to realise which 'they' she was talking about. 'They are?'

'Yes!' Lilah ran forwards and pulled her to her feet.

Aisha gave Maryam an apologetic look as she was dragged from the room. Then the three sisters headed down the corridor, their footsteps in sync.

It had been months since Aisha had seen the rest of her family, and she didn't know if she would laugh with joy when she laid eyes on them or bawl her eyes out.

'What were you doing with Maryam?' Safiya asked when they were a good distance from her chamber.

Aisha had known the question was coming. 'Talking.'

Safiya stared at her. 'While holding hands?'

'We weren't holding hands.' Aisha didn't mean to

sound quite so defensive. 'She was showing me some breathing techniques.'

Lilah looked between them. 'What did I miss?'

'Yet another early-morning meet-up between Aisha and Maryam,' Safiya said. 'That makes seven days straight, am I right?'

Nothing got past Safiya.

When Aisha didn't respond, Safiya said, 'Did you think we wouldn't notice?'

'That my *attendant* visits my chamber? Why on earth would you care?'

Safiya grabbed Aisha by the arm, forcing her to stop. 'What are you hiding from us?'

Heat rushed to Aisha's face.

'Wait. You have a secret?' Lilah asked, sounding genuinely crushed. 'From *us*?'

Guilt tore through Aisha. She had always shared everything with her sisters. While she couldn't tell them about Maryam, she also couldn't bring herself to lie to their faces. 'Please don't ask me anything else, because there is a secret, but it's not mine to share.' She looked between them. 'Please.'

Safiya crossed her arms. 'That's not the only secret you're keeping from us, is it? Maryam visits your chamber in the mornings, and *Tariq* visits at night.'

More colour flooded Aisha's cheeks. Satisfied, Safiya resumed walking, leaving Lilah and Aisha standing there.

'It's probably best that Zara doesn't know about the prince's nightly visits.' Lilah said.

Aisha opened her mouth to deny it, but the lie got stuck.

'I won't say anything,' Lilah said before following Safiya.

They reached the receiving room, a chamber used for prestigious guests. A guard opened the double doors as they approached. Inside, the windows were open to the courtyard gardens and sunlight poured in. Aisha's gaze landed on the dark-haired boy in the centre of the room.

'Omar.'

A smile split his face at the sound of Aisha's voice, and he took off at a run towards her. She opened her arms as he flung himself at her, nearly knocking her over.

'You're too big for that now,' Aisha laughed. She kissed the top of his head over and over as his arms wrapped tighter around her.

'I thought you would be waiting at the port,' Omar said.

'I'm sorry. If I had known you were arriving early, I'd have been there.'

Omar pulled back from her. 'The captain of the ship said the wind was in our favour. Where's Tariq?'

'Likely still in the training yard.'

'And it's *Prince* Tariq,' Yasmin said, all but pushing him out of her way. 'Now let the rest of us greet her.'

Aisha looked her youngest sister over before pulling her into an embrace. She smelled like sunshine and saffron.

'Have they been nice to you?' Yasmin whispered.

'Yes.' It was the only answer she would ever give her.

Aisha spotted Zara standing on the far side of the room, watching them. Zara gave her a weak smile, and she could see the toll the past few months had taken on her. When Yasmin released her, Aisha went to Zara, throwing her arms around her. To her surprise, her older sister hugged her back with equal enthusiasm.

'I told Omar not to run inside the castle,' Zara said into her ear.

Aisha drew back with a laugh. 'I'm sure you did—multiple times.' She kept hold of Zara's hands as she looked her over. 'You made it.'

Zara released a breath. '*We* made it.'

The familiarity of family was blissfully overwhelming.

'Come,' Lilah said, gesturing to Yasmin and Omar. 'We'll go see Baba, and then we'll take you to meet Mira.'

'Can't we meet Mira first?' Omar asked as they headed for the door.

'No,' Lilah and Safiya replied in unison.

Aisha and Zara were left alone in the chamber.

'So,' Zara said, letting go of Aisha's hands and strolling towards the window. 'This is your new home.'

Aisha looked around the room. 'This is it.'

'And it's really going well?'

'It really is.'

Zara stopped and turned to her. 'I received your letter the day before we departed. It must have been quite the shock when Zahvik showed up—at your Binding Feast, no less.'

'It was, but we managed. Thankfully, his quarters are as far from ours as they can be. And he's been so busy with King Hamza, none of us have seen him since.'

Zara dropped her gaze. 'I haven't told Baba.' She sounded almost ashamed. 'I should have, but I was worried he wouldn't get on the ship if I did.'

Aisha nodded slowly. 'Where is he?'

'Where do you think?' Zara swallowed. 'He greeted King Hamza and Queen Farrah on arrival, then wanted to go to the guest quarters to rest. He told me he couldn't handle the noise.' She brushed a finger down her nose. 'But there was barely any noise at all.'

Aisha was silent a moment. 'When he learns that Zahvik's here—'

'It will break him,' Zara said matter-of-factly. 'We'll need time to piece him back together, so the sooner we tell him, the better.'

Aisha thought for a moment. 'You did the hard work of getting him here. Let me tell him.'

Zara looked like she was about to object, but then she appeared to change her mind. 'If he sees that you're unaffected, he'll draw strength from you. He wants to do his part.'

She didn't doubt it. 'How was he? Outside the walls?'

'He was…' Zara lifted her shoulders in a small shrug. 'Adored. People were crying in the streets. And you know what he's like. He just cried right along with them.'

The burning in Aisha's throat was relentless. She had to look away and collect herself.

'This marriage has given people hope,' Zara said. 'We must ignore Zahvik's presence and stay focused on why we're all here.'

That made Aisha smile. 'All right. Take me to see Baba.'

* * *

Aisha waited for her father's guard to announce her. When he returned to the door and gestured for her to enter, she stepped into the dark room. The heavy curtain had been drawn across the tall window. She peered through the dark and found her father seated in a high-backed chair on the other side of the room with a blanket draped across his knees. He looked smaller than she remembered, like a man trying to disappear into himself.

'Aisha?' His voice was fragile, uncertain.

She went to him, dropping to her knees at his feet and taking his hands in hers. 'I'm here, Baba.'

He studied her face in the poor light, eyes flicking across her features. 'Our beautiful Aisha.'

The 'our' made her chest constrict. 'I'm so glad you're here.'

He reached up, his trembling fingers brushing her cheek. 'You look well,' he said softly. 'I was worried you would fade without Avanid's sunshine.'

Aisha smiled through the ache in her throat. 'Turns out there's sunshine in Gruisea some of the time. I'm learning to embrace the cooler weather.'

He nodded. 'Good. And Prince Tariq? He treats you kindly?'

'He does,' she said. 'He's a really good man, and he's going to make a wonderful king one day.'

Bilal exhaled, his shoulders sinking with relief. 'I prayed for that.'

That made her smile. 'Well, the gods delivered.' She glanced over at the window. 'Do you mind if I open the curtain a little? So I can see you better?'

Even in the dark, she saw the worry on his face. 'Just a little.'

She got to her feet and walked over to the window. 'You should see the gardens, Baba. Different from what we have back home, but no less beautiful. And you can smell the ocean from here.'

He blinked against the light. 'Maybe later.'

Returning to him, she took hold of his hands once more. 'There's something I need to tell you.'

With his brow creased, he waited for her to speak.

'Zahvik Barakat is in Gruisea.'

Nothing.

'He's here at Azura Castle, and he'll be at the wedding.'

At first, it seemed like Bilal didn't understand. But then his hands went rigid in hers, and he looked past her. 'No.' The word was almost voiceless. 'It is not safe. You must leave this place. We must all leave.'

'Baba.' She tightened her grip on him. 'Look at me.'

His gaze returned to hers. 'What fool would allow him into these halls? I will speak to the king. I will—'

'He's a guest here.' She kept her voice soft.

'A guest?'

She nodded. 'But he cannot touch us here. Tariq won't allow it. The court won't allow it. The people here are entirely invested in this love story. If the sectarian does anything to upset this union, the whole kingdom will turn on him.' She didn't really know that. Maybe they would cheer him on.

His shoulders eased slightly. 'Love story?' The idea seemed to calm him down.

She squeezed his hand. '*Yes*. It's so much more than a political marriage.'

The lines around his mouth softened, and he breathed out slowly. Aisha rested her forehead against his knuckles.

'Have you seen him?' he asked after a moment of silence. 'Zahvik?'

She nodded. 'Yes. And you will too, at some point.'

He fell silent for a long time. 'I told myself that if I ever saw him again, it would be his last day alive.'

She pressed her eyes closed. 'I think we all told ourselves the same thing at some point, but here we are.'

'He cannot be trusted.'

She straightened to look at him. 'Of course not.'

Bilal's expression darkened. 'You cannot let them take it.'

'It?'

He gripped her hand so hard she flinched. 'They take things, slowly. And by the time you realise what is happening—'

'They don't get anything else,' Aisha said firmly. 'They've taken enough.' She held his gaze. 'Nothing else.'

He sagged back into his chair, breath shallow. 'Nothing else.' It was clear he was done.

'You need some rest.' Aisha patted his hand. 'I'll come back later.'

He nodded, seemingly distracted.

Rising, she walked to the door, then glanced back. He was staring at the open window, and she knew he would draw the curtain the moment she left. 'Rest up, Baba.'

She exited the chamber and closed the door behind

her, swallowing the lump in her throat. 'Keep a close eye on him,' she instructed the guard.

He bowed his head. 'Your Highness.'

She walked slowly down the corridor, eyes on her feet as she processed the conversation with her father. She looked up when she heard footsteps coming in the other direction, then froze when she locked eyes with Zahvik. He stopped also, clasping his hands behind his back as he took her in. A single guard stood behind him.

A single witness.

'Princess,' he said. 'Have you been to see your father?'

She didn't answer. *Couldn't* answer.

'It is the first time he has left the palace walls in many years, is it not?' His voice was smooth and leisurely.

Aisha forced herself to respond. 'Yes.' It was the best she could do.

Zahvik watched her carefully. 'I do hope he is coping.'

Her gaze fell to the fragile skin of his neck, and she imagined ripping it open with nothing but her fingernails. Such a thought should have brought shame, but it didn't.

'The mind is a delicate thing,' he continued. 'We must always protect it.'

Again, she didn't reply.

He tilted his head. 'You remind me of her, you know.' He said it almost gently. 'Your mother.'

She stopped breathing.

'Perhaps you do not remember—'

'I remember,' she said, cutting him off.

They stared at each other for a long moment.

'Aisha?'

She flinched when someone said her name. Looking

behind her, she found a sweat-soaked Tariq approaching with Kaidon following at his heel. He looked like he had just stepped out of the training yard. The prince looked from her to Zahvik, and his face hardened. She immediately went to him, forcing herself not to run. When she reached Tariq, he moved in front of her.

'Are you lost, Your Holiness?' he asked, his tone cold.

The sectarian's mouth curved up. 'Not at all. I am on my way to see King Hamza.' His gaze shifted to Aisha. 'Princess, please tell your father that he is welcome to join us.'

When she didn't reply, he resumed walking.

Aisha closed her eyes as he passed by. Only once he had disappeared around the corner did Tariq turn around, taking a firm hold of her shoulders.

'Did he say or do anything to you?' he asked.

He hadn't said anything unkind or made any sort of threat. It was more the *way* he said things that unsettled Aisha—and his general presence. 'No. Nothing.'

His grip on her relaxed.

'I'll organise for one of the guards to shadow the princess,' Kaidon said. 'At least until Zahvik's gone.'

'That's not necessary—'

'Do it,' Tariq said before Aisha could finish objecting. 'I should have done it the day he arrived.'

Nodding, Kaidon disappeared to make the arrangements.

'I'm sorry I wasn't here when your family arrived.' Tariq wiped his face. 'How's your father?'

She checked to ensure they were alone before answering. 'Tired. Overwhelmed.' She swallowed. 'I'm worried he won't make it to the temple.'

'He will.' Tariq gestured for her to start walking, then fell into step with her. 'Until then, we keep Zahvik well away from your entire family and make the whole thing as easy as possible. Whatever he needs, we'll provide it.'

Aisha stopped walking.

Tariq turned to her with a questioning look, damp hair clinging to his temple.

'I know this isn't the right time,' she said, keeping her voice down. 'But you keep making room for me and my family, and I need you to know…' She swallowed. 'That I love you. You don't have to say it back. I just needed to say it.'

For a beat, he simply stared at her. Then, with complete ease, he said, 'I love you too.' His hand found hers, thumb grazing her knuckles. 'You're the best thing I've ever imported.'

Aisha let out a shaky laugh, then laced her fingers through his. Together, they walked on.

CHAPTER 24

The new arrivals spilled across the pale stone paths, draped in the finest fabrics and smiling politely to one another. From a shaded balcony above the gathering, Aisha stood with Zara, Lilah, and Safiya, watching them. Zara had insisted they assess all opportunities beforehand.

When Queen Farrah suddenly stepped out onto the balcony, they immediately straightened and bowed.

'Your Majesty,' they all said, exchanging glances.

Farrah looked out at the view, then shifted her gaze to Zara. 'What a superb hunting spot.'

Zara feigned confusion. 'I'm afraid I have no idea what you mean, Your Majesty.'

'I am quite certain that is not true.'

Aisha had felt somewhat differently towards the queen since the Binding Feast—ever since she had leaned in and told the king to give the toast. While Aisha had no proof that it was an act of kindness, she couldn't come up with another reason for it. They had barely exchanged more than a few words since then, but the tension between them seemed more tolerable than usual.

Below, a herald announced the arrival of a tall figure in black robes. His presence was like a crack of thunder in the garden. Everyone paid attention to him.

'The new King of Cogalla, Rakan,' Zara said. 'His father recently died in what some are calling a suspicious hunting accident.'

'His first act as king was to execute his mother's lover,' Farrah added. 'An act he carried out himself by all accounts.'

A look of horror settled on Lilah's face.

Safiya took a step forwards to get a better look. 'Why's he just walking by without greeting anyone?'

'Because he's the King of Cogalla,' Farrah said simply. 'They dominate the iron ore, tin, and copper trade. People have to smile at him.'

'Unmarried,' Zara said, 'but rumoured to have his sights set on Imperial Princess Ranya.'

'The Emperor's daughter?' Safiya asked.

Farrah interrupted them. 'Actually, he has shown little interest in marriage. It is the Emperor who is pushing his daughter in the king's direction.'

Safiya exhaled sharply. 'No surprises there given Cogalla controls all the materials needed to produce weapons.'

Another new arrival was announced, and they all leaned forwards slightly—even the queen.

'The Crown Prince of Makan,' Farrah said. 'Majid.'

'And who's that behind him?' Safiya asked.

'His younger brother, Prince Taim,' the queen replied confidently.

Zara glanced sideways at her. 'Currently second in line for the throne—until Majid's children arrive.'

'I think I've heard of him,' Safiya said. 'He's supposed to be a great swordsman.'

Zara didn't comment.

'Prince Majid is betrothed to Princess Nalia of Montia,' Farrah said pointedly.

'Betrothed is not married,' Zara replied bravely.

They all fell silent for a moment, until a familiar figure entered.

'Is that Nasir?' Lilah asked, perking up. 'I didn't know he was coming.'

'He's the head of the diplomatic mission to Avanid,' Zara said. 'And the bride is from Avanid, so I'm not surprised.'

A throat cleared behind them, and they all turned around. Tariq stood there casually, arms crossed, looking very princely. The corners of Aisha's mouth turned up at the sight of him.

'Why are you not down there greeting our guests?' Farrah asked, as if she weren't herself an equal host.

'I was just on my way.' He stepped onto the balcony. 'Who are we spying on?'

Farrah appeared immediately offended by the question. 'The very accusation... I am going to do my duties, and I suggest you and your betrothed follow.' She left the balcony.

The relationship between Aisha and Farrah hadn't yet

progressed enough for the queen to refer to Aisha by her name. For now, she remained 'your betrothed'.

Zara ushered Safiya and Lilah inside. 'Come. We need to check on Yasmin and Omar before we join the gathering.'

That left Aisha and Tariq alone on the balcony.

The prince's gaze drifted downwards. 'You look as beautiful as ever.'

The deep tone of his voice had Aisha's insides melting. She needed to get a grip. 'Thank you, Your Highness.'

He closed the distance between them and kissed her in a way that made her not want to go downstairs. When he broke the kiss, he said, 'Kaidon tells me your father isn't coming.'

'No.' She rested her hands on his chest. 'But he assures me he will be at the wedding.'

Tariq angled his head, studying her. 'You sound rather certain.'

She lowered her voice. 'That's because I *saw* it.'

'You saw our wedding?'

'Sort of.' Her hands fell away. 'When I visited him last night, I had a vision of him standing in the temple, dressed in his formal robes. Naturally, I asked him what he planned to wear, and he showed me what his attendant had laid out for him.' She paused, feeling pleased with herself. 'It matched my vision perfectly.'

What she didn't tell him was that it had been her first attempt at summoning a vision. It had been a chance to practise what she had learned. There had been a window of opportunity while her father's focus was elsewhere, and she had taken it.

He searched her face. 'And have you recovered all right?'

'Yes. I was better by morning.'

His face relaxed after hearing that.

She hated that she couldn't tell him everything. Her new knowledge and skills felt like a dirty secret. She trusted him completely, but she couldn't break her word to the woman who had helped her understand herself.

Tariq leaned in and kissed her forehead. 'Shall we go greet our guests?'

'Absolutely.'

When he offered his arm, she wrapped herself around it.

* * *

The garden was even more crowded by the time they entered. Guests formed elegant circles around shaded tables, and musicians plucked softly at their instruments. They went first to King Rakan, who Tariq had met a number of times over the years—*before* he was crowned.

The king had the darkest eyes Aisha had ever seen. He wore no ornamentation beyond a thick leather belt.

'Your Majesty,' Tariq said, bowing politely. 'It's good to see you again.'

Rakan nodded once. 'And you.' His assessing gaze drifted to Aisha.

'Allow me to introduce Princess Aisha of Avanid,' Tariq said.

Rakan didn't offer his hand, merely inclined his head. 'Princess.'

'Your Majesty.'

'I heard your father's here,' Rakan said, looking about. 'But I haven't seen him.'

She had been expecting those types of comments, so her smile never faltered. 'He's resting ahead of a big day, Your Majesty.'

Tariq guided the conversation in a different direction, and Aisha was content listening to the two of them speak about everything from ships to copper.

At one point, Aisha saw the king's gaze drift, then shift entirely. Curious as to what had caught his attention, Aisha followed his line of sight all the way to... Lilah. She was standing by a citrus tree, inspecting the leaves, no doubt wishing she could pluck some for her bag.

Rakan smoothly returned his attention to the conversation, and Aisha pretended she hadn't noticed a thing.

After a few more minutes of copper discussions, Tariq told the king to make himself at home, then excused them so they could continue making their rounds.

When they were a good distance away, Tariq whispered, 'I've heard rumours that their military is developing a new type of weapon.'

Aisha frowned. 'I don't know whether that's a good or bad thing.'

'I suppose it depends on whether Slevaborg get their hands on it or not.'

She stopped walking when she heard a ripple of noise moving through the crowd. A low murmur that dropped to a hush. She looked around.

'What's wrong?' Tariq asked.

Aisha grew uneasy. 'I'm not sure.'

A moment later, he quietly said, 'Aisha,' then pointed discreetly towards the garden's main entrance, where a figure stood at the edge of the lawn.

Her heart sank when she spotted her father. He was wearing his royal robe, but it hung loosely from one shoulder. His hair was uncombed and his sandals... there was only one sandal. He was frozen in place, staring at something or someone—

'Zahvik's here,' Tariq said.

Just the name had Aisha's stomach tightening. She looked in the direction her father was staring and found the sectarian staring right back. Her lungs faltered as she headed straight for her father. Zara reached him first, gracefully turning him around and guiding him away from Zahvik and the other guests. Safiya and Lilah got to him at the same time Aisha did. All eyes were on them, and the silence was loud.

Bilal's guard appeared, out of breath, like he had been running for some time, which he probably had. He gave Zara an apologetic look, and she glared back at him.

'Let's go, Baba,' Lilah said.

Bilal blinked at her, his brow creasing. 'I heard music.'

'You should have sent for us,' Zara replied.

Bilal tried to look back. 'He was right there.'

Zara nodded. 'We must ignore him, remember?'

His worried gaze went to Aisha. 'I do not want to embarrass you.'

'You could never embarrass me,' she said, her throat closing.

'Go back to the party,' Zara told Aisha. 'You too, Lilah. Safiya and I will join you as soon as we can.'

Zara always seemed to know the next right move. The guests had enough to whisper behind their backs about without the entire family being absent. It was on Aisha to return and show everyone that all was well.

She stopped walking, and Lilah stopped a few paces after her. They watched their father's retreating back until he disappeared through the door of the castle. Only then did Lilah turn to Aisha with eyes full of sadness.

'He'll be all right,' Lilah said. 'You saw him in his wedding clothes. He'll be fine after a good night's sleep.'

Aisha nodded, barely, then turned around and walked back to the party.

CHAPTER 25

Tariq braced for an onslaught as he and Aisha stood before the twin thrones. His father was leaned forwards, his crown glinting under the lantern light, and his mother sat with a disapproving expression next to him. The air in the audience chamber was thick with unspoken scrutiny.

'Do you have any idea how this court appeared today?' Hamza's gaze moved between Tariq and Aisha. 'A king, confused and wandering through my gardens, shouting at shadows—'

'He wasn't shouting,' Aisha said, clearly feeling the need to defend her father.

'He was missing a shoe,' Hamza continued, knowing she couldn't contradict that. 'The guests saw it. The emissaries saw it. And Zahvik, who will be reporting directly to the Emperor, most definitely saw it.'

Aisha dropped her gaze, and her humiliation had Tariq's temper flaring. 'If you wanted him in the right mind to select footwear, then perhaps you shouldn't have invited the man who killed his *wife*.'

Hamza's fingers tightened around the arms of his throne. 'Mind your tone.'

Tariq drew himself up and kept going. 'He has earned the right to stumble. The man buried his queen, watched his kingdom suffer for it, entrusted his daughter to us, and this is how we repay him.'

Farrah spoke up at that. 'We empathise. However, he is still the King of Avanid, and his presence reflects upon all of us.' She rose from her seat and stepped down from the dais, hem whispering against the floor. 'Do you understand what is at stake with this union? Tomorrow, the eyes of the entire empire will be upon us. If that man does not walk his daughter down the aisle and give her to you —in a sane manner—we will be the subject of ridicule.' She paused for effect. 'Royal weddings are not sentimental occasions. They are statements of strength and alliances. These displays weaken us both.'

Aisha continued to stare at the floor, and Tariq couldn't bear it anymore.

'Kaidon, please see the princess to her chamber,' he told the guard.

That had Aisha looking up. She went to object.

'Go,' he told her.

Hamza's face turned red. 'We are not done here.'

'You are done with Aisha. Everything else you want to say you can say to me alone.'

Aisha appeared torn about leaving him, but when Kaidon approached, she went with him. Tariq waited until the door closed behind them before resuming the conversation.

'You're worried about humiliation?' He looked between his parents, eyes blazing. 'Then perhaps I should relay the conversation I had with envoys from Rogritis this afternoon, who are refusing to trade with us due to our exploitation of children. Now *that* was humiliating.'

Hamza's jaw tightened, but he said nothing.

'You are treading dangerously close to insolence,' Farrah said.

'Then I'll not tell you about my conversations with envoys from Ukrocia and Montia for fear of crossing a line,' Tariq said. 'But understand this: People will remember compassion far longer than they remember some protocol.'

Farrah turned around and made her way back to her chair.

Hamza waved a hand at Tariq. 'You are dismissed.'

Bowing stiffly, Tariq strode out of the throne room. On his way to his chambers, he ran into Kaidon returning from escorting Aisha.

'How is she?' Tariq asked.

'Worried about you, actually. How did it end in there?'

'I held up a mirror to them, and they didn't like it.'

Kaidon grinned at the floor.

There was something Tariq needed to take care of before the wedding. 'Could you fetch Maryam for me? Ask her to come to my quarters?'

Kaidon looked up. 'Now?'

'When she's finished with Aisha for the evening.'

Kaidon bowed his head, then headed off in the direction from which he had just come.

Exhausted, Tariq made his way back to his quarters to wait for Maryam. It was around an hour later when she appeared at his door, head bowed and hands folded. 'You sent for me, Your Highness?'

'Yes.' Tariq gestured for her to come inside, then closed the door behind her. 'I'll get straight to the point, as I know it's late.' His hands went to rest on his hips. 'From now on, I no longer require updates about Princess Aisha. If I wish to know something, I'll ask her directly.'

Maryam appeared slightly surprised by this.

'When you first came to me, you told me you felt the gods were calling on you to act,' he said. 'You've more than fulfilled that duty.' His eyes creased at the corners. 'Tomorrow is our wedding day, and I plan on starting our new life together with trust and transparency. I want you to know that I've kept my word and haven't revealed your gift to Aisha. You're safe here at Azura and will remain so.'

Maryam's hands tightened slightly. 'I see,' she said quietly. 'I appreciate that, Your Highness.' Her uncertain gaze remained on his.

'Was there something else you wanted to say?' Tariq asked.

She hesitated. 'There is one thing. I cannot, in good conscience, let you go into this union with a lie between you—or between us, for that matter.'

He waited for her to continue.

'Aisha knows,' she said. 'She knows what I am. That I'm a covenweaver—like her.'

Her words seemed to land one at a time. 'She...
knows?'

Maryam nodded. 'She discovered it herself, through a
vision. I had no choice but to tell her the truth. Since then,
I have been helping her understand and control her gift.'

He just stood there, trying to absorb this new information. 'You've been teaching her?'

'Yes.'

'She never said a word about...' He didn't finish his
sentence. Of course Aisha never said anything to him. She
would never tell another soul, no matter how much she
trusted them. It was simple maths. The more people who
knew, the higher the risk of exposure.

'She was struggling,' Maryam said, 'and in need of
guidance. Guidance her mother would have provided if
she were still alive.'

He paced a few steps over to the table and held on to
the edge. 'What exactly does she know?'

'I have not told her of any cooperation between us.
Nor of the visions that brought the two of you together.
However, I trust her. So if you wish to begin your
marriage with transparency, you are free to tell her whatever you like.'

Tariq straightened and drew a long breath. He looked
back at Maryam, nodding slowly. Yes, he would tell
Aisha, because she deserved to know everything—especially about the visions that had brought them together.
He was confident she would understand every decision
he had made up to that point, the same way he understood hers.

'Thank you,' he said.

Maryam bowed her head. 'May the gods bless you both with a lifetime of happiness, Your Highness.'

Tariq went to the door and opened it for Maryam. As she was exiting, he noticed Aisha standing several paces away, her body still and expression confused.

Maryam froze when she spotted Aisha. For a beat, no one spoke. Then Aisha brought a hand to her forehead as though struck by a sharp pain. Turning, she walked away.

Tariq dragged a hand down his face before going after her. 'Aisha, wait.'

When he caught up with her, she spun to face him. 'I didn't mean to interrupt.' Her tone was cold.

He was conscious of the fact that they were in a public space, so he kept his voice low. 'Let me explain.'

'Explain why Maryam was in your chambers at this hour?'

He blinked. 'Not for the reason you think.'

'You either have her spying on me or you're sleeping together. Which one is it?'

'Sleeping together?' His voice was too loud that time.

'Spying on me, then. What was so important that it couldn't wait until morning?'

He scrubbed a hand through his hair. 'The conversation wasn't supposed to go like this.'

'We're supposed to be getting married tomorrow.'

He stepped closer. 'Will you just listen, please?'

'What exactly has she been reporting? When I sleep? What I say? What I—'

'Stop.' He gripped her shoulders firmly but not roughly. '*Listen to me.*'

She fell silent.

He checked their surroundings before continuing. Even Maryam had fled the scene. 'I know about Maryam. Everything you know, I know. There are a million reasons why we've both been keeping secrets, but that all ends tonight.'

Aisha's breath came fast, her chest rising and falling beneath his hands. 'You know?'

He nodded. 'She's the reason I was able to find you. She saw our future long before our paths crossed.'

'She told you about her visions?' Her voice was thick with shock.

His gaze never left hers. 'I swore to protect her secret, but I don't want to keep secrets from my *wife*. That's what I was speaking to her about.'

She stared at him in the quiet corridor—then threw herself at him. He caught her, his arms instinctively wrapping around her as she pressed her face to his chest.

'Thank the gods,' she said, her breath shaky with relief. 'No more lies. No more secrets.'

He was completely taken aback by her response. 'That's it? That's your response?'

She pulled back just enough to look up at him, eyes shimmering. 'This is the best wedding present I could ask for.' Her head returned to his chest. 'I wanted to tell you. You wanted to tell me. All three of us were trying to do the right thing.'

He stroked her hair for a moment. 'So, we're still getting married tomorrow?'

'Yes.'

He released a slow breath, full of relief. For the first time ever, they were truly standing on the same side.

CHAPTER 26

The sun came out the morning of the wedding. It shone through Aisha's window, throwing patterns across the floor. She stood in front of the mirror while her sisters moved around her, fastening clasps, smoothing fabric, and adjusting jewellery.

'You look like a painting,' Lilah said when she stepped back to admire her.

'A nervous painting,' Aisha replied, touching the corner of her lips.

Yasmin looked over from her perch by the window. 'It may not even go ahead.' She was playing with Mira instead of preparing the flowers for Aisha's hair like she had been instructed. 'You could be nervous for no reason.'

Everyone stilled and looked in her direction.

'Why would you say that?' Lilah asked. 'Of course the wedding will go ahead.'

Yasmin took in everyone's expressions. 'I simply meant if Baba doesn't show up—'

'Have you finished those flowers yet?' Lilah asked, cutting her off.

Yasmin placed the cub on the ground with a huge sigh, then began sorting and trimming the flowers.

'She's not completely out of order,' Safiya whispered to Lilah.

Lilah gave her a look that translated to *stop*. 'Don't listen to them,' she told Aisha. 'Zara will get him there.'

There was a soft knock at the door before it eased open. Maryam stepped inside, carrying a tray of tea. Her gaze met Aisha's in the mirror. 'Something for the nerves.' She placed it down on the dressing table.

'Thank you,' Aisha said.

Maryam bowed her head, then left the room.

Lilah went to pour the tea for Aisha. As she poured, she sniffed the air. 'What tea is this?'

'The usual, I imagine.' Aisha slipped the chain of her token over her head and tucked it into her dress. 'A blend of lavender, fennel, and balm, I think.'

Lilah lifted the cup to her nose and inhaled deeply, her brow furrowing instantly. 'And something else.' She gave it another careful sniff. 'What *is* that?'

Safiya rolled her eyes. 'Maybe we figure it out *after* the ceremony.'

'I think there's Miraji root in here,' Lilah said as if Safiya hadn't spoken.

Aisha gave her a doubtful look. 'I don't think so.'

Lilah continued to take long inhales of the steam. 'Certainly smells similar.'

Miraji was a rare silvery-green root native to high-altitude forests. It was used to loosen the mind.

'*You*, especially, shouldn't be drinking it,' Lilah added.

What she meant was someone with the Sight.

A knock at the door made them all still. Lilah set the teacup down, then went to the door. 'I told you he'd be here.' But when she pulled the door open, the smile fell from her face.

It was Zara.

Alone.

Her face was calm, but her eyes were a little too wide. She stepped inside and closed the door quietly behind her. 'He was dressed and ready,' she said. 'But then the music started outside... I tried everything. I'm sorry.'

Yasmin pushed the tray of flowers aside with a sigh. 'So much for Aisha's vision.'

'She saw him in his wedding clothes,' Lilah said, her face slack.

Zara looked thoroughly uncomfortable. 'And he was wearing them—before he changed his mind.'

Aisha's throat was painfully dry suddenly.

'So I'll be walking you down the aisle,' Zara announced, trying to sound confident.

At first, no one responded.

'I don't want to rain on anyone's parade here,' Safiya said, 'but you know how much these people pride themselves on tradition.'

'I'm well aware,' Zara said, stress creeping into her tone. 'However, they'll have to make do with the next best thing—and that's me.'

It wasn't only that her father wouldn't be giving her away that had Aisha blinking back tears, but the fact that he wasn't even going to see her marry the man she loved more than she could have ever imagined.

'We're not doing tears,' Zara told Aisha. 'There's zero chance of them tolerating a crying bride on top of this, so I need you to focus.'

Swallowing hard, Aisha held Zara's gaze, siphoning strength from her—as she had done her whole life. 'Even if they allow it, people will talk.'

Zara took her hands. 'Let them talk. There's nothing they can say about our family that hasn't been said behind our backs already.'

'She's right,' Safiya said. 'We have to try. If this wedding doesn't go ahead, this will all have been for nothing.'

That wasn't true. No matter what happened, loving Tariq would never be a waste.

Aisha walked over to the dressing table, drank the tea Lilah had poured for her, then placed the empty cup back on the tray. 'I'm ready.'

The sisters all exchanged surprised glances.

'I'll fetch Omar,' Yasmin said, climbing down and snatching up the tray of flowers. She thrust them into Lilah's hands. 'Here.'

Lilah watched her leave, then looked down at the tray. 'Right.' She cleared her throat. 'Let's get these flowers in your hair.'

* * *

'Are you trying to give Tariq a heart attack?' Kaidon whispered to Aisha when she arrived at the temple. 'The guests are growing restless.' He looked around at her family. 'Where's King Bilal?'

'Time for us to go in,' Lilah said, ushering Safiya, Yasmin, and Omar towards the door. Zara and Aisha remained to update Kaidon.

'He's not coming,' Zara said bluntly. 'He has asked me to walk Aisha down the aisle and bless the union in his place.'

Kaidon looked between them. 'Is this a joke? Because I have a *very* good sense of humour, and this isn't funny.'

Neither of them responded.

He cursed under his breath. 'Who else knows?'

'Only you at present,' Zara said. 'It was a rather last-minute change.'

Leaning in and lowering his voice, Kaidon said, 'They'll halt the ceremony.'

'Would it be better to *not* go in?' Zara asked. 'Leave the prince standing before the altar?'

A tense moment of silence passed as they stared each other down. It was broken when Nasir exited the temple. He was dressed in formal robes of deep indigo, with Slevaborg's diplomatic seal gleaming at his shoulder. The High Verran looked between the three of them. 'What's the problem?'

'There's no problem as far as we're concerned,' Zara replied, eyes on Kaidon.

Nasir gestured to the temple. 'Then perhaps Princess Aisha should make her way to the prince waiting inside to marry her.'

Kaidon exhaled. 'What a mess. I'll go and let him know you're on your way.' He went to leave, but then looked back at Aisha. 'You look lovely, by the way. Forgive me. I should have led with that.'

Her mouth stretched into a smile. 'Thank you.'

Kaidon returned inside.

'I gather by his reaction that King Bilal isn't coming?' Nasir asked with genuine concern on his face.

Zara took Aisha's hand and placed it on her arm. 'I'm afraid not.'

Nasir straightened when he caught sight of something behind them. 'It appears that you're wrong.'

Aisha whipped her head around and found her father standing in the middle of the pathway—dressed in his wedding clothes. He looked tall and composed. His guard stood a few paces behind him, looking quite pleased with himself.

'Baba,' Aisha breathed. She practically ran to him, wrapping herself around his middle. 'You're here.'

'Sorry I am late,' he said.

Zara looked heavenwards on an exhale, then muttered a prayer.

'Come,' Nasir said to Zara, gesturing ahead of him. 'I'll walk you in.'

Zara touched the corner of her eye before going with him.

Aisha stepped back from her father to look him over. 'You look so handsome.'

'And you...' There was pain in his smile. 'I wish she could see how beautiful you look today.'

Aisha swallowed down the burning sensation in her throat.

'Ready?' he asked, offering his arm to her.

She took it, unable to hold back the smile that followed. 'Ready.'

Together, they walked into the temple.

The music changed when they entered, prompting Tariq to look towards the door. The prince's posture relaxed when he saw Bilal, and his eyes creased at the corners when he saw Aisha. He stood at the front of the assembled guests, dressed in ceremonial robes. He looked at her like she was the only thing in the temple worth seeing.

The crowd was silent as she made her way to the altar, her father steady beside her. Nobles and dignitaries lined their pathway, but Aisha barely saw them. She looked only at Tariq, just like he'd told her to. She stopped when she reached him.

Tariq carefully took Bilal's hand when he forgot to offer it, paying his respects to the king. 'Thank you,' he said when he rose.

Bilal looked somewhat confused, but then Zara appeared, gently guiding him to a nearby seat—on the opposite side from Zahvik. Aisha snuck a glance at King Hamza and Queen Farrah. Their silence was their approval.

'Eyes on me,' Tariq reminded her. 'Only me.'

She looked back at him, and everything else dimmed.

Jamil stepped forwards to begin the ceremony. 'We are gathered today to witness a sacred union.' His voice carried over the couple. 'A vow not only between a man and a woman but also between kingdoms and their rulers.'

Tariq's hand tightened around hers as the speech went on. Finally, it was time for the vows.

'I vow to protect your name and your honour,' Tariq said. 'To build a future with you, stone by stone.'

She soaked up every word he spoke until it was her turn. 'I vow to be your strength,' she told him. 'To be your light in the darkness.'

When she had finished, Jamil looked over at Bilal. 'And who here gives this woman and blesses this union?'

Aisha braced for the possibility of silence, but instead heard her father say, 'I do.'

The relief was enormous. He had done everything that was necessary, and she could finally breathe all the way out.

'I shall invite His Holiness, the Sectarian of Slevaborg, up to light the ceremonial flame,' Jamil said.

No one had mentioned that part.

Tariq squeezed Aisha's hands so that she focused on him. She didn't even look in Zahvik's direction. They were so close to being done, to being married, and she wasn't going to let that man ruin any part of it.

'Eyes on me,' he mouthed.

Aisha didn't even look in her family's direction, because she trusted Zara to handle their father, or if need be, discreetly extract him.

Zahvik walked gracefully to the altar, picking up one of the candles and using it to light the symbolic fire. When the flame was stable, he turned to Aisha and Tariq. 'May this flame forge you together.'

How dare he speak of flames at her wedding. She did her best to block him and his ugly words out. All that was left was the obeisance with King Hamza and Queen Farrah.

Aisha went first to the queen, a hand over her heart as she bowed. Farrah gave her blessing. She moved on to the king, kissing the back of his hand before touching her forehead to it. In her distracted state, she forgot to limit contact. So when her forehead touched the king's hand, everything vanished. The vision, sudden and sharp, gave her no time to pull away. Someone was lying on a bed in an unfamiliar room. Around them stood Farrah, Tariq, Jamil, and—

The real world rushed back in. She was in Tariq's arms, and he was kissing her. She heard applause in the distance. No, not in the distance. Around them.

Tariq broke the kiss and brought his lips to her ear. 'I need you to stand up,' he whispered.

That's when she realised he was holding her entire weight, which might have been considered romantic if it were not a royal wedding.

Concentrating, she anchored her feet. He took a small step back, searching her eyes for confirmation that she was all right. Aisha used all of her strength to smile, then turned to face the applauding guests. The applause grew louder.

It was done.

Gruisea had their future queen.

Aisha's gaze drifted unwillingly to King Hamza, who was also clapping. She looked down at his robes... the same robes worn by the person lying on the bed in her vision.

CHAPTER 27

The wedding feast was underway in the grand hall. Music and laughter drifted through the side doors to the balcony, where Aisha stood talking with Zara. The celebration felt far away.

Bilal had already retired to his bedchamber, too exhausted to endure the feast. He'd given everything he had left to walk her down the aisle. His part was done.

'I watched you fade as soon as your head met King Hamza's hand,' Zara said. 'Your new husband is a genius, by the way. He just swept you up like he couldn't wait another moment to kiss you. The guests were literally gasping.'

Aisha leaned against the rail. 'He's going to need every trick available to him in order to keep this secret. We both know that even the title of queen comes with no guarantee of protection.'

They both fell silent.

'Do you really think it was King Hamza lying on that bed?' Zara asked.

The image flashed in Aisha's mind, and she nodded. 'Yes.'

'Sick?' Zara lowered her voice. 'Or dying?'

Aisha shook her head. 'I really don't know. I didn't even see his face.'

Zara's gaze drifted to the door. 'Have you told Tariq?'

'Today has been stressful enough. He deserves to enjoy the next part.'

Zara took hold of Aisha's shoulder. 'Perhaps you should forget what you saw. Say nothing more about it to anyone. Because if anything does happen to King Hamza, you might be implicated.'

The balcony doors creaked open again, and Lilah stepped out.

'There you are,' she said, sounding out of breath. 'I just did forty laps of the hall looking for you.'

Aisha took in her expression. 'What is it?'

'I checked the tea, and I can confirm it contained Miraji root.'

Aisha's mind scrambled to catch up. 'What?'

'The tea Maryam has been giving you, *multiple times per day*.' Lilah waited for a reaction, and when she didn't get it, she added, 'She's either attempting to induce visions or trying to make your mind more accessible to others.'

Aisha shook her head, mostly because she didn't like what she was hearing.

'I think she's a covenweaver,' Lilah whispered. 'But I think you already know that.'

Aisha had made a promise to keep Maryam's secret. She would not expose her without having all the facts first. Her first thought was that it had something to do with her previous arrangement with Tariq. But she had given Aisha the tea that morning.

A look of deep concern settled on Zara's face. 'That means Maryam knows about you.'

Shouting reached them from inside the hall. The music stopped, and the heavy beat of footsteps followed.

'What on earth is going on?' Zara said, rushing over to the doors and looking through them. The others followed at her heels.

Aisha was terrified of what she would see.

'Clear this space!' she heard Tariq shout.

The edge of fear in his voice had her stumbling forwards into the grand hall, looking around. Mere moments ago, the room had been brimming with music and laughter. Now there was nothing but stunned silence. Plates lay abandoned. All eyes had turned towards the platform at the head of the room, where King Hamza lay on the floor beside an overturned chair.

Aisha's heart thundered painfully in her chest as she took in the scene. Queen Farrah was on her knees beside the king, barking commands at nearby attendants, all the colour drained from her face. Tariq was kneeling opposite, two fingers pressed to his father's neck, searching for a pulse. His jaw was tight and shoulders rigid. Kaidon stood behind him, hands in his hair, watching.

Aisha saw Nasir standing nearby and went to him. 'What happened?' she whispered, eyes fixed on the king.

'He collapsed. One moment he was eating, and the next he was on the floor.' Nasir shook his head. 'They've sent for the royal physician.'

Aisha began weaving through the stunned crowd until

she reached the edge of the platform, where Hamza lay painfully still.

'Stay back,' the queen hissed at her.

Aisha took in her expression. It was pure distrust.

Tariq looked at his mother with surprise.

The physician arrived in a flurry of dark robes, kneeling swiftly beside the king. A heavy silence fell over the room as he checked for signs of life. Tariq took a few slow steps back, bracing for what was coming.

The physician sank back on his heels and lifted his gaze to the queen. 'He is gone, Your Majesty. I am so very sorry.'

Aisha's hand flew up to her mouth. The collective intake of breath from those around her seemed to use up all the air in the room. Somewhere, a goblet hit the floor with a clang. Someone else began crying. Aisha looked over at Tariq and watched as the weight of a kingdom settled on his shoulders.

The wedding feast had ended with servants running to and fro as guests filed out of the hall in stunned silence. Tariq had instructed Kaidon to take Aisha to her chamber to wait for him there, no doubt realising that her remaining there wouldn't end well. Zara had offered to take Aisha so that Kaidon could remain with Tariq, leading her sister from the room and away from the queen's accusatory glare.

Aisha was in her chamber now. Yasmin and Omar were playing cards on the bed, and the rest of her siblings were scattered about the room. Lilah sat cross-legged on the rug, staring at the door. Safiya paced, with Mira attached to her ankle, enjoying being dragged back and forth. Zara sat at the table, looking down at her hands.

'He was fine one moment, then—' Safiya snapped her fingers. 'Gone. Heart failure, perhaps.'

'Or poison,' Lilah said.

Zara looked over at Aisha. 'Let's hope not. We all know who they'll blame.'

'Tariq knows you would never do such a thing,' Lilah said.

Safiya stopped pacing. 'Tariq knows, yes. That trust doesn't extend to all of us.'

'Yes, it does,' Aisha said.

Safiya tilted her head. 'Be reasonable. The timing alone—'

'Don't say it.' Aisha pressed a hand to her temple. 'Please.'

That quieted them all for a minute—except Mira, who was gnawing on Safiya's foot.

'Interesting that Maryam is nowhere to be seen,' Lilah said. 'I would have thought she'd be here with her famous *tea*.'

It was too much for Aisha to think about. 'I'm sure there are a million things to do under these circumstances,' she said, despite having had the same thought earlier. Her mind was spinning with possibilities.

Zara turned in her chair to face her sisters. 'We should all prepare for the possibility of being called before the court to answer questions.'

'No one's being called before the court,' Aisha said, trying to sound confident.

They lapsed into silence again, each lost in her own thoughts, until a knock at the door brought them all to their feet.

'Who is it?' Safiya called through the door.

'Kaidon,' came the reply.

Safiya opened the door, and Aisha thought he looked twenty years older suddenly. She walked over to him. 'How is he?' she asked.

'About as well as one can be after watching his father die at his wedding.'

She swallowed but didn't look away.

'He's at the king's bedside. If you would like to pay your respects, now is the time.' He paused before adding, 'He's alone.'

Aisha nodded, then glanced back at her sisters before stepping out into the corridor and closing the door behind her. The two of them walked to the royal wing of the castle.

The palace had never felt so quiet. Or so cold.

They stopped before the large carved door of the king's bedchamber. The door was slightly ajar. Aisha stepped closer, her fingers grazing the edge of the wood as she peered into the room. A chill broke out across her skin when she recognised the room from her vision.

She was about to enter when someone grabbed her arm. Whipping her head around, she expected to see Kaidon, but instead she found herself face to face with Farrah. The queen's features looked as though they were carved from granite. She pulled the door closed, then dragged Aisha away from it.

'Your Majesty,' Kaidon said, following them.

'Leave us,' Farrah instructed.

'Your Majesty, Tariq is waiting for—'

'I said *leave us*.' Her voice cut in like steel.

Kaidon hesitated, then cast an apologetic glance at Aisha before leaving them.

The queen's grip on Aisha tightened as she pulled her further away from the door, away from Kaidon, clearly not wanting anyone to hear what she was about to say.

'You're hurting me,' Aisha said, panic rising in her chest.

Farrah stopped and turned to stare at her. 'You have some audacity to complain to me.'

The hatred in her voice was paralysing. 'What?'

'You could not even wait *one day* to take my place.'

Words jammed in Aisha's throat, with nowhere to go.

'When the physician told me he suspects poison, I did not need to think too hard about who might do such a thing.' She leaned in. 'A covenweaver. Yes, I *know* what you are.'

Aisha pulled her hand free and cradled it. 'You think I murdered the king?'

Farrah tilted her head. 'Zara would be *so* proud of this little innocent act of yours. What a wonderful performer you are.'

She's grieving, Aisha reminded herself. 'I understand you're in a lot of pain right now, so I'll do you the courtesy of forgetting this conversation ever happened.'

Farrah took a fast step towards her, and Aisha steadied herself on the wall.

'A covenweaver should never be trusted,' Farrah said. 'I told Tariq that when he brought you here.'

Aisha held her gaze because looking away felt like an admission of guilt.

'He really thought he knew better,' Farrah added.

There was nothing Aisha could say to alter the course of the conversation, so she remained silent, enduring every word.

'You should have stayed in Avanid,' the queen said coldly. 'When the cause of death is confirmed, all eyes will turn to you.'

The door to the king's chamber opened, and soft light spilled out into the corridor. Farrah turned and walked away, disappearing into the darkness and leaving Aisha consumed by nausea.

'Aisha?'

She turned and saw Tariq standing in the doorway. 'Yes.'

'What are you doing?' His voice was thick with exhaustion. 'Where's Kaidon?'

She promised herself in that moment that she would protect his heart and mind while he grieved his father and king. Whatever Farrah said to her would remain between them.

'Here I am,' Kaidon said, reappearing.

His steady gaze met Aisha's briefly, and she realised that he would protect Tariq too.

Drawing a shaky breath, she went to join her husband and pay her respects to the king.

CHAPTER 28

The world felt both too loud and too quiet. Every sound in the castle seemed wrong. Even the air strained under the weight of loss. Tariq couldn't decide whether to scream or stay silent. His father was dead, his mother was angry, and amid it all, he had become king.

King.

The word didn't quite fit him.

After Aisha had paid her respects to the dead king, the pair had slipped out into the garden for air, walking in silence with his fingers closed around hers. She kept him tethered to the world. He was grateful for the absence of conversation. There was nothing she could say to untangle the noise in his mind.

Once he could breathe again, they returned indoors, ready to make a plan for the next day. He was confident he could stretch his brain that far, just not beyond it. He wanted to forget the throne, the crown, the whispers circulating through the castle, and just be with his new wife. But time to grieve was one of the few luxuries a new king wasn't entitled to.

They were almost to his quarters when Kaidon found them. One look at his face told him his plans were about to change.

'What is it?' Tariq asked.

'The queen wants to see you.' Then, realising his mistake, he added, 'Your Majesty.'

It seemed too soon for such an address, but he understood the importance of immediate transfer of power. Exhaling, he looked at Aisha.

'Go,' she said. 'I need to find Maryam.'

He kissed her forehead. 'I'll be as quick as I can.' Then, to the guard by his door, he said, 'Go with her, and stay alert.'

He made his way to his mother's quarters, bracing for the conversation ahead. Yes, she would be grieving, but she would also be making plans of her own.

They arrived at Farrah's receiving chamber, and the guard opened the heavy doors without announcing his arrival.

'Good luck,' Kaidon said quietly.

Tariq found her staring out the window despite it being too dark to see anything. He could almost see her mind churning. 'Mother?'

She turned, looking him over. 'How are you doing?'

'Probably about as well as you.' He was surprised to find her alone at such a time. 'Where are your attendants? You shouldn't be alone right now.'

'I sent them away.' She touched a delicate finger to her

forehead. 'There are some things we need to discuss in private.'

'If it has to do with funeral arrangements, it can wait until the morning.'

'I already have people working on that.' She stared at him for a long moment. 'I wanted to speak to you about the Avanid princesses.'

He already didn't like the direction of the conversation. 'What about them?'

She walked to the table and retrieved a piece of parchment. 'This is the report from the physician.' She held it out to him. 'Your father was poisoned.'

Tariq had known it was a possibility. Walking over to her, he took the report from her and began to read.

Residual traces of toxin. No struggle observed. Rapid circulatory collapse.

His death had been silent, almost peaceful. No convulsions, no cry for help. Just a steady slowing of breath until nothing remained. The kind of death one prays for.

He looked back at his mother. 'What does this have to do with the princesses?'

She held his gaze. 'I believe they did it.'

It took him a moment to register the accusation. 'You think them killers? You can't be serious.'

'They're covenweavers. Maybe not all, but definitely some—including your *wife*.'

He remained composed, knowing that any reaction would confirm it.

'You must have suspected it after she told you to clear that mine before it collapsed,' Farrah continued. 'That *was* her. Correct?'

He couldn't decide what surprised him more, the fact that she knew or that she had kept it to herself. One thing was for sure: If she suspected the family's involvement in the king's death, she wouldn't be keeping any secrets now.

'Why do you think I tried to prevent this marriage?' Farrah asked. 'Look at where we have ended up on the first day of your union.'

He waited until he could speak calmly. 'You cannot lay blame at their feet without proof, and you know it.'

She didn't so much as blink. 'You want proof? All right. Your bride's sister was witnessed handling and mixing herbs in her chamber minutes before arriving at the feast. *Minutes* before the king's collapse.'

That couldn't be true. 'The princesses were coming and going because they were caring for their father.'

'It was Lilah, in case you were wondering.'

He laughed at that. 'If you had said Safiya, I might have paused to consider the possibility. But Lilah? Come on now.'

Farrah took a step towards him. 'One of the servants informed me that she arrived here with a bag full of witchery.'

He rubbed tiredly at his forehead. 'Apparently you've forgotten how many people were angry at the king. He might have been tolerated by the nobles, but he was *loathed* by the miners.'

Her composure fractured, but only for a beat. 'His body is barely cold, and you dare speak ill of him.'

Tariq's face went slack. She was right. Now was not the time for those conversations.

'You want to believe they're all innocent,' Farrah

continued. 'I understand that. Except you are *king* now. You are loyal to the throne above all else.'

Tariq looked away, his jaw aching from the tension.

'You trust Kaidon, do you not?' Farrah said. 'Send him to investigate if my word means so little. Doing nothing is not an option for someone in your position.'

For a moment, neither of them moved. The only sound was the gentle crackle of the fire.

'I'll look into it,' Tariq said, realising he had no choice. 'Including a thorough investigation of Zahvik Barakat.'

Farrah sighed. 'You are a smart man. You know the Emperor wanted Hamza on that throne for as long as possible.' Her expression softened. 'If you had been killed, on the other hand, he would have been first on my list.'

He hated that she was right.

When she turned back to the window, Tariq folded the physician's report in half. 'Try to get some rest,' he said, then left her chambers.

Kaidon was waiting for him when he exited, a mirror of his own exhaustion. 'Well?' he asked.

The request Tariq was about to make felt like betrayal. 'I want you to search all the rooms of the Nazari family.'

It took Kaidon a moment to respond. 'What am I looking for?'

He handed the physician's report to him. 'Lethal herbs,' he replied, then drew a steadying breath. 'I want everything done properly so I never have to have this conversation with my mother again. Understand?'

Kaidon ran his eyes over the note, then looked up. '*All* of the rooms?'

Tariq nodded slowly. 'All of them.'

Aisha failed to find Maryam anywhere. The other servants had confirmed sightings of her throughout the day, but no one knew where she was. Exhausted, Aisha gave up the search and went to speak with Zara about her encounter with Farrah.

She sat on the edge of a low settee with her hands clasped tightly in her lap while Zara sat opposite folding a piece of linen with absent-minded precision. Omar and Yasmin were now in their own beds in the adjoining room.

'I think you need to leave as soon as possible,' Aisha said quietly.

Zara set the linen down. 'Abandon you with this mess to clean up?'

She shrugged. 'It's technically *my* mess. And I just don't trust the queen right now. She's clearly grieving and desperate for someone to blame.'

A look of resignation settled on Zara's face. 'You're right. I'll send word to the ship's captain. I doubt anyone will question the urgent departure given Baba was absent from the wedding feast.' Her expression softened. 'I wish you were coming with us.'

'Can you imagine what people would say if I left now?' A faint smile came and went. 'Baba won't survive the weight of all this. A quiet departure is best. No ceremony or elaborate farewells.'

Zara searched her eyes for a moment. 'I—'

The chamber door swung open, and two guards marched in. The women shot to their feet.

'What's going on?' Zara demanded, moving to block their path.

'A search, Your Highness,' said one. 'You need to step aside.'

The other had already flung open Zara's trunk and was now searching through her belongings.

'What search?' Aisha asked, stepping past her sister. 'On whose orders?'

Omar wandered into the room, rubbing his eyes. 'What's going on?'

Zara gestured for him to come to her, never taking her eyes off the guard in the process. 'You both need to leave —now.'

'We'll be as quick as we can,' the guard replied calmly.

Aisha walked over to the man going through the trunk. 'Did Queen Farrah order this?' If she had, Aisha would go directly to Tariq, and he would put a stop to the craziness.

'The king ordered the search,' came a voice from the door.

Aisha turned to see Kaidon standing in the open doorway, looking remorseful. 'He ordered a search of my sister's chamber?'

A nod. '*All* of the chambers.'

Aisha looked at Zara, whose shocked expression mirrored her own, shaking her head in disbelief. Tariq would never… Except he had. Kaidon was no liar.

One of the guards passed by her, going into the adjoining room. He lifted the lid of Omar's chest and began pulling clothes out. Aisha felt sick.

She made up her mind to go and speak with him and headed for the door. 'Where is he?' she asked Kaidon.

'Aisha…'

She stilled. 'You will address me correctly.'

His nod was almost sad. 'Your Majesty, he's in the west gallery with one of the foreign envoys. He said he would—'

She was out the door before he could finish, and to his credit, he didn't try to stop her.

Moving quickly through the winding corridors, still in her wedding garment, she focused on the conversation ahead. She needed to see his face and hear his voice so she could try to understand what was going on. They would talk, regroup, and move forwards together—just like they had planned.

As she rounded the corner of the guest wing, a figure emerged from the far corridor. It was Maryam. The attendant paused when she caught sight of Aisha. The kind of pause someone makes when they've been caught doing something wrong.

Aisha waited in her path for her to stop and look at her properly. 'Where have you been?' The question was choked by tears. 'The king dies, and you're nowhere to be seen.'

The shame in Maryam's eyes made Aisha uneasy.

'I know about the Miraji root you've been putting in my tea,' she said, testing the waters.

Maryam nodded. 'I know. I… saw it.'

Neither of them moved.

'I saw a lot of things I wish I had not.' She practically whispered that part.

Aisha swallowed. 'I trusted you.'

'I know.'

An impulse gripped Aisha. Lunging forwards, she seized the attendant's wrist and mentally reached for anything she could get. Maryam flinched, her mouth parting in shock. Then the world slipped sideways.

Aisha's vision slammed her senses. Maryam stood before Zahvik, her shoulders hunched in defeat and tears pouring down her face. Zahvik appeared unmoved, fingers steepled like the villain he was. Maryam's knees buckled, and she collapsed to the floor.

The vision shattered.

Aisha stumbled backwards as the corridor came rushing back around her. The cold stone and poor light. The weight of her own body. Maryam rushed forwards and caught her around the waist.

'Come with me,' she said.

Aisha pushed her off. 'Let go of me.' She then lost her balance because she hadn't had enough time to recover.

Maryam caught her—again—and looked her straight in the eye. 'You cannot let them see you like this. Not now.'

Aisha didn't push her away this time.

Maryam led her to a nearby unoccupied room, ushering her inside and closing the door behind them. Aisha collapsed onto the floor, careful not to take her eyes off the attendant.

'You have to be more careful than that,' Maryam said. 'You have some very difficult challenges ahead of you that require you to keep your cool and be smart. That was not smart.'

Panting, Aisha said, 'Don't stand there and pretend to be my friend.'

'I *am* your friend.' Maryam's throat worked, and her eyes glistened. 'But I am also a covenweaver trying to survive this world.'

With everything that was happening, all Aisha wanted to do was lie down and cry, but she needed to get to Tariq and protect her family. 'I have to go to Tariq.'

'Not like this. If they see you—'

'I'm not listening to you anymore. You drugged me. You drugged me, and I saw you with Zahvik. I...' A sob rose up her throat, but she forced it down. 'What is going on?'

Maryam's eyes filled with tears. 'Because he told me to.'

'Who told you to?'

She blinked, and a tear escaped. 'Zahvik.'

A loud ringing sounded in Aisha's head. '*What?*' She shook her head, rejecting the answer.

Maryam brushed tears off her face. 'They have eyes everywhere. *Everywhere.* You had not even arrived in Gruisea yet, and they were at my family's door.'

Aisha took a hurried breath.

'He wanted insight into your intentions, your thoughts,' Maryam said. 'I was instructed to extract whatever information I could.'

Aisha stared at her in horror. 'And you did it.'

'I did what I had to and nothing more.'

Aisha covered her face with her hands, trying to steady her thoughts. 'He knows you're a covenweaver.' Her hands fell away. 'And he knows about me.'

'No,' she said firmly. 'He suspects, but I have never confirmed it. I swear to you.'

Silence pulsed between them.

'I can't believe you agreed to help him,' Aisha said, feeling utterly broken. 'Why? He'll dispose of both of us.'

Maryam closed her eyes. 'I did not have a choice.'

'Of course you did.'

When Maryam opened her eyes, they were full of pain. 'No, I did not.'

A realisation dawned on Aisha then. 'What did he threaten you with?'

Maryam swallowed audibly. 'He has men watching my family. All the time. Every day.' She paused. 'He knows what side of the bed my sister gets out of. That she sings when she does laundry.'

Aisha felt her body slump.

Maryam sniffed. 'You know better than anyone the lengths one will go to in order to keep their family safe.'

She did know better than anyone.

'The gods know I never wanted this,' Maryam said. 'I thought I could keep everyone safe.' She continued to wipe at the tears falling down her cheeks. 'Even you.'

Aisha watched her a long moment before asking, 'Did you… kill King Hamza?'

'Gods, no.'

Slowly, Aisha got to her feet. 'They're pointing the finger at my family.'

Silence.

'But I bet you already know that. All that tea to raid my mind.'

Aisha's question was met with sympathy. 'It does not matter who did it,' Maryam said. 'It matters who they *say* did it.' She paused. 'Tariq must uphold Gruisea's laws.'

Aisha searched her eyes. 'You know something.'

'I know he loves you and will protect you with his life.'

'Did you see that in a vision?'

A sad smile came and went on her face. 'I do not need a vision to tell me that.' She moved closer to Aisha. 'I know you do not trust me at this time, but please listen to what I have to say before you leave this room.'

Aisha fought the urge to flee and slam the door behind her.

'You need to take the blame for King Hamza's death,' Maryam said.

Of all the things she guessed her attendant would say, that wasn't among them. Aisha blinked, stunned. 'Have you lost your mind?'

'No,' Maryam said sadly. 'I saw Lilah marched into the courtyard by the guards.' She released a shaky breath. 'Your sister will stand accused of the king's murder.'

Aisha felt like she had been struck. Her mind seemed to freeze for a moment. 'That's impossible. She had nothing to do with it.'

'I know.'

Lilah. Sweet Lilah.

'I've no reason to believe what you're saying,' Aisha said, despite sensing the truth in her words.

Maryam looked even more sympathetic. 'If you confess, Tariq will find a way to protect you, and your family will be free to return home. I cannot think of another solution that keeps you all alive.'

Aisha looked away. 'This is all getting out of hand. I need to go find Tariq.' She smoothed down her hair and dress, then stepped past Maryam.

'If I am exposed for cooperating with Zahvik, I will be labelled a traitor and sentenced accordingly,' Maryam said.

Aisha stopped, her hand hovering over the door handle.

'I deserve that,' Maryam continued, her voice softening. 'But my family will pay at the other end of this. And they do not deserve any of it.' Her voice cracked when she said that last part.

Aisha's throat tightened. 'I have to go.'

She left with no plan.

No power.

And no idea what was ahead of her.

CHAPTER 30

Tariq abandoned his formal robes and replaced them with a cream tunic and trousers. He was desperate to see Aisha but forced himself to wait until the searches were complete—until he could face her with all the facts. They could then face his mother as a united front.

A knock at the door had him rising from his chair. Kaidon entered with a bag in hand. Dread pooled in Tariq's belly as he recalled the bag of 'witchery' his mother had mentioned. He reminded himself that a bag of medicinal herbs wasn't evidence of murder.

Kaidon placed it on the table and opened it. A sharp, earthy scent filled the room. 'This was among Princess Lilah's belongings,' he said. 'Various dried leaves and roots.' His tone remained neutral.

Tariq stared down at the open bag. Aisha had told him herself that Lilah was knowledgeable with herbs. They weren't hiding anything.

'Take the bag to the physician and find out what all

these are. I want to know their uses and what they're capable of.'

Kaidon didn't move. 'Then what?'

That was a very good question. 'Then we do the next thing.'

Still, Kaidon did not move. 'There are rumours circulating.'

'Of course there are.'

'Your mother has witnesses claiming Lilah was burning herbs in her bedchamber while the feast was underway.'

Tariq brushed a finger down his nose. 'One thing at a time.'

'She'll be labelled a covenweaver and—'

'Burned,' Tariq finished. 'I'm well aware of our laws.'

Kaidon bowed and headed for the door. When he pulled it open, Aisha was standing there, face pale and hair loose. And her expression…

Gods, her broken expression. A tight mask of restraint barely holding back exhaustion.

Her eyes landed on the bag in Kaidon's hand.

'That bag belonged to my mother,' she said, her voice frayed.

Tariq gestured for Kaidon to go. The guard slipped past Aisha, taking the bag with him. She watched it leave.

'She's an herbalist,' Aisha said. 'You know that.'

Since she didn't appear to want to come in, he walked over, meeting her at the door. The tension coming from her almost repelled him.

'I'm sorry,' he whispered.

She slowly lifted her gaze to his. 'Lilah would never

hurt anybody. She heals people, just like Mama did. She was helping people the day she died.' Her eyes filled with tears. 'And they burned her alive for it.'

He reached up to touch her face, and she drew back. He lowered his hand. 'My father is dead. There are processes I have to follow.'

She searched his eyes. 'This isn't the wedding day we envisioned.'

He shook his head, his chest tightening. 'No.' He swallowed. 'You know how this looks, right? The king dying on the day of our wedding?'

Frustration sharpened her features. 'Zahvik has to be behind this.'

He wished he could believe that. 'Me on the throne, with you as queen, is the last thing they wanted. They know everything's about to change.' He leaned against the doorframe, watching her. 'Give me some time to sort this out. If we do everything properly, we'll only have to do it once.'

She looked at him like he was a stranger. The love and trust they'd built seemed to be dissolving before his eyes.

'We'll both do what we need to do,' Aisha said.

With that, she turned and left.

Aisha returned to Zara's quarters, her breath shallow and mind racing. Her sister was frantically packing.

'Where have you been?' Zara asked without looking up. 'They confiscated Lilah's bag. The gods only know what conclusions they're drawing.'

Aisha peered into the adjoining room, where Yasmin and Omar were asleep.

'I've sent word to the captain, informing him that we need to leave at first light,' Zara said. 'Hopefully that's enough time to gather supplies.'

Aisha looked around at the mess. 'Have they searched Baba's chambers?'

'Yes.' Zara straightened. 'Lilah and Safiya are there trying to settle him. As soon as we're packed, we'll head straight to the ship. We need to get as far from Azura as we can—and quickly. I've got a bad feeling.' She fell silent to look at Aisha properly. 'What's going on? Why are you so calm?'

Aisha drew her eyebrows together. 'I'm not calm. I'm far from calm.' She sank down onto the chest, gripping its edge. There were things she needed to say, and she didn't know where to start or how much time they had.

'You're scaring me,' Zara said. 'And you know I don't scare easily.'

Aisha looked up at her. 'They're going to arrest Lilah. They may have even done it already.'

Zara's eyes widened, then darkened. She moved to leave, but Aisha seized her wrist.

'You need to listen to me first,' she said.

Zara shifted her weight in Aisha's direction. 'Then you better speak quickly.'

Aisha wet her lips. 'They're going to arrest Lilah for the murder of King Hamza, but they're not going to hurt her, because I have a plan.'

Zara never looked away. 'Go on.'

'I'm going to confess to the murder.'

Zara pulled her hand free. 'No, you're not.'

'They'll kill her.'

'They'll kill *you*!'

Aisha rose to her feet. 'Tariq won't let them.'

Zara laughed. 'Your naivety is mind-blowing.'

'I trust him.'

Zara leaned in, lowering her voice. 'Then you're a fool. It doesn't matter how much he loves you. He's the King of Gruisea. He'll do what he must for his kingdom. It's not up to him.' She drew back. 'You'll be executed.'

Aisha swallowed.

Zara turned in a slow circle, hands on her hips as she thought. 'You have to come with us.' She stilled and looked at Aisha. 'If we all leave together—'

The door opened, and Safiya entered, looking as tired as Aisha felt. She pushed her messy braid over her shoulder, glancing between them and around the room. Frowning, she looked into the adjoining room where her siblings were sleeping. 'Where's Lilah?'

'What do you mean, where's Lilah?' Zara said. 'She was with you and Baba.'

'Baba's not well. She went to fetch medicine for him.' Safiya looked uneasy now. 'What's going on?'

Zara squeezed her eyes shut as Aisha's blood ran cold.

'Tell me,' Safiya said, losing patience.

Aisha walked over to Safiya and wrapped her arms around her. 'I need you to listen to me very carefully.'

CHAPTER 31

Tariq sat on the edge of the bed, elbows on his knees and head in his hands. The room was silent except for the low crackle of the dying fire. His body felt heavy, as though his bones had absorbed the grief. He pressed his palms to his eyes until stars burst behind them. He longed for silence inside his skull, but all he could hear was his father's last breath, his mother's accusations, and Aisha's heartbreak.

A sound reached him—distant at first. A door. A voice. It took a few seconds for his mind to return to the present and the words to take shape through the fog. When he lifted his head, he realised Kaidon was before him. He blinked hard, forcing his focus to return.

'What?' His own voice sounded strange in his ears.

Kaidon's expression was urgent. 'They're holding her in the east courtyard.'

He shook his head, confused. 'Who?'

'Lilah,' Kaidon said. 'The queen has ordered her detained.'

He shot to his feet as the cloud covering his mind lifted. 'What?'

'She said she had enough evidence to order her arrest.'

The fatigue burned away under a surge of adrenaline. He ran out the door, moving fast. Servants flattened themselves against the walls as he passed them.

'They were preparing to flee,' Kaidon said, keeping pace.

Tariq glanced at him. 'Lilah?'

'The whole family.'

Tariq lengthened his stride. 'Where's Aisha?'

'I don't know.'

Voices echoed through the stone archways as Tariq turned the final corner and took in the scene before him. Guards stood in a semicircle, holding back a crowd of spectators. At the centre stood Lilah, her wrists in shackles and hair clinging to her face. His mother was nearby, dressed in black mourning garb, contrasting Jamil's white thobe.

'Oh, that's not good,' Kaidon said, coming to a stop beside him.

Tariq's eyes narrowed on Safiya, who stood facing the line of guards, a sword pointed in their direction. There were at least five weapons pointed back at her.

He moved towards them, shouting through the noise. 'What's happening here?'

Farrah looked in his direction, and her face pinched. 'The princess was found with enough illicit herbs to kill a man. Or rather, a *king*.'

'She's a healer!' Safiya shouted. 'That's not a crime!'

'She is a *covenweaver*,' Farrah replied calmly. 'And that most certainly *is* a crime.'

Murmurs rippled through the crowd. When Tariq looked around, he spotted Zahvik far back in the shadows, likely thrilled by what he was seeing.

'If she is innocent, she has nothing to fear,' Jamil said, gesturing for calm.

Safiya let out a harsh laugh. 'Nothing to fear? You must be joking.' Her blade moved slightly, enough to make two of the guards shift forwards.

Tariq raised his hands. 'Stand down.'

The guards took a tentative step back but kept their weapons raised.

Safiya took a defiant step towards one of the swords, her chest inches from the tip of the blade. 'You dragged her from her chamber like a criminal.'

'Safiya,' Tariq said. 'This isn't the way.'

Her gaze shot to his. 'She trusted you.'

A whimper came from Lilah when one of the guards adjusted his grip on her.

'Careful!' Safiya screamed at him.

Farrah's patience snapped. 'Take them both into custody.'

'No,' Lilah sobbed. 'Tariq, please.'

Farrah didn't like that. 'That is the king you are speaking to. You will address him as such.'

The guards moved to disarm Safiya.

'Step back!' Tariq shouted at them.

They froze and looked in his direction. Then their attention shifted. Aisha approached at a fast pace. Her hair was now smoothed back and secured tightly at the nape of her neck, her face scrubbed clean. All eyes followed her as she stepped into the centre of the conflict, her gaze burning towards the guard holding Lilah.

'Let her go,' Aisha said.

Farrah stared in disbelief. 'How dare you—'

'I am the Queen of Gruisea,' Aisha said, turning to her. 'And you will address *me* as such.' She held Farrah's gaze before turning to Tariq. 'My sister had no part in your father's death. She did not poison anyone.'

There was nothing but truth in her eyes, but that wasn't enough. He couldn't simply take her word for it, and she surely knew that.

'Of course you would say that,' Farrah said, going to stand beside Tariq.

Aisha was supposed to be at his side. It was supposed to be the two of them against the world.

'It's true,' Aisha said.

More people had gathered to see what was happening. All eyes were on Tariq, watching to see how he would conduct himself as the new king.

'It was me,' Aisha continued, her voice dropping. 'I had Lilah unknowingly mix the poison, and then I put it in your father's food.'

The shock on Lilah's face likely mirrored Tariq's.

'You have my confession. I killed King Hamza,' Aisha said. Though the words were softly spoken, they seemed to ring out like bells through the courtyard. Sharp and undeniable.

Tariq didn't move—couldn't. Nor could he breathe. The words were like a noose around his neck.

'I killed King Hamza.'

A rush of heat surged through his chest, followed by a cold sensation that left his fingers tingling. His feet shifted as feeling returned.

It couldn't be true.

No one spoke. Or he didn't hear them. No one seemed to know quite what to do with that confession—not even his mother.

Tariq couldn't look away from Aisha. His gaze was locked with hers, searching for some glimmer of truth or flicker of a lie. This had to be an attempt to protect her sister.

She stood tall like a queen. *His* queen. All the love he carried for her sat uselessly inside him. Heavy. Pointless. He struggled to recognise this version of her, this queen who had just signed her own death sentence in front of witnesses.

In front of Zahvik.

'Take them both to the tower,' Farrah instructed. 'And clear this courtyard.'

'I acted alone,' Aisha said, turning to Farrah. 'My family are innocent.'

That brought Tariq out of his trance.

'Princess Aisha has confessed to the crime,' he said, drawing the attention of the entire courtyard. His fingers brushed over the token hidden beneath his tunic. 'The rest of her family is free to go.'

Farrah's mouth flattened into a thin line, but she had the good sense not to speak. Perhaps referring to Aisha as a princess instead of a queen had appeased her.

Tariq's gaze found Aisha's again, and he could barely believe what he was about to say. He had vowed to love and protect her. They had unified their *souls* before the gods.

'Take her to the tower.' The words clawed at his throat on their way out.

The guards moved in decisively now.

'I want two men guarding that cell,' Farrah said. 'Covenweavers are notorious escapees.'

Tariq blinked slowly as a fresh wave of whispers passed through the crowd. Aisha stood still as a guard approached, tugging her arms behind her back. She surrendered to all of it. There was not the slightest struggle as they led her away. She didn't fight. Didn't speak.

Didn't look back.

CHAPTER 32

The iron grip on Aisha's arm tightened as guards escorted her out of the courtyard. The stone beneath her feet felt foreign.

'You can't lock her up without a trial!' Safiya shouted behind her.

Aisha kept her eyes forwards. Safiya had known what was going to happen, and yet still she fought the inevitable.

Footsteps came at a run behind her. 'Aisha.' It was Lilah. 'What have you done?'

She wasn't talking about the murder, because she knew Aisha would never do such a thing. She was talking about the confession.

'Go with Safiya,' Aisha said over her shoulder. 'Now.'

Zara, Omar, Yasmin, and her father had already left for the port. The plan was that Safiya would follow with Lilah once she was freed.

'She's lost her mind,' Lilah told Safiya.

Safiya grabbed Lilah's arm and pulled her in the other direction. 'Let's go.'

'We can't leave her.'

Aisha didn't hear Safiya's reply, because she was marched through the tower door before it groaned shut behind her.

Darkness swallowed her.

The air inside the tower was colder. It tasted different. Torchlight flickered across damp stone walls as she was led up a winding staircase. The shadows seemed to reach for her. No one spoke, one guard ahead and one behind. The rhythm of their boots matched the pounding of her heart. She tried to slow it down, tried not to fall apart.

The staircase finally gave way to a corridor with a single iron-banded door at the end. One guard pulled out a ring of keys to unlock it. The scrape of metal on metal was loud in the small space. The door creaked open, and she was guided into a cell with one tiny window at the top. A single cot sat against the far wall, with a folded woollen blanket on the end. The floor had been swept clean. It felt like a tomb.

The door clanged shut behind her, and the guards retreated to the other end of the corridor. Aisha walked slowly over to the cot, brushing dust off it before sitting down. Her hands trembled in her lap as she looked around, and her mouth was so dry. She reminded herself that she had lied to save them. Her sisters, her father, and Omar—the future King of Avanid. But the cost of that decision was being locked in a cell and praying Tariq wouldn't execute her.

The cot creaked beneath her weight. There was no warmth. No comfort.

Shuffling back, she leaned against the wall and pulled her knees up, dropping her forehead to them. A tear slipped down her cheek and was soaked up by her robe. She didn't lift her head again, because there was nothing to see but stone and shadows. So she closed her eyes and waited for dawn.

The cold crept in overnight, and Aisha woke with a sharp jolt. For a moment, she didn't remember where she was. The walls were unfamiliar, and the bed was harder than anything she'd ever slept on. Her gaze went to the small window above, where pale grey light finally filtered in.

It was morning.

Her throat ached, and her body felt sore from being tense all night. She ran a hand through her hair as she moved to the edge of the bed, her feet meeting the chill of the floor. And that's when she felt it. That sense of being watched.

She looked up.

Tariq stood on the other side of the door, watching her. He looked as if he hadn't slept at all. The hollows beneath his eyes were the darkest she had ever seen them, and his jaw was dusted with stubble. He looked… brittle.

Aisha slowly stood, waiting for him to speak.

'Your family's ship departed Gruisea an hour ago.' His voice was low. 'Everyone made it aboard. I thought you'd want to know.'

There was relief, but there was also crushing grief. 'Thank you.'

Her gratitude seemed to agitate him. 'I had no reason to keep them here, since you apparently acted alone in killing my father.'

'I'm sure your mother would have preferred to see us all locked up.'

Tariq's expression didn't change, his cold eyes staring at her. 'I would have investigated the situation thoroughly.'

'I saved you the trouble.'

He took a step closer, so that his face was almost touching the iron bars. 'I need to hear it from you, one last time, before I meet with the council. Did you kill my father?'

Aisha's pulse thundered in her ears. 'Yes.'

The disappointment on his face crushed her.

'Were you really in such a rush to be queen?' he asked.

'I did it for both of us.' The lie came out easier than she thought it would. 'So we could change all the things we planned to change. Save lives.'

His jaw worked. 'Last chance to take it back. Once the council rules, a sentence will be passed.'

Aisha's hands twitched at her sides. 'I'm sorry. I wish I could tell you what you want to hear.' That part was truthful.

'You're sorry.' He shook his head. 'They'll sentence you to death. And I won't be able to stop them.'

I know he loves you and will protect you with his life. Maryam's words came to her. Aisha had no choice but to trust the woman who had deceived her.

'Will you take care of Mira?' she asked.

Tariq's eyes filled with anger. 'You have a lot of audacity asking for favours.'

She swallowed guiltily.

Without saying another word, Tariq turned and left, the heavy scrape of his boots fading down the corridor. A bolt slid shut in the distance. Aisha remained where she was, breath jammed in her throat, knowing the last thread between them had snapped.

She returned to the cot to sit and wait once more.

Hours passed slowly. Aisha attempted to count them by the shifting light from the window. A guard brought her food and water, and she ate it despite the absence of appetite. Eventually, the light turned golden as the sun slipped westward, before dimming completely.

Then time lost all structure.

She didn't sleep that night, not properly. She drifted in and out of dreams, her body too tense and her mind too busy.

In the morning, she sat with the blanket wrapped around her shoulders. She had managed to braid her hair back despite her fingers fumbling from the chill. It gave her something to do and something small to control. Rising, she paced slowly from one end of the cell to the other, again and again. She tried not to think of her family now far away. They would be so worried about her. She whispered a prayer for courage.

A noise broke the stillness.

A door closed far below, followed by heavy boots. Voices. Muffled at first, then clearer as they entered the corridor.

She stood in the centre of the cell, blanket still wrapped around her, gripping it tightly. The key scraped in the lock, then the door at the end of the corridor opened. Jamil stepped into view and spoke quietly with the two guards posted there. His hair was perfectly arranged, his robes pristine. He met her gaze through the bars as he spoke, and her stomach dropped.

'Your Majesty,' he said, making his way over to her. The address felt patronising. 'I have come to inform you that your sentence has been decided.'

Aisha said nothing. She didn't trust her voice.

Jamil gestured to one of the guards, and they came forwards to unlock the cell door. 'A ruling by His Holiness Zahvik supersedes any ruling made by royal decree,' he continued. 'Queen Farrah welcomed the decision in hopes of sparing King Tariq further stress.'

Zahvik.

Aisha stepped back as the guard entered her cell. 'Wait. Tariq doesn't know?'

'Her Majesty has insisted on a private execution, shielded from the masses, out of respect for your station.' Jamil said that last part as if he were delivering good news.

Aisha's hands were seized and shackled behind her back once again. She didn't fight, but this time she really wanted to.

The torchlight blurred as she was marched along the corridor and down the narrow staircase. They didn't exit through the door they had come through, instead turning left at the landing and walking through a narrow corridor that sloped downward. There were no windows in this part of the castle—or air, for that matter. It opened into a small courtyard Aisha had never seen before. She froze when she laid eyes on the pyre in the centre of it, stacked high with dried wood and straw. Off to one side stood a solemn Queen Farrah, wearing her mourning veil—and Zahvik Barakat.

The guards pushed Aisha forwards to get her walking again, but her body refused to cooperate. Her steps faltered. She tripped, so they dragged her, not stopping until they were a few feet from the wooden mound. Her eyes locked on the metal post embedded in the centre of the pyre, chains hanging from it. Panic exploded inside her.

'Where's Tariq?' she shouted, looking over at Farrah.

The queen drew her veil back. 'The king has suffered enough. Would you not agree?'

'He would never allow it to happen this way, and you know it.' Her gaze flicked to Zahvik. 'If you do this, he'll never forgive you.' When she didn't respond, Aisha added, 'There are a thousand other ways to end my life.'

'There is only *one* way to execute a covenweaver,' Zahvik said, speaking for the first time. 'The king will be informed once it is done.'

It.

Burning her to death.

'You confessed of your own volition,' he continued. 'Before witnesses.'

This was the ultimate outcome for Zahvik, who had travelled to Gruisea to destroy everything.

Jamil moved closer, looked heavenward, and said a quiet prayer. Then, clearing his throat, he turned to

Aisha. 'You sought a poison and used it knowingly to murder King Hamza. The act was carried out with the precision one expects from a covenweaver.' His tone was thick with disgust. 'Now you will pay the price for bringing this evil to our shores and taking the life of our king.'

It wasn't supposed to end this way. She had never considered the possibility of a sentence without Tariq's knowledge. Her trust in him was meaningless if he didn't even know of her fate.

For a moment, she considered telling them the truth. Even if they didn't believe her, it might delay her execution. But as she looked over at Zahvik, she realised he'd never accept an outcome where they all lived. If he couldn't destroy their alliance from within Gruisea, he would find a reason to go to Avanid instead. He could take his pick of her family there.

'Well?' Jamil asked.

She realised she had missed the last thing he said. 'What?'

He appeared agitated. 'I asked if you have any last requests.'

She had barely wrapped her mind around the fact that she was about to die. She tried to concentrate on the question. What did she need in her final moments?

'Yes.' A tear slipped down her cheek. 'I want you to tell my family that my death was quick. Tell them I lost consciousness before the flames reached me. That I didn't feel a thing.' Her mother's scream rang out in her mind. She looked over at Farrah. 'Please. Promise me you'll do everything you can to ease their pain.'

Farrah's expression had turned from hateful to something more human. She nodded her consent.

'So be it,' Jamil said before stepping aside.

One of the guards pushed Aisha towards the pyre. It wasn't even a forceful push, but she stumbled anyway. She had no choice but to climb the wooden steps to the narrow platform at the top. The men secured her shackles to the post using the available chain. They produced a second chain and wrapped it around her ankles. She remembered how stoic her mother had been the day she died and channelled that energy, hoping it would ease the fear.

Once she was secured, the guards made their way back down the steps and positioned themselves well away from the pyre.

It was Zahvik who lit the torch and carried it to the pyre. Zahvik who lowered it to the debris and teased the edges until smoke rose.

Aisha closed her eyes, and the faces of her family flashed in her mind. Early memories too. Her father humming as he carved ivory. Her mother watching with a sleeping Omar pressed to her chest. Life had been beautiful once.

Then she saw Tariq. His barely there smile, the one that betrayed his restraint. The warmth in his eyes when he looked at her. She could almost feel the weight of his hand against her back. Maybe if she held his gaze for long enough…

A faint heat bloomed around her feet. It was the kind of heat one holds their hands to for warmth. She made the mistake of opening her eyes to look, and they immediately began to water. When she looked up, her eyes met Farrah's. The queen stood with her hands clasped, her veil catching in the draft from the tunnel behind her. There was no disdain. No gloating or satisfaction. Only tightness around her mouth and something resembling pain in her eyes.

Hers was the last face Aisha saw before she closed her eyes—tightly this time. The kindling crackled louder below her, and the heat thickened against her skin.

The world narrowed, and Aisha refused to scream.

CHAPTER 33

Tariq stood atop the eastern wall, hands braced on the cold stone embrasure and eyes on the tower in the distance. The morning was cold and bitter, the sky the colour of ash. The view was deceptively peaceful.

Once again, he had barely slept. Every time he closed his eyes, he saw Aisha's face or heard her voice—the conviction in her tone.

'Your Majesty,' Kaidon said behind him. The guard had barely left Tariq's side since the feast.

Tariq looked tiredly over his shoulder. Kaidon gestured to someone on the wall walk. It was Maryam—moving fast. When Tariq registered her panicked expression, he straightened and headed in her direction.

'What is it?' he asked.

'Your Majesty.' She fell to her knees before him. 'I have come to beg you not to go ahead with this execution.'

Tariq's eyebrows came together. 'That's a little premature. Aisha hasn't even been sentenced yet.'

Maryam looked up. 'Yes, she has.'

A cold sensation crawled along Tariq's spine.

'Where's that smoke coming from?' Kaidon walked over to the embrasure for a better look.

Tariq looked over at the plume of smoke rising into the sky. Then he was running.

'What's wrong?' Kaidon asked, following him.

Tariq bolted for the stairs, every footfall pounding in his ears like a war drum. He took the steps three at a time, his cloak flying behind him. His breath steamed in the cold air as he pushed himself faster. 'Move!' he roared at the guard standing at the bottom.

Kaidon managed to keep up. When they reached the tower, he yelled, 'Open the door!' at the slightly panicked guard watching their fast approach.

The man fumbled with a ring of keys, pushing the door open just as they reached it. Tariq leapt up the stairs, heading for the corridor that led to the lower courtyard, where the smoke had been coming from. The smell of it hit him full in the face as he slammed through the gate and sprinted down the final corridor.

The next door was unbarred, and when he burst through it, the world narrowed. Shackled in the centre of the pyre was Aisha. A motionless figure amid smoke, eyes pressed closed, surrounded by a ring of flames. They hadn't reached her yet, but they were nauseatingly close.

Zahvik, Jamil, and his mother stood off to one side with some of the guards. Every head turned in his direction when he entered.

Kaidon skidded to a stop beside Tariq, taking in the scene. 'Gods above.'

Adrenaline surged through Tariq. 'You!' He pointed at the guards. 'Put out the flames!'

The guards hesitated at first, but when Kaidon roared, 'Obey your king!' they leapt into action.

The fire crackled, climbing higher. Tariq sprinted forwards, eyes locked on Aisha.

'Wait!' Kaidon shouted.

But there was no time. Heat swallowed Tariq as he leapt over the fire, his cloak brushing the blaze. The scent of scorched fabric followed as he landed hard atop the wooden platform. It groaned beneath his weight. Shackles clinked as Aisha startled, her eyes snapping open. She stared at him as though she was trying to figure out if he was real or not. He moved behind her, wrestling with the metal, fingers fumbling with the locking mechanism.

'Shit,' he hissed. The cuffs were already heating up, and smoke blurred his vision as pails of water were thrown over the flames.

'Leave,' Aisha pleaded, her voice hoarse. 'Before you die here with me.'

'Not a chance.'

With a final twist, one of the shackles snapped free. He dropped to a crouch to attack the chain around her feet. It burst open and clattered against the wood. Tariq scooped her into his arms, shielding her with his body as he looked for the best exit.

'This way,' Kaidon shouted. The guards had managed to extinguish a small section of the fire.

The heat clawed at Tariq's back as he made his way towards Kaidon. 'Cover your face,' he told her. Then he leapt, hitting the ground below with a grunt and twisting to cushion her from the impact.

Kaidon doused Aisha with water, cursing the entire time.

Still cradling Aisha in his arms, Tariq looked her over. 'Are you burned?'

She shook her head, dazed. 'I don't think so.'

'Keep working!' Kaidon shouted at the guards as he pressed a water flask into Tariq's hand.

Tariq lifted it to Aisha's mouth. 'Drink,' he told her.

She did, tears spilling from her red-rimmed eyes as she swallowed. 'They'll hate you for this,' she said when he lowered the flask.

'Yes, but that's not for you to worry about.'

His emotions were all over the place. Part of him wanted to cradle her forever, and the other part wanted to place her on the filthy floor and walk away. He couldn't bear her death, but what was the alternative? A life locked in the tower? Or banished to the countryside, perhaps? Her mere existence would serve as a permanent reminder of everything she had done and all he had lost.

Footsteps approached, led by Zahvik. Smoke swirled in his wake.

'You have offended the gods,' Zahvik said.

Tariq slowly stood, lowering Aisha's feet to the ground while keeping her pressed against him. 'And you have offended me and this court by collaborating behind my back.' His glare flicked to his mother, who at least had the decency to look guilty.

'She is a covenweaver,' Farrah said. 'We had no choice.'

'You have no proof of that,' Tariq replied. '*You* should have been first to object.'

She raised her chin. 'I was trying to spare you further pain.'

'Liar,' Tariq said. 'You wanted to make yourself feel better and appease *him*.' He set his gaze on Zahvik. 'Well, that stops today. Pack your things, gather your men, and get out of Gruisea. You're no longer welcome here.'

Nothing changed on Zahvik's face. He simply tutted. 'The devil has hold of your soul. The woman you defend is both a covenweaver and a murderer.'

Farrah looked at Aisha, who was limp in his arms. 'She has bewitched you.'

Tariq shook his head, his breath shaking with anger. Anger at his mother, but also at himself, because she was right. Aisha *had* bewitched him. Body and soul.

'Your Majesty,' Jamil said, 'justice must be served.'

'It will be.' He looked between the three of them. 'But it will be served as *I* see fit. Your opinions are now void.'

He sounded much more confident than he felt. He needed space from all of them—even Aisha. Releasing his hold on her, he stepped back.

'You cannot protect her from her own actions,' Farrah said. 'There are consequences when you go around killing kings.'

He had no right to decide Aisha's fate while still so shamefully in love with her. And yet, because he had the power to do so, he would.

When he looked at Aisha, he saw she was shaking. The flames hadn't touched her, but they had scorched something far deeper. She had nearly died the same death as her mother.

'Take Aisha back to her cell and remain there with her,' he told Kaidon. 'No one in. No one out. Understood?'

Kaidon stepped forwards and gently took hold of Aisha's arm. 'No one in. No one out,' he repeated.

Tariq backed away from Aisha, and her eyes followed him.

'Where are you going?' Farrah asked.

He turned away and left them all standing there, ignoring the questions. He entered the smoke-choked corridor with a single-minded purpose: to get his wife out of Gruisea. Not just for her, but for himself. If she stayed, she'd die. If she stayed, he would unravel piece by piece.

The shipyards. The patrol schedules. He knew them all. All he needed was an opening wide enough to smuggle her to the port. It was his only option, because the three people behind him would stop at nothing to see her destroyed.

Tariq moved through the castle grounds like a man possessed. The air was refreshingly cold against his face. Once indoors, he crossed the lower hall and took the back stairs to avoid the main corridors. The further he got from them all, the clearer his mind became. He wasn't just reacting anymore.

He was planning.

CHAPTER 34

The smell of smoke on Aisha's skin was fading, but it was woven into her mind. She sat cross-legged on the floor, her back against the cell door. The wool blanket covered her legs.

On the other side was Kaidon, knees drawn up and arms slung over them. They hadn't exchanged more than a few words as they each stared at their own patch of stone wall. Aisha found herself watching the slow shift of dust in the light, willing her mind to be blank instead of racing in fractured loops.

'I saw a covenweaver burned in the city once,' Kaidon said, his voice flat. 'A simple shift in the breeze had it over and done with rather quickly.'

Aisha pressed her eyes closed.

'You know, this might be the messiest wedding in history,' he continued. 'Historians will give it a dramatic name and write it into their books. You'll be forever referenced as a warning to young lovers.'

She opened her eyes. 'The Poison-Pyre Wedding.'

'The Ashes and Arsenic Affair,' he replied.

'The King Killer's Nuptials.'

'The Torch-and-Treason Ceremony.'

'That one is catchy,' she said.

Kaidon let out a long breath. 'Except I don't think you killed King Hamza.'

His words dropped like a rock into still water.

'But I understand why you took the fall,' he said. 'I'm a little surprised it was you, though. You're the only one perfectly positioned to help the rest of your family. You're no good to anyone dead.'

Aisha didn't reply. She was afraid if she did the lie might come undone.

Footsteps sounded on the stairs below.

'Thank the gods,' Kaidon said, getting to his feet. 'I'm starving.'

Aisha rose also, backing up when she heard the door at the end of the corridor open. Tariq stepped into view, wearing the soot-covered clothes from earlier. He didn't look at her until he reached the door.

'No food, then?' Kaidon asked.

Tariq's gaze remained on Aisha. 'You're leaving. Pack your things.' His voice was low and measured.

Aisha looked around. 'I don't have any things.'

'Even better.'

'Are you going to let me, your bodyguard, in on the plan here?' Kaidon asked.

Tariq's gaze shifted to him. 'There'll be a gap in the outer patrol shortly. We're going to use it.' He pulled a plain black scarf out of an internal pocket and pushed it through the bars. 'Put this on. Cover your face.'

Aisha stepped forwards and took it. The wool was much softer than the cell blanket. 'Where are you taking me?'

'Far away from here.'

Kaidon's eyebrows rose. 'A smuggling mission?'

'Yes.'

'What happens if you're caught?' Aisha asked.

He ignored the question. 'Open the door.'

Kaidon hesitated. 'You sure about this?'

Tariq levelled him with a stare. '*Open the door.*'

Exhaling, Kaidon fished the key from his pocket and unlocked the cell door.

'Let's go,' Tariq said to Aisha. 'We don't have much time.'

She threw the blanket onto the cot, then exited the cell, following Tariq.

The torchlight in the corridor flickered as they moved, creating shadows that made Aisha feel as if they were being chased. She kept close to Tariq, the scarf covering most of her face, with Kaidon trailing a few paces behind.

They didn't take the main stairs but veered left at the first landing, ducking into a narrow side corridor she hadn't noticed before. He led her down a tight spiral stair-case that smelled of damp stone. At the bottom, they exited through a crooked doorway into a part of the keep where cobwebs danced above them. Tariq slowed when they reached an iron gate that sat ajar, then pushed through it, glancing back to ensure she was still behind him.

'Where does this lead?' Aisha whispered.

He kept his eyes forwards. 'There's a passage that cuts behind the granary and opens near the southern watch gate. From there, we'll take the cliff path down to the harbour.'

Hope sprouted inside Aisha. 'The harbour?' *We're leaving Gruisea.*

'The watch gate will be guarded,' Kaidon pointed out.

'Yes, but the sentries are always distracted during the changeover,' Tariq replied.

'Then they need a good talking-to.' Kaidon checked over his shoulder as they pressed on. 'Tomorrow—after we've snuck by them.'

The passage narrowed, and Tariq ducked his head beneath the low beams. His shoulders occasionally brushed the stone on either side. Aisha concentrated on not tripping on the uneven ground.

Finally, they emerged into the mouth of a short tunnel, and the smell of grain greeted them. Tariq paused at the edge of the tunnel, eyeing the watch gate ahead.

'When the outer bell chimes, the sentries will change posts,' he said. 'Then we go.'

Kaidon stepped up beside him. 'I thought all ships to Avanid had been suspended.'

Tariq nodded. 'They have.'

'Then where are we sailing to?' Aisha asked.

'*We* are not sailing anywhere.' Tariq finally looked at her. '*You* are sailing to Montia. From there, you can make your way inland to Avanid.'

Of course he wasn't going with her. Why had she said 'we' like an idiot?

Before she could ask anything more, the bell rang. One sharp clang echoed across the quiet grounds.

'Make sure you stay close and keep your head down,' Tariq told her.

She nodded.

The trio slipped from the tunnel, weaving through the edge of the orchard and past the grain bins. The watch gate loomed ahead, partially open. The guards inside moved slowly, exchanging banter. Tariq led the way through, his posture calm but commanding. The guards barely noticed them as they griped about the cold. Aisha held her breath as she passed by them.

A few moments later, they were out.

Tariq didn't slow down. He continued around the stone wall and down the embankment where the ground turned from stone to dirt. At the base of the slope, covered by trees, waited two horses. It was a short walk to reach them, and Tariq mounted the closest one, then immediately reached for Aisha, lifting her up behind him. She had barely landed on the horse's back before it lurched into a canter.

Aisha kept her head down as they rode, using Tariq's back for protection from the wind. She wondered if she was too close for his liking, for his state of mind. She soaked up those final moments with him, memorising his shape, scent, and the exact rhythm of his breath. There would be no more moments once she boarded the ship to Montia.

The harbour appeared below them, a single narrow dock curling into the bay. Two ships sat at anchor, but only one flew Montia's flag.

They rode down to the edge of the dock, and Tariq lowered Aisha to the ground before dismounting. A man wearing a thick cloak and a sun-bleached scarf approached, hand over his heart as he bowed before them. 'Your Majesties.'

Plural. Even as she was being expelled.

'Everything in order?' Tariq asked.

The man nodded.

'This is Captain Harun,' Tariq told Aisha. 'He'll see you safely to Montia.'

The captain's weathered face seemed stuck in the same expression. 'Wind's in our favour,' he said. 'If all goes well, we'll dock at Virelin in two days.'

Aisha lowered her scarf so she could speak. 'I appreciate you taking me on your ship, Captain.'

He bowed his head. 'Your attendant is waiting for you.'

'Attendant?' Aisha looked past him.

'Told her to put that animal in a cage, but she insisted on holding it.'

Aisha's gaze landed on Maryam, standing at the base of the gangway. The hem of her cloak was lifting in the breeze, and in her arms was Mira. Aisha was painfully conflicted about having Maryam as a travel companion while simultaneously thrilled that Mira would be going with her. She knew her relationship with the attendant couldn't be salvaged, even if her reasons for the betrayal were justifiable. Aisha had only kept quiet about the treason for the sake of Maryam's family. But silence didn't equate to forgiveness.

'No one else would care for the leopard,' Tariq said. 'We have enough problems.'

Aisha looked at him, knowing that wasn't the only reason he had sent her along. 'I understand that doing this is going to create more problems for you. I'm sorry you'll have to wade through the mess alone.'

'Are you?' His eyes were like two dark storms—grief, confusion, and anger swirling together.

'Yes.'

His gaze returned to the ship. He really couldn't look at her for long.

The wind dragged her cloak around her ankles. 'I should go.'

Tariq didn't move. He stood rigid, his jaw set and eyes ahead. When he finally spoke, his voice was low and tight. 'You've destroyed everything.'

Her lungs stilled.

'I don't know whether you killed my father or not,' he said, 'but it barely matters now. The damage is done.' A bitter breath escaped through his teeth. 'I might not have the strength to watch you die, but if you ever return to Gruisea, you'll be imprisoned, then executed.'

She forced herself to breathe.

'I fought for you,' he said. 'For *us*. I faced down the entire court and never regretted a moment until...' He shook his head, unable to finish.

Her throat felt like thorns were jammed in it. 'I never wanted—'

'It actually doesn't matter what you wanted.' Anger had crept into his tone. 'It matters what you *did*.'

Silence lapped between them again.

Aisha took a much-needed breath, trying to hold herself together. Now wasn't the time to fall apart, not when he had risked so much to get her out. 'I'm sorry.' The words fell flat.

Tariq's gaze flicked briefly to hers. 'Go.'

She walked as bravely as she could towards the ship, the wind harsh against her skin. She didn't dare look back. Tears began falling despite her best effort to hold them in. She was halfway to the ship when she heard him call her name.

'Aisha.'

Her feet instantly stopped. She turned, stupidly hopeful despite having no reason to be. He walked towards her, hands fisted at his sides. He didn't say anything when he got to her. Reaching up, his fingers brushed the skin of her neck, and for one naïve moment, she thought he was being tender with her, that maybe he had changed his mind and wanted to fight for them all over again. But then his fingers closed around the chain hanging from her neck, and with one sharp tug, it broke. The token was taken from her. The action left a stinging sensation on the back of her neck, a reminder of their final severing.

Aisha's hand went instinctively to the place the token had rested.

'Now you can go,' Tariq said, his voice quiet. He turned and walked away before she had a chance to move, the chain curled in his fist.

Aisha watched him for as long as she could bear it. Then she slowly turned and went to join Maryam. She noted the dark circles around the attendant's eyes. Mira wriggled in Maryam's arms when she saw Aisha. She took the cub from her.

'Your Majesty,' Maryam said, her hand going over her heart as she lowered her head.

Aisha stared at her for a long moment, then made her way up the gangway, one step at a time, ready for the wind to carry her away.

Water stretched in every direction, blue-grey and endless. The ship creaked as it cut through the sea, its sail drawn taut. Salt clung to Aisha's skin. She sat on the mid-deck, her cloak pulled tightly around her, staring at the horizon. It was day two at sea, but it felt more like day thirty thanks to the ever-present nausea.

Mira dozed at her side while Maryam sat a respectful distance away, occupying a shaded corner closer to the stern. She was seated on a crate with her face tilted to the sky. They had barely spoken since their departure. There was no hostility between them, but no warmth either. Just silence. A growing heaviness between two people simply trying to survive.

Yawning, Mira moved to Aisha's lap, nuzzling her hand. Aisha obliged, her thoughts circling back to Tariq as they had done so many times. She recalled his tense body and icy tone. The finality of his words. She knew she would survive it, but she didn't know who she would be at the end of it all.

The hours passed in a slow, sun-drenched haze. While the nausea dulled, it never truly left. She remained in that spot, with Mira sprawled across her thighs. Occasionally, a crew member passed by and nodded a greeting, but they didn't stop. No one knew what to say to the king's exiled bride.

By mid-afternoon, the clouds thinned and the coast-line appeared. *Montia*. Aisha moved to the ship's rail, watching as the sun-bleached stone buildings of Virelin became clearer. Maryam appeared beside her as the ship began its slow turn towards the bay. The lines under her eyes had deepened with fatigue.

'What's the plan when we disembark?' Aisha asked.

Maryam bent to pet Mira. 'I am certain the captain knows more than we do.' She straightened. 'I will remain with you until you are safely home, then return to Gruisea.'

'You don't have to take me any further than this,' Aisha said, trying to sound brave.

Maryam's soft eyes met hers. 'It is not safe to cross Montia by yourself.'

They fell silent for a while.

'Are your family still safe?' Aisha asked, looking out at the water again.

'Yes.' Maryam swallowed. 'Thanks to your silence.'

Aisha didn't say anything further.

The ship docked right before sunset. The smell of brine and wood smoke drifted up as the dockhands secured the ropes. Captain Harun disembarked briefly to speak to the harbourmaster, then returned to talk to Aisha.

'The harbourmaster is arranging an escort for you,' he said. 'The pair of you wait on the dock, and he'll come find you.'

Aisha frowned. 'I'm afraid I don't have any coin to pay them upfront.'

Harun waved a hand in her direction. 'That's all been taken care of. The king more than covered it.'

Of course he had. Despite the enormous amount of anger he must have felt towards her, he had still ensured she was safe for the entire journey.

'I will fetch our bags,' Maryam said, disappearing.

'There's an inn nearby,' Harun told her. 'I suggest you rest there tonight and leave in the morning.'

Aisha nodded. 'How many days is the journey to Avanid?'

'Five to seven days, depending how long you can last in the saddle.'

She felt herself deflate. Home was still so far away.

Harun tipped his head once, then turned away, calling to the crew to begin offloading the crates.

Maryam returned a few moments later with their bags. When she saw Aisha's expression, she asked, 'Is everything all right?'

'As well as a disgraced, seasick queen charged with murder can be.' She attempted a humoured smile. 'Let's go.'

They disembarked, both grateful to be on solid land again.

'Why does it feel like the dock is moving?' Maryam asked.

Aisha's mind went to her arrival in Gruisea months back, and her lips curved up at the memory. 'You have to get your land legs back.'

'My what?'

Aisha placed Mira on the ground and took one of the bags from Maryam. 'It'll pass.'

The harbour bustled as twilight deepened, lanterns flickering to life along the pier. The women waited together near a stack of cargo crates, cautiously watching their surroundings. Thankfully, the dockhands paid them little mind.

Eventually, a local man, wearing a Montian leather vest, approached. He had a shortbow slung across his back and a slight limp.

'Evening,' he said, frowning at Mira as he stopped in front of them. 'I see you brought your own meat. We have plenty here in Montia, you know.'

Aisha picked Mira up and held her close. 'She's a companion animal.'

His eyebrows rose. 'What, no dogs in Gruisea?'

'Are you the escort?' Maryam asked.

'That's me.' He looked between them. 'Which one of you is the princess?'

'*Queen*,' Maryam corrected, gesturing to Aisha. 'Queen Aisha of Gruisea.'

He looked her up and down, his expression sceptical, and didn't bother to bow. 'Right. My name's Rafiq. Captain says I'm to take you to the Stonehill Inn for the night.'

'I'm quite looking forward to sleeping in a bed that doesn't sway,' Aisha said.

Rafiq chuckled. 'And a wash, judging by the look of you.' He began walking. 'This way.'

The two women exchanged an amused glance before following.

Virelin was quieter than Aisha had expected. It had narrow stone alleys, packed with faded houses and shutters already drawn for the night. Lanterns glowed in doorways.

The inn sat at the top of a hill, nestled between an apothecary and a wine merchant. Its stone façade was chipped along the archway.

'Wait here,' Rafiq said before disappearing inside. He emerged a few minutes later. 'Everything's settled with the innkeeper.' He pointed to the ground. 'I'll meet you at this very spot at first light. Don't be late.' He then limped away.

Inside, the courtyard smelled of roasted meat and cardamom. A pang of hunger hit Aisha. Arched walkways lined the courtyard, each leading to a heavy wooden door or a curtained sleeping alcove. A tired woman rose from a bench when she spotted them, setting aside her teacup and bowing politely. She crossed the worn rug to reach them.

'My name is Maryam,' the attendant said. 'And this is—'

'Princess Aisha of Avanid,' Aisha finished.

Maryam didn't correct her.

'Welcome,' said the woman. 'We don't get a lot of royal

visitors. Or wild animals, for that matter,' she added, looking pointedly at Mira.

Aisha smiled politely.

'We would love to put our bags down,' Maryam said.

'Of course.' She bowed again. 'This way.' She led them along a pathway before pushing open one of the doors. 'This one's yours.'

Aisha peered inside. The room was small but clean, with two cots and a washbasin.

'Let me know if you need anything,' the woman said before leaving them.

Aisha entered first, placing Mira on the bed before going over to the window and pulling back the curtain. Lights flickered across the town.

Maryam organised the bags near the wall. 'I will get us some food,' she said, then slipped quietly out the door.

Aisha was relieved to be alone for a few moments. She went to fetch a clean set of clothes from the bag Maryam had packed on her behalf. As she was digging around in search of clean linen, her fingers brushed against something soft. She drew out a small suede pouch. Something clinked inside as she lifted it. Untying it, she found gold dinars and a folded piece of parchment tucked in with them. Pulling it out, she opened it, running her thumb over Tariq's familiar handwriting.

In case you need it.

. . .

No signature. Nor was it needed. She pressed the note to her chest, closed her eyes, then tucked it back into the pouch and buried it at the bottom of the bag.

Aisha had just finished washing and changing when Maryam returned with a tray of food and some fresh water. The smell of spiced lentils filled the room.

'They gave me some goat ribs,' Maryam said, placing them on the ground for Mira.

The two women sat opposite each other on their cots, watching the cub gnaw noisily. They were too tired for conversation, and Aisha didn't know what to say anyway.

When the food was gone, Mira curled up on the foot of Aisha's bed while she lay there appreciating the silence. No men shouting or creaking timber.

The last thing she saw was Tariq's face as he had torn the token from her neck. She pressed a hand to her chest before sleep took her.

CHAPTER 36

The road to Avanid was a winding ribbon of dust and stone, carved through hills that rolled endlessly in all directions. It was day five of their journey, and the horses were moving at a steady walk. Aisha's thighs ached, her shoulders were tight, and her hands were raw where the reins had rubbed her skin. Even Mira, who had grown accustomed to the saddlebag contraption they had made, twitched with restlessness.

'How much further to the border?' Aisha asked Rafiq.

It was clear from his expression that he was sick of the question. 'One hour less than the last time you asked.'

Maryam rode her horse up beside Aisha's, adjusting her scarf to cover her wind-chapped lips. 'Do you need a rest, Your Majesty?'

What she needed was for the journey to be over. 'I'm fine to keep going.' She fixed her cloak, blinking grit from her lashes.

When the sun began its descent, turning the sky to

bronze, hunger kicked in. They hadn't eaten anything but a handful of almonds all day.

Finally, Rafiq turned in the saddle. 'We'll make camp at the next clearing.'

Aisha almost wept with relief when he said that.

They rode for another fifteen minutes before Rafiq guided them off the road into a sheltered hollow surrounded by boulders and scrubby trees. It provided enough cover for them to get a good night's sleep, though Aisha suspected she would sleep through a storm in her current state.

Rafiq dismounted and unslung his saddlebag, dropping it on the ground before wandering off to fetch kindling for the fire.

When Aisha slid down from her horse, her legs buckled beneath her. Luckily, she was still holding the saddle. When Maryam dismounted, she crumpled straight to the ground.

'Are you all right?' Aisha asked.

Maryam laughed, but it sounded tired. 'I am afraid I will be useless to you until the feeling returns to my legs.'

'We're really not built for this life,' Aisha said, holding back a smile.

'Give me a comfortable castle any day.'

Aisha took Mira out of the saddlebag, then hobbled over to help Maryam to her feet. Moving slowly, they secured the horses, unsaddled them, then walked clumsy laps of the clearing, willing blood flow to return to the deprived parts of their bodies.

Rafiq returned and built a fire, the timing perfect, because as the sun dropped, so did the temperature. The women sat closer to the flames, eating the last of their cheese with their nuts.

'I don't think I'll ever be able to eat nuts again,' Aisha told Maryam.

Rafiq fed and watered the horses, seemingly unfazed by the cold.

Seeing that Maryam was shivering, Aisha moved closer to her, spreading her blanket across both their legs.

'Thank you,' Maryam said quietly.

Mira was done with her adventuring and padded over to curl up between them. They sat in silence, watching the flames.

'I would kill for some tea,' Maryam said after a long silence.

Aisha shook her head. 'I bet you would.'

Realising what she had said, Maryam sighed. 'I should think before speaking.'

Aisha didn't respond.

'I cannot recall if I have said this enough times,' Maryam said, 'but I am sorry.'

'For drugging me or spying on me?'

Maryam swallowed. 'Both.'

Aisha wriggled her feet in front of the fire. 'Once we separate, they should hopefully leave you alone. You'll be of no value to the Emperor or his spies then.'

The worried expression remained. 'Until the next time they need a covenweaver. They know what I am, so I will never be free of them'

Aisha stared hard at the flames. 'Do you know one of the hardest parts about all this?'

Maryam looked at her.

'It confirms what we've all long suspected. It's not about eradicating covenweavers—it's about controlling them. We're quite useful under the right circumstances.'

'And when we are not, *then* they eradicate us.'

The wind whistled through the rocks above them.

'If you had come to me with the truth, I would have kept your secret,' Aisha said.

Maryam nodded gently. 'That was not a risk I could take before.'

'Before?' Aisha turned her head.

'Before I knew I could truly trust you.'

'You mean, when I learned your secret?'

Maryam's brow furrowed. 'No.' Her eyes filled with tears. 'When you found out about Zahvik and *still* chose to protect my family—even when you were drowning in my betrayal.'

In the firelight, Maryam looked older than her twenty-eight years.

'There was no point in anyone else getting hurt,' Aisha said.

Maryam stroked Mira's coat. 'You could have pinned King Hamza's death on me. King Tariq would have believed you.'

Aisha nodded. 'Except you didn't do it.'

'And neither did you.'

Aisha looked back at the fire. 'We should get some sleep.' She lay down, facing away from Maryam. She really had no right being angry at Maryam for what she did to keep her family safe.

What a hypocrite Aisha was. Look at what she had done to Tariq in order to keep her own family safe. Lied to his face and robbed him of a queen, a wife. A person to survive this world with. She had made him hate her.

Behind her, Maryam prepared for sleep. 'Goodnight, Your Majesty.'

Aisha blinked. 'Goodnight.'

* * *

The cold hit hard in the morning as Aisha peeled her eyes open and looked around. The warmth of the fire was long gone. Mira yawned and stretched beside her, blinking awake. She was surprised to find Maryam up and already packed. Rafiq was readying the horses. Two were saddled, and he was working on the last one.

Aisha sat up slowly, every joint stiff. She noticed Maryam's leg bouncing nervously. 'Are you all right?'

Maryam jumped at the sound of her voice. Her leg continued to bounce as her eyes filled with tears. 'No, actually.' She glanced over at Rafiq before saying, 'There is something I need to tell you.'

A bad feeling washed over Aisha.

'I made contact with Rafiq earlier,' Maryam whispered. 'I suppose I was curious about the rest of our journey.'

She'd had a vision. And judging by the trauma in her eyes, it wasn't good.

Maryam opened her mouth to speak, but then closed it suddenly, looking off in the distance. That's when Aisha heard the faint sound of hooves. Maryam shot to her feet.

'What's going on?' Aisha asked, scrambling upright and looking around. 'Maryam—'

'We have to go.' Maryam ran over and began snatching up Aisha's belongings. 'Grab Mira—quickly.'

Aisha shoved the blanket into her bag, then scooped up the cub. 'Who's coming?'

There was no colour in Maryam's face. 'I do not know.'

'You don't *know*?' Aisha exhaled. 'We're not the only ones using this road.'

Maryam's head snapped towards the sound, eyes wide. 'Aisha, get on your horse—now.'

The fact that she had called Aisha by her first name was enough reason to take her seriously. She headed for the horses. 'Rafiq,' she called, 'we have to go.'

He looked in their direction, frowning. 'What's going on?'

'We have to leave,' Maryam said. 'Right now.'

His confusion solidified. 'I haven't finished securing the packs.'

'It does not matter,' Maryam said, reaching for the reins of her horse. 'We will carry them.'

Nostrils flaring, Rafiq placed his hands on his hips. 'What's the hurry?'

'There are people coming!' she shouted at him.

'I think you need more sleep,' he replied, turning back to the horse.

'Get on your horse,' Maryam told Aisha. 'We are leaving.'

Aisha had just finished putting Mira into the saddle-bag. 'We can't just ride off without Rafiq. He's the only map we have.'

Maryam's breath hitched, and her voice broke as she said, 'He is going to die!'

The world stilled.

Rafiq froze, eyes narrowing in confusion. A faint whistle cut through the air and—

Aisha gasped as an arrow buried itself deep in his throat. He staggered backwards, clutching at the shaft as a wet gurgle came from his mouth. The gelding he was holding reared.

Maryam pushed Aisha towards her horse as Rafiq crumpled to the ground. 'Ride,' she said. 'As fast as you can.'

Aisha clambered onto her horse and gathered up the reins. 'Why aren't you getting on your horse?'

'You are going to ride north,' Maryam said. 'It is one straight line to the border from here.'

Panic seized Aisha by the throat. 'I can't outrun them.'

'You can.'

'I'm not leaving you—'

'Go!' Maryam slapped the rump of her horse. 'Ha!' The horse took off, kicking up dirt behind it.

North. Aisha looked to the rising sun to get her bearings, then back at Maryam, who was standing dead still, watching her.

She really wasn't coming.

Aisha rode as hard as her fresh horse could manage. The next hour was a blurry haze of pounding hooves and shallow breaths. Her legs screamed in protest, but she didn't dare slow down. Fear drove her forwards.

Mira had buried herself in the saddlebag, letting out the occasional soft growl. Aisha didn't reassure her. She was too afraid that the scream lodged in her chest might escape if she spoke.

She was feeling hopeful of reaching the border when the road abruptly ended. 'Whoa.' She pulled the heaving, sweat-soaked animal to a stop as she took in the river before her. The banks were steep, the current fierce, and all that remained of the bridge were its two ends on either side. The rest had been washed away.

Her horse stepped sideways, nostrils flaring as it eyed the rushing water. Aisha didn't know what to do. She didn't even know if she was being pursued. All she knew was that Rafiq was dead and Maryam had chosen to remain behind.

'Ride. As fast as you can.'

She had to trust Maryam's vision.

Dismounting, she led her horse along the riverbank in search of another crossing. Her boots slipped on the damp ground. The minutes stretched, and her breathing quickened. If she couldn't find a crossing, her only option was to go back.

The river eventually narrowed upstream. A cluster of half-submerged stones formed a broken trail across the water. It was no bridge, but it was a chance.

Aisha pressed her forehead to the horse's damp neck and whispered a shaky prayer. Then, guiding the gelding with slow, coaxing steps, she began to cross.

Her boots skidded slightly on the slick surface, and the horse threw its head up behind her, snorting at the churning water. She kept a firm grip on the reins and murmured some reassurances. Mira let out a low, uncertain growl from the saddlebag, but Aisha kept her eyes focused on the path in front of her. Water rushed around her calves as she moved from one rock to the next, testing each one before shifting her weight. The current pulled at her cloak and skirts as her teeth began to chatter. She was halfway across when her foot landed on a moss-covered stone. It slid out from under her, and in an instant, she went under.

The cold hit like a slap, water closing over her with a roar. The weight of her cloak dragged her down, but she clung desperately to the reins with both hands. Miraculously, her horse held its ground. Aisha surfaced, coughing and heaving as she clawed her way back towards the rocks.

But then the current carried her away once more.

The horse threw its head up in response and took a trembling step backwards. Aisha used the opportunity to grab hold of a rock. Finally, she found some footing beneath the surface and climbed back up onto the crossing. Soaked and shaking, she crawled the rest of the way to the riverbank, the horse staggering after her. The moment she was clear of the water, the horse leapt up the bank, dragging her through the mud for a few paces before swinging around to face her.

'That went well,' Aisha muttered as she got to her feet.

She went to check on Mira, who wasn't happy. The cub whimpered, despite only having some water spray on her face.

Aisha looked down at her sodden clothes and boots full of water. At least they had made it across. She looked up at the sun again to get her bearings and wondered how much further the border was. After emptying the water from her boots and wringing out her clothes as best she could, she climbed stiffly into the saddle. Her muscles were sluggish from the cold, and her clothes stuck to her skin. The sun continued to rise, but it offered no warmth. She nudged the horse into motion, clutching the reins with numb fingers.

'Almost there,' she said—mostly for her own benefit.

The landscape began to slope down. Aisha urged the horse faster while checking over her shoulder every few minutes. Hills in every direction.

She rode for another half hour before a village appeared in the distance like a mirage: low stone homes and smoke curling into the air. As she got closer, she caught sight of a pale blue banner fluttering in the wind, a distinct desert rose symbol at its centre.

Avanid.

The relief came out as a sharp laugh. 'We did it.' She clapped her hand on the horse's neck, then nudged it forwards. 'My sisters are never going to believe this story.'

Another mile and she would be across the border.

She whipped her head around to look when she heard horses coming at a fast canter, dust lifting into the sky behind them. Her stomach dropped when she recognised the white surcoats banded with scarlet. Holy warriors. She sank her heels into the horse's sides, and the gelding responded with a surge of speed.

'Just a little further,' she told the horse, holding the reins so tightly her palms burned.

Mira's frightened cries were muffled by the rush of wind.

She risked another glance over her shoulder and saw that the warriors were closing in. Leaning low over the horse's neck, she said, 'Come on, come on…'

The gelding's hooves struck the road as they flew towards the village. A farmer in the fields turned at the sound, his hand lifting to shield his eyes from the sun. He looked from Aisha to the warriors behind her.

'Help me!' she shouted as loudly as she could. 'Please!'

The man dropped the plough he was holding and turned to shout in the other direction. Two more figures appeared. Aisha's horse stumbled on some uneven ground but recovered well, sides heaving as they reached the edge of the village. She continued towards the men, blindly hoping they would protect her. Her horse skidded to a halt in front of them. The tall man with the greying beard was holding an axe and looked ready to cut her down from the saddle.

'I'm Princess Aisha, and I need help,' she blurted.

The younger man looked from her mud-streaked face to her wet clothes. The man from the field came running over.

'We don't want trouble here,' he said, out of breath.

'She claims she's a princess,' the young man told him.

'I am.' She slid off her horse. 'I swear before the gods.'

The warriors were closing in.

A door creaked open nearby, and a woman stepped out of a house. Her hair was wrapped in a scarf, and flour dusted her forearms. Her gaze travelled from Aisha to the warriors riding towards them.

'I need help,' Aisha said, her voice cracking. 'I can pay you.'

The woman looked her over. 'Come inside.'

Aisha pulled Mira from the saddlebag and ran for the

house. 'Thank you,' she breathed when she reached the door.

'Get that horse to the stables,' the woman called to the younger man. 'Go on.' She turned to Aisha, frowning at the cub in her arms. 'Stay inside no matter what.' The door banged closed between them.

Aisha leaned against the wall, sliding to the ground. Her heart continued to thud against her aching ribs. Outside, she heard the horses pull up, then the voices of the riders, muffled and angry. They carried all the way to the house. Feeling brave, she pressed one eye to a crack in the wall.

'You think we're fools?' one warrior shouted. 'We saw her go in there.'

'Actually, I think you're trespassers,' the older man replied. 'You've no authority here.'

A door slammed, and another man appeared holding an axe. 'You heard him. On your way.'

More doors opened. Then another, and another. A chorus of villagers stepping up to protect their homes and one another. Someone was shoved. Someone cursed. A horse squealed. Then the warriors were mounting their horses and riding away.

Aisha leaned her head against the wall, exhaling a shaky breath. A minute later, the woman returned, closing the door behind her.

'They're gone,' she said, crossing her arms and looking down at Aisha. 'Why are you wet?'

Aisha swallowed. 'I went for a swim in the river.'

Frowning, the woman walked over and crouched down in front of her. Her eyes were steady and searching.

'The money's in my saddlebag,' Aisha said, holding Mira close.

The woman sighed as she scrutinised her. 'Are you really Princess Aisha?'

Aisha nodded. 'Yes.'

Her expression softened. 'Must have been some wedding.' She rose to her feet. 'We don't want your money. We want our kingdom back.'

Aisha's throat was coated in dust. 'We're working on it.'

The woman nodded slowly and looked out the window. 'Up you get. Let's get you dry and warm, then see about getting you home.'

Home.

She was going home.

CHAPTER 37

Incense hung heavy in the air of the temple—resin, sage, and some other scent Tariq couldn't place. Gruisean nobility sat in rows according to importance, something his mother had insisted on. Silence pressed down on Tariq as he stood in the centre, robed in ivory and deep blue. His back was straight, his features steady. Farrah stood nearby, still dressed in mourning black despite it being over a month since King Hamza had passed. Though she had her veil pulled back for the occasion.

It was Coronation Day.

Jamil stepped forwards, a carved staff in his hand. He looked at Tariq with grave intensity. 'This crown is not only inherited,' he began, his voice low and carrying. 'It is also earned. It is given. And it may be taken.'

Interesting way to open.

'Tariq, son of Hamza,' he continued, 'do you swear to govern with wisdom, to hold the good of Gruisea above your own ambition, and to shelter your people from harm?'

Tariq's voice was steady as he answered, 'I swear it before the gods.'

Jamil turned to the pedestal beside him, where the iron crown rested on blue velvet, and lifted it carefully. 'Then, by the authority of the temple and the will of our forebears, I name you king.'

The crown was placed on Tariq's head, and he could feel his mother exhale. Every noble in attendance bowed their heads in a silent nod of allegiance.

Jamil stepped back and lowered his staff. 'Rise in fire and rule in light, Tariq of Gruisea.'

Guests rose from their seats, responding in a unified cry, 'Long live King Tariq.'

Nothing moved on Tariq's face. Nothing moved inside him either.

It was his turn to speak. They were the same words spoken by every king before him. Assurances of peace, loyalty to tradition, and the promise of strength and prosperity. The nobles applauded politely, no doubt trying to figure out how much of his father lived on in him.

His mother was the first to approach, kissing the back of his hand, then touching her forehead to it. 'Your Majesty.' She straightened with what appeared to be pride in her eyes. 'Well done.'

Tariq bowed his head, his gaze drifting to the arched doors where sunlight was pouring in. Aisha should have been standing beside him. His queen.

'Your Majesty,' Kaidon said. 'I'll be right behind you.'

His mother looked towards the exit. 'As will I.'

Next came the procession from the temple in the heart of the capital to the castle. It wound its way through stone streets, which were lined with pennants and banners. People gathered, cheering and tossing petals in his path. Tariq sat atop his horse, waving at them. It was muscle memory more than spirit.

When he finally dismounted at the castle, there were more displays of obeisance and well-wishes as he made his way to the feast in the great hall. The room hadn't been used since his wedding day. Long tables overflowed with meat, rice, pomegranate stews, and honey-soaked pastries. Cups were filled and refilled, servants moving between the guests with military precision. Laughter rang out. Cups clinked. A musician played.

Tariq sat at the head table, his mother on one side and Jamil on the other. He barely ate but sipped frequently from his cup, welcoming the numbness the wine provided. He responded politely when addressed and accepted every blessing with gratitude. And when dancers entered the hall, veiled and spinning, he watched them without seeing.

One thought persisted through the numbness.

Aisha.

It should have been a day for both of them.

Aisha.

He sat through the first toast.

Aisha.

Then the second.

Aisha.

He was finally free to leave.

Farrah reached for his hand as he stood. 'Stay a little longer. They will notice if—'

'Let them notice.' He gently pulled out of her grasp and walked out of the hall, Kaidon a few paces behind him.

They passed through the corridors, where guards bowed and servants stepped aside. Tariq slowed as they neared his quarters, waiting for Kaidon to catch up.

'Tomorrow, I get to work,' Tariq said.

The guard nodded. 'I figured as much.'

'We start with the mines, as planned.'

'Remove every child under the age of sixteen.'

'No exceptions,' Tariq said firmly. 'Every single one of them will return to their schooling.'

'And families will be compensated through the transition. Don't worry. I've not forgotten the plan.' He flicked his gaze to Tariq. 'And you're prepared for the backlash?'

Tariq looked over his shoulder, half expecting to find his mother behind him. 'They'll adapt.'

They came to a stop.

'Then we hit them with the Ashwaq Mine closure,' Kaidon said, crossing his arms, 'sending people spiralling once more.'

'Correct.'

Footsteps approached down the corridor, and even without looking, Tariq knew they were his mother's. Her gown trailed like a shadow, and her veil was lowered once again. She stopped before them, looking between the two men with blatant suspicion.

'Commander,' she said. 'Might I have a private word with the king?'

Kaidon inclined his head. 'Of course, Your Majesty.' He gave Tariq a look that translated to 'Good luck' before leaving them.

Farrah waited until he was far away before speaking again.

'What is it, Mother?' Tariq asked, already losing patience. 'It has been a long day.'

She studied him for a moment. 'First, congratulations on an exceptional coronation. I have heard nothing but praise from everyone I have spoken to.'

'And second?' Tariq asked.

'With the coronation now behind us, I need to know what you plan to do about the failed marriage.'

It took all his effort not to recoil at her words.

'The nobles are whispering, and soon the foreign courts will follow. With the crown secure, you must annul the marriage quickly and reassert control of the narrative before the Emperor twists it to his advantage.'

Tariq had known the conversation was coming, but that didn't mean he wanted to have it. 'The Emperor will say and do whatever he pleases, regardless of my actions.'

'At least give the people something else to talk about. Why not take a new bride? Create a new alliance. Show people that you have a plan.'

'I do have a plan.'

Her eyes moved between his. 'One that you plan on sharing with your council, I hope.'

'Yes. First thing tomorrow morning.'

Farrah studied him a moment. 'You cannot remain married to the woman who killed your father and king. Please tell me you understand that.'

She was right, of course. He couldn't stay married to Aisha. The union was beyond broken, and staying in it would ultimately damage trust with his people. And yet the annulment seemed so… final.

'You cannot let sentiment dictate your reign. You are king now.'

'I am well aware of my position.'

She looked doubtful. 'Thank the gods the marriage was never consummated. It should be a straightforward process.'

Tariq made the mistake of looking down.

Farrah narrowed her gaze. 'The marriage was not consummated because there was no opportunity between the ceremony and your father's death. Correct?'

That part was true. 'Correct.'

Her eyes sharpened like a hawk sighting prey. 'I am well aware of the visits to her chamber that took place at all hours of the night before the wedding. But we are going to forget all about those, yes?'

Those moments were burned into his brain and weren't going anywhere. 'My memories are one of the few things you can't control.'

Farrah pressed her lips together. 'My point is, no one else need know. Do you understand me?'

Tariq simply blinked.

'You will annul the marriage,' she went on. 'Quietly, respectfully. Let the scribes handle it. Then you will never speak of her again. Understood?'

He was agitated now. 'You're forgetting yourself.'

'No. You are forgetting how inexperienced you are.

This is no longer a matter of the heart. This is governance. Now get some rest. As you said, it has been a big day.' She left before he could respond.

Tariq remained there, every muscle tense, until she disappeared from sight.

CHAPTER 38

Aisha lay in a hammock in the garden, an arm draped over a dozing Mira. The cub had grown considerably in the month they had been in Avanid. Her sleek, heavy body sprawled over Aisha's legs, a blanket of muscle and fur. Aisha scratched behind Mira's ear absent-mindedly, eyes half-lidded against the midday sun.

One month home with her family.

One month without word from Maryam.

One month without *him*.

It had taken three days to get from the border to the palace, but at least they had travelled in a wagon instead of on horseback. She had fallen, crying, into her sisters' arms when she'd finally made it. Even Zara's composure had cracked that day. Her father had cupped her face in trembling hands, his eyes watery as he looked at her. Omar hadn't left her side for three days, sleeping in her bed with Mira, just like when he was little.

Despite the soft landing, the ache in her chest lingered, worsening whenever she thought of Tariq for too long.

She wondered if he missed her. While she stood by her choices, she carried the weight of them everywhere.

Lilah appeared at the edge of the garden, barefoot, holding a fig in one hand and a book in the other. She used the book to shield her eyes as she approached. 'There you are,' she said, sitting on the edge of the hammock and swinging it gently.

'I can't move until Mira does.'

'Oh, that's the rule?'

Aisha nodded.

Lilah reached over to stroke the leopard, her expression turning serious. 'But you're all right?'

Aisha lowered her arm. 'Yes.'

'Because you're allowed to feel bad about the empire thinking you're a murderer. And you're allowed to miss him.' A sigh slipped from Lilah. 'You're not required to put on a brave face for our benefit.'

Aisha didn't reply straight away due to the lump in her throat. 'It's not for your benefit. It's for my sanity.' Her arm went over her eyes again. 'I'm out here trying not to drown.'

Lilah held the half-eaten fig out to her. Aisha took a bite from it and passed it back.

'To be clear, we have no intention of letting you drown,' Lilah said.

Aisha swallowed her mouthful, then held her hand out for another bite.

'Finish it,' Lilah said, passing it to her. 'I'll get another.'

'A pity fig. Perfect,' Aisha said as she took it.

The sound of footsteps coming at a run broke the moment. Safiya burst into view.

'What is it?' Lilah called to her.

'There's a courier here,' she shouted. 'He has a letter from Gruisea.'

It felt like someone had thrown a pail of water over Aisha. She climbed off the hammock, Mira grunting in protest as she tumbled off her lap. This was it. The annulment they had all been waiting for.

'Has someone told Baba?' Lilah asked.

Safiya was already running back in the other direction. 'Zara's fetching him now.'

Aisha and Lilah made their way to the front of the palace, arriving just as Safiya took the envelope from the courier. Aisha eyed the Gruisean seal as they waited for their father to arrive. Losing patience, Safiya held it up to the light, trying to see the words written inside.

'Stop,' Lilah said, taking it from her.

Safiya snatched it back and held it out of reach. A throat cleared. The three of them turned to see Zara and Bilal approaching.

Safiya immediately extended the envelope towards their father, who tutted as he stepped up slowly and took it. He broke the wax and pulled out the thick, folded parchment. Aisha leaned forwards slightly, but a glance from Zara had her straightening again.

Bilal's lips moved soundlessly for a moment as his eyes scanned the page. Then, finally, he read it aloud:

'To the esteemed house of Nazari,

Let it be known that, on the first day of the month, the Crown of Gruisea passed peacefully to its rightful heir.

Tariq, son of Hamza, has been crowned king in the Temple of the First Light in Gruisea's capital.

In accordance with the rites of our ancestors, he was named and confirmed by the sectarian and the noble houses present.

Gruisea endures, and its future is secure.

Faithfully,

Commander Kaidon ibn Gharan, Royal Guard of the Crown

On behalf of His Majesty King Tariq of Gruisea.'

When Bilal finished reading, he slowly lowered the letter. Silence followed. Aisha stared at the page in his hands, confused that there wasn't more. It couldn't just be news of the coronation.

'So…' Safiya said, equally as confused. 'Is the annulment on the back or…?'

Bilal turned the page, even though they all knew it was blank. 'That is all it says,' he confirmed.

Lilah looked at Aisha. 'I guess you're still the Queen of Gruisea.'

'They're likely working through formalities one at a time,' Zara said. 'I assure you the annulment is coming.'

'If my spouse killed my father,' Safiya said, 'I'd hand him the annulment right before his execution—out of spite.'

The tightness in Aisha's chest intensified.

'It's clear he can't bring himself to end the marriage,' Lilah said.

Bilal reached out and patted Aisha's arm. 'You do not need a piece of parchment to move forwards.'

She needed *something*, because she was entirely stuck.

Bilal slid the letter back into its envelope, kissed the top of Aisha's head, and turned to go inside. Safiya and Lilah dispersed, leaving Aisha and Zara standing there.

'Walk with me,' Zara said.

Nodding, Aisha followed her.

They walked in silence for a few minutes, until they found themselves beneath a corridor of trees.

'Self-pity won't rebuild Avanid,' Zara began. She stopped walking and turned to face Aisha. 'You should be grateful he got you out, because any other king would have happily watched you burn under those circum-stances.'

'I know that.'

'Do you?' Zara gave her a doubtful look. 'You seem to have forgotten that the entire empire thinks you're a king killer. We're no closer to any sort of independence. In fact, we're further from it. We're one future queen down.'

Aisha made a face. 'Ouch.'

'Who in their right mind would marry you?'

Her sister's words stung, but they were true.

'Unfortunately, we don't have time for broken hearts,' Zara said, softening her voice. 'If we don't act fast, there will be nothing left of Avanid to save.'

'I know that,' Aisha said, guilt creeping in.

'The palace is purely symbolic at this point.'

Aisha made an exasperated noise. 'I know. I failed. Do you think I don't realise how dire things are after being pursued across Montia? I've been carrying the weight of my failure since I got here.'

'Then carry it forwards.' Zara took hold of Aisha's

hands. 'Lilah must be the focus now. We need an alliance secured, and it needs to be the most spectacular alliance we can fathom.'

Carry it forwards. Move on. Forget all about him. These were all variations of the same nightmare. Aisha's heart and mind refused to let go. It was the plan none of them wanted but had all agreed to. 'You know I'll help in any way I can.'

Zara squeezed her hands before letting go. 'I appreciate that. I shall leave you to think on it.'

Aisha forced a smile, holding it until Zara left. She was underwater, drowning.

And she didn't know how much longer she could hold her breath.

CHAPTER 39

Smoke drifted from tall burners in the corners of the reception chamber. Tariq sat at the head of the crescent-shaped table, dressed in a blue robe trimmed with orange thread, the same formal robe his father used to wear when greeting foreign dignitaries. His mother sat at his right, wearing colour again, her mourning clothes finally packed away.

The Slevaborg delegation sat opposite, wearing their bold national colours. Their spokesman, a fox-faced man named Hadrik, had spoken at length about trade, tariffs, and piracy in the southern passage. Tariq wondered if they mentioned the piracy in every court they visited, just to keep people afraid. He listened with the detachment of a man observing a game he didn't care to play.

'We received your correspondence regarding next month's reduction in supply,' Hadrik said, his stare meaningful. 'We trust this is temporary and Gruisea's commitment to the empire's supply chain has not been impacted by the transfer of power?'

Tariq held his gaze. 'Gruisea remains committed to *Gruisea*. We have some internal reforms underway.'

Hadrik leaned forwards. 'Such as?'

'For a start, our mine in Ashwaq will soon be decommissioned.'

A short silence followed, and Tariq made no effort to fill it. It was better to let everyone sit with the discomfort.

'That site accounts for a quarter of your limestone output,' the younger envoy said, as if Tariq was unaware.

'The yield is declining.'

Hadrik shifted atop his cushion. 'I suspect that is because the number of workers has been reduced.'

'Children,' Tariq said. 'Children have been removed entirely.'

Farrah cleared her throat. 'His Majesty was eager to see them return to their education.'

'And, of course, the men also now have more flexibility, including the option of pursuing other occupations.'

Hadrik made a low, thoughtful sound, as if tasting something. 'We understand the pressures of domestic change. However, sudden drops in output have a ripple effect, and Slevaborg has infrastructure projects and deals in motion throughout the empire.'

The audacity to mention those deals—the ones Gruisea should have been making directly.

'We'll negotiate new quotas.' Tariq's tone was neutral but final. 'Which won't be at the pace you've grown accustomed to.'

His mother was doing her best to remain quiet, which was the condition under which she was allowed to attend the meeting.

The envoys exchanged a glance before Hadrik said, 'We will convey your position to the imperial office.' He adjusted the sleeve of his robe. 'Though I must say, I am a little surprised by all this, especially given the state of your alliance with Avanid. I thought you would be falling over yourselves to keep your only trading partner happy.'

Tariq inclined his head. 'You needn't concern yourself with Gruisea's relationship with Avanid. All you need to know is that we no longer intend to break our backs, or the backs of our children, for the benefit of others.'

Hadrik gave him the longest, darkest stare. Then, nodding, he reached for a pomegranate seed and rolled it between his fingers. 'Before we finish, the Emperor wanted me to once again express his condolences and despair at your father's passing. I pray you find comfort in the fact that nightbarrow is very effective. Quick and quiet—or so I have heard.'

Farrah stiffened, prompting Tariq to look at her. She sat utterly still, unblinking, her cup hovering in the air.

'Apologies, Your Majesty,' Hadrik said. 'I should have thought before mentioning your late husband's death. It must still be quite raw.'

Tariq's gaze remained on his mother, noting the tension in her jaw and the way her hand had gone white around the stem of her cup.

What had he missed?

Farrah finally blinked, and that single motion seemed to bring her back to life. 'Yes, nightbarrow is indeed effective.'

Then it hit him. Nightbarrow had never been

mentioned. Certainly not to a foreign envoy. The man knew something he shouldn't have.

Tariq sat back, watching the man through new eyes.

'The fact that his murderer escaped Gruisea unscathed must be devastating to all of you,' Hadrik continued. 'Did you ever find out how she got out of the castle?'

It was clear by his arrogant expression that he already knew the answer to that.

'We know she departed with her attendant' was all Farrah said.

His mother had never asked Tariq directly if he had smuggled Aisha out of Gruisea, because like Hadrik, she also knew the answer.

Hadrik's penetrating gaze shifted between the two of them. 'Well, I think we have imposed enough on you for one day.' He rose to his feet with a practised bow, the others following. 'We thank you for your time, Your Majesties.' Then to Tariq, 'And we look forward to seeing the revised trade draft.'

Tariq got to his feet, inclining his head in place of a reply.

A few more courtesies were exchanged, then the men left, the heavy doors closing behind them. Tariq's eyes remained on the chamber doors as silence filled the room. For a long moment, neither he nor his mother spoke. When he finally turned to her, he noticed that her hands were clasped tightly in front of her. He could almost see the threads forming in her mind behind that steady mask.

He struggled to ask the question. 'Have the medical records been amended since we met with the council?' he asked, already knowing the answer. 'Because the report I saw made no mention of nightbarrow.'

Farrah dragged her gaze to his. 'No.'

'The report included a list of herbs in Lilah's possession, but stated that the exact poison used couldn't be identified, correct?'

She nodded. 'Correct. There was no mention of nightbarrow.'

Tariq took an unsteady step back from her as all the pieces fell into place.

Aisha.

Her face flashed in his mind. Her expression when she had confessed, delivering the lie with such conviction. She had truly come prepared.

He swallowed, finding the inside of his mouth dry. 'I knew she didn't do it,' he whispered. He had felt it all along, but he hadn't been able to do a damn thing about it. Now his mother knew it too. Grief and fury stirred in her eyes.

'I have to go,' he said, heading for the chamber door.

His mother didn't try to stop him.

Outside, Kaidon straightened, watched him march by, then jogged to catch up with him. 'That bad, huh?'

The corridors of the palace were quieter than usual, but Tariq walked as if he were being chased.

Kaidon fell into step beside him, reading his mood. 'What the hell happened in there that has you in such a state?'

'I want you to find out everything you can about the herb nightbarrow,' Tariq said without preamble. 'Every known use. Every known source. Who handles it.'

'Understood. Am I permitted to ask why?'

Tariq stopped at the doors to his private quarters, a hand pressed to the carved wood. 'She didn't do it.'

'Who didn't do what?'

He took a few painful breaths before looking at him. 'Aisha didn't kill my father.'

Pity flashed on Kaidon's face. He stepped back from the door. 'I'll bring you everything I find.'

It was late in the afternoon when the knock came at Tariq's door. He rose from behind his desk, where he had been trying to work since the meeting—and failing. 'Come in.'

Kaidon entered, looking windblown and still in his riding cloak.

'Well?' Tariq asked.

The guard closed the door behind him before launching into his findings. 'It's indigenous to the highlands of Slevaborg. We don't grow it here, and trade was banned nearly forty years ago. Even on the black market, it's rare.'

Tariq leaned on the desk, waiting for him to continue.

'If someone wanted to smuggle it in, they'd have to know how to dry it properly first. It rots within hours unless treated using a very specific process.'

The tips of Tariq's fingers pressed against the table. 'What sort of process?'

'That's the interesting part.' Kaidon walked closer. 'No

one knows. The method's kept by the imperial alchemists in Slevaborg.'

Tariq's mind raced. 'Then it's highly unlikely that Aisha or her sisters would have access to the herb or know how to process it if they did.'

'Slevaborg alchemists sharing their secrets with coven-weavers? It would never happen,' Kaidon said.

Tariq exhaled, slow and steady. The relief was as heavy as all the lies. But then the anger hit. The Emperor had found a way to kill his father, destroyed his marriage, and severed their alliance with Avanid, all without blame or consequence.

'I gather from all this that the delegates knew things about your father's death they shouldn't have,' Kaidon said.

Tariq closed his eyes for a long moment. When he opened them again, his vision sharpened. 'We were duped.'

Kaidon crossed his arms with a sigh. 'So what are you going to do about it?'

'Stop playing the Emperor's game.' He straightened. 'Halt all trade with Slevaborg, effective immediately.'

Kaidon appeared taken aback by this. 'What?'

'You heard me.'

'That will be viewed as an act of open defiance.'

'That's exactly what it is.' Tariq knew it would send shock waves through the empire, but he didn't care. He moved around his desk and sat on the edge of it. 'Let him feel it. Let the whole empire feel it.' His mind was no longer heavy with doubt, but with something far more dangerous: resolve. 'Fetch the scribe. I have some messages to deliver.'

CHAPTER 40

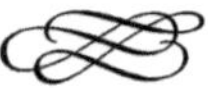

Aisha noticed the change in Zara the moment the guard announced Nasir's arrival at midday. It was subtle—a smoothing of her braid and a quick glance at the brass mirror mounted beside the archway—but for someone like Zara, it was telling. She stood a little straighter, her fingers laced neatly behind her back. Aisha saw a flicker of something very close to anticipation cross her face.

'Are you all right?' Aisha asked as they walked to the audience chamber together.

Zara glanced sideways at her. 'Why do you ask?'

Aisha gave a small shrug. 'You just seem a little on edge.'

'I'm always on edge when there's news from Slevaborg.'

Aisha let the subject go.

Nasir entered the chamber with the same serious expression he always wore, because he never delivered good news. His two guards waited for him by the door.

'Your Highnesses,' he said with a small bow.

'High Verran,' Zara replied, addressing him formally.

His gaze cut briefly to Aisha. 'Forgive the intrusion.'

The irony of his statement was seemingly lost on him.

'Should I send for some refreshments?' Aisha asked.

He shook his head. 'Please don't trouble yourself. I'll get straight to the reason for my visit.'

They waited, trying not to appear anxious.

'I wanted to inform you that Gruisea has recently cut all trade with Slevaborg. Every route.'

Zara's brow lifted. 'Oh.'

'Why?' Aisha blurted, stepping forwards.

Zara levelled her with a stare that had her moving back. She tried again. 'I mean, what reason have they given?'

'No official reason was given.' Nasir paused. 'Though there have been some rather big changes there of late. The closure of Ashwaq Mine and the banning of child labour, to name a few.'

Aisha's hands went to her chest, where her token had once sat. 'He actually did it.'

Both Nasir and Zara looked at her.

A laugh escaped Aisha. 'He got the children out of the mines just like he said he would.' The smile fell from her face when she saw Zara's pointed stare. 'Apologies.'

Zara turned her attention back to Nasir. 'What has the Emperor's response been to the halt in trade?'

'You know I can't share those details, but I'm sure you can imagine. There will be a push for Avanid, along with other kingdoms, not to engage with them.'

'Isolate them, you mean?' Aisha said, unable to hide her irritation.

Nasir looked at her. 'I can't imagine that will be too much of an issue for Avanid given the current state of your relationship with Gruisea. You're wanted for the murder of King Hamza, are you not?'

Something in his tone and expression hinted that he didn't believe it.

'If you do have any ties to Gruisea at present, I recommend severing them,' he said. 'Or you risk provoking the Emperor.'

Of course *he* would say that.

'I'm sure you understand that we make decisions in the best interests of Avanid,' Zara said, feigning the freedom to do so.

Nasir frowned. 'Perhaps you can tell that to Zahvik when he arrives. He's on his way to Khorasan Palace.'

'What?' the two sisters said in unison.

'That's why I came here—to warn you.' Nasir looked between them. 'He'll be here in the morning.'

Aisha's mouth fell open. 'Why on earth would he think he's welcome here? The man tried to *burn me*.'

'And you murdered a king,' Nasir replied. 'With a potion.'

Aisha rolled her eyes. 'Clever use of "potion" there. Sounds much more covenweavery than poison.'

Looking heavenwards, Zara gestured for calm.

'We don't want him here,' Aisha said. 'Tell him that.'

'He already knows,' Nasir replied calmly. 'He'll be coming to you under the guise of a pardon, but make no mistake, he wants loyalty in return.' He looked between them. 'If you trade with Gruisea, you'll fall with Gruisea.'

Neither Aisha nor Zara spoke for a moment. Aisha was trying to imagine her father receiving Zahvik into his *home*. How on earth were they going to protect him from the harm this visit would cause? Khorasan Palace was the only place he felt safe.

'I wanted to give you some time to prepare,' Nasir said, his voice quieter this time. He gave a short, formal bow. 'Good day to you both.'

Zara bowed her head but didn't say anything as he turned and left, his guards following him out. The two sisters stood in stunned silence.

Aisha was first to speak, her voice a whisper. 'We don't have to let him in, do we?'

Brushing an invisible strand of hair back from her eyes, Zara replied, 'Of course we do.' Her eyes searched Aisha's. 'But we can be smart about it. Keep Omar well away from him for a start. We'll tell Zahvik he's unwell.'

'And Yasmin.'

A nod. 'And Yasmin.' Zara exhaled and looked around the room. 'We'll need to find a way to get Baba there—at least for part of it.'

Aisha nodded, barely.

'Let's not panic,' Zara said. 'Let's prepare.'

They began walking slowly towards the door.

'If he wants to pardon you, great,' Zara continued. 'We'll take the pardon.'

They exited the chamber and continued down the corridor.

'Even Nasir admits he's not coming to pardon me,' Aisha said.

'Of course not. He's coming to remind us who holds the leash.' When they reached the staircase, they started to climb. 'I'll leave you to break the news to Safiya and Lilah.' She drew a slow breath. 'I'll go tell Baba.'

* * *

The palace was quiet. Too quiet. Even the fountains seemed to hush as the gates creaked open and Zahvik's carriage entered the palace grounds. His visit had caused complete chaos as everyone scrambled to prepare. Now they all stood in practised formation, guards lining the marble paths with the Nazari family at the top of the steps, dressed in ceremonial silks—minus Omar and Yasmin. They were under guard at the far end of the palace.

Aisha leaned forwards to check on her father. He stood with his spine straight and hands balled into fists. His face twitched, and small beads of sweat were already forming across his brow. Zara had her arm threaded through his, just in case. She looked in Aisha's direction, giving her the smallest nod, which was meant to reassure her.

'Here he comes,' Safiya said.

The procession was completely unnecessary for someone of his rank. Anyone would have thought the Emperor himself was coming. Boots struck stone in perfect rhythm as two rows of scarlet-cloaked holy warriors marched towards them. Behind them were the banner-bearers with their bright red flags embroidered with a black sun. Then, finally, the carriage, six horses pulling it when two would do. It rolled to a stop at the bottom of the stairs. A footman positioned a stool before opening the door. Then, from a dark hole, Zahvik emerged.

Aisha took in his smug, clean-shaven face, and a familiar anger rose inside her. But it dissipated when a second figure stepped out of the carriage.

Maryam.

The chains connecting her hands and feet clinked softly as she stepped out. Aisha's stomach turned at the sight. She was dressed in the pale grey uniform of an imperial servant, and her once-vibrant eyes remained locked on the ground because she wasn't permitted to look up.

Aisha instinctively moved towards her, but Safiya grabbed a firm hold of her arm before she had even taken one step.

'That's exactly what he wants,' she whispered. 'Don't give it to him.'

Aisha slowly moved back into line with the rest of her family.

Zahvik made his way to the foot of the steps, then paused to say a prayer. When he opened his eyes, his gaze moved over them one by one before settling on Bilal.

'Your Majesty,' he said as he climbed the steps, Maryam following him silently.

The king merely inclined his head.

Since everyone at the palace had objected to having him in their home, Zara had made the decision to host him in the garden, where the scent of citrus might drown out the stench of evil.

Aisha couldn't take her eyes off Maryam.

'This way, Your Holiness,' Zara said when he reached the top, taking immediate control of the meeting before he extended his hand and expected anyone to kiss it. She led the way to the garden.

Low couches had been arranged with far more space between them than was necessary. Dates and sugared almonds sat on a polished tray next to a steaming pot of tea. These were clearly refreshments for a *short* visit.

Zahvik sat, crossing one leg over the other as he looked around. Maryam stood behind him, the length of her chains clinking softly as they settled around her feet.

Aisha was desperate for Maryam to look up so she could look into her eyes, but she kept her chin firmly tucked to her chest and her gaze pinned to the ground. Aisha buried her hands in her lap to hide the angry tremble in them. It was clear Zahvik wanted to remind them who was in control. Maryam was an example of what happens when a woman steps out of line.

'Tea?' Zara asked.

Zahvik nodded. 'Thank you.'

Zara poured it and placed it down in front of him. Maryam stepped forwards and carefully picked up the cup. She sniffed the tea, then took a sip. A moment later, she handed the cup to Zahvik with a bow. The chains barely rattled as she returned to her place behind him. He didn't speak to her or acknowledge her in any way.

It wasn't unreasonable for him to think the Nazari

family might try to poison him after everything he had done. The thought had definitely crossed Aisha's mind.

Aisha glanced at Lilah, who looked as distressed as she felt.

'What is the purpose of your visit?' Bilal asked.

Zahvik took a sip of tea before replying. 'I came here for two reasons.' He looked up. 'First, Gruisea's recent actions have created some trading turbulence, and unfortunately, such turbulence can be problematic for the whole empire. I wanted to let you know that the Emperor will be stationing ships at your ports to ensure Avanid's coastline is protected.'

Bilal shifted in his chair. 'Gruisea poses no threat to Avanid.'

'I would be very surprised if that is true given your daughter killed their king.'

Safiya couldn't contain her agitation. 'The actions you're taking sound an awful lot like a blockade.'

Zahvik turned his gaze to her. 'You have no army of your own. You should be grateful for the Emperor's ongoing protection.'

Aisha almost laughed at the ridiculousness of that statement. The Emperor was the reason they no longer had an army.

'You cannot assert control over our harbours without my consent,' Bilal said.

Everyone looked in his direction. Aisha couldn't have been more proud. For a brief moment, she glimpsed the man he was before losing his queen.

'Consent is a luxury in times of unrest,' Zahvik replied.

'This is just a precaution—with Avanid being so vulnerable and all.'

Bilal's knuckles turned white on his knees. 'And the second thing? You said there were two.'

'Ah, yes.' He placed the cup down. 'I am prepared to pardon Princess Aisha for the heinous crime she committed in order to safeguard our alliance.'

The silence that followed rang in Aisha's ears. Did he actually believe they considered Slevaborg an ally? Perhaps he wanted to give that impression to Gruisea, which suggested Tariq had successfully poked the bear.

'The thing is,' Zara began, 'Avanid has its own ties to Gruisea.'

A patronising smirk came and went on Zahvik's face. 'If you are referring to Princess Aisha's infamous one-day marriage—'

'It's Queen Aisha,' Aisha said, surprising even herself. 'Whoever told you the marriage only lasted one day was either ill-informed or has intentionally misled you.'

Bilal pulled out a handkerchief and touched it to his brow.

'Forgive me,' Zahvik said, his voice silky and low. 'One would assume the marriage ended the moment you *killed* King Hamza.'

'There has been no annulment.' She was too angry to concede. 'And history has shown us that some crowns grow sharper the longer they're worn.'

Maryam looked up at that. It was brief, subtle, but when her eyes met Aisha's, all the hairs on her arms rose. Zahvik must have sensed it, because he glanced over his shoulder for the first time. Maryam's gaze dropped the moment he started to move, a picture of obedience once more. Aisha was desperate to speak to Maryam, but there simply wasn't a way.

Bilal's gaze had drifted to the palace walls. 'We cannot lose any more.'

Aisha's heart twisted as she looked at him.

After a few seconds, Bilal blinked, as if startled by something, and his brow creased with confusion. 'Why are we all outside?'

Zara immediately rose from her seat. 'This heat,' she said smoothly. 'It certainly takes its toll. Come, Baba. You have that meeting to prepare for.' She gently took his arm to help him up. 'Forgive us, Your Holiness. My sisters will see you out.'

Bilal didn't resist as she led him away, and he didn't look in Zahvik's direction again.

The sectarian watched him until he was out of sight. 'Caring for family is very important.' He paused. 'Especially when they are *so* fragile.'

Safiya bit down on her lip.

'We thank you for the pardon,' Lilah said, rising. 'Was there anything else you needed to discuss before departing?'

Taking the hint, Zahvik slowly stood and straightened his robes. 'I think I have said all that needs to be said.'

Aisha's gaze flicked to Maryam again. She stood like a beautiful statue of a prisoner, both composed and defeated. Aisha wanted to demand the chains be removed —or at least say her name aloud. But if Zahvik had brought her as bait, as provocation, then she refused to give him something else he could weaponise.

Zahvik began his walk back through the garden, and Maryam followed like a shadow. He passed close to Aisha, his last chance to try to intimidate her. Aisha refused to look at him. She couldn't tolerate his smug face a moment longer. But she did look at Maryam. She was so close that Aisha could touch her.

In a moment, she would be gone.

Acting on an impulse, Aisha reached for her, fingers closing around Maryam's wrist. The chains stilled, and time cracked open.

The scent of salt hit first, sharp and thick. The creak of wood straining against water and sails flapping under a black sky. When she looked up, she saw a red flag with a black sun.

A shoreline appeared.

A shoreline covered in bodies. Dozens. Hundreds, maybe. Holy warriors alongside soldiers in blue uniforms, strewn across a blood-soaked beach like discarded dolls.

Aisha returned with a jolt and found Lilah at her side, holding tightly to her arm. Maryam was walking away.

'This way,' Safiya said, keeping Zahvik focused on leaving.

He passed beneath the garden arch and disappeared from view. Just before Maryam crossed the threshold, she looked back at Aisha. Then she was gone.

Aisha swayed, then sank onto the couch, unable to stay upright.

Lilah sat with her, keeping hold of her arm. 'Have you lost your mind? He could have seen you. Aisha, he's a sectarian.'

'I'm sorry,' Aisha breathed. 'I had to see.' Her tongue felt numb.

Lilah wore a worried expression. 'And what did you see?'

Aisha swallowed a few times, her gaze flicking cautiously to the archway. 'I saw… warships.'

'Warships?'

'War,' Aisha said, recalling the bodies on the beach. 'I saw war.'

Lilah searched Aisha's eyes. 'Here? In Avanid?'

Aisha shook her head. 'No.' Though she had recognised the beach in her vision.

Lilah waited.

'Gruisea.' Aisha's voice cracked as she spoke. 'Slevaborg's going to attack Gruisea.'

CHAPTER 41

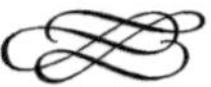

Tariq stood atop the northern wall, letting the wind cool him down after his training session. He was watching the movement in the barracks below. He hadn't meant to stay long. Guards had come and gone in the time he was there, giving him a wide berth as they changed posts.

He was brought back from his daydreaming by the sound of his mother's footsteps, measured and composed.

'There you are,' Farrah said. 'Anyone would think you are avoiding court.'

'Come look at this,' he said, keeping his gaze forwards.

She approached the embrasure. 'What exactly am I looking at?'

He closed his eyes. 'Listen.'

She fell quiet.

The chaotic noise of the barracks drifted up to them. It was the sound of his childhood. He used to watch the soldiers from the walls when he was young, imagining what it would be like to fight alongside them, knowing they would protect him at any cost.

'It is not a sound I thought I would hear again in my lifetime,' Farrah admitted.

Opening his eyes, they watched and listened together for a moment.

Eventually, Farrah turned to him. 'The stewards need your signature on the salt tariffs.'

'I'm sure it can wait until this afternoon.'

'It *is* the afternoon.'

He looked up at the sun, then at his mother. They had barely spoken since the visit from the Slevaborg delegates. There were so many things they needed to say but hadn't.

Farrah let out a soft breath. 'I am pleased to see soldiers back in the barracks, but we need trade to continue if we are to fund this new army of yours.'

'New army of *ours*,' he corrected, eyes returning to the barracks.

'With so much uncertainty, you really must be seen at court,' she continued. 'They need to know you are reliable in order to trust your leadership.'

He rested his forearms on the stone embrasure. 'I've shown more strength and leadership in the past few months than my father did in the last five years of his reign. The only person doubting me right now is *you*.'

She didn't respond straight away. 'It might seem like doubt, but it is, in fact, worry.' She studied him a moment. 'You forget that as well as being one of your advisers, I am also your mother.'

He continued to stare straight ahead.

'Have you written to her?' she asked after a long silence.

The question caught him off-guard. He turned to her, eyebrows drawn together.

'Your wife,' Farrah said, as if it needed clarification. 'Have you written to her?'

Hearing the term 'your wife' was too much. 'No.'

'Why not?'

The conversation was starting to sound like a mother-son talk. It was unfamiliar territory for him. 'Because she's settled and safe in Avanid.' He shifted his weight. 'And I've no intention of disrupting that.'

Farrah's expression softened. She didn't respond right away, instead looking back at the barracks as she gathered her next words. 'You miss her, deeply.'

Tariq's throat tightened, and he wasn't sure what to do with his hands suddenly.

'I thought it was infatuation. A distraction,' she continued. 'But then I saw you start to trust her. I saw you *love* her.' Another pause. 'It was easier to believe she had fooled you, cast some sort of spell, than accept a relationship I did not understand, one I deemed inappropriate because it was not my experience of marriage.'

He didn't speak for a moment. 'You let that man *burn* her.'

A solemn nod. 'Yes.'

Another silence stretched. This one felt tired.

'I cannot change how I have handled things up to this point,' Farrah said. 'But I can see now what I refused to see then.' She waited until he looked at her. 'That despite the family she came from, and all that has transpired, she might, in fact, be the right queen for Gruisea.' Her voice softened. 'And perhaps… the right wife for you.'

His shoulders fell an inch. There was a strange relief in hearing her finally say it. For the first time in his life, it felt like she was seeing *him* instead of just the crown on his head. 'I appreciate everything you just said, but I won't disrupt her peace and safety.'

Farrah moved closer to him. 'No one is safe with Emperor Hassan in power. Least of all Aisha, whose father is completely incompetent in his role.'

'Mother—'

'I know you do not wish to hear it, but you know it is the truth. The only thing holding that kingdom together is the eldest sister and the memory of a great queen who will eventually be forgotten.' When Tariq didn't dispute it, she added, 'Aisha belongs here, at your side. As the Queen of Gruisea.'

Tariq stared at his mother. He hadn't allowed himself the luxury of such thoughts. There was only so much disappointment he could bear. But now hope seeped through the cracks of his restraint, drowning everything else out.

'You are clearly committed to fixing this kingdom,' Farrah said, 'but perhaps you should fix your marriage first.' She released a heavy breath. 'I will not interfere with your relationship again. You have my word.'

Tariq searched her eyes for any sign of insincerity, but all he saw was an exhausted mother—trying. 'She may not want to come back.'

Farrah nodded. 'That is a possibility. There is only one way to find out.' She turned and left.

Tariq remained on the wall, the wind pressing at his back. He hardly felt it. What filled him now was a quieter force. Aisha's laugh came to mind—not the polite one she offered at court, but the real one that took over her entire face. He'd made it his personal mission to earn that sound again and again. He remembered the way she looked at him when no one else was watching, with curiosity and love. She had a way of seeing every truth he tried to bury. If he concentrated really hard, he could almost feel the weight of her fingertips on his wrist.

Her absence suddenly felt unbearable.

Tariq released a long, steady breath. It was time to stop watching the distance and start closing it.

It was time to make a plan to bring his wife home.

CHAPTER 42

The tea on the table had long gone cold. Aisha sat cross-legged on the floor of her bedchamber, her back resting against the lounge where Lilah and Safiya were seated. Zara stood by the window, twisting a ring on her finger as she watched the orange sky. It was the day after Zahvik's visit, and the four of them were still trying to figure out what to do with Aisha's latest vision.

'How many ships do you estimate?' Zara asked.

Aisha slowly shook her head. 'I saw a fleet, but I couldn't say exactly how many. But enough.'

'And you're sure the beach was in Gruisea?' Safiya asked—again.

'I recognised the coastline.' Aisha blinked at the memory. 'And some of the men wore blue uniforms.'

Safiya appeared sceptical. 'And where did these magical soldiers supposedly come from? The barracks weren't even functional when we were there.'

Aisha looked up at her. 'The mines. It was always his plan.'

Silence.

Lilah was first to break it. 'We have to at least warn them. We owe the king that much.'

Safiya scoffed. 'And how do you propose we get a message to Gruisea right now? The Emperor has eyes everywhere these days. Besides, Tariq would likely set fire to any message with Avanid's seal.'

'I don't think so,' Lilah said. 'You're forgetting that they're still married. If the king wanted to cut all ties with Avanid, he would have done so by now.'

Safiya leaned in. 'And *you're* forgetting that Aisha was exiled for the murder of his *father*. Even if he's not ready to let go of her completely, do you honestly think he's going to believe a word that comes out of her mouth now?'

Zara turned to face them. 'Enough.'

A plan was taking shape in Aisha's mind. She got to her feet. 'I'll deliver the warning in person. He'll have no choice but to listen to me.'

All three sisters turned to her with matching horror-stricken expressions.

'Did the vision impair your brain?' Safiya asked. 'Tariq made it perfectly clear when you left that place that you're not welcome back.'

'It doesn't matter,' Aisha said. 'I have a responsibility to—'

'You have no such responsibility,' Safiya snapped.

Lilah reached for her hand, attempting to calm her down. 'What Safiya's trying to say is that it's too danger-ous. You barely survived the last journey.'

Aisha looked between them. 'Many people are going to die.'

'And you can't change that,' Zara reminded her. 'You can't change the future, only see it. Those people are going to die whether you make the journey or not.'

'That's true, but what about all the other people *not* on that beach?' When no one spoke, she added, 'I don't just owe him, I owe the entire kingdom.'

Safiya rose from the lounge. 'Say, by some miracle, we got you across the border and you made it there. What's your plan if he throws you into the tower? Or his mother tries to set you alight again?'

'Even if both those things happen, I know Tariq. He'll take the warning seriously. At least they'll be better prepared.'

'And you'll be dead!' Safiya fired back.

Zara raised a hand, gesturing for calm.

'It's not just about what I've seen,' Aisha replied. 'I'll be able to see what's ahead.' She looked between them. 'Remember, if Gruisea falls, the ripple effect will be devastating. You all know I'm right.'

No one argued the point.

'I'm not asking for permission,' Aisha said, softening her voice. 'I'm asking for your help to get me there.'

They were all silent for a moment.

Zara drew a slow breath. 'We could get you out via Ukrocia.'

Safiya's eyes widened. 'Zara!'

'It's a smart suggestion,' Lilah agreed. 'The Emperor's focused on the coast and our shared border with Montia right now.'

Safiya looked between them. 'I can't believe you're both indulging her.'

'Does Ukrocia have ships that go to Gruisea?' Aisha asked.

Zara shook her head. 'Not at present, but that doesn't mean they can't.'

Safiya rubbed at her temples.

'I won't let you go alone,' Lilah said. 'I'm coming with you.'

Safiya let out a laugh with no humour in it. 'The two of you won't last five minutes.' Her hands fell to her sides. '*I'll* go with her.'

Lilah gave her a grateful smile. 'I'm sure we can spare a guard or two for the journey.'

Zara looked between her sisters. 'All right. I'll make the arrangements.'

Aisha looked at Safiya. 'Are you sure you want to come with me?'

'Of course I don't want to.' The frustration in her voice had turned to defeat. 'But someone needs to ensure you make it back alive.'

'I'll reach out to my contacts,' Zara said, walking over to the door, 'and gently break the news to Baba.'

Lilah was already tearing up. 'Promise me you'll both return safely.'

'I've no intention of dying on foreign soil,' Safiya replied. 'I'm going to pack.'

Lilah followed her. 'I'll help you.'

Aisha looked down at the cold tea, a mixture of nervousness and excitement swirling in her chest.

She was going back to Gruisea.
She was going to *him*.

CHAPTER 43

The council chamber smelled of ink and paper despite the windows being open to the morning breeze. The maps on the table blurred slightly the longer Tariq stared at them. He shifted in his seat and blinked twice, listening to the discussion taking place around him.

'If the barracks are to hold more than four hundred men, we will need to extend them beyond the southern ridge,' his mother was saying. 'Unless we build up instead of out.'

'Building up costs more,' said Parveen, another of Tariq's councillors, 'and takes longer. Time is the issue here, because we have so many people eager to join.'

Jamil just listened, since this was not his area of expertise.

'We can have the stone cleared by week's end,' Malik said. He was heading up the project. 'If you sign off on it, Your Majesty.'

All eyes went to Tariq. He pushed back from the table and straightened. 'Where are we with the water supply?'

'We're now diverting from the creek,' Malik said. 'Plenty to meet demand.'

Farrah said something, which Tariq missed, because his thoughts had drifted again. He was due to depart for Avanid the following day, and it was all he could focus on —laying eyes on his wife. He needed to see her more than he needed to breathe.

'Your Majesty?' Parveen prompted.

Tariq looked at him. 'Sorry, what?'

'I was asking if we should proceed.'

Tariq had no idea what he was agreeing to, but his mother appeared to be on board with it, so he nodded. 'Yes, proceed.'

Parveen wrote something down.

A knock interrupted the meeting. Kaidon opened the door and stepped inside, red-faced and slightly breathless. 'Forgive the intrusion, Your Majesty, but a ship has arrived from Ukrocia.'

'Ukrocia?' Farrah said.

Tariq couldn't remember the last time anyone had travelled from the small kingdom to Gruisea. 'Do they have diplomatic papers?'

'Yes, but there's more than papers on board.'

Tariq walked around the table towards him. 'What?'

'Not what, but *who.*'

'For goodness' sake, Commander,' Farrah said sharply. 'Can we skip the riddle, please? Tell us who is on board.'

The corners of Kaidon's mouth lifted. 'Queen Aisha and her sister Princess Safiya.'

The room went still. Tariq thought he must have misheard. 'What did you say?'

'Your queen.' Kaidon couldn't hold back the grin. 'Your wife is here in Gruisea, Your Majesty.'

Aisha.

He headed for the door, her name repeating in his mind. 'Excuse me,' Tariq said over his shoulder before bursting from the chamber at a near run.

He tore down the castle steps and across the cobbled courtyard, startling two servants who barely had time to bow.

A stable hand jumped aside as Tariq marched into the stables, untying the first horse he came across wearing a saddle. He mounted in one fluid motion and left the stables at a canter.

'Wait!' Kaidon called after him, gesturing to the stable hand for a horse.

But he wasn't waiting for anyone.

Hooves struck stone as they headed for the castle gates, guards scrambling to clear a path. Then he was weaving through the city.

The moment he was free of it, he leaned into the speed, the wind cold on his face. Trees blurred past, and the road stretched before him. He rode like a madman until he caught sight of a group of riders ahead. His eyes narrowed on a woman wearing a green cloak, and his horse slowed instinctively to a careful trot before stopping completely.

The group came to a halt as well, and the woman lowered the hood of her cloak and looked at him. It was Aisha. Safiya rode beside her, and they were flanked by two guards. Aisha eased her horse towards him, the details of her face growing clearer with each step. The wind lifted strands of her dark hair as she came to a stop directly in front of him.

Neither of them spoke.

Tariq was overwhelmed by the sight of her. She seemed unsure, but she never looked away. She was close enough for him to see the rise and fall of her chest with each breath. His mind ran through every possible word he could say to her, but none of them seemed worthy.

To his relief, she spoke first.

'I know I'm not welcome here,' she began, 'but I really need you to hear me out.'

The breeze carried her voice to him like a long-awaited prayer.

Dismounting, he walked towards her, and Aisha's grip on the reins tightened. She was afraid, and he didn't blame her.

When he reached her, he lifted her from the saddle and pulled her straight into his chest. She went rigid at first, startled, but when his arms closed around her, the tension melted from her frame. Her arms slid around his waist, her face pressing into his tunic. He closed his eyes, letting the closeness of her steady him. The sensation of her grounded him. *Undid* him. For a few blessed seconds, nothing existed but the shape of her.

A horse came to a skidding halt nearby. It was Kaidon.

'What did I miss?' he asked.

'Aisha here was about to tell the king why we've travelled all the way to Gruisea—again,' Safiya said.

Aisha slowly, reluctantly, drew back from Tariq and looked up at him. 'Hello.'

His eyes moved between hers. 'Hello.'

'You haven't even made it through greetings yet?' Kaidon asked.

Safiya shook her head.

'What did you come all this way to tell me?' Tariq asked.

Aisha put some distance between them, and that's when he realised it was serious.

'There's a fleet of Slevaborg ships coming to Gruisea,' she said. 'Many people are going to die.'

Tariq glanced back at Kaidon, who wore the same shocked expression he did.

'So I came here to warn you,' Aisha continued, 'and help in any way I can. I know I'm probably the last person in this empire that you trust, but I couldn't stay in Avanid knowing—'

'I trust you,' Tariq said with his entire chest.

Aisha swallowed. 'Oh.'

'Get back on your horse,' he said. 'We're going to the castle.' When Aisha didn't move, he realised that she didn't trust *him*. 'You're safe,' he assured her. 'You have my word.'

Aisha stared into his eyes, then turned back to her horse. 'All right. Let's go to the castle.'

Aisha couldn't ignore the nerves in her belly as she entered the gates of Azura Castle. It was late in the afternoon, and the high walls cast shadows over them. She tried not to shrink in the saddle as she passed the curious stares of the guards and servants.

Once they had dismounted, they followed Tariq across the courtyard, through the great doors, and into the cool corridors of the castle. Their boots sounded impossibly loud on the polished stone as they made their way to the council chamber looming at the end of the hall. The heavy doors swung open at their approach, revealing a long table covered in maps, scrolls, and parchment. Several faces turned in their direction. One of those faces belonged to Queen Farrah.

Aisha froze in the doorway when their eyes met.

Farrah rose slowly from her seat. The last time they had been face to face, the queen had ordered her to be burned. The memory sat heavy in Aisha, threatening to break her apart from within.

Safiya stepped up next to Aisha, staring defiantly at Farrah.

When Tariq realised Aisha wasn't behind him, he returned to her. 'What did I tell you? There's nothing and no one to fear. All right?'

She was melting under Farrah's scrutiny, but nodded. Only as she entered did she realise that Jamil was there too. Double the bad memories and discomfort.

'Right,' Tariq said, looking around at his council. 'Listen carefully.'

He then proceeded to tell them about the ships coming their way while Aisha watched the colour drain from their faces.

'We should double the coastal patrols,' Kaidon suggested.

Farrah nodded. 'Agreed.'

Jamil looked over at Aisha. 'Tell me, Princess, how did you learn of their plans?' His tone was thick with suspicion.

Everyone in the room was now looking straight at her, waiting for her answer.

'Come now,' Safiya said. 'You don't actually expect us to reveal our sources, do you?'

'And it's *Your Majesty* when addressing the queen,' Tariq said, staring the sectarian down. 'You would do well to remember that.'

'How much time do we have?' Farrah asked.

Aisha shook her head. 'I'm afraid I don't know.'

'It seems your source was a little light on important details,' Farrah said.

'I want patrols running day and night,' Tariq told Kaidon. 'And tell the harbourmaster that no vessel is to dock without approval.'

Kaidon bowed, then strode from the room.

'The rest of you are dismissed,' Tariq said.

Jamil and Parveen bowed and murmured their farewells before leaving.

Farrah looked between Tariq and Aisha, then turned to Safiya. 'Princess Safiya, I would really value your thoughts on a portrait I had commissioned. I wonder if I might steal you away for your opinion.'

Confusion was Safiya's first reaction, but then she must have realised the reason behind the invitation. 'I'm *full* of opinions, Your Majesty. It would be my honour to judge your taste in art.'

The pair left the chamber, and the doors closed behind

them, leaving Tariq and Aisha alone in the echoing chamber.

'I see your sister hasn't changed much,' Tariq said.

A ghost of a smile came and went on Aisha's face. 'You mean at all.'

He studied her for a long moment. 'I know you didn't do it.'

'Do what?'

His throat bobbed. 'Kill my father.'

That explained the warm welcome. She went to speak but didn't know what to say.

'Tell me I'm right,' he said.

At first, she couldn't seem to find the words. Every instinct told her to tread carefully, to guard herself while in Gruisea. But his pleading expression melted her resolve. 'Maryam saw Lilah's arrest. She warned me. I did what I had to in order to protect my family.'

'You sacrificed yourself.'

'Not really.' Her eyes filled with tears. 'Because I knew you wouldn't let them do it.'

He wandered closer. 'If I hadn't got there in time—'

'But you did.'

He nodded. 'I would have believed you if you told me the truth.'

'I couldn't take that risk.' She paused, watching him. 'How did you find out?'

He looked around the room. 'The truth always comes out, eventually. The Emperor's envoys might all be master manipulators, but they're sloppy liars.'

So it had been them after all. 'I don't understand. What did they gain from it?'

'I've thought about that a lot. It was clever when you think about it. They managed to sever ties between Gruisea and Avanid without anyone suspecting them.' He shook his head. 'We should have turned Zahvik away the moment he got here.'

'No one turns that man away.' Aisha pressed her eyes closed. 'Not even us.' She opened her eyes on an inhale. 'He has Maryam.'

Tariq's eyebrows pinched together. 'What?'

They were so past secrets now. 'She's been enslaved.'

'I don't under—'

'She was a spy.' The next words stuck in her throat. 'For Zahvik.'

He didn't move.

'He has people watching her family,' she explained.

A look of understanding passed across Tariq's features, and he finally drew a breath. 'What a mess.'

A question burned on Aisha's tongue, and she had to ask it. 'How long have you known it wasn't me?'

Shame overtook his expression. 'A while.'

She had been afraid of that. 'You could have written.'

'I could have—should have.' His hands opened at his sides. 'I was planning to come to Avanid.'

A sad laugh fell from her. 'You really don't have to say that to make me feel better.'

'It's true.'

'I mean, we're beyond repair anyway.' She didn't know why she said that.

It took him a moment to reply. 'You think we're beyond repair?'

Her eyes searched his. 'I think… there's a lot to fix.'

He took a step towards her. 'Aisha—'

The doors burst open, and Kaidon entered, his jaw drawn tightly. 'Forgive me, but I've just received a report that there's a fleet of ships about twenty miles off the coast.'

A cold sensation washed over Aisha. It wasn't enough time to prepare.

'How long do we have?' Tariq asked.

'With the wind at their backs?' Kaidon's jaw worked as he thought. 'Maybe two hours.'

The room seemed to shrink.

Tariq stood very still. 'Tell the High Marshal to ready the soldiers. No one gets ashore.'

* * *

It wasn't enough time, but it was more than they would have had if Aisha hadn't risked her life to come and warn him. He wondered what she'd been thinking travelling to Gruisea with no idea how she would be treated at the other end.

'You'll remain here at the castle,' he told her as they exited the chamber.

'No, I'm coming with you.'

'It wasn't a request.'

'Why does everyone assume I'm asking for permission?'

He stopped and turned to face her. 'Please. I don't have time to argue about this.'

'Then don't. If you take me with you, I can guide you through this. I can see what's coming before it gets here.'

He checked their surroundings, worried someone might hear her. 'There's going to be a battle, and I don't want you anywhere near it.'

She held his gaze as she said, 'I'm not going to hide away while your men die—not when I can help.'

She had no idea what the thought of her out there, with steel swinging and arrows flying, did to him. 'I can't fight properly with you in danger.'

Her expression softened. 'I'll be in far greater danger if they reach the castle.' She reached for his hand. 'Let's stop them at the beach. You're going to need every advantage you can get.'

He took hold of her face. 'You risk exposing your abilities.'

'I think being labelled a covenweaver and tied to a burning pyre might have already clued people in.'

He exhaled, and it felt a lot like defeat.

'And you're not going without me,' Safiya cut in.

They looked in her direction. She was standing in one of the doorways with her arms folded, clearly listening in.

'I've waited my whole life to fight those dogs.' Safiya walked over to join them. 'I'm not missing this chance.'

Tariq shook his head. 'This isn't the time or place—'

'This might be the only time and place,' she replied.

The harrowing sound of a horn rang out through the castle grounds. Tariq looked between the sisters, weighing the risks. He muttered a curse under his breath. 'Fine, but you listen to me—*both* of you. You follow every instruction, and if I tell you to fall back, you fall back. Understood?'

Aisha's reply came without hesitation. 'Understood.'

Safiya drew her shortsword and inspected the blade. 'You know me. I'm always respectful of rules.'

'You're not getting close enough to use that, by the way,' he said, gesturing to the sword. 'Can you shoot a longbow?'

'As well as any man.'

Aisha tugged off one of her gloves and looked up at Tariq. 'Catch me if I fall.' She then proceeded to take hold of his wrist, and her eyes glazed over. She disappeared to some place he couldn't follow her. He tried to be patient as he waited for her to return to him, but his fingers twitched nervously. Finally, she let go, blinking hard as she drew a sharp breath. He held her steady.

'There's a narrow beach,' Aisha panted. 'The cliff curves like a hook around it. The rocks are black, and the water's rough.'

He thought for a moment.

'Kharid's Maw' came Farrah's voice from the same doorway Safiya had emerged from.

Everyone looked in her direction.

'It is rather dangerous for ships,' she continued casually, as if she hadn't just seen Aisha disappear into a vision. 'They likely think they are being smart because no one would expect them to come ashore there.'

'Then let's surprise them with a welcome party,' Safiya said.

Farrah stepped out into the corridor, her silks whispering across the floor as she looked between the three of them. 'Good luck.'

CHAPTER 44

*L*ight bled into the bay, pale and cold. Tariq stood at the edge of the beach, the salty air burning his lungs, eyes fixed on the horizon. The fleet sat like blackened teeth in the morning mist. Their army had remained there all night.

Patient.

Waiting.

A shout broke across the shore, and Tariq saw a glowing ball emerge from the haze.

'What *is* that?' Aisha asked, her voice fatigued from broken sleep.

Kaidon took a few steps, squinting. 'A boat.' He looked over at Tariq. 'On fire.'

More of them appeared, each piled high with brushwood and tar-soaked sailcloth, engulfed by flames. The fire turned the water into molten gold as the boats drifted lazily towards the beach.

'Why are they burning their own boats?' Safiya asked.

Tariq didn't have an answer yet. 'I'm sure we're about to find out.'

His soldiers ran along the shoreline, hauling pails from the shallows, their shouts lost beneath the crackle of burning wood. Tariq's shoulders tensed. No commander wasted boats on such a crude gesture unless it served a greater purpose.

He narrowed his eyes, trying to peer through the shifting plumes of smoke. Hulking galleys edged forwards, oars dipping in perfect rhythm. Not fast enough to draw attention, but enough to bring them closer.

'They want us focused on the fires, not them,' Tariq said. 'The burning boats are their shields.' His fingers curled around the hilt at his hip as he watched the creeping dark shapes move closer.

'You're right,' Safiya said. 'The fire's a curtain while they close in.'

Tariq looked up at the northern cliff face. From that position, his bowmen could fire straight down onto the decks before the enemy reached the shore. It would be a punishing welcome.

'Kaidon,' he called.

The guard moved closer to listen.

'I want two dozen archers.' He gestured to the cliff. 'Right now.'

Kaidon jogged away.

Tariq took Aisha's hand and pulled her in the other direction. 'You don't leave my side.' He looked at Safiya. 'And you don't leave your sister's side.' He picked up his pace.

Wind whipped at their clothing as they started up the cliff. The noise from the beach faded, replaced with the sound of their feet. The path narrowed as they climbed, the cliff face pressing in on one side and dropping down on the other. As they reached the top, Tariq studied the flat area covered in scrubby grass, then pointed his men to positions along the lip.

'Nock and *wait*,' he instructed.

'Finally,' Safiya said, preparing to join the soldiers.

Tariq caught her by her cloak. 'What did I say?'

Exhaling noisily, she took up a position close by.

Aisha looked out at the boats below. 'Will your archers make that distance?'

Kaidon took up his longbow and drew an arrow from the quiver on his back. 'Normally, no. But we have gravity on our side.'

Tariq retrieved his own longbow, eyeing the black hulls through the haze. 'Stay here,' he told Aisha.

'Before you go.' She reached a hand up, touching his cheek. Her breath hitched, and she was gone again, returning a few moments later. Her hand went over her ear as though in pain.

'Get everyone back from the edge,' she said. 'Now.'

He didn't hesitate. 'Fall back!' His voice tore across the clifftop.

The archers looked back at him, confused.

'You heard the king,' Kaidon said. 'Move!'

The soldiers began scrambling back from the cliff's edge.

The first impact came with a sound that didn't belong

to this world—an unholy whistle that tore the air apart, followed by a violent crack as a flaming stone slammed into the cliff. The ground shuddered, and dust burst upwards in a choking wave. Another followed, this one landing just short of the soldiers.

They were firing burning rocks the size of heads. Shouts erupted as more landed.

Tariq dragged Aisha back out of harm's way and called to her sister. 'Safiya!'

The princess returned to Aisha.

'They're firing them from the ships,' Kaidon shouted in disbelief.

Another rock struck a weak seam in the cliff, and the edge gave way. One of the archers went over the edge with it. His scream was brief, swallowed by the crash of stone against the sea.

'Back!' Tariq said as another fiery projectile struck, scattering shards of molten rock across the ground.

Tariq looked down at Aisha. Her face was pale, her hair plastered to her cheek by the wind. She had saved dozens of his men's lives.

'Get down there and see if he survived the fall,' Tariq told Kaidon.

With a nod, Kaidon set off back down the path.

'Everyone else, with me,' Tariq said. 'We'll take position further down, where there's cover.'

Safiya took Aisha's other arm, since her legs weren't cooperating yet, and they descended at a controlled run. Below, the roar of the fires and the shouting grew louder. They reached the lower slope, a narrow shelf of earth and stone that overlooked a jagged stretch of shoreline. While they could no longer shoot at the galleys in the water, they could reach some of those closer to the shore.

'Form a line!' Tariq instructed.

Archers spread out along the shelf, feet braced and bows steady. Once Safiya was sure Aisha could stand without support, she loaded her longbow.

'Loose!'

Arrows whistled through the air. Shouts erupted from below as the holy warriors lifted their shields. One boat began to spin, its oarsmen thrown into the foamy waves. Safiya's arrow struck clean into him. Her hands shook as she lowered the bow, the reality of taking a life setting in.

'I need to see what's next,' Aisha said. But when she touched Tariq this time, nothing happened.

'What's wrong?' he asked.

'I don't know.' She looked around at the archers. 'Can you take me to the archers?'

He really didn't want her to move from that spot, but he also didn't want his men to die. 'Stay behind me.' Nocking an arrow, he moved out.

As they moved between the men, Aisha's fingertips brushed over the soldiers until she found one who gave her what she needed. Tariq watched down his arrow as boats lodged themselves in the sand below.

'Draw! Loose!' he shouted, joining in the shooting this time.

The second volley fell, but it didn't slow the warriors splashing up the beach under the cover of smoke.

'You all right back there?' Tariq asked Aisha.

When she didn't reply, he glanced over his shoulder

and saw that she had moved to another archer. Her breaths were short, and her legs wavered. 'Gods damn it,' he muttered as he moved to cover her. 'That's enough,' he told her.

'I'm fine,' she insisted, reaching for the next soldier.

'Aisha, fall back,' he said.

But she was mid-vision now, head jerking.

'Safiya!' he called.

She looked over in their direction, then came at a run. She got to Aisha just as her knees gave out.

'Cover us,' Tariq instructed a nearby soldier. He flung his bow over his shoulder and turned to Aisha, horrified to discover blood dripping from one ear. Scooping her into his arms, he carried her away from the edge to a large rock that offered partial cover.

Safiya followed. 'Why is her ear bleeding?'

'She's overdone it.' He lowered Aisha to the ground as gently as he could and placed a hand on her chest. 'She's not breathing.' He couldn't keep the panic out of his voice.

Safiya dropped to her knees beside her sister. 'Damn it, Aisha. You need to breathe.' She gave her sister a shake. 'Breathe!'

Finally, Aisha's chest rose sharply, and her eyes fluttered for a moment before clearing. She grabbed hold of Tariq's arm as she caught her breath, but the contact pulled her back under again.

Tariq tore his arm free, and Aisha returned with a gasp, this time rolling onto her side and retching.

'For the love of all the gods,' Safiya said.

Aisha lifted her head to look at Tariq, and her expression frightened him. He brought his face closer to hers. 'What is it?'

'It won't be enough.' Her eyes struggled to focus on him. 'You'll have to fight hand-to-hand.'

'That's all right,' he assured her. 'We're ready for that.'

She shook her head. 'Not here.' Then she coughed. 'In the castle.'

The world returned in nauseating flashes. Aisha could see the shock on Tariq's face as the weight of her words settled. The sounds from the beach were getting louder—shouting, crying, steel clashing. He rose to his feet and looked down the hill.

'Go,' Aisha said. 'They need your help.'

Tariq looked torn.

'I'll stay here with her,' Safiya said. 'Keep her hidden.'

That seemed to ease the tension in Tariq's shoulders a little. 'Don't move from this spot. I'll come back for you.'

He gathered the rest of his men, and they headed off down the slope towards the beach—gone from sight.

Safiya propped Aisha up against the rock. Aisha's head still swam, but she didn't tell her sister that. From that position, they could see part of the beach below. The real fighting was well underway.

Safiya nocked a fresh arrow and crept forwards to see what was happening.

'Can you see him?' Aisha called to her.

Safiya looked around. 'He probably hasn't even reached the beach yet.'

Even in her weakened state, Aisha found the energy to go and look for herself.

Safiya groaned. 'Will you get back there and rest, please?'

It was pure chaos below, but eventually Aisha found him. He moved like a current, cutting down every warrior he encountered. The sun flashed off his blade each time it came down. Men fell into the surf, turning the water red, but plenty made it ashore.

Nearby voices drew Aisha's gaze to the left. Three holy warriors appeared over the crest, immediately spotting the two women.

'Safiya,' Aisha said.

Her sister was focused on the fighting below. 'What?'

'Incoming.'

Finally seeing the men, Safiya immediately swung her bow in their direction. 'Stay back!'

The warriors ignored the warning and continued towards them.

Safiya released the arrow, but the men were ready, and it missed. Panic surged through Aisha. She reached for the sword at Safiya's hip, her fingers clumsy on the hilt. Her hands shook so violently she nearly dropped it. She knew the basics of sword fighting, but she had never used a sword outside of a training yard before—and certainly not straight after a vision.

The closest of the three warriors raised his shield and charged towards them. Aisha got to her feet—barely—and tightened her grip on the sword. Safiya fired a second arrow at his leg, this time hitting her target. He went down, clutching his leg as he slid a few feet down the slope. Safiya's next arrow hit the man behind him before he could get his shield up. He toppled backwards, collecting the third warrior on his way down.

The sword fell from Aisha's hands. 'Thank the gods one of us is useful right now.'

Safiya snatched the sword up and returned it to its sheath. 'Next time, don't grab my blade unless you mean to use it.'

That was completely fair.

'We need to leave,' Safiya said.

Aisha looked around. 'Is there another way down?'

'We'll make one.' She looked Aisha over. 'Can you walk by yourself?'

'Yes,' Aisha replied as confidently as she could.

'Follow me.'

They forged another path to avoid the warriors. Safiya kept her bow trained ahead as they half ran, half slid towards the bottom. Aisha fell over more times than she cared to admit, but thankfully Safiya didn't seem to notice.

By the time they reached the bottom, Gruisea's line had fractured. Soldiers were scattered all over the beach, some fighting with blades, others wrestling in the surf, some sprawled unmoving on the sand. There was no safe place, no fixed point of retreat. Only chaos.

A warrior caught sight of Aisha, and his eyes widened with recognition. He came for her, not with a weapon, but with hands outstretched. She was far more valuable to them alive.

Aisha stumbled back out of his reach. 'Safiya!'

But Safiya was already locked in another fight. 'Run.'

Even if she could run, there was no way she was going to leave her sister behind.

She spotted a sword lying in the sand nearby and swooped down to grab it.

The man stopped and laughed. *Laughed.*

Aisha suddenly wished she had taken training as seriously as Safiya had growing up. Instead, she staggered around, messy and weak.

The man lunged at her. She swung her sword at him, and the tip of it sliced the back of his hand. He didn't seem to notice, because he lunged for her again.

A shadow cut between them.

That shadow was Tariq.

The king drove his weapon through the man's neck, steel bursting through flesh. The warrior's eyes widened in shock before he crumpled to the ground, blood spilling out on the sand.

Aisha looked from the dying man to her own useless weapon. Her hands were covered in flecks of blood. When she looked down, she saw that the rest of her was also sprayed with blood. She dropped the weapon.

'Are you hurt?' Tariq's voice drowned out the noise around them.

She looked around for Safiya and found Kaidon with her. They were safe. All she needed to do now was to keep it together.

'No.' She looked at him properly for the first time and saw that he was covered head to toe in blood. 'Oh, gods.'

'Most of it's not mine.'

'Most?'

'I'm all right,' he reassured her. 'Really.'

She looked from his blood-soaked clothes to the shrinking pockets of fighting around them. The beach was covered in corpses, just like her vision.

'Have they broken the line?' Aisha asked.

Tariq shook his head.

That didn't make sense. Perhaps her visions were unreliable in her current state.

'Take some men and go to the castle,' Kaidon told Tariq. Blood streaked his jaw and covered his sword. 'We can handle this.'

Tariq hesitated.

'Your mother's there,' Aisha said.

He wiped a hand down his face, then took Aisha by the arm as he gestured to Safiya. 'Let's go.'

* * *

Aisha prayed the entire way back to the castle that her vision had been wrong. But when they arrived at the gate, her stomach clenched. Not one voice called down to them, and not a single sentry was visible atop the wall. Tariq slowed the horse, looking around.

'This isn't right,' he said quietly.

The courtyard was silent, the usual clatter of hooves on cobblestone replaced by stillness. No groom or stableboy ran out to meet them. The castle's steward was nowhere to be seen.

The party dismounted and drew their weapons, and Tariq pulled Aisha to his side. 'Stay close.'

Aisha nodded, her throat like sandpaper. She looked over at Safiya, who also had her sword drawn. They led their horses into the stables, looking around.

'Where is everyone?' Safiya asked no one in particular.

A rustle from the far stall had them all spinning around. A young boy emerged from behind a pile of feed sacks, his face ghostly white and eyes wide. 'Your Majesty…' His gaze darted nervously about. 'You shouldn't be here. It's not safe.'

Tariq sheathed his weapon and went over to him. 'What's happened here?'

The boy swallowed noisily. 'Men came over the wall —*dozens* of them.' His voice cracked. 'They killed some guards…' He broke off and shook his head as if trying to expel the imagery from his mind. 'They're dead.'

Aisha closed her eyes.

'You can't go in there,' the boy said, sounding genuinely terrified. 'They'll kill you too.'

'I'll be all right.' Tariq signalled for one of his men to remain with the boy before leaving the stables with Aisha, Safiya, and the rest of the soldiers.

They made their way across the courtyard towards the tall double doors of the Audience Hall, which sat ajar. Tariq pushed them open. Sunlight streamed through the windows, printing long golden beams across the polished marble floor. It was too bright. Too still.

Aisha froze when she noticed some Gruisean guards against the wall. Their shoulders sagged, and their eyes were fixed on the ground, where their weapons lay discarded.

'What on earth is going on?' Safiya whispered.

Aisha's skin prickled as she took in the scene. Then her gaze snagged on a white robe.

Her lungs stilled.

Zahvik stood calmly at the front of the room. Beside him, *on her knees*, was Farrah. Her wrists were bound and her mouth gagged. The pins in her hair had come loose, and it hung messily. Despite the degraded state she was in, her chin remained high in defiance.

'What the hell is this?' Tariq asked, a dangerous rumble in his voice.

Zahvik's gaze settled on him. 'There you are, Your Majesty. We were all worried you might not make it back.'

Tariq's hand rested on the hilt of his sword. He squared his shoulders as he stepped forwards into the light. 'You better start speaking.'

Zahvik nodded, his expression bordering on sympathetic. 'I am here under the command of Emperor Hassan. I bring terms for you.'

'Terms?' Tariq looked around the room. 'Go on.'

'You may yet keep your throne if you prove yourself obedient to the empire,' Zahvik said.

It was eerie how the Gruisean guards kept their eyes down on the ground despite their king standing before them. Whatever Zahvik had said or done to them had clearly been effective.

The sectarian pressed the tips of his fingers together. 'First, you will dismantle your army. Every sword, every bow, every weapon will be handed over. You will no longer command a force of your own.'

Aisha glanced over at Safiya, who was still holding her sword firmly, her eyes burning in Zahvik's direction.

'Second,' he continued, 'you will reopen Ashwaq Mine so the men who lay down their weapons have somewhere to go.' Zahvik paused. 'The limestone belongs to the empire—though Emperor Hassan is generous enough to compensate you for the work carried out to retrieve it.' He looked up at the ceiling and opened his hands. 'I pray the gods help you return to a righteous path.'

Aisha felt sick. Tariq had worked tirelessly in his short time as king to achieve everything he had. It would be devastating to see his soldiers forced back into those tunnels.

She looked back at Farrah. There was something deeply unsettling about seeing the proud queen in that position.

'And third,' Zahvik said, drawing attention back to him, 'you will return to the trade agreement signed by your father before his death. All embargoes and restrictions will be lifted. Ships will once again sail from your harbour under the Emperor's protection.' He fixed Tariq with a stare. 'Failure to accept these terms will result in your removal from the position. The Emperor will select a new ruler for Gruisea in your stead and show your people what proper governance looks like.' He blinked. 'And he will not hesitate in making examples of those who resist.'

The soldiers they had brought with them from the beach were all looking at Tariq, waiting for his reaction. The next few seconds passed in silence. The only sound was the shallow breaths of the guards lining the walls.

Aisha slowly reached for Safiya's sleeve. When her

sister looked at her, she whispered, 'Watch. Don't look away—no matter what.'

Safiya's eyes narrowed in question, then relaxed with understanding. Aisha's fingers enclosed her sister's hand, and she went hot, then cold, as she welcomed the first vision...

Holy warriors poured into the room, settling into position. The first clash rang out, deafening as the space turned to disorder.

Air rushed back into Aisha's lungs as she returned to the room.

'You will not dictate terms in my home,' Tariq was saying.

Aisha stepped closer to him. 'Soldiers. Fifty or so. They'll enter from both doors.'

It took him a second to realise what she was doing. He flicked his gaze to her shaking hands before saying to his men, 'Eyes on the doors.'

Irritation flashed on Zahvik's face. 'I am warning you—'

Aisha didn't hear the rest, because she took Safiya's hand once more and disappeared into the storm that was her mind, determined to remain in it for as long as she could. Her vision blurred, and her pulse roared in her ears. The fight unfolded ahead of her. She saw Tariq with his sword raised, and the glint of a dagger arcing towards his exposed side. The image fell away as she returned with a gasp.

Warriors were now flooding into the room, exactly like her vision. The guards lining both walls burst back to life, snatching up the weapons on the ground and joining the fight. They needed the numbers.

Safiya led Aisha away from the fighting, pressing them both up against the opposite wall.

Aisha watched Tariq carefully until she recognised the moment coming. 'Dagger on your left,' she called to him.

He spun, sword flashing just in time to catch the strike. Blades crashed, then Tariq shoved the warrior back and cut him down with a single brutal stroke.

This was how it continued, Aisha holding on to her sister as visions slammed her.

'Duck!' she cried.

Tariq dropped as a sword whooshed over his head, embedding in the column behind him. The king thrust his sword upwards.

In her next vision, Kaidon was there, and there were even more Gruisean soldiers in the room. She saw him lift his sword to deliver a blow, unaware of the spear headed for his spine.

Her temples pounded as she came back to the room. The floor tilted beneath her feet, but she held on, one hand flattened against the wall, the other clutching her sister.

'Kaidon's on his way,' she called to Tariq. 'Hold on.'

He had no other choice.

After what felt like minutes, but was probably only seconds, the door flew open, and Kaidon and his men joined the fight. Aisha released a shaky breath.

'Thank the gods,' Safiya said.

Aisha watched Kaidon this time, recognising the exact

moment he turned his back to the enemy, the exact angle of her vision.

'Kaidon, behind you!'

Kaidon twisted around and, to Aisha's astonishment, caught the spear that was about to strike him. He tore it from the warrior's hands, then, with a roar, drove it through the man's chest. He returned to fighting before the man had even hit the floor.

'Aisha,' Safiya said, her voice full of concern. 'Your eyes are bloodshot.'

'Don't look away,' Aisha said, grabbing her sister's hand once more.

She saw sunlight flashing off blades, men shouting and crying out. Zahvik stepped up to Farrah, fisting her hair as he drew a blade from within his robe. The steel gleamed as he lowered it to her throat.

A scream tore from Aisha's chest as she returned to the room.

Safiya grabbed hold of her. 'Your nose is bleeding.'

Aisha barely heard her. She looked around for Tariq and found him fighting for his life in the corner. Pulling free of Safiya's hold, she stumbled forward.

'Where are you going?' Safiya shouted.

Aisha couldn't form words and walk at the same time. She continued forwards, flinching at the cries of men as she passed by them. She fixed her gaze on Farrah.

It happened just as she had seen.

Zahvik didn't like that he was losing. He grabbed the queen by her hair, pulling her head back as he reached inside his cloak. Farrah's eyes widened as she realised what was happening.

Somehow, Aisha found it in her to run. It was sloppy, but it got her to where she needed to be. With no weapon and no real plan, she threw herself at the sectarian with all the strength she had left, colliding with his side. Down he went, not one god willing to soften his fall as he collided with the floor. Of course, she went down with him, landing beside him with her face mere inches from his.

The fighting seemed to fade into the background, but not because of a vision. Aisha was a girl again, standing in a town square in Slevaborg. Acrid smoke filled her nostrils as she watched the flames consume her mother. Zahvik was unaffected by her screams.

Aisha lay frozen on the cold marble floor, her body present but her mind trapped in the memory of her mother's death. Zahvik's eyes bored into hers as he lifted the dagger still in his hand. Aisha didn't have the strength to stop him. The steel glinted above her, and she waited.

A shadow fell across them, and the dagger was kicked clean from Zahvik's hand, landing some distance away and skidding across the marble. Tariq towered over them, sword in hand and eyes ablaze. The muscles in his arm knotted as he raised his weapon, his murderous gaze fixed on Zahvik.

'No!' Aisha shouted, the word coming out hoarse. She raised a trembling hand, palm open to Tariq. She could feel blood dripping from her nose and ears as she struggled to breathe. 'Not like this.'

At first, Tariq appeared confused, but then his features softened with understanding. Lowering his weapon, he stepped back, his chest rising and falling sharply. 'Get him out of here,' he instructed the two soldiers who appeared on either side of him.

Zahvik was dragged across the floor and disappeared from sight.

The clash of steel dulled to cries of surrender as Gruisean soldiers forced the last of the warriors to their knees. Sweat and blood were all Aisha could smell, the floor slick with it.

Safiya appeared, dropping to her knees. 'What the hell was that?'

Aisha's eyes met Farrah's as Tariq went over to remove the gag from his mother's mouth and untie her hands. They stared at each other, two women stripped bare by terror, exhaustion, and the things they had nearly lost.

In that stare was an understanding deeper than words could ever carry.

CHAPTER 46

The courtyard was packed to its edges at dawn, a sea of bodies pressed shoulder to shoulder. The scaffold of wood had been built high, a pyre for all to see. Zahvik stood at its centre, bound to a stake. His white robes were filthy, his face gaunt but unrepentant. His eyes were fixed defiantly on the horizon. Hungry torches flared at the edges of the pyre.

Tariq stood tall at Aisha's side, his jaw hard and eyebrows lowered. Kaidon was also nearby, still bloodied from a long night of sorting and imprisoning warriors. Safiya had found time to wash but hadn't slept a wink—none of them had. Together, they watched as the first torch was lowered to the kindling.

A hush fell over the courtyard as the flames curled around the dry wood. The fire spread quickly, climbing. It wasn't long before they could all feel the heat.

That was the moment Zahvik began to pray.

'Take this flesh to cinder and my breath to oath. Let my ash ride the wind to Emperor Hassan's hand.'

Safiya rolled her eyes. 'Just die already.'

'If I have failed, make my ruin a whetstone for those who follow. If I am weighed, weigh me by devotion,' he continued, the pitch of his voice increasing.

His words had no impact. There was no empathy to be found, no forgiveness.

A scream tore from him as the flames climbed his body, a sound so raw it seemed to split open the air. No one looked away. Aisha breathed in the smoke, the justice, feeling the heaviness lift from her shoulders. She had seen what she needed to see—heard his fear and pain, as she had once heard her mother's.

That was enough.

It was done.

Turning from the pyre, she walked away. The crowd stirred, and faces turned towards her. Then, like a tide pulling back from the shore, they parted, clearing a path for her. One by one, men and women pressed a hand to their hearts as she passed them. Aisha's throat tightened at the gesture.

As she neared the archway, the final spectators at the back moved aside, revealing a lone figure at the end of the path. It was Queen Farrah, all cleaned up with her hair pinned back and a gown as regal as always—though her wrists still bore the bruises of their binding.

Aisha came to a halt when their eyes met across the distance. For a breathless moment, neither of them moved. Then, slowly, Queen Farrah came forwards. She stopped in front of Aisha and, before everyone present, took her hand. Bowing, she kissed the back of it before pressing her forehead to it. She remained in that position for several seconds before finally letting go.

'Your Majesty,' Farrah said, stepping aside and looking around at the crowd. 'Gruisea, bow to your queen.' Her voice cut through the courtyard, rising above the fire, strong and clear.

Aisha could barely breathe through the sight that followed. Turning in a slow circle, she watched as hundreds of people bowed before her. It was overwhelming, terrifying, and achingly beautiful all at once. She found Safiya among them, her eyes shiny with tears and mouth set in a proud smile. Without looking away, her sister placed a hand over her heart and bowed.

Soldiers and citizens, nobles and servants, all in the same pledge of fealty. Aisha remained at the centre of it all, the fire's glow behind her and the people of Gruisea before her.

A hand slid into hers, warm and steady. She turned her head, eyes meeting Tariq's. His grip tightened, firm and grounding. Then they both took another look around, side by side, king and queen.

From the eastern wall, Tariq and Aisha could see most of the city sprawled out below. The rooftops were painted in the familiar golden light that came only when the sun set. In the distance, the sea burned orange.

Tariq rested his palms against the cool stone and looked at Aisha. Her bloodshot eyes were the only visible sign of the trauma she had endured.

He had thought himself immovable once. Iron-willed, made only of Gruisea. But she had shown him he was made of other things, like devotion. He had nearly lost her once, and he had sworn never to let it happen again. The sight of her on that marble floor, blood dripping from her eyes, nose, and ears, Zahvik's dagger raised over her, would haunt him until his death.

'I'll send word to the Emperor,' he said, breaking the silence. 'I'm sure he'll want his warriors back. Let's see what we can negotiate in return.'

Aisha looked at him. 'A guarantee of peace would be nice.'

'It would—if we could trust his word.'

She chewed her lip, looking like she wanted to say something.

'What is it?' he asked.

She released her lip. 'Do you think we could request Maryam as part of the deal?'

He searched her face. 'If that's what you want.'

'It is,' she replied confidently.

He tucked some loose hair behind her ear, and she turned into his touch. 'My brave queen,' he murmured. 'You've changed the course of history, and I'm forever in your debt.'

Her eyes searched his. 'I guess we weren't beyond repair after all.'

He dropped his forehead to hers, eyes closing. 'We're unbreakable. Whatever comes.'

She tilted her face up and kissed him. He savoured every sensation, every breath. This kiss was binding, sealing something no crown or empire could touch.

Breaking the kiss, Tariq reached inside his tunic, pulling out the token he had removed from her neck the day she left. It was threaded on a new chain. He reached around to fasten the clasp.

Her hand lifted instinctively to the token, and he laid his palm over his own beneath his tunic.

Below, lanterns flickered to life in the narrow streets. Gruisea breathed with hope again.

Tariq pulled Aisha to his chest, certain for the first time in his life that the future was bright.

EPILOGUE

*D*usk gathered at the same shore the Slevaborg ships had invaded. The water glistened copper as people filtered down the dunes, carrying their lanterns. Soldiers, miners, women wrapped in shawls, children holding parents' hands. The elderly with their careful steps.

The beach had been washed clean by countless tides.

Aisha stood at the edge of the water with Tariq, wishing her sisters had been able to visit as planned, but the Emperor's growing control over Avanid's coast was making travel and trade more difficult than ever. Tariq was forced to send soldiers with every shipment to ensure deliveries landed in the right hands. But even then, around half the limestone was being intercepted by rogue ships they all knew were funded by Slevaborg.

Farrah moved through the crowd at an unhurried pace, accepting greetings. She was there for the same reason everyone else was, to pay her respects to those who had lost their lives defending Gruisea's shores. It was a ceremony to honour the dead as they emerged from trauma and grief. The names of the lost rose and fell in low voices. Everyone present had someone to send off.

Mira tumbled into Tariq's leg, a silky bundle of muscle and mischief bounding all over the beach.

'Easy,' Tariq told her, righting her with his foot and watching her trot away.

She had arrived on a ship a few months earlier, smuggled out of Avanid like a criminal, which was a fairly accurate description of the young leopard. Time had evolved her from lanky adolescent to something larger and more powerful. But her eyes were the same pale gold as the cub Aisha had discovered in that den a year earlier.

The pair watched as she dropped into an exaggerated prowl, tail flicking, then sprang at a crab.

'She has no respect for solemn occasions,' Aisha said.

Tariq laughed quietly and shook his head. 'As long as she's not hunting the children, she's welcome.'

Torches were passed down the line, and one by one, the lanterns lit up, their paper faces coming to life. The first to be released in the shallows were carried out by the families of the wall guards. Hands pressed to hearts as the flames bobbed free. More lanterns followed. Then more.

Aisha balanced her lantern against the breeze. The paper was pale blue, ringed with a delicate ink line of waves. One of the children had made it for her. She angled the lantern towards Tariq, and he shielded the small flame as he lit it.

'This one's for your mother,' he said quietly.

The sting in her eyes was instant. She breathed her mama's name into the flame as she walked into the shallow water and set it down. When she let the lantern go, the tide took it, the sea unhurried. It rocked gently, then drifted away to join the others.

Mira joined Aisha in the shallows, sending water spraying in all directions. 'Stop,' Aisha scolded, ushering her towards the sand.

A tut drew Aisha's gaze over her shoulder. She found Farrah standing a few feet away.

'She is a true menace,' Farrah said.

A smile broke out on Aisha's face. 'Come, Your Majesty. We'll light a lantern for King Hamza.'

Farrah's lips flattened, and she looked like she would dismiss the offer. But then she walked over to Tariq, who took another lantern from a nearby basket and held it out to her. She accepted it with a small nod, the stiffness at her shoulders easing.

Aisha returned to the sand as Tariq lit it. He looked at her over the lantern's glow, his lips briefly turning up in appreciation.

'Must I get wet?' Farrah asked.

'Yes,' Tariq and Aisha replied at the same time.

The three of them entered the water together, the hems of their clothing soaking up water as they did so.

Farrah placed the lantern in the water and whispered, 'For King Hamza.'

The tide lifted it and carried it away, its light joining the slow, shimmering procession across the darkening sea.

A spray of foam rushed at their ankles, and Mira bounded after it with indecent enthusiasm. Farrah turned to the leopard. 'Come, Mira. Before you soak all the lanterns.' She clicked her tongue, and to Aisha's absolute surprise, the leopard followed her back to the sand.

Further along the beach, Kaidon was crouched down, helping a young girl light the wick of a lantern twice the size of her head. When it finally blazed, she clapped and looked up at him as if he had kindled the sun.

'This beach will never be a place of death again,' Tariq said, staring out at the water. 'From now on, it's a place we come to remember who we are.'

'And who we refuse to be,' Aisha added.

He wrapped an arm around her shoulders, and she leaned into him.

They stood for a long time, watching the lanterns and listening to the whisper of names around them as the sun continued to descend.

'The Emperor won't stop,' Tariq said quietly. 'Avanid's under a blockade, even if no one's brave enough to call it that.'

He was right, but she didn't know what else they could do. They needed more support. Zara was, of course, working on that.

'You need a counterweight he respects,' Tariq said. 'You need Cogalla.'

Aisha stifled a laugh. 'Now *that* would be a great ally. If only Cogalla wasn't entirely independent and their king averse to most people.'

Mira had escaped Farrah's control and was now dragging a coil of rope she had stolen from gods only knew where across the sand. The sight drew laughter from the grieving.

'She'll not forgive me for the bath she's about to need,' Aisha said.

Tariq shook his head. 'Good luck with that.'

Kaidon approached, his boots sinking into the damp sand. 'Excuse me, Your Majesties, but I've just been informed that a ship has anchored.' Something flickered beneath his serious expression. 'The cargo has been brought safely ashore.'

Aisha tilted her head. 'What cargo?'

Tariq pointed to the line of trees at the back of the beach. '*That* cargo.'

Aisha took a few steps forwards, focusing hard in the dark. There stood Maryam, smaller than Aisha remembered.

Their eyes locked, and a shocked laugh came from Aisha before she crossed the beach, skirts dragging through the wet sand. Maryam met her halfway, stopping a few feet away and bowing low, hand over her heart.

Aisha stepped forwards, pulling her into a hug. 'Welcome home.' She held Maryam's small frame until Maryam hugged her back. There was no need for words, just silent recognition of all they had survived together and apart.

Maryam released her and stepped aside as Tariq appeared.

'Queen Aisha's looking forward to having you back in her service,' he told her.

Maryam bowed her head. 'I am honoured, Your Majesty.'

Mira bounded in, nearly bowling Maryam over with her overly enthusiastic greeting.

'Safe to say she remembers you,' Aisha laughed.

Once Mira had settled down, Aisha and Tariq returned to the water's edge, watching the lanterns navigate the small waves. The tide reached for their feet, then slid away. Tariq took her hand again, and she marvelled at how his touch could reorder the world. Fingers wove through hers, palms meeting.

As the sun slipped below the horizon, a rider appeared on the beach, dismounting fast. A messenger. Kaidon strode across the beach towards the breathless man, and Aisha watched their exchange. When Kaidon looked in her direction, the change in his expression made her stomach drop.

'Something's wrong,' Aisha said.

Tariq followed her line of sight to where Kaidon was now making his way over to them.

'What is it?' Tariq asked.

Kaidon waited until he was standing right in front of them before speaking. That was surely a bad sign. He looked at Aisha, an apology in his eyes. 'Your Majesty.'

Her pulse slowed.

'I'm sorry to inform you that Princess Lilah is missing,' he said.

A wave broke, then retreated with a hiss. The last bit of light vanished, leaving behind a black sea and turning lanterns into stars.

ACKNOWLEDGMENTS

I am endlessly grateful to the many people who helped bring this book to life.

First, thank you to my readers. Your enthusiasm and support allow me to keep doing what I love most. To Mr B, thank you for cheering me on and holding down the fort when writing steals me away. You're the best.

To Kristin and the wonderful team at Hot Tree Editing, thank you for shaping this manuscript into its best self. Thank you to my eagle-eyed proofreader, Rebecca, for catching those last slippery typos. And of course, to Stuart Bache for creating yet another gorgeous cover.

And finally, to my incredible Launch Team, your support means the world to me. You are all simply amazing.

9 781764 121958